with the
Ice
catching
Twilight

Ice with the catching Twilight

NELLY ALIKYAN

To my future husband.
May I always be your very pretty princess.

ALSO BY NELLY ALIKYAN

Catchers Series

With the Flames Catching Midnight

With the Rains Catching Dawn

With the Ice Catching Twilight

With the Storms Catching Dusk

With the Winds Catching Sunlight

With the Ashes Catching Daybreak

Whittle Magic Series

Alluring Darkness

Beholding Darkness

Claiming Darkness

Desiring Darkness

ALSO BY N. ALIKYAN

Buttercup Baby

Promise of A Lifetime

SOUNDTRACK

1. Big Bad Handsome Man by Imelda May

2. Forgotten by From Ashes to New

3. Emerald Eyes by Anson Seabra

4. Carry You by Ruelle ft. Fleurie

5. Worth Fighting For by Emily Hearn

6. Us Against the World by Westlife

7. Everything I Need (film version) by Skylar Grey

8. Where I First Found You by Forest Blakk

9. I Can't Hate You Anymore by Nick Lackey

10. You Are the Reason by Calum Scott

11. Wherever You Will Go by The Calling

PROLOGUE
ISLAND NATION RESIDENT

*R*un, *run, run, you run to save yourself.*
Run, run, run, we don't turn back, no.
Run, run, run, it's live or be killed.
Run, run, run, no love left if I'm dead.

It was the mantra every Islander was taught from the moment they were conceived, sung straight down to the belly, then reminded every night until they too, brought about children.

Run, run, run.

The Island Nation was a savage one, where politics worked by death, and men killed to have what they wanted.

Most were raised to respect the highest, but there were always others who wanted to take what they didn't have. Eli knew that was what he was running from—someone wanted what they didn't own. His home.

You run to save yourself.

Parents always reminded their children in the Island Nation that they saved themselves first until they had children to protect. Children were the only ones to save before yourself. Eli always wondered if that meant leaving behind the person you loved.

Papa loved Mama a lot. And Eli knew Mama loved Papa a lot. Sometimes, he thought they loved each other more than they loved him, but he knew that wasn't true. Because he was...

Run, run, run.

Eli tripped on a stair as he tried to make his way up as the screams of his parents filled the house. He turned for only a moment to see the blood splattered everywhere.

We don't turn back, no.

Eli's eyes scanned up, his heart sprinting as he took in the monster above his father's slit body.

The monster was a big, tall man. And he was covered in blood. It leaked from his face and his body.

Eli's eyes dropped behind the monster to see his mama's dead body. Tears bridled to his eyes, but he didn't have time to cry.

Run, run, run.

Eli sprinted up the stairs and across the hall to the last room—his parents'. He could hear the man's steps behind him as he readied a rope pulley his father left for emergencies out the window in order to jump away.

He was out of the house, hands and thighs burning as he slipped down the rope when the pulley jumped. Eli looked up to find the man holding the top of the rope.

He had long gashes down his face, and he grit his teeth as he worked as if any bit of effort was too painful for him. Eli wondered in that split second if all of that blood wasn't his parents. The monster looked worse off than his parents had.

And there were tears in his eyes.

Eli held his breath as he released the rope before the

monster could pull him up, took a final glance back, reminding himself that monsters could not cry, and ran.

It's live or be killed.

He was only six years old, but he'd been born in this house and lived his every day in it. He knew the woods around it like he knew what air was. Knew the spots where branches jumped out to trip the passerby and the angles the leaves met branch. Knew which way led to town and which way led to the darker depths. Knew neither was a safe spot for him.

No one would intrude as the monster killed him because in the Island Nation, it was all for themselves.

And an animal's attack would be worse than the dagger of the monster.

Run, run, run.

Eli jumped over the twigs that tricked the eye and ducked under branches that hung too low. He moved as fast as his little body could move.

But still, he heard the monster behind him.

It was only when a pull on the back of his shirt lifted him through the air that Eli realized he wasn't as ahead of the monster as he'd thought.

It turned Eli around and crouched so they were eye to eye, and again, Eli swore there were tears in the monster's eyes. They didn't run down his face the way they ran down Eli's, but they looked sad.

The monster's bloodied thumb brushed the tears from Eli's cheek as he whispered, his voice guttural and rough, "I'm so sorry."

The dagger sliced through Eli before he could wonder why.

No love left if I'm dead.

CHAPTER 1
ROSAELIA

She could still hear him—Miels trying to convince her not to brashly talk of leaving because of his relationship with Etel. He insisted that they would not be so public to rub it in her face.

It made her smile, his desire to keep her around. But not in the way it would've months ago. Now, Rosaelia only saw Miels as a good friend. No more silly crush.

And she truly thought him a perfect match to Etel's quiet nature. Hopefully he believed her because her decisions truly had nothing to do with him or any relationship he found himself in.

The water rocked around her as Rosaelia stood on the edge of the ship she'd snuck onto, as she thought of the rest of her little family, the Posse they were called. Sparrow, the closest man to a brother she could fathom, and his new wife, Rosaelia's twin sister, Evony, had thought her ludicrous to want to come to the Island Nation. Rosaelia knew they'd said so out of love. That they believed her naivety in walking to the local town unprotected still lingered.

The memory of that night, of walking through town giddy to finally be out on her own, lingered. Rosaelia still felt the stares on her that she'd been stupid enough to believe were those of love like the love she had for her people. She still remembered walking too far and into an alleyway and feeling a blush come along her cheeks that this was the closest town and she did not know the layout at all. Then turning to see the men. The anger still filled her at how stupid she truly had been when she saw them and didn't immediately think of danger.

Not until they stepped closer, telling her she wasn't going anywhere.

Rosaelia couldn't explain the relief that flooded her when Evony's cool presence entered that alleyway. She'd been a moron, and it shamed her how clear that one night made it.

But she'd learned since then. Trained, both with the others and by herself. She would never be so weak again.

While she'd learned hand-to-hand combat and started the use of daggers, held swords and ran laps, felt the true impact of a spare with the Posse, Rosaelia had taught herself archery.

It had started as a silly challenge when she'd been upset, only moments after leaving her first fitting for training wear after Sparrow had found out about her night out in town. She'd felt so humiliated, so weak, so pathetic. It was an emotion Rosaelia never wanted to feel again.

So as she'd passed the end of the training yards, and her gaze had landed on the bow and arrow, she'd felt the need, deep within, to take the two pieces. She'd run deep enough into the surrounding forest to not be heard while still close enough to go home if needed.

Then she'd set up and shot the arrow away in the opposite direction to the palace to keep from inadvertently hurting anyone.

And directly away from her target.

Which only happened after her weak arms had been able to pull at the bow at all.

As Rosaelia watched the water lap as it hit the side of the ship, she laughed. How weak and naive she truly had been.

But no longer.

Now she wore her bow and arrow on her back, in the least impressive of all her dresses so as not to go noticed, and in a cloak of low quality. It was thick enough to keep her warm in the cold nights of the Island Nation she'd only heard of, but nothing compared to what her Princess's cloak would've gotten her.

Her Princess's cloak.

Her Princess's mentality.

Her Princess's naivety.

She would never go back to such stupidity. Never allow herself to be the center of such embarrassment.

And though she was angry with herself for the person she had been, Rosaelia could not find an ounce of herself to be angry with her father, the King. He'd done everything to protect her and give her the life Evony had gone without.

Rosaelia also couldn't find it in herself to be angry with the men in her life—Sparrow, Tristan, and Miels. They'd all done it out of love as well, wanted to protect her because of how much they loved her and nothing more. No part of their actions had been vindictive.

As she thought about the four men she loved more than life itself, a sadness entered her again. For leaving them. For going away with nothing but a note she'd hidden.

Rosaelia let them think her rash, jumping with the need to come to the Island Nation and find her mother, the past Queen of the Northern Lands who wanted to kill her twin and her father. Who wanted to take from Rosaelia everyone who mattered to her.

But not Rosaelia herself.

Because she was no threat to the Queen. Rowena had not found her impressive enough to even entertain stopping. It had been the final thrash of the nail within Rosaelia's heart.

The Posse believed her soft enough to be angry for her people; to be angry for the Posse; to be angry for herself; to be angry. But never to do a thing about it.

She could not blame them. In her time believing it was her twin sister who was betraying them in leading the rebellion in the North, Rosaelia had done nothing about it but go to the four men she loved. Trusted them to take care of matters.

Well, now it was her turn to take care of matters.

While the Posse believed her to be locked away in the Southwest library she loved to venture to, Rosaelia had gone there only to leave the note within the one book she always pulled out when she was there. Sparrow knew the one.

They believed they'd been able to talk her out of her plans to stop her mother, to wait a few weeks until they had things settled within the politics of the palace before going after her. What they didn't know was that she wasn't the same Princess she'd been at the beginning of the year, or even a month ago.

It would be another week, possibly two if she was lucky, before they didn't hear anything and went looking for her. It would be then that after searching the library and sleeping quarters for her, Sparrow would pull out the book to find the note she'd left behind, the one telling her family how much she loved them and how much responsibility she felt not only to her people in the Northern Lands but the people of the Island Nation to stop her mother.

Rosaelia could already picture how truly angry they would be. How Evony would cloak them to come up to the Island Nation and find her, because Rosaelia had no doubts they would come immediately for her. Which only meant she had about two weeks to take care of this problem. Three if she were lucky.

Hopefully, that would be plenty enough time for her.

Time to protect herself with the archery she'd forced herself to hone in, and while she wasn't yet a professional, Rosaelia knew she was well off enough. Especially after the tips she'd nondescriptly received from Evony's most favored people, Gemma and James, Rosaelia was sure she'd do just fine. She had to. She had no other choice.

It was time to be off on her own and show the world she was no damsel. Show them that her Princess status meant nothing because she was not feeble. Show them that she could handle matters on her own, that she did not *need* the others. She, who traveled across the oceans on a ship she'd boarded without permission. She, who was running to the enemy—both her mother and the Islanders—and ready to fight. She, who would come out victorious.

Time to bring together the bridge between the Island Nation and Northern Lands. Find a way to take the savage politics of the Islanders and mesh them with the civility of the Northern and Southern Lands.

And most importantly, time to find Queen Rowena and kill her.

CHAPTER 2

ROSAELIA

Getting off the ship was just as terrifying as getting on it. Rosaelia didn't know how anybody would react to the Princess's presence, now not in the Northern Lands. Would her people from the boat treat her the way those men in the alleyway had tried to before Evony showed up? Would they stop them if the Islanders tried something?

Luckily she didn't need to find out because she jumped off the ship and ran up to hide behind a large shed as the Northern men emptied their ship of delicacies from her homelands, then began filling the boat with the Islanders delicacies.

Rosaelia especially loved the baked goods made of a special cocoa that the Islanders especially thrived on. She wondered if any one of the crates they carried onto the ship now held those brownies.

As she watched, Rosaelia was shocked to find how much the two sides got along. After all she'd heard of the Islanders, they were barbarians. These men by the ships seemed the farthest from barbarian—though they definitely were scarier looking than even the toughest of Northerners. Scarier even that Sparrow because of the more rugged way they appeared.

But as Rosaelia stood in hiding, she was equally shocked and pleased to see the two sides grin to one another like seeing old friends. Watched them laugh and sing together. Exchange stories of how the families were doing.

Rosaelia crouched in her spot for a long while, thinking how very wholesome the whole exchange was.

When they finished with the exchange of delicacies, instead of getting back on the ship and awaiting morning to leave as Rosaelia had always assumed they did, the Northern men followed the Islanders to what looked like a pub only about a hundred feet from the waters. These men were all truly friends.

It was astonishing and heart-warming all at once. Maybe Rosaelia's plan to close the bridge between the two nations wouldn't be as difficult as her family seemed to believe.

Only after the last man disappeared into the pub did Rosaelia allow herself to stand, too on edge about getting caught to risk anyone seeing her. There was a forest only a few yards out that she needed to run to. She'd heard talk of how it led to the towns while the Northerners and Islanders discussed their regular topics. Only problem was the open space she needed to run through to get there.

And the fact that the temperature was dropping quickly.

She'd had her cloak off her shoulders as she'd sat about watching the men interact in the early summer day, but as the day grew later, the chill that was known of the Island Nation set about.

And it wasn't yet very late.

Rosaelia's heart hammered within her chest as she brought her cloak in close and made sure her bow and arrows were properly secured before running. She didn't allow herself to turn to see if she was spotted. Only ran, ran, ran.

She didn't stop until she was a few dozen yards within the forest.

As she turned to see if anyone had spotted and followed her, Rosaelia's heart calmed. Entirely alone.

In the middle of a forest.

In the Island Nation.

Known for its savagery.

Her heart's speed picked up slightly, but she relaxed herself at the fact that she was alone. Maybe the past few weeks had truly screwed with Rosaelia's mind because she was the twin who preferred the indoors, libraries and nooks and walls, while Evony jumped from tree to tree in the forests. She had no business running around a whole Island she wasn't familiar with.

Rosaelia fought the urge to run back to the ship and sail back to the North, throw her entire plan away and wait for the Posse to do what they'd planned to in a few weeks. As she began her walk deeper into the forest and hopefully to the other side, to town, she convinced herself she would figure out this nation and a way to protect herself while she was at it.

As she took her first steps toward where she hoped pointed to town, Rosaelia's heart began to race a little faster. She needed to be quiet lest she draw unwanted attention. She needed to keep her senses alert unless an animal came out at her. She needed to fight the Princess upbringing asking her what she'd been thinking coming to the Island on her own.

"Your family thinks the idea ridiculous," she whispered to herself. "Father needs to protect the North. The King cannot leave. The others need to protect the palace. Rowena's weak now which means they can take a bit of extra time to plan out how to get to her, but I know that we have to get her while she's weak!"

Her mother was on this land, hiding away and trying to recover from the betrayal of the Master Sorcerer—Sparrow's mother. It was all so incredible, the fact that both of them had found long dead mother's.

And a bit incredible that they both turned out to be not-so-great people, though the Master Sorcerer had partially made up for her part by betraying Rowena and allowing them off.

It all led to the one thing Rosaelia could not get her mind off of—her own mother. The way she had caused a rebellion within the Northern Lands, messing with people's minds to get to her goals. Rosaelia was saddened by the foolishness of those people—those who believed things would be 'better' with their new ruler only to turn around and have the worst of people take over.

But she could not judge them. She was once naive too.

Maybe she still was.

'What do you know about what she'd be like as a ruler?' the soft Princess inside her—the part of her trying to find the good in people—asked.

"I know that she led all those people into a battle to die for her, and she didn't care an ounce for them. Leaders protect their people!" she argued with it.

She also felt for the Islanders—people who already had it tougher and were now being used as a pawn on the chessboard. Rosaelia wanted to protect them.

After seeing the way her people interacted with the Islanders, her desire to protect them only grew. Whatever Rowena had planned with the North, Rosaelia could imagine she would do whatever she pleased to the Island in order to get it. She couldn't allow for that.

Rosaelia brought the cloak in closer as her feet crunched and she realized the land was turning icy. She slowed her gait so she wouldn't make any noise and made sure she was as hidden as possible between trees as her heart raced. Maybe growing up as the Princess of the Northern Lands gave her some privileges, but she doubted any Northerner wouldn't be afraid to walk in foreign lands.

In Islander lands.

The chill grew around her. She hadn't realized it would grow this cold at the start of summer. She could only wonder how cold it got in the winters.

"Rowena's using the Island as a hideaway, a safe place. She must be near the shores to keep an eye on the North," she mumbled under her breath. "Now, Ro, you just need to find a way to get an Islander to give you a map of the place without giving away that you're not from the area. Then you can figure out the towns that make the most sense for her to organize this mess. Hopefully, you don't have to go through each one individually otherwise your family will definitely get here before you find her. Then, you protect your twin, your father. Simple."

She scoffed at herself, then breathed in as she made sure she didn't hear anything from around the forests.

Maybe it was stupid of her to think of her mother when she should be focused on not dying in these forests, but she couldn't help it. She was here for one reason.

It was another five minutes into her walk, all the while hashing out what excuse would best get her that map of the land without giving herself away, when an arrow flew through the air and landed in the tree two steps beside her.

Then another on the tree barely above her hairline.

Rosaelia panicked as she turned and ducked right in time for another flying directly toward her chest.

Someone had noticed her. They were trying to kill her. She'd been so silent. How had they found her? How was she supposed to outrun men who knew these forests?

She needed to calm herself down and figure this out. This

was only the start of the challenges she would be dealing with alone in a foreign land.

Then another few arrows flew into trees five feet away from her, where only two landed into tree bark, and as Rosaelia rose, she noticed the arrows weren't meant for her. They were hunting deer.

And from the looks of it, two large ones and a smaller one had been hit. Plenty of meat for whatever these men had planned. Or to pass to locals for regular meals.

Rosaelia moved slowly toward the animals—which were in the direction she'd been headed—when a hand shoved into the front of her cloak and rammed her so hard into the body of a tree that the air left her. And she was no longer in the sight of the animals.

Or the men moving toward them.

Rosaelia's gaze landed on the hand still bunched at the front of her dress and cloak, then followed the calloused muscle covered in blood up slowly, slowly, oh so slowly.

And into the eyes of a monster.

Two scars lined his face, one running straight down from his right forehead, over his eye, down his cheek to his jawline and the other beginning at the bottom of his left eye and down his cheek to that perfect jawline.

He snarled at her, but something in her core liked it. Rosaelia's breath came out harshly from both fear of now seeing what everyone meant by barbarian and something else. Pounding. Different. The feeling in her core lowered to between her thighs.

He was the most handsome monster she'd ever seen.

CHAPTER 3

KILLIAN

He hated the men who needed to waste so many arrows to get their kill, but Killian enjoyed watching the constant failure. It was an odd sort of comfort to know that he could take the kills right out from under all of those men.

That is, in normal circumstances when there weren't any soft-dressed women about. The women who came into these forests were dressed for it, ready for the hunt. The bow and arrow on this one's back didn't hide that she was not one of those women.

She hissed at the impact of her weapons at her back hitting the tree, but Killian hardly cared. She was only moments from becoming the next prey for these men, and Killian now needed to keep her hidden until they walked off with their wins.

"Are you trying to get yourself killed?" he growled against her soft cheek, his hand tightening into her clothes as the other landed beside her head, caging her from any man who decided to turn through the trees toward them.

She looked up at him with wide eyes. "I didn't know anyone was hunting."

He scoffed against her. "What kind of imbecile doesn—" The affronted and defiant look in her eyes gave her away—she was not from there. "Where are you from?"

She pushed him away, but the impact didn't move him even an inch. "Get your hands off me!"

"I think you need to keep your voice down, love," he snarled the last word. "My hands are hardly on you, but believe you me, if those men find you here unprotected, hands *will* be on you."

On that body that was probably soft in all the right places. She was well covered, but he could already imagine the divinity beneath it all simply based on the beauty of her features. Features that looked... familiar?

The girl looked angrier now. "*Unprotected.* Because all women need a man to save them."

The girl had some bite to her. It was impressive, especially against the snarling scars on his face. She definitely didn't know of him. She definitely wasn't from around there.

"I didn't say that, princess. Women are mighty able to protect themselves. You, on the other hand, are not." He bit the words out, but every part of him took notice of the way her body froze at the use of a certain word.

Princess.

The Island Nation didn't have Princesses.

The Southern Lands didn't have Princesses.

Only one land had a Princess and it was the one that kept the Islanders away from the rest of people.

"Princess," he snarled into her cheek again, their breaths mixing as hers hitched. He knew now why she looked familiar. "What the fuck is the Northern Princess doing here?"

Her breathing came out harshly as she tried again to push him away. "I don't know what you're talking about!"

Understandably, she was not expecting an Island man to know of her. And if it weren't for his nonas, Killian wouldn't have.

"Give it up, Princess"—his finger, still covered in the dried blood of one of Keir's men he'd killed, trailed her cheek—"what was it?" The memory of the stories his nonas had told him of the Northern Lands and the royalty came back to him. "*Rosaelia?*"

It was obvious she was trying not to react, but there was a slight hitch in her breathing that Killian was finding himself obsessed with noticing. "I'm not—"

"Princess Rosaelia?" He smirked. "I'd beg to differ. But what I'd really like to know is what you're doing here? On enemy lands."

"I'm not—"

She was cut off as the laughter of the men with the kills came closer, and Killian realized they were turning right for them.

Immediately he pushed away from her and pulled on her cloak, the hood falling over her long black locks and covering most of her face. Killian brought her into his side just as the men turned and paused at the sight of them.

"Well, well, what do we have here?" one laughed.

"C'mon, mate." Another chuckled around his ale, thankfully barely paying any mind to them as he seemed ready to head home for more. "Quite obvious they're rutting."

Rosaelia froze at his side, and Killian had to dig his fingers into her side to keep her silent and release the tension from her body. He really wasn't in the mood to kill all these men right then.

"Nah." Another gave a disturbing grin. "This is that Black-wood boy. He doesn—"

"What I do with my woman is none of your business," Killian snarled and brought the girl closer into his side.

It probably wasn't bright of him to claim her as his own. Word would get around that he'd claimed a woman, even if these men couldn't see what she looked like now.

"Your w—" one went to question, the shock evident on his features. Definitely not smart to have claimed her. He would now be expected to have a woman, even if no one would dare question him about it.

Though maybe not. Maybe these fuckers were too drunk to remember this.

"Mine," he growled and a possessive side of him wrapped his arm tighter around her waist. His nonas would owe him for this because there was no way they'd ever allow a Northerner to be left out here on her own.

"If this is your woman," the original one spoke with an ale-infused smile. "Why rut in the forests?"

That was a stupid question. Islanders always rutted in forests.

A growl deep within his throat escaped Killian. "What part of 'what I do with my woman isn't your business' did you not understand?"

They all seemed to get the message then. He wasn't joking. Men never joked when claiming a woman in the Island, but it was obvious that none had expected it from Killian.

"Now move," he snarled before pushing Rosaelia to move faster than her small legs could muster, his long ones moving with ease. They needed to get out of the forests.

"Where are we going?" she whisper-hissed at him when they were far enough away. As if she had any right to be angry with him.

"Home." *I'm taking my woman home.*

Killian snarled at himself. The fucking Princess was most definitely *not* his woman.

SHE WAS WALKING by his side until they were out of the forest and moving around the edge of his home when she tentatively whispered, "Thank you."

He scoffed to himself before throwing her against the side of the house, caging her in on both sides. Those wide, green eyes looked up at him with a mix of fright and something else, and it made Killian chuckle. "Afraid of me, Princess?"

"Not the word I would use," she whispered, her chest distracting as it hit his.

He narrowed his eyes at her. "Tell me who you are."

She looked irritated at his command yet still stared at him with defiance. "You already know."

Killian licked his lips, biting down on the bottom one and fixating on the way her gaze latched on to it. "I want to hear you say it."

Her green orbs jumped to meet his dark ones. "Princess Rosaelia of the Northern Lands."

"*Princess,*" he whispered the word with some ridicule. "I hope you know what you've gotten yourself into coming here. We don't cater to the spoiled and bratty."

Those eyes narrowed with a bit of hate. "Don't worry about me, *barbarian.*"

He chuckled, letting his lips skim hers, trying to see how far he could take it before her royal heir became too frightened.

"You may let me go now," she said strongly, seemingly unaffected though her cheeks grew pink in the dim light of the growing moon. "Thank you for your help, barbarian, but I will see myself about the land."

His chuckle was completely laced with ridicule now. "You're not going anywhere, sweetheart."

He pushed off the house and roughly grabbed for her arm, a savage part of him hoping it bruised, before he continued around the home.

Inside, the chill of the air was long gone, and the scent of Nona Eleni's soup was strong. It was warm and inviting, and Killian could not wait for a bath and a hot meal.

But first, he had a certain someone to take care of.

A certain someone who fought against his hold with every step they took inside.

Both nonas looked up as he moved into the house, their inviting smiles dying on their lips at the sight of another beside him. Her hood still covered her face so they only looked on with trepidation and intrigue. Of course they did. They wanted him to claim a woman more than anything.

Killian didn't release his tight hold on her arm, though she continued to struggle as he turned to her. "Take the hood off." When she didn't move, he growled. "Now!"

He could see the hate in those defiant eyes, her jawing gritting in what he assumed was annoyance at being told what to do before she shoved his hand off of her and reached for the hood. She was slow to remove it, her bravado obviously a ruse in this foreign place she'd brought herself.

As the hood fell, Killian watched both nonas' eyes light with recognition.

"Princess..." Nona Eleni started.

"Rosaelia?" Nona Tereza finished.

Rosaelia's eyes widened. "How could you possibly know with a look?" Her wide eyes turned to him, the question loud within them as she took a step back.

Killian didn't know why, but he decided to ease her worry rather than allow it to play out the way he normally would. "Islanders wouldn't know who you are. My nonas are a special exception. Islanders wouldn't even know your name. Or your father's." He wouldn't say 'the King's'. He didn't have a reason to respect the man so.

A sense of ease settled into her, but it was quite clear she didn't trust them as she turned back to the nonas. "So how did you know?"

Nona Tereza looked between the two of them without answering. She was analyzing them with a spark in her eyes. One Killian recognized immediately and needed to put an end to. He ground his jaw and began to move before she could say a word. "Don't even think it, Nona."

She wanted him to claim a woman more than Eleni. By only a slight margin.

As much as he wanted to bathe, he pushed out a chair at the table by the hearth and sat, waiting for the rest to do so as well before he could turn on his little princess. He was curious about the Princess's business here more than he wished for clean skin.

Rosaelia still stood by the door, looking unsure whether to move. She watched him warily, mistrust for what *he* might do to her clear within her green orbs. As she analyzed him though, it was clear she knew if she turned for the door, he would be at her back, caging her in again. The monster in him grew hard at the idea of her fear as he whispered into her ear, her back pressed against his front as he locked her in.

Her innocence was invigorating in a land where it wasn't seen often.

As he waited for her to move, Killian surprised himself with how much he wanted her to turn for the door.

Run, little princess, run. Your monster will catch you.

Nona Tereza smiled that old, sweet smile toward the girl. "Come, dear. Come, sit next to Kill. Let us feed you."

Her eyes shot to Killian as she slowly moved. "Kill?"

He smirked. "Apt, isn't it?"

She looked like she was trying to read him when Nona Eleni answered, "Killian. A strong, beautiful name. Do you not think, dove?"

Rosaelia took her seat around the corner of the table so she was beside him, but not directly. She faced the nonas like she was ignoring him on purpose as she answered, "Very beautiful."

Killian noticed the way her fingers fidgeted in her lap, away from view. But still, she held herself perfectly. No doubt the Princess upbringing coming in handy.

Nona Tereza's old hand shook a moment before placing the bowl of soup before the Princess. As Killian sat up, preparing for his own, Nona Tereza's gaze latched to his. "She must finish first, son."

Rosaelia's questioning gaze met his as he ground his jaw. "I told you to not even think it, Nona. That isn't happening."

Even though he'd already technically claimed her in the forest, even if those men were too drunk to remember it.

It was an Islander man's tradition that a woman claimed as his must finish her meal before he could begin during moments of long travel or tough days. And this would constitute as both a long travel for the Princess—if she had just arrived as he expected—and a tough day.

But he hadn't meant it in the forest. He was only protecting her knowing his nonas would have his head had he not—because she was the little Northern Princess, but also because she was a defenseless woman in those forests. It was obvious with a simple look she was nothing like Norya.

Again, that innocence made her foreign to Killian. She was

an inherently good girl. There weren't many of those in the Island. At least, not many who were good *and* defiant like her green eyes told him she was.

Nona Tereza's look said not to play with her, and when Killian turned to Nona Eleni for help, he saw the mirror image.

"What is it?" Rosaelia's voice was soft, her hands in her lap unmoving.

Killian's gaze shot to her, annoyed that she hadn't reached for her meal yet. He gave a rough sigh as he leaned back. "Eat, Princess."

"Stop calling me that!" Her voice remained gentle as she bit the words out.

A cunning smirk rose on his lips, glad that he'd gotten under her skin at least a bit. "Eat, Sael."

Her gaze narrowed at the shortened version of her name, but she finally moved for the bowl before turning to the nonas, effectively ignoring him again. "So, if I may ask—how did you recognize me?"

Nona Tereza smiled, the more talkative of the two, as she waited for Rosaelia to get two spoonfuls in before answering, "We were long ago friends with your grandmother, child. You are her likeness. Your name, we asked the Northern sailors for."

Her eyes widened as she ate. "But for you to be friends, you'd have to be..."

"Northerners," Tereza answered. "Yes, dear. We lived our first quarter life in the North before moving up here."

"Why move?" She leaned in but, to Killian's delight, didn't stop eating.

"Back then, travel between lands was allowed. I had fallen for a man from here, deary. I moved for him, then about a decade later, we were stuck, not allowed to come back any longer. Didn't matter all that much seeing as we had no other family but one another"—she pointed to her sister—"but it was disheartening."

"I'm sorry," Rosaelia whispered, a gleam of shame lining her eyes.

"For what, deary? You were nowhere near conception."

"For my grandfather's ruling. My father's ruling," she answered. She looked like she wanted to say more but stopped herself. Then picked up. "What happened to your husband?"

Tereza grinned sweetly as the haunted memories took root in her eyes. "Wretched man he turned to be after a dozen or so years, but no matter, we got our Killian from it."

Nona's children, one of whom was Killian's mother, were just as wicked as his grandfather had been.

"What happened to them? To your children?" Rosaelia asked, her bowl halfway through.

Tereza's gaze met his, both of them lost in the memory before she gave Rosaelia a less convincing smile. "Eat, deary. Then we'll get you washed up."

It was obvious the Princess could tell something was remaining unsaid in the room, but she didn't push it. She finished her soup in the silence of the room, the hearth the only sounds past the chill outside.

When she finished, she smiled at both nonas. "Thank you."

Nona Eleni looked especially pleased, but again, it was Tereza who answered, "Of course, deary."

Tereza took Rosaelia's finished bowl and filled it again, a growl coming from Killian in the process. Both nonas ignored it.

The final part of the tradition—the man would eat from the empty plate of his woman.

Nona Tereza placed the bowl before him, a cunning smirk on her innocent, wrinkled features. "Eat, son."

Rosaelia looked confused at the exchange as Killian sighed and took the bowl.

He was halfway through it when Rosaelia pushed her seat back. "I should go now."

The room moved quickly, both nonas freezing in their seats as Killian's hand grabbed her arm and held her in place. "You're not going anywhere."

There wasn't a bit of fear in her as she looked at him, a concept so new to Killian he didn't know what to do with it. He couldn't remember the last time someone, especially a woman, wasn't afraid of him.

Though as her gaze traveled to his hand still latched to her arm, Killian felt her pulse accelerate. She wasn't afraid of him, but maybe she was smart enough to be afraid of what a male, especially a barbarian male, might do to her body.

Then she turned to the nonas. "I do not wish to be a burden. Thank you for the meal but I must—"

"Where are you staying?" Tereza interrupted softly. "Killian can walk you there."

Rosaelia swallowed as her gaze shot around like she was looking for some excuse. It was clear with a glance toward his nonas that she didn't have anywhere to stay.

"You will stay here, Princess," Tereza finalized.

"I do not wish to be a burden."

"Nonsense, deary." Tereza smiled softly. "You will stay here for as long as you need. We would never let a fellow Northerner attempt to learn these lands on her own."

She didn't ask the question they all wanted the answer to —what the Princess of the Northern Lands was doing in the Island Nation. And annoyingly, Killian realized they wouldn't be asking.

He also knew they would both turn on him if he tried to. He would have to settle for whenever the Princess deemed them worthy enough to know. Damn nonas and his need to please them.

The tension in Rosaelia's jaw never eased, but she relented to the nonas' offer. When her body settled back into the chair, he released his hold on her wrist and continued with his meal. She was tense beside him, eyeing him like she was trying to figure out if he might hurt her, as he emptied his bowl and handed it over for a refill.

Before it was placed in front of him, Killian turned to the Princess. "Go get cleaned up, *Sael.* I need to wash up too, and I don't intend to wait for you then as well."

That defiant look sprang to her eyes before she turned soft ones to the nonas, and Eleni silently rose to lead her to the washroom.

When they were away, Tereza narrowed her gaze on him as he began on his second bowl. "Killian Rhys Ira Blackwood, you be kind to that girl!"

He quirked a brow but didn't dignify the command with a response.

She didn't drop her gaze as they challenged one another before Killian said, a sarcastic tilt to his tone that he knew would annoy his nona, "I'll be the definition of welcoming, Nona."

She growled but didn't say a word more as he finished his meal.

CHAPTER 4

ROSAELIA

It was later in the night. Her bath having been much nicer than any she'd expected to have while in the Island Nation. It wasn't as advanced technologically as the North, but it was more than the river baths she thought she'd have to take while hiding away and looking for her mother. Never had Rosaelia expected to be invited into anyone's home, better yet for them to know exactly who she was, and to be given food, a bath, and warm clothes to change into.

The bedroom she'd been given was cozy, and again, far more than she'd been waiting for when coming to the Island Nation.

But instead of spending the rest of her night in it, Rosaelia sat in the most comfortable armchair in the corner of the living space with a piece of paper over a book and a pencil in hand.

She wasn't yet sure what to make of these people who had opened up their home to her. She was thankful, surely, but was she so stupid as to believe they simply wanted her to stay because she was a Northerner? Were they not resentful of her family for making it impossible to go back to their motherland?

The nonas looked sweet, and they smiled at her lovingly, like they could tell there was something about her they wanted to protect. Was it simply Rosaelia's appearance that screamed she needed protecting? She was tired of needing to prove she'd be fine.

Though they looked at her sweetly and Killian harshly, Rosaelia still wasn't convinced she should be staying there that night. Killian was a large beast of a man, had been covered in blood when he'd thrown her against that tree, and had a snarl about his lip that made it seem like he was about to attack. He was handsome, surely, but that didn't mean he wouldn't hurt her. Rosaelia had learned only a couple months ago that the appearance of a man did not matter. The memory of being surrounded by those men in the alleyway before her sister had come out to save the day still haunted her. Would Killian do that to her?

Would the barbarians do that to her?

Her heart raced with the thought of it, had been the only reason she'd said okay when this family insisted she stay with them. She would bar the door to her room with a chair—though she knew if Killian wanted to, he could easily break through it—and sleep with her weapons beside her.

It had always been the one fear she'd had with coming to the Island on her own, but had she left it to her family, they'd be allowing Rowena to heal for another month or two, allowing Rowena to come back to the North before they did anything. They'd keep Rosaelia hidden away while *they* handled matters.

Rosaelia had handled her responsibilities at the palace—which mostly consisted of the running of the place with the head housekeepers—before she'd come. She knew that though there was a lot to handle at the palace, especially with the recent attacks, at least half of her family would've been able to do the same and come with her. Simply put, at the end of the day, they didn't see Rowena as such a big threat. Now that she was weak from the Sorcerer's potion. Or maybe there was something more going on that her family was still hiding from stupid, naive Princess Rosaelia.

And maybe she wasn't as big as Rosaelia was making her out to be, but she could help the need to figure this out.

Rosaelia hadn't known what she was going to draw as she began with the pencil in hand, but that was normally how her sketches came about—she drew until there was something on the page. So it was only when Killian emerged from his bath with a cold stare in her direction that she realized she'd subconsciously been drawing the handsome monster, splatters of blood around the page because she knew instinctively he was a killer, properly named.

It was only a light sketch, time needed for the details to show themselves, so while she sat back and added those details—the hard edge to his eyes, the distinctness of each scar, the coils and strength in his arms—she thought about her father in the North.

King Edmund, having taken the title when he was Rosaelia's current age, was an only child who was raised by parents who had brainwashed his way of ruling. It was why he had continued the ban on magicians and sorcerers, and why had he known of his second daughter's birth, of a magician's birth, Evony would not have lived longer than a few hours. There wasn't much to thank her mother for, but they were all thankful she had chosen to hide Evony though none of them knew why. Why hide her and risk her own life if she were caught if she was going to turn around two decades later and try to kill said daughter?

But Edmund wasn't that man any longer. Now, and for

many years past, he'd been in an insufferable amount of meet-ings in order to peel back those laws to first allow magicians from the South in. It was more difficult to do so now because of the different mindsets in the North who would need to believe, as was the truth, that magicians were simply peers with special capabilities and nothing more. Things needed to be done slowly so a true uprising didn't take place.

Then maybe they could allow sorcerers as well. Rosaelia could look into them while she was in the Island Nation, see if sorcerers were in the same stance as magicians.

But Rosaelia loved that her father had long ago had the change of heart. He said love was what had changed him. He always said the changes started with her, with the love he had for her, but when Rosaelia questioned where it ended, he looked away and changed the conversion. It made her wonder what it was her father was hiding.

Rosaelia analyzed her drawing, the image the perfect representation of a blood-splattered Killian, but something felt off about it, so her hand moved again, already knowing what to fix even if Rosaelia herself wasn't yet sure.

While her hand worked, Rosaelia thought of Sparrow, Master Assassin, and her favorite man outside her father. He had always been like a brother to her, but now married to Rosaelia's twin, he truly was. Their children would truly be cousins by blood as well as through love.

She was thankful for the relationship he found and espe-cially thankful it was with her blood sister, because he had been grumpy Mr. Assassin for far too long. Now he smiled, laughed, kissed Evony publicly against his Northern upbring-ing. He showed everyone, proudly, how in love he was, and it made Rosaelia proud of him for it.

Then she remembered how angry he'd been with her for

going into that town, naive as she was, and her heart sank. If he had been that angry because she'd gone into a town with simple Northern men, he was going to be furious that she ran up to barbarian nation on her own, this time without her sister for protection.

Times like these—when his anger was going to be too great—Rosaelia was especially thankful for Evony. Because she would calm him down and at the same time, encourage Rosaelia to be a strong and kickass Princess.

A small smile was on her lips as her hand continued, thoughts now moving to the most important matter to her at the moment, and the one she truly had no ideas how to go about. Her mother.

How was she going to find Rowena?

A benefit of this family finding her was now she didn't have to worry about asking Islanders for a map, though she wasn't yet sure if she wanted to ask this family for a map. Maybe they were only playing with her and would lead her to her death if she informed them of her reasoning to being in the Island. Maybe they were working with Rowena, so they took her in to keep an eye on her.

The thought was so plausible it almost made Rosaelia get up and leave the house altogether.

Then she remembered the men that had surrounded her and Killian in the forest, and she knew she wasn't going anywhere. Had she been naive to think she could handle herself on the Island? Probably. But that would be the only thing she would be naive about with her time here.

Come morning, she would go into town, and she would find the first piece to getting to her mother. Maybe she would find her mother.

As the thought of seeing Rowena again filled her thoughts, Rosaelia forced it out of mind. The thought was too much to drown in at the moment. The woman whom Rosaelia had always assumed had died loving her was actually the woman who had sent men to kill her, the woman who had come to the palace to do so herself.

When she came out of her thoughts, her gaze latched to the completed drawing of the barbarian. His eyes, now those of a true monster's, frightening and lethal, and his mouth curled up in a cruel grin like he was going to drink the blood of his victims.

The cruel barbarian.

The handsome monster.

Rosaelia was lost staring down at it, shivers running down her body as she imagined this Killian touching her—a thought so random, Rosaelia was frozen, lost by it—so she didn't realize until the sheet was stolen off her lap and held up too high for her to reach that the actual man was beside her.

"What do we have here, Princess?" He smirked as he took in the drawing of him as the animal he probably was.

"I told you to stop calling me that!" She shot up to her feet, book and pencil falling to the ground around them, and reached for the drawing. "And don't take my art."

"Your art of me?" His lips curled into that cruel smirk that was somehow still handsome. "Are you already in love, Princess? I told you, we don't cater to the spoiled around here."

"I'd rather wear those scars on *my* face than love you, barbarian!"

He stepped up closer, lowering his head so they shared breath. "That can be arranged."

She really needed to be careful before he did something to her.

"Kiss my ass," she seethed, surprising herself with the phrase. She never spoke like that, but this barbarian was bringing it out of her, this savageness.

His smirk grew, and those eyes darkened as he stepped closer, now only a couple of inches between them. "Bend over and lift that dress for me, my innocent. Little. Princess."

Goose bumps skittered across her flesh, and for once in her life, Rosaelia was especially thankful for her long locks that covered her now peaked breasts. She didn't know this reaction, but her core was on fire and a throbbing was beginning between her thighs as she stared up at him.

What would happen if she bent over with her skirts around her waist? Did she want to find out?

The spark in his eyes told her he saw that she considered it, even for a moment. He licked his lips, which made her skin tingle with... need?

Her head clouded, trying to figure out this reaction before she swallowed and seethed, "I'm not your anything!"

"Bend over for me, and you *will* be my princess, Sael."

Rosaelia stepped back, needing the space to breathe. "I'm going to bed." She held out her hand. "My drawing."

Those lips looked to permanently hold that smirk as he focused on the drawing of him as a monster, then back up at her. "I think I'll keep this."

He winked and walked off to his bedroom, leaving her grinding her teeth so she didn't attack him with her limited training. At least she could be thankful that both nonas had gone off to bed when she was finishing her drawing, so they hadn't been around to witness what their savage grandson had done.

Rosaelia sighed, and whispered to herself, "You're in barbarian nation, Ro. Remember that."

BEING the Princess had made her an early riser. With all of the teachings she'd gone through as a child, she'd needed all of the hours that could be spared, and even after stopping said lessons, her body continued to wake at early hours.

It came in handy with her arrival to the Island Nation because she'd heard word of the people's early days in order to combat the chill that came when the sun began to set.

And because she was up early, she caught Killian preparing to head into town before he was gone. Rosaelia hadn't taken no for an answer when she insisted on going with him, and she delighted in the irrigation she saw in his eyes. He deserved it after the night before.

Along with the irritation, Rosaelia saw another emotion— one she hadn't seen aimed toward her but had noticed when Sparrow looked at Evony when she'd first arrived at the palace. If she wasn't mistaken, it was desire.

But she could be entirely mistaken.

And most likely was. It was likely mistrust. Sparrow definitely hadn't trusted Evony at first.

That was it.

Probably? Definitely? Absolutely.

Killian hadn't slowed for her as he walked toward town only a half mile from his secluded home, so Rosaelia had to jog at a light speed to keep up. The obnoxious, ginormous man was infuriating.

He laughed as she tried to keep herself poised like she was speed walking rather than lightly jogging. "Are we running, Princess? Shall I run too? Leave you out here to deal on your own? That was the original plan, wasn't it?"

"Go ahead," Rosaelia ground out. She wanted desperately to bash him over the head with something.

He glanced over at her with a glint in his eyes before he moved into the bushes with his dagger out, and Rosaelia witnessed him shoving the weapon into the greens. She heard the squeal a moment before he lifted his hand with a small rabbit on his dagger.

He walked it over to her and shoved it nearly into her face. "Hungry, Sael?"

Rosaelia tried not to step away, not to back down. "You're a savage!"

"I'm a hunter!" He dropped the animal and got in her face.

"You're not hunting! You're trying to scare me! That poor animal didn't *need* to die!"

He took his bottom lip between his teeth and made her body swarm with what she now recognized as desire even though she didn't want to feel it.

He took her jaw roughly in his hand, forcing their eyes to meet. "Trying? Have I not succeeded, *Rosaelia*?"

He certainly had, but she wouldn't be informing him of that. "No."

His thumb ran across her pulse point as he laughed. "Don't worry, love. I don't always kill. Just last week, I only broke a man's arm."

"Savage!" she gritted around the tight hold he had on her face.

"You're in barbarian nation!" He got so close to her, their lips were touching. "Welcome."

Rosaelia wanted to push him away, get the monster away from her.

She wanted to pull him in, cling to him, allow him to do things to her body she had never fathomed.

He finally pushed away, cleaned off his dagger on his trouser leg, left the animal on the ground, and continued on toward town. Without waiting for her.

Rosaelia followed, no longer trying to catch up with him, but keeping him within her line of sight.

When they reached town, he didn't inform her about the dynamics of the townsfolk, he simply lost himself in the booths before she could question him about anything, so Rosaelia was stuck to discover on her own.

Which was completely okay. It had been her original plan after all.

And she didn't know how much she trusted what he'd have to say.

She needed this chance to get a look at the town, the people, get a grasp on whether her mother may be around here or in another part of the nation altogether. Logically it had to be here with its proximity to the North, but Rosaelia didn't want to close off any possibilities.

In her new clothes which the nonas had given her, with a cloak that would be indiscernible, Rosaelia fit right into the market.

She remained mostly around the edges to observe for the better half of an hour. The way people behind booths chatted to spend time. The way women moved around the market without fear that a man may try something. The way men moved around the market like they were kings themselves, especially those carrying meats she assumed were a prized possession in these homes.

And for a bit, Rosaelia thought all the rumors of the savagery were just that, rumors. These people were surely rougher than Northern or Southerners, but things looked normal.

But as time passed, she realized her imagination had not been wild enough for the Island Nation.

She saw two men fighting off to the edge of town, a group of seven or eight others standing around throwing bets.

She saw an older woman smack a child so hard he hit the

ground before getting up without a reaction and moving about his day. As if he deserved it and was used to it.

She saw... her cheeks flushed, and Rosaelia pressed herself to a tree at the edge of the market. She saw a woman against a tree with a man between her legs. They were clothed, but it was quite clear that they were... what was the word the Islanders had used before? Rutting?

Yes, rutting.

Out at the edge of town.

And though Rosaelia knew she wasn't the only one to notice, no one seemed shocked or appalled or even taken aback. Was this so common?

It must've been because not five minutes later, Rosaelia caught another couple, this time with the man taking her from behind as she clung to a wooden pole at another outer aspect of the market. Her moans were louder, so even through the ruckus of the market, Rosaelia could pick up bits of her pleasures.

Then again. This time, Rosaelia watched the tryst begin with the man kissing his woman, his hands fondling her, before dropping to his knees and hiking her skirts up. He disappeared within them, and Rosaelia was stuck watching the woman cling to his hair, her head falling back as she moaned.

Rosaelia was innocent. More so than most everyone her age. Not because she was a Northerner, but because she had always been too embarrassed to ask about it. She'd only ever had men close in her life, so she hadn't felt entirely comfortable speaking with them about the matters. Northerners were more reserved on the matters of sex, which meant they had plenty of it but questions must be asked of in order to learn more. Rosaelia had simply never had anyone she could do that with. She did not know the specifics of what was happening between the couple she was watching, but it seemed her body instinctively recognized it as something to desire.

She flushed at being so affected by the sights, but she was glad to have her dress on so no one would notice her press her thighs firmly together to ease a bit of the friction she craved.

The memory of Killian as he'd slammed her into the tree came to mind. Then again onto the side of his house when he'd stood over her with that cruel grin. She could imagine him hiking up her skirts and disappearing beneath them. Could imagine him pulling on the ties of his trousers only enough to show his manhood to enter her.

Rosaelia didn't understand the feelings that came with these movements, but from the sounds of her friends and family at home, rutting was the best of experiences.

And she was imagining them with that monster?

Imagining his tongue slithering down her body. Imagining his teeth grazing her skin until she prickled with sensitivity. Imagining his rough hands running over her smooth skin.

She was a Princess, but her family held no rules about who she must be with. Her father had abolished that ruling after Rowena had been 'killed.' He'd found that he wished to have married for love, and he wouldn't force Rosaelia to marry for a transactional arrangement.

She had always loved her father for doing so.

As she stood there, watching that couple while she pictured it was her against the tree with the scarred monster between her legs, she knew she didn't wish to marry the man.

But feeling him—all of him—on her, in her...

Rosaelia snapped herself out of her ridiculous thoughts and continued moving around town, trying to erase the image of Killian between her legs, whether with his mouth or his... cock.

Damn. That one simple word made the feeling between her

legs grow with a throbbing persistence. She'd only voiced it in her mind, and still, it made her want it. Want Killian's in particular.

She was meant to be searching the town's center for anything that may relate to her mother, not fantasizing about having that barbarian take her virginity.

But she couldn't help it.

And like every time she'd caught members at the palace *rutting*, her cheeks flushed bright. Another reason to be embarrassed—everyone could see her reactions on her face.

Rosaelia was so lost in mind that she didn't realize she'd walked directly into a man until she'd bumped into him. As she moved to apologize, she got the awful feeling that this man was more similar to those in the forest, those in the alleyway back home, than to Killian or her brother.

And still, she didn't find herself completely prepared for what he said.

"Shit, darlin', if you want to fuck, just say so."

He reached for her, but Rosaelia pushed his hand away. Her instincts from those trainings the Posse had put her through kicked in and she had the man on his knees, his hand twisted behind his back before she could think about the actions.

She knew a large reason behind her ability to drop him was because he never would've expected it, but still, Rosaelia was proud of herself for being her own protector. Evony would be extra proud.

"Don't even think about touching me," she seethed into his ear.

He grumbled but nodded before Rosaelia let him go. He didn't argue with her, so maybe he wasn't like those men in the alleyway after all. Maybe he simply thought she wanted to rut. She *was* in the Island after all, she couldn't keep to Northern logic.

Rosaelia walked away on high alert to make sure he didn't try anything while she had her back to him. As she moved and realized no one else attempted to touch her, Rosaelia felt a lot more like her sister. She could imagine Evony would've handled that encounter quite the same because though she was the Master Magician, that twin of hers preferred beating grown men with her hands.

And Rosaelia had to admit, it was thrilling.

CHAPTER 5
KILLIAN

He'd been ready to storm across the square and rip that fucker's head from his body. Killian hadn't heard what he'd said, but he knew by the look on Rosaelia's face that it hadn't been a nicety.

He'd been two steps in when she knocked the fucker to his knees and twisted his arm behind his back. Even from a distance, Killian could tell it was so far back that the man's shoulder may have come completely out of place.

It'd given Killian a great sense of pride to watch her do it.

Though it shouldn't have because she wasn't his woman.

She was a spoiled little Princess using others to get to her goal, whatever fucking goal that was that they apparently weren't deemed trustworthy enough to know even though the woman was living under their roof.

Killian had racked his mind all night but hadn't been able to come up with a concrete theory. She could be here in order to get a look at the sorcerers since they were the largest reason the North had cut off ties with the Island. She could be here to get a look at the Islanders to see if they were as savage as the

North expected, to see how safe it might be to reopen borders. She could be sent to steal or bargain for something specific that she doesn't wish for his family to find out about.

But none of that made sense because the Princess wouldn't be sent for any of those matters. She would be too precious to send, especially on her own.

Too precious, too pure, too good.

It almost made Killian laugh how plainly it was written on her features—she was a girl who never got in trouble, who always made others happy, who wanted the best for everyone. It was a purity Killian was unaccustomed to growing up on the Island.

The memory of her touch the day before, every single time he'd touched her, didn't make him gag. It'd been so long since the touch of a woman hadn't made him sick. But it was clear in her soft features—she didn't hold the same greed and ill will as the Island women he'd seen. There were many beautiful women on the Island, but most of them were too like Killian— too savage, too barbarian. And the good ones were too soft.

This Princess, from a land known for its etiquette, was surprising and invigorating to Killian. She was good, that much was clear, but she wasn't soft. She held a determination in her eyes that made him want more of her.

He didn't want any of her.

He needed more of her touches. Needed her purity to wash away his cruelty.

He didn't need any of her.

But she was his responsibility in this market. The Princess was innocent. Unable to peel his gaze away from her as she'd moved around the market, Killian had affirmed that much. He'd seen exactly when she'd caught sight of the savagery of Islanders.

Then as she caught sight of the desires of Islanders.

Her bright green orbs had widened at the first sighting, and Killian had enjoyed himself immensely watching her process the happenings before her. Then again with the second couple she saw.

Then again at the final with the male dropping to his knees. Killian wasn't sure if he'd imagined it, but he was certain the Princess had pressed her thighs together beneath that dress. She enjoyed what she was seeing, though her flushed cheeks proved her embarrassment at such feelings as she hurried to move, removing her stares from the couples.

All the while, Killian delighted in every moment of watching her from a distance.

Until he didn't.

But it was thrilling to know that though she was a delicate Princess, Rosaelia could protect herself. At least the crown hadn't left her completely defenseless sending her here.

After her little debacle with the man, Rosaelia caught Killian's stare from across town square, and those green orbs narrowed with suspicion as she eyed him from head to toe. It made his cock impossibly hard.

So hard, he'd never felt so uncomfortably tight in his trousers and in such desperate need of a wank.

He knew she was affected too by her slight change in breathing as her gaze latched to his lips which he purposefully teased between his teeth. Her tongue darted to wet her lips as she lost herself staring at his mouth, and Killian knew with certainty that the little Princess had fantasies.

He had fantasies too. Very new and very vivid ones all centered around taking the good little brat and tying her up, spanking her and spitting on her, biting her and coming all over that body.

When her eyes finally met back with his again, they were darker than before.

But still, she narrowed those orbs and continued on with whatever she was doing in town.

It was impossible to get himself to focus on his reasoning for being there with her around. The reminder that though she could protect herself against that fucker, a larger one or a group of men wouldn't be something she could get herself out of was constantly sitting on his shoulders. Though, realistically, that wasn't his problem. The Princess had come to the Island Nation on her own, she would need to figure out how to survive on her own.

Plus, a large reason as to why their people were enemies was because of her royal family, so Killian especially had no reason to want to protect the prissy little thing.

But he couldn't help following her with his gaze the entire time she moved around the market, obviously trying to 'not notice' the rutting couples.

It was a heaven send when she finally made her way back toward his house a little over two hours after arriving to the market. It was only then that he turned to the booth he'd needed and began his business.

It was late before Killian was finally able to make his way home. Later than he'd planned, but he also hadn't planned to spend hours watching a fucking Princess stroll around town square.

He wondered if the girl would fear a walk like this—late and in the cold air. Wondered if she would have had to take one had he not found her. Wondered where she would hide herself from the frigid temperatures without his nonas' safety to rely on.

Part of Killian wanted to throw her out of the house and watch her attempt her foolish original plan, whatever it had been.

But only part. The other, much louder, part wanted to throw her against a tree and fuck her until she couldn't walk any longer.

He smirked. Then maybe he'd walk away and watch from a distance as she attempted to make her way home.

Killian scoffed to himself as he moved leisurely past the final parts of town square and began the route home. He shouldn't be thinking of that spoiled *Princess*.

Sure, she was beautiful but Killian would have expected that from any Princess. Nothing though, would have prepared him for his cock's response to her. To those curves that weren't as common on Island women; to those defiant eyes; to that endearing tongue always ready to battle with him. It'd been so long since his friend down south had reacted, and never with so much vigor.

His princess.

Killian rolled his eyes at his cock's little name for the girl— not her title, but an endearment—then paused his walk slowly as his senses latched on to his sides, and he waited as five of Kier's men walked out. It'd been a while since they'd tried anything, and Killian was shocked that they'd start again now.

"My night's been a good one," Killian opened as they circled him. "Trying to make it better by allowing me to kill the lot of you? I'd tell you to tell Kier I'm thankful, but I think he knows."

The one before him grimaced. "Kier didn't send us."

He quirked a brow. "Oh? Free agents now, are we?"

Another one growled. "I knew I should've killed you long ago. It's finally time to be gone with yuh."

Killian smirked, smelling the ale off of them through the

chill of the night. These fuckers always drank too much, most Island men who were stronger than the women but nowhere near Killian or Kier's strength drank far too fucking much.

"If my death is what you'd like, then please"—Killian lifted his arms wide open—"kill me."

As the fucker moved for him, more fat than muscle, Killian ducked out of the way and behind him, stealing the dagger from the back of the man's trousers and spearing it into his ass cheek. Just because he could.

Killian turned to smile at the others as the man screamed and reached back to dislodge the weapon. "I'll finish him in a moment. Who's next?"

The others' wide eyes showed Killian just how useless these men were. He had no clue why Kier would want them around, but that wasn't his problem to think of.

He took a single step forward and the four scurried off, leaving their friend behind as they ran for Kier's estates at the other side of town. Killian had made sure to find himself a place far from that fucker and his games.

But now, Killian turned to Fatty and watched as he pulled the dagger out. He hardly moved as the man came for him. He simply broke the man's arm back so he slashed the blade through his own chest, blood squirting all over Killian.

And for some reason, the blood smattering his skin made Killian angrier as he forced the man's hand still gripping the dagger across his genitals. "I don't understand why any of you fuckers think you can come close to me. I've learned a lot since Kier."

The man's screams filled the air, but no one would come. Islanders didn't work that way.

Killian forced the dagger one final time to the man's throat and slashed through it, covering himself in another spurt of blood before allowing the body to drop.

He stared at it a moment, annoyed that his night had been interrupted before he turned and continued his walk home.

Killian moved for the bathing room first, taking the back entrance so he didn't make a mess within the house. He needed to clean himself and just head to bed already.

The blood was quick to rinse off his skin in the bath, but the frustration still clung to his shoulders. Killian didn't know why those fuckers thought they could mess with him, but he would kill every one of those fuckers, he didn't care how long it took.

He was out of the bath in record time and in his low-hanging sleeping trousers he kept in a drawer off to the side especially for nights like these. He hardly saw the scars that decorated his body through the steam that clung to the mirror within the bathing chamber, but he knew where every single one was. Remembered receiving most of them.

He sighed out his frustration as he left the bathing chamber and moved for his room at the other end of the hall. He'd had both nonas take the rooms upstairs so they'd be farther away if anyone were to try attacking.

As he moved across the hall, Killian momentarily paused at the door to the room Rosaelia was given. The only other bedroom within the home.

He had a gnawing urge to barge in there and fuck her until she couldn't walk anymore. It was her fault he'd run into those fuckers and ruined his mood anyway. Had she not come to town and distracted him, he would've been home hours ago and not felt this hostility in his muscles.

Though, he admitted as he forced himself to continue walking, had he not run into those fuckers, he wouldn't have had the opportunity to kill one. And he greatly appreciated the fact that he'd killed yet another of Kier's men.

Maybe he should be more thankful toward the Princess.

He had barely gotten himself to calm a bit when he opened the door to his room and found the object of his thoughts and desires standing within it.

He was in no mood at the moment for whatever she wanted to bark at him about.

"Princess," he breathed out darkly.

CHAPTER 6

ROSAELIA

She had no idea where she'd found the confidence to come into his room, but she stood there now with his eyes trained on her, and she wouldn't back down.

"Barbarian," she answered his call.

He looked down at her like he was trying to gauge her motives as he slowly closed the door behind him, enclosing her in with the monster. "Aren't you afraid I'll bite, Princess?"

He stood shirtless with a few small, light scars across his chest and arms, and those two prominent face ones. He was more than handsome. She didn't think handsome accounted for the things simply looking at him did to her body.

Rosaelia swallowed back her nerves, and held her head high as she said, "From what I've seen from those within my family, I imagine biting is part of the reason I'm here."

His brows furrowed, but there was a shine to his dark honey-colored eyes as he moved a few steps toward her. "And what is that reason, *princess*?" He said that final word with mockery, but something instinctive in Rosaelia knew he didn't mean her title.

She forced her breathing to calm but saw the way his gaze latched on to her chest, taking in every one of her reactions. "You know why."

At least, she was sure he'd guessed.

He moved again until he was so close to her, he forced her back until she hit the wall. Then, like the day before, his arms settled on either side of her face, and he dropped his head so they were eye to eye. "I think we both know I want to hear you say it, *Sael*."

That nickname, and the way it came from his lips, affected Rosaelia in a way she'd never experienced.

"I want you to..." She inhaled and swallowed again, unsure of the words to use. She'd never used words like these. "I want you to..."

"To what, princess?" That grin was dark. He was enjoying himself. Mocking her.

"To... do whatever you'd like to me. With me." When he quirked his brow, she finished. "Sexually."

That grin was dark and cunning. "And if I made you get on your knees and suck my cock?"

Her breath hitched at his choice of words, but the delight of said words rushed through her, and she knew he could see it in her eyes. "Anything you want to do to me."

He chuckled darkly as he leaned into the nook between her neck and shoulder, licking at the skin there. "Don't tease me with such temptation, princess." He growled like he couldn't believe the taste of her.

His tongue on her skin sent her to a different world, and a whimper left her immediately. It was far better than she imagined it in the hours she'd waited for him to get home.

He chuckled again at her response, his breath hot at her ear. "You sure you want a barbarian to take your virtue, Princess?"

"What makes you think you'd take my virtue?" Somehow, her voice was only slightly affected by how close he was, where his mouth was.

He pulled away and gave her a dark smile. "You're telling me someone else has been between those legs, Princess? Come into that pretty little mouth of yours?"

"I'm not saying anything." She couldn't control her breathing any longer, it was coming in quick sprints at the simple vision of him doing any of those things to her.

"Then say it," he ordered, dark and guttural.

Rosaelia merely looked up into his eyes with defiance. Only slightly distracted by the way he bit his bottom lip as he took her in.

"If you want me to fuck you, princess, say it."

Infuriating, despicable man.

"No one's ever been between my legs. Come into my mouth." Somehow, the words were controlled as they came out.

"Has anyone ever touched that little mouth, princess?"

She wasn't sure why he was asking, but she figured knowing her history would help with the events that occurred next. "I've kissed a couple of boys. But it's... been a while."

His gaze darkened. "Boys. So no experience then."

"I just told you—"

"That you kissed boys. I imagine I'm giving you more pleasure right this moment than any of their mouths or tongues did in those kisses." He sounded slightly angry but composed as he spoke.

"Fine," she huffed. "No experience."

"And yet you want my cock between your lips," he said it as a statement, not a question.

And she heard the words that went unsaid. *Lips.*

Rosaelia had heard women refer to parts of their nether regions as lips.

His eyes shined as he realized she understood his words. His cock would end up between the lips of her mouth and her cunt.

She nodded. "Very much."

"You think I'm so fucking stupid that I'd jump into bed with a spoiled little princess? One who won't even tell me of her purpose? If I was that desperate, I'd go to a whorehouse."

Her head shook on its own. "I see the way you look at me."

He scoffed as his lips upturned. "You want me to spoil your innocence? Why?"

His hands were fisted at her sides, and Rosaelia had to assume controlling himself from taking her the moment she asked for it was more difficult on him than he was letting on.

"I've never been so attracted to anyone before." It wasn't a lie. Miels didn't even compare in her eyes. "Never felt this way between my legs before. This... throbbing."

There was a war in his eyes, one where the devil encouraging him to get a taste of the Princess obviously won out because it didn't take long for Killian to give her a dark, wicked grin as his hand finally moved and he grazed her lips with his knuckles. "Don't worry, Sael, we'll fix that ache. Plenty of times."

She didn't know what those words meant, but loved the promise behind them.

Then his lips were descending and before she could think, his mouth was on hers. Kissing her.

And he'd been right, this was nothing like anything she'd ever experienced before. His mouth was both rough and gentle and pulled a moan out of her.

He chuckled against her lips which made her smile, an opening he seemed to enjoy as his tongue slipped in. It was a thrilling shock to her system to have him take control of her mouth like that, and Rosaelia never wanted it to end. She pulled at his hair as if their meshed bodies could get any closer.

She clung to his neck, the tips of her fingers digging into his cropped dirty-blonde hair, as she pulled herself into him. She hated herself in that moment for having her sleeping gown on so her bare chest couldn't touch his.

A long moan came out of her when his hands dug into her scalp and pulled her head back so he could lick his way down her throat.

"You taste fucking delicious, princess."

Her fingers dug into his hair, and she pulled. She was sure it was only the shock of the moment that allowed her to dominate and pull his head back.

But then her mouth was at his neck, licking at his skin. It was amazing. "You taste better, barbarian."

He chuckled as he yanked her head back, a moan riding out of her at the mix of pleasure and pain as his lips descended, and he bit into the side of her neck. "Is this a competition now, princess? Because I will win."

With the way his mouth sucked at her neck, she couldn't answer. All she knew was that she needed him inside her. A primal part of her knew it even if she didn't entirely know what she was doing.

"Killian," she moaned. "Killian, please."

He slammed her into the wall. "Say my name again." His teeth pulled at her bottom lip.

She caught his gaze, glad to be having an effect on him. "Killian."

"You're making it difficult to go slow, princess. And trust me, you want it slow your first time."

That much she knew.

"Sorry." She smirked, unaware where all this confidence was coming from. Maybe it was how desired he made her feel.

"Me too," he said with the same smirk, and before Rosaelia could question why, his hands fisted to the front of her dress and ripped the thing in two.

She gasped, both at his strength and at the air that now touched her naked body as the dress slipped off her shoulders.

And at the feeling of his eyes on her bare form. No man had ever seen her so. She wanted to cover up on instinct, but forced her arms to remain by her sides, fingers clinging to the banister that lined the walls of the room.

His eyes looked black in the dim lighting of the room as they met hers again. "I saw the way you watched the towns couples." He kissed the spot by her collarbone, and she fell back into the wall to hold herself up. "Is that what you want?" He kissed the valley between her breasts causing a gasp mixed with a whimper of pleasure. "Me on my knees." He fell to his knees and kissed her stomach. "Pleasuring you." He kissed her right hip bone. "With my tongue?" Her left hip bone. "Making you come into my mouth?" He kissed the spot low on her stomach.

Rosaelia held on to the banisters, breathing hard and finding these new sounds escaping her mouth.

Then his gaze snapped up. "Answer me, *princess.*"

"Yes," she gasped, needing his mouth to continue on her body. Whatever he was doing. She didn't care. She just needed him to continue.

Another cruel smirk erupted as his shoulders pushed her legs apart. He growled, and even she smelled her arousal fill the room.

"I can already taste you in the air." His hands skimmed up her legs, leaving shivers behind in their absence, before stopping at the apex of her thighs. He watched her every reaction as his thumbs moved to her cunt, slipping through her slit and collecting the arousal there.

Killian brought one thumb to his lips and sucked on it, his gaze remaining on Rosaelia's as he growled, "I must've done something right in this world to deserve such a delicacy."

"Please," she begged.

"What?"

"I don't know, Killian. Just, please!"

He chuckled, and it was the sexiest thing Rosaelia had ever heard. "You know what you want. Tell me, Sael."

"Lick me, Killian! Please."

"See. That wasn't so difficult." His thumbs spread her folds apart. "And I think we're all aware the Princess gets whatever she wants."

Then his tongue was on her, and Rosaelia's head fell back. She didn't care that he was technically an enemy as an Islander. Didn't care that he was a savage barbarian. Didn't care that this beautiful monster had probably done some horrific things in his life. All that mattered was the way his tongue lapped at her juices.

The way his tongue entered her. Her hands dropped from the banisters and clung to his hair. She pulled at it like the girl in the town had as screams flew from her mouth without her permission. This was better than anything any imagination could've come up with.

Then his finger slipped through her folds and into her opening and she gasped at the intrusion as he thrust that finger within her. His eyes shined as he watched her reactions, and his mouth found its way to that nub between her legs.

He sucked at it, thrusting his finger into her before adding another. Her cries barely left space for breath as she pulled on his hair and scratched at his scalp.

Then he curved his fingers within her as he pumped and

continued his steady suck of her clit and her head fell back hard into the wall as she cried out with her climax.

It lasted years, decades, millennia. She was in the stars and then she was floating back, his tongue still working at her cunt to lick up every drop.

"Fuck, Sael, you came all over my face." He licked at her like a starved man. "Fuck, you taste so good."

"Kill..." She could barely get the words out. "Killian, please."

She felt empty.

She needed him inside her.

And from the way he looked up at her, finally stopping his assault to her cunt, face shining from her arousal, he knew it.

He swiped his hand across his face to get the access arousal off, then to Rosaelia's shock, licked his hand clean.

He smirked up at her reaction. "Can't let any go to waste. There's nothing in this world so fucking sweet."

She swallowed, her legs shaking from the thought of walking to the bed.

Killian rose to his feet and had her legs wrapped around his waist in seconds. He slammed her into the wall and attacked her mouth.

Rosaelia could taste herself on his lips and had to agree she tasted good. But everything within her told her that he would taste better on her tongue.

But not tonight. Tonight, she needed him inside her.

"Please," she cried and tugged at his hair.

He gave her a genuine smile before pulling from the wall and walking her to his bed. He dropped her to it, his hands immediately reaching for his trousers.

Rosaelia didn't know why since he'd just had his face between her legs, but she felt the need to close them now as she backed up on the bed. His eyes tracked her the entire way.

Then his trousers were on the ground, and his cock out and looking as hard as a rock.

She swallowed. "That's..." *Supposed to fit inside her?* "Impossible."

He grinned as he fell onto the bed, pushing at her knees to open her up. "Trust me, Princess, very possible."

She grimaced at him. "I told you to stop calling me that. Barbarian."

"But you are a princess." He kissed her stomach. "The same way I am a barbarian." He kissed the edge of one breast as she fell back onto a pillow.

He gripped the base of his cock and slipped the tip through her folds, coating it in her arousal, and causing her back to arch from the pleasure.

He lined his cock to her entrance, then paused. His hands moved for hers and he wrapped them around his neck. "Your hands go no lower. Understood?"

She nodded, but then that defiant part of her came back. "As long as you understand that I'm Sael." Surprisingly, that was the name that came out. Not Rosaelia or Ro, but Sael. His nickname.

He smirked and rammed into her without warning. Then paused as his cock buried to the hilt with a bellowing groan.

"My princess," he whispered against her skin.

She was too clouded in the moment to pay attention to his words.

Because she'd been right. Impossible. He was huge and her cunt nowhere near large enough for him.

It hurt. Coursed through her like she was being split in half as she tried to move her body to adjust to him.

He groaned as he bit at her neck and kissed down her chest. His lips helped distract her. Especially when they latched on to a nipple and sucked.

She cried out in pleasure as her hips thrust up, then the feeling within her wasn't just pain. "Oh my lords. Killian," she moaned.

His teeth pulled at her nipple before moving for her mouth. "Feel better now, princess?"

"Please, barbarian." Even in the depths of pleasure and pain, she would be as petty as him. "Fuck me!"

"There's my woman," he growled as he hiked her knee up and thrust his hips into her. Again and again and again. Every time rubbing her clit in the most delicious way.

Then his mouth was on hers, and his tongue thrusted into her mouth in time with his cock. "Fuck, princess, you're going to be the fucking death of me."

She wasn't coherent enough to form words as she cried out, his own growls and groans matching hers, then she became louder still as one of his hands played with her nipples and the other moved down her body. His fingers rubbed her clit, then pinched it and without warning, Rosaelia was flying again.

Out into the stars.

Her nails dug into the back of his neck as she screamed, his thrusts becoming rougher and less controlled.

She was barely down from her high when he pulled out and stroked himself once before his own climax hit. His cry was as loud as hers, though rougher in nature, as his arousal fell over her stomach, coating her, marking her. She loved the sounds he made. They made her wetter between the legs, made her want more of him.

When he came down, he fell back on his haunches and watched her lie, legs spread, before him. "I've never seen a prettier princess, Sael. You should wear my cum more often."

Her cheeks flushed from embarrassment, but her body liked the sound of that. "Whatever you want, barbarian."

CHAPTER 7
ROSAELIA

Rosaelia woke in a bed she felt comfortable in for the first time since leaving her home a few days prior. She wanted to wallow in the sheets and pretend like the day wasn't starting. Wanted to drown herself in this scent she wasn't altogether familiar with.

Though a memory of the scent did cling to the back of her thought—one of getting thrown against the side of a tree with a monster hovering over her.

Rosaelia's eyes snapped open to find herself alone in the room as images from the night before came crashing back to her.

He'd told her he didn't sleep with his fucks, but Rosaelia had only looked at him defiantly, her new signature apparently. He'd just made her finish twice, she would not be leaving his bed.

So she'd merely turned to her side and gotten comfortable for sleep as he'd grumbled around her.

But he hadn't left. Only settled himself beside her.

She'd smirked. Point one for her at least.

But now she was alone. And her dress from the night before torn in a heap on the ground.

Rosaelia grumbled as she forced herself out of the confines of Killian's bed and moved for his drawers, the soreness between her legs a momentary shock, before taking a shirt for herself. Thankfully, he was twice her size, so the shirt covered far more than that dress from the night before had.

And it smelled of him. This new smell that she would associate with the night before. Of the beautiful monster between her legs.

Rosaelia tried to be silent as she left his room since their rooms were on the lower level and she already heard the nonas in the other room preparing for the day. It was ridiculously early, Rosaelia hadn't overslept, and yet, she was still the last awake.

She moved for her room silently, not needing the nonas to know what happened between herself and Killian the night before.

Rosaelia dressed in one of the dresses they'd given her— one that matched the locals perfectly so she didn't stand out. As she did so, she lost herself in memories of the day before, of the hours before he'd come home.

She hadn't fully known what she'd wanted until after coming out of the bath she'd taken to wash off the sweat from being in town all morning. She'd been headed for her room when her gaze fell to Killian's door at the end of the hall, and she'd been stuck, hand on her knob, watching that room. Every fiber in her body had wanted to move to it rather than her own room.

But she convinced herself out of it like the proper Princess she was.

Then, after spending hours with the nonas helping around the house and learning more about the geography around the

Island Nation—the only reason she'd come back at all—and specifically around their part of the Island Nation, where Rosaelia highly suspected Rowena to be in order to remain near the North, she'd been left alone with her sketches once more.

This time, when her hand drew the image she wasn't quite sure of yet, it had been Killian on his knees looking up at her like that man in town square had looked up at the woman.

She'd been extra happy to be alone, both nonas having gone out to a neighbor's for trades, when she recognized the image she'd drawn. She'd folded that sketch up and hidden it before Killian could come home and see it.

But that had also gotten her back to thinking about him coming home.

And how badly she wished to be waiting for him. How badly she wished to get him in that position she had him in her drawing.

It hadn't been a conscious decision, like drawing him was never a conscious decision, but she'd been in his room moments later, waiting.

Nervously waiting.

So very nervously.

But one look into his eyes when he'd shown up awoke every fiber of her body, and she was thrumming with the need to be with him.

Rosaelia tied a piece of cloth in her hair to keep most of it off her face as she forced herself to come back from the memory before she got lost in what happened after he'd closed the door to his room the night before.

Then she moved for the living area where the nonas worked, Eleni preparing food and Tereza organizing materials. So far they'd shown themselves to be lovely, and Rosaelia would be sad to be leaving them.

They both smiled warmly up at her.

"Good morning," she opened.

"Morning, deary." There was a spark in Tereza's eyes.

Rosaelia furrowed her brows as she cleared her throat. "I wore the clothes left in the room because I couldn't find the ones I'd traveled in. If I can have those back, I'll change and be out of your hair."

Tereza's grin snapped down. "Where?"

"I don't mean to be a burden on your family..." *And as sweet as you two are, as sexy as your grandson is, I can't tell if it's all a ruse. I need to protect myself.*

Tereza took her hands. "I promise you, deary, we would never hurt you. You are safe with us. I do not know your reason for being here, but this will be your safe house. Do whatever you need during the day but come back here. Eat, sleep, be warm and safe from the Island."

Rosaelia went to argue when Eleni simply added, so uncommon to hear her voice since the woman hardly spoke that it shocked Rosaelia for a moment, "Sit and have some breakfast, dove."

They looked so genuine, Rosaelia wasn't sure what to think. Were they simply amazing actors? Her instincts told her no. Her gut told her she could trust these two women above all else on the Island.

"Okay," she complied, hoping she wasn't making a stupid decision, then sat with the women, and prepared herself a light plate of grits and fruits they'd left on the table. She ate her meal in silence before realizing that Killian wasn't around the house as she'd assumed.

"Where is he?" Not that she cared, but she did wonder what had him gone so early in the morning. And if she could've followed, learned more about the Island Nation and some way to find Rowena.

"Hunting. Days he hunts, Kill likes to leave before the sun comes up," Tereza answered. "But not to worry, deary. He'll be back in bed beside you by nightfall."

Rosaelia choked on her water. "What? No, no, that's not why..."

They both watched her with cheeky grins, Tereza's more wicked than her sister's. "You are not from here, child, so we understand your hesitations, but your nightly activities are nothing to be ashamed of."

Rosaelia was left open-mouthed. "I... we... no..."

"These walls, dove," Eleni said, "do not hide sound like the palace."

"Though even the palace would have trouble covering at a certain point," Tereza joked.

Rosaelia took a moment to try to understand what they meant before realization knocked into her and she felt her cheeks flush a color so deep, she worried it would burn her alive. "You..."

"Heard?" Tereza grinned. "Yes, deary, and it is nothing to be embarrassed about. What you do with your man is entirely your own. We do not mind hearing our boy so enthralled."

Her cheeks heated even more as she shook her head. "That's not what..." Rosaelia didn't know how to get out of this one.

Tereza laid a soft hand over Rosaelia's. "We were Northerners too, deary. We understand the reaction. But know that we do not mind your relationship with him. Be as loud as you'd like." Rosaelia's eyes widened more as she finished, "Especially in Killian's celibacy, I did not think he would claim a woman ever."

Rosaelia still did not understand what claiming a woman meant. It obviously couldn't be sleeping with her since Killian had most definitely slept with women in the past, and from

Tereza's wording, claiming sounded like it was only done once.

"He's celibate?" She didn't know why those were the words she chose to focus on.

Both nonas nodded.

"Until you, of course," Tereza added, her hand giving a gentle squeeze of Rosaelia's.

"Why?"

They looked to one another with sad eyes before turning back to her. "It is something he will tell you, deary. I am sure of it."

THE REST of breakfast passed quietly, but as Rosaelia walked back toward town square where the nonas had mentioned the Northern delicacies shop was, keeping to the edges of the trail to hide within the trees, she could not get her mind off of a few things. One, Killian's celibacy. Two, the memory of how loud she had been the night before. And three, and most importantly, the need to keep her head focused with finding Rowena.

She hadn't been thinking about the other residents of the home or the fact that her octave could've been heard by passersby to the thicker walls of her room in the palace so this home's walls would definitely do nothing to hide her cries.

But Killian hadn't told her to be silent, hadn't warned her of the sounds that would tell his nonas exactly what they'd been doing. Though he *was* an Islander, and apparently, these things didn't matter to Islanders. Unsurprising considering what she'd witnessed in town only yesterday.

Then Killian's celibacy came back to her. Why was he celibate? And what was so important about the matter that made both nonas go silent about telling her? Was it a safety measure? Rosaelia couldn't fathom how it could be, but what else would've made them clamp up?

Nonetheless, he was celibate. Well, he had been. She didn't know for how long or for what reason, but Rosaelia delighted in knowing he'd broken that celibacy for her. In knowing he was so attracted to her that he would break an act of celibacy because she'd given him her virginity—her virtue, in his words —and now she had something sacred of his too.

She didn't see her virginity in the same manner—a virtue. She'd simply never been around a man who made her feel that throbbing, pulsing feeling between her legs before, so she'd never engaged in the act. Yes, conversations about the topic had made her blush when in the palace—still did—but she hadn't held out for virtue's sake. She'd simply waited until she reacted to someone. More than how she'd reacted to Miels. He'd been a crush. She'd wanted more, needed to feel her body's reaction before she allowed herself to see if that act was as pleasurable as the Posse back home made it sound. Rosaelia could imagine Evony and Gemma would be proud of her for taking this plunge and heading to Killian's room.

Rosaelia was halfway toward the town square, stuck to the sides of the trails, and lost in her thoughts of sex with Killian— and how much she'd like to repeat the entire night—as a way to distract herself from this mission. She was nervous she had no idea what she was doing but had convinced herself she'd figure it out.

Maybe she was a moron.

She tried to push both topics out of her mind so she had a clear head when a fog lifted around her. It was so sudden and so unlike any other area of the forests that it made her freeze.

When she turned to her right, away from the trail and deeper into the forest, she saw the fog continue on through the trees, requesting that she follow along. She knew it was idiotic, but something instinctual told her to trust the white puffs of air around her legs.

So Rosaelia took a large breath and hoped she wasn't being stupid in doing so. Her hands settled on the bow and arrow on her back, and she prepared the weapon, ready to shoot and protect herself if need be.

Which scared her too because Rosaelia didn't know if she *was* ready to kill anybody. Even if her life depended on it. She was afraid she'd freeze up if she needed to release her arrow. She wasn't her twin, killing wasn't as simple to her as it was for Evony.

Her hands grew sweaty where they held the bow and arrow in place, but Rosaelia moved after the fog anyway. She was in the Island Nation to find her mother and kill her. There'd be far more dangerous situations than following a bit of smoke.

She walked, on edge, for a couple of minutes before she came into a clearing where the fog lined the edges but left the middle empty of smoke. At the other end of the clearing stood a cloaked woman. And even cloaked, Rosaelia recognized her.

"Master Sorcerer," she gasped but didn't drop her weapon.

"Princess," the Master spoke kindly, nodding her head forward with respect as she gave a slight smile.

Rosaelia's eyes narrowed. "What are you doing here?"

"I'd ask you that question, my girl. You are on enemy lands. I am home."

"You're a Northerner too."

"But I have lived here for over two decades. I am well known and this is home." She gave a smile that said she knew the answer to her next question but she wanted to hear it anyway. "What are you doing here, Princess?"

"Why did you betray my mother?" Rosaelia diverted, needing to know the answer to this before she said any more.

The Master's grin was close-lipped but still present and sweet. "You know why."

Because Sparrow was her son.

"I need you to say it." To be sure of it.

"For my son, Princess." She stood calm, but there was the slightest change to her breathing, like saying so made her nervous. But not in a way that indicated lying. Rather, in a way that said the words felt surreal to her.

"Then why leave him in the first place?" Too many thoughts were running in Rosaelia's head. A top one being whether the Master Sorcerer could truly be trusted.

"I had my reasons, Princess, as I'm sure you have yours for being on enemy grounds. Am I to presume my son doesn't know you're here?"

I would assume by now he might, Rosaelia thought. Though she'd only made it to the Island two days prior, it had been a week now since she left the libraries. If she were lucky, she still had another week before they found her note. Then at least a few days for them to travel up here as well. She hoped they believed she needed time with her thoughts since they continued to deny her request to come up to the Island. That way, they wouldn't yet expect correspondence, and she might have a bit longer before they go checking on her.

Rosaelia only shrugged but didn't drop her weapon. She knew, deep in her heart, she wouldn't be able to kill the Master Sorcerer if it came down to it. It made her fear her end in being in the Island Nation—when she came face-to-face with her mother, would she be able to do it?

She knew the answer and hated to even think it.

"You are my son's sister. I will not hurt you. You may drop your weapon." She didn't say that Rosaelia wouldn't be able to release the arrow to actually hurt her, but Rosaelia could see by the look in her eyes she knew it.

Rosaelia swallowed and slowly dropped her arms. "Why did you call for me?"

"What makes you think I called for you, and you did not merely follow some fog into a clearing, and I happened to be here?"

Rosaelia narrowed her eyes again. "I am a Princess, not a fool."

The Master let out a small laugh. "Yes, Rosaelia, I'd wager you a great Princess."

Rosaelia sucked in a breath at hearing her full name on the Island Nation. She knew most everyone here didn't know of the Northern Princess's name, but it still froze her every time.

But she didn't say anything in return.

"You are here for your mother," the Master stated and didn't wait for Rosaelia's response as she added. "I am here for the same thing."

"You want your ally back?" Rosaelia was impressed by the hard tone she kept.

This time the Master didn't try to keep her laugh at bay, though she remained graceful as she did so. "I will not allow that woman anywhere near my son and his wife. Being that they're Masters and your mother a power-hungry woman who will stop at nothing, I do not intend to allow her to continue living."

Rosaelia's heart raced. Could her luck be turning so positively already? "What are you saying?"

"I have led you here, Princess, so that we may begin plans to kill your mother."

She held her breath, and slowly let it out. "How can I trust in you?"

The Master shrugged. "It is difficult to call upon a mother's love for her child as your mother has not been of great example, so I ask you to call upon a father's love for his child. Both yours and Sparrow's fathers raised you alone, they loved you. Trust in a parent's desire to protect his children."

Trust that her mother was an anomaly because Rosaelia knew that to be a fact.

"All right, Master Sorcerer." Rosaelia stood tall, hoping, once more, that she didn't regret this decision. "Let's find my mother and kill her."

If I ever came up with such bravado.

"Alana."

"What?" Rosaelia questioned.

"Call me Alana."

ROSAELIA'S MIND was now sufficiently clouded with the fact that she had an unlikely ally. She'd been planning on having no allies since she knew no one on the Island, and they considered Northerners the enemy since the North was the reason Islanders couldn't travel. She'd been fully prepared—though scared—to be completely alone in her mission.

Killian's family had covered her problems with where to stay—which she was convincing herself would be fine—but Rosaelia had definitely thought she'd be alone in fighting off Rowena.

Now she had an ally.

One who had once been Rowena's ally, so Rosaelia was extra cautious. Things weren't working out in the way Rosaelia thought they would. She had no idea what she was doing, but she was figuring it out.

Now, she was headed for the Northern shop by town—the

one that sold a bit of all of the delicacies dropped off by the ships—in hopes to find something about her mother. When the nonas had been telling her about this shop while speaking of the geography of the Island, and especially this town closest to the North, the first thing Rosaelia had thought of was how much she'd like a raspberry-filled pastry—one she knew got shipped to the Island. And that thought had brought about another—if she was already missing Northern delicacies, there was a high likelihood her mother had frequented the shop in order to get her fill constantly.

Rosaelia didn't expect to find her mother there, and she knew she looked more like her father's side than her mother's so she wasn't sure if her looks would help with her line of questioning, but she hoped she could get the shopkeeper to understand who she was in search of.

The shop, named North's Share, was larger than Rosaelia had been expecting. It was made of wood as most of the buildings here were and there was a large sign hanging from an awning with the name painted in red lettering.

Inside, the place was filled with tables and displays of all sorts. Most of the stuff was food related, but to the sides, Rosaelia saw fabrics and books, and smaller items. There was a sense of nostalgia being in the space. She expected the nonas loved this place as much as she found herself loving it, as much as she suspected her mother likely loved it.

Rosaelia traveled around the others within the shop, looking for the old man the nonas had told her owned the shop. He was on the shorter side with white hair that was so far retreated, it made him look even older. His skin was wrinkled, but he always wore an infectious smile. Rosaelia recognized him immediately. He drew attention with his happiness.

Rosaelia waited until he was finished with the two women he was speaking with, then moved in his direction—where coincidentally the raspberry-filled pastries were—and began filling a baggie with two.

"Well, look at the beauty we have here." The man's voice carried to her. "I don't believe I've seen you in my shop before, lovey."

Rosaelia gave him a smile as she got a closer look at the man. He was an Islander for sure with the scars lining his skin, smaller than Killian's face ones but similar to the ones on his body. "What a shame to have missed out on this delicacy in all this time. I just traveled to this town."

"Ah." He smiled. "From?"

He was infectiously happy. So different from the other Island men she'd met. "Redding." She pulled the name from the geography lessons the nonas had given.

"Well, girl. I hope you remain. We, here, are the best town."

She laughed. "And you the best shop?"

"Of course!" He laughed.

She handed him the coin for her pastries. Noticing the markings on his finger, the one Northern and Southerners would put a ring. "May I ask you a question, Mr. …"

"Geppetto. And of course, my dear."

"Mr. Geppetto. I am actually in town looking for my cousin." Rosaelia knew they had enough similarities about them that Rowena still needed to be referenced to as family. And she most certainly didn't wish to call her a mother. "I was told she frequents this shop often. She is quite a bit older so we never grew up together, but I wish to know her. I simply cannot seem to find her."

"Of course, of course. I know all of my customers, especially the ones that frequent often." He gave her a cheeky grin. "Her name, child?"

Would she use a different name in the Island? Would she

use a different name in this shop specifically? Rosaelia had to risk it. "Rowena."

He paused. "You are family to Ro—yes, yes. I see a bit of the similarity. Well, of course, I know Rowena. She comes here every week."

Rosaelia smiled. "She's a routine girl."

Mr. Geppetto laughed. "No. She never comes the same time or day. That would be too easy." He leaned in. "That cousin of yours has certain pastries she especially loves and grows angry when we run out before she makes her visit. I told her if I knew when she was coming, I could save her some, but she always ignores me. That one you have there"—he pointed to the raspberry-filled pastries in her baggies—"is one of her favorites. A family taste, I see."

Rosaelia's grin dropped, but she forced it back up. She didn't want any similarities with her mother.

"Would you happen to know where she comes from? Or goes after her visit?"

"I do not know where she goes, per se. I always figured home to drop off her buys. But I have seen her time and again come in with red stains about her dress. I assume she comes from the Bloody Fields on those days, though I couldn't fathom why anyone would want to spend time there."

The Bloody Fields. The nonas mentioned that in their little lesson. It was a bit farther out than town but closer to this shop than Killian's home on the other side. It was a field of flowers that had been crushed and now never grew the same. The red of the flowers were known to stain so most people stayed away from them since those stains were impossible to get out and Islanders didn't exactly have the abilities to constantly be buying or making new clothes.

"The Bloody Fields," Rosaelia repeated. "Would you mind giving me directions?"

He eyed her clothes. "Are you sure?"

She gave a warm smile. "I will change into already ruined clothes before traversing." Though she had no plans of actually getting close enough to get stained. "And maybe, if you remember, the days you see her in those stains. Is it normally earlier in the day or later?"

"Midafternoon, love," he answered, then began the directions to get there from this shop.

"Thank you," she said with finality as a few kids came running for him with a list of things they needed for their families, and Mr. Geppetto was back to helping his shoppers.

Midafternoon meant Rowena conducted her matters morning to early afternoon. It was already too late in the day to head to the Bloody Fields. By the time Rosaelia got there, she may have missed her mother. She'd try later, but this was a huge start.

She left the shop with the pastries, then hesitated as she brought one to her lips. She brushed her thoughts aside and bit into it. She couldn't control if she had similarities with that woman. At the end of the day, they were blood.

CHAPTER 8
KILLIAN

The taste of her still lingered on his tongue as he pulled an arrow out of one carcass and his dagger out of another. Killian didn't know what had brought on the night before, but he assumed the girl's obvious attraction to him and the fact that no one in the North would hear of it had her curious for more.

He was glad she'd listened to that side of her brain rather than the logical one because it was the best fuck of his life.

And not because of his seven-year celibacy train either. In his twenty-eight years of life, he didn't know anything could taste so good. And it saddened him in a way Killian wasn't accustomed to feeling to know that he would not get another taste. To know that the Princess had wanted him to sate her desires and curiosity, but that would be all he would be receiving.

He growled as his cock fought against his trousers to be let out and into Sael's cunt again. It desired to know what her mouth would look like wrapped around it, what her tongue would feel like on its tip.

Killian shut his eyes hard, hating that he hadn't even thought to question his celibacy the moment he'd realized what she was in his room for. Hadn't thought to question anything, not her purpose for showing up and coincidently finding her way into the one house that would protect her or her true purpose for being in his bed. Nothing past the fact that he *needed* to be inside her any way she would allow it.

It had been foolish.

Foolish to allow her to get near him. Foolish to drop to his knees for her. Foolish to swallow every drop from that divine pussy. Foolish to take her to his bed and lose his cock inside her. Foolish to lick and bite and taste every inch of her, to cry out with how amazing it felt.

Killian growled again as he threw his dagger through the air and watched it land into the gut of a squirrel. The small ones normally got traded in for whatever his nonas wanted. The larger ones, he looked down to the three large bodies beside his feet, he either kept all to himself for his family's meals or traded for larger purposes.

He had been ridiculously foolish touching her not yet knowing what the fuck she was doing in the Island.

Even though he knew that much, Killian convinced himself the night before hadn't been a stupid mistake that would get him killed. The girl was not from the Island Nation, and she was gentle as a *literal* fucking Princess. He would be safe. His family would be safe.

And he most definitely wouldn't be inside her again.

Killian loaded the animals to his pulley and continued on his trek, knowing a few animals would be stupid enough to show themselves with the smell of all this blood, and he would get those kills to add to his pile.

He would hunt until he was forced to go home because in

reality, he only wanted to find the Princess again for another taste, so he needed the distraction.

"C'mon, Kill," he muttered to himself as he pulled the animals. "She's a fucking Princess. The girl uses and throws out. It's what she's used to. You're not getting another taste." *And you most certainly don't want it.*

He needed to talk himself out of it now. Before he saw her again and all reason was lost.

She wasn't his claim, no matter what he'd said to those men in the forest or what his nonas thought. Especially after hearing them the night before and knowing of his celibacy, Killian knew the nonas would expect nothing more than for Sael to be a claimed woman now. His claimed woman.

As he pulled the heavy load, he wondered if it would be such a bad thing—to claim a Princess that would soon be off to her palace. He would get the benefits of claiming her—which really only meant that everyone would know whose she was and no one would try to touch her. It was something he had thought through thoroughly—she was a beauty, and other men would notice soon enough, especially if she became more comfortable walking about town.

But he could easily claim her now, then be done with her when she went home. It would at least ensure no one else would touch her and that he could touch her as much as he'd like.

"The problem there, tough guy," he growled to himself. "Is that the Princess isn't going to want any more of your touch. Do not fall under fucking Northern-Southern fairy tales of coming together because you fucked. And especially not with the fucking spoiled brat."

And though he'd enjoyed the night before immensely, he wanted to be rougher with her, more barbarian. He wanted to do things to her so everyone knew who she belonged to. So maybe it wasn't such a bad thing she wouldn't come back for more.

"She doesn't belong to you, fucker," Killian mumbled again as he dropped the pulley and threw his dagger directly between the eyes of a medium-sized wild cat species. It had smelled blood and come for an easy meal. Killian would be the first and last lesson it learned—nothing in life came easy.

With it added to his pulley, Killian observed his lot for the day. Four larger ones and three small should be plenty enough for a day of hunting. With the day closing to night soon, he needed to get these to the shed behind his home and begin skinning them for trade or meal.

Killian huffed as he stared at his latest kill, his hand moving on instinct to the back of his neck where he still felt the fresh wounds of Sael's fingernails. He couldn't help but smile to himself for a moment, knowing this was a set of scars he wouldn't mind, though he knew these would be gone soon.

He dropped the smile. It was ridiculous to be doing so at all when thinking of the girl. Especially not knowing whether it had been her plan all along to be found by the one family who was guaranteed to protect a Northerner.

Luckily, Killian ran into no other problems on his walk home and was quick to skin and wash off the animals and himself so the smell of blood didn't attract any more.

They were stored in the back closest that grew colder than the Island's frigid nights, then he finally moved for the back entrance to the bathing chamber. He needed a thorough washing. Then maybe a long soak and a few visits between his cock and his hand, the image of Sael in blissful throws still clinging to him. The memory of her covered in his cum placed to the forefront of his thoughts.

CHAPTER 9
ROSAELIA

Rosaelia jumped, reaching for the closest piece of cloth to cover herself. "What are you doing in here?" she raged at the barbarian.

"Don't yell at me, princess." Killian closed the back door and moved into the room. "It isn't my fault you didn't lock the door. How was I meant to know there was anyone in here?"

"I-I didn't know."

He one-handedly swung his blood-soaked shirt off, catching all of Rosaelia's attention. "Still not my fault, princess."

He reached for his trousers and Rosaelia backed up. "What are you doing?"

His trousers dropped, and his hardening cock was out as he leisurely moved for the tub she had been filling. "Taking a bath. What else would I do in the bathing chamber, blood-soaked as I am?"

"You can't!"

His smirk, even on that scarred and dirty face, was enticing. "Says who? I can do anything I please."

"I was going to take a bath, Killian. Wait your turn!"

"You may join me, Sael. I have absolutely no problem with that." He touched the still filling water, then turned it slightly cooler as if her temperature had been too hot.

Rosaelia wrapped the cloth around herself and moved for him, pushing him away from the bath. "Stop that! Stop touching anything and get out!"

He licked his bottom lip. "You think my sleeping trousers are doing any work in covering up every piece of skin I've already tasted, princess? Or is this your way of making me head to bed naked? Want another round already?"

Rosaelia's head snapped down, and that's when she realized it had been his sleeping trousers, normally left in the bathing chamber for him to change into after his baths, that she'd grabbed. It was the leg of his sleeping trousers that she held over her breasts and the other leg that fell over her cunt.

She caught his gaze once more. "Don't confuse my earlier stupidity and curiosity for desire, barbarian. Look at you, covered in blood like that. You're an animal!"

He gave her a cruel laugh. "Don't shy away now, *princess*."

Rosaelia knew the term of endearment—men calling their women 'princess' to signify that they ruled over the man's heart. But Killian used it in such a derogatory tone it was almost worse than when he called her by her station. Never could she have fathomed she would have wanted 'Princess' back over 'princess.'

"Call me what you truly want to," he continued. "Monster. Go ahead, *Rosaelia*. I'm a monster."

"Don't boost your ego, barbarian. You're savage and impossible and an animal, but you're not scary in the slightest."

He collared her throat and pushed her into the wall so hard the trousers fell from her hands so they were skin to skin, his still somehow hard cock pressed into her stomach. "I think you need to be schooled about where bratty little Princess Rosaelia has found herself."

She matched his dark stare with one of her own. She wasn't afraid of him. "What did you do? Kill a few people, barbarian? My brother is the Master Assassin. That doesn't scare me!"

That cruel laugh touched her cheek, his teeth skimming down her skin until he reached her ear. "I haven't only killed people, princess. I continue to do so."

Rosaelia kept her head held high. "My brother is the Master Assassin."

His teeth scraped her cheek again as he made his way to her lips, then tilted his head back to catch her eyes. "Did your Master Assassin kill his entire family?"

Rosaelia didn't know how to comprehend that question. "What?"

"Why do you think it is only me and the nonas? Did you ever wonder where my grandfather was? My aunts and uncles? Cousins? *My parents?*"

Rosaelia's heart stopped. "You're lying!"

"Am I?" He moved his free hand so his index skimmed her cheek, down her neck until his hand pressed into her chest. "You're afraid because you know I'm not lying."

"I'm not afraid of you!" Stupidly, idiotically, moronically not afraid of him.

"Your heart begs to differ." His hold around her neck tightened a bit as he pressed into her chest. "Afraid I'll kill you too, princess?"

"You're lying!"

He smirked as he leaned down to take her bottom lip between his teeth. He tugged on it until it swelled with evidence he'd been there. "Ask the nonas. They'll tell you I wore each of them blood splattered on my skin like medals."

Rosaelia hated her betraying heart as it sped up, both because of the fear creeping in and because of what he'd done to her lip. His proximity hadn't gone unnoticed by her body, and half the reason behind her racing heart was knowing they were both naked, skin to skin, and she wanted him closer still.

Stupidly, idiotically, moronically.

"I told you not to give your virtue to a monster, princess."

"Let go of me, barbarian!"

He chuckled as his hand moved up, holding her jaw as he forced her head back, then leaned down and licked her from that dip between her collarbones to her lips. "Still refusing to see the monster before you, huh? Maybe the Princess is spoiled *and* stupid."

He released her and turned back to the bath like she meant nothing in the world. He lowered into the water and ignored her as he dipped completely under to get the blood and sweat off his face and hair. Rosaelia wanted to move for him and keep him under that water until he drowned, but she wasn't so stupid to think her strength came anywhere near his.

She ground her teeth together, grabbed for the small robe, and put it on as she moved for her room. She wanted to slam it but she wasn't a child so she wouldn't. She absolutely wouldn't give Killian that ammunition.

And she didn't need the nonas to know something was the matter.

She fell into her bed and grumbled into the pillow, especially annoyed that her body was awake and wanting to go back and allow him to continue licking her. She was throbbing between her legs, and her peaked nipples were incredibly sensitive as they brushed against her robe.

She yelled into her pillow, then tried to calm down as she

hugged it, and made herself forget about the barbarian as she fell into sleep.

BECAUSE HE'D STOLEN her bath the night before, Rosaelia woke early to take it in the morning. It was only ten minutes of quietude before she was dressing in her room and she heard the others waking for the day, but she enjoyed every moment of it.

As she dressed in her simple dress and tied her hair back with a cloth, Rosaelia sighed with the thought of seeing Killian again. She was already stressed about locating her mother and finding the courage to kill her, the very last thing Rosaelia needed was this barbarian ridiculing her.

To make matters worse, she wasn't meant to be seeing the Master Sorcerer until the next day so she had this entire day to spend. She had plans to follow what that shopkeeper told her the day before and see if she could find Rowena. Or a trail that led to her. Her heart raced at the prospect of finding the woman so early on. She'd never done anything like this, being so unlike the others within the Posse, and she hated herself again for the sheltered, spoiled life she truly had lived before.

When she turned into the common spaces, Killian was sitting at the table with a large plate before him, the nonas around the table as well.

"Well, if it isn't my princess up for breakfast." He still wore that wicked grin.

Both nonas smiled at her, then beamed at Killian's declaration. Rosaelia wanted to smack him with a pan, but she didn't want to upset the nonas so instead she forced a smile—poorly, for once even her Princess training unable to hide her annoyance—and took her seat at the other end of the table.

Her poorly constructed smile, Killian's cruel one, and the tension filling the space between them made both nonas' grins drop as they snapped their gazes between the two of them while Rosaelia readied her plate and quietly ate.

Killian continued to throw her cocky looks throughout the silent meal, but Rosaelia ignored him and instead memorized the instructions she'd been given the day before.

When he finished his meal, Killian took his plate to the wooden bucket used as a washbasin, then moved for her.

Rosaelia didn't have time to react before he had a hand clasped to the back of her neck and forced her head back. When she met his gaze with her defiant one, he gave that dark chuckle and kissed her temple, then loudly said, "I'll see you tonight, princess."

He was making fun of her *and* his nonas' desire for them to be together. He was a savage animal!

Both nonas watched her as Killian left the house. While Rosaelia tried to ignore them in order to avoid trouble with the family, she felt their stares burn into her.

She ate silently, then moved for the washbasin, taking Killian's and her own plates to clean. All the while, she felt the nonas staring at her.

When she finished, she gave them a light smile. "I will see you two tonight. Thank you again for your hospitality."

They gave her warm, unconvinced smiles, but she left before they could question her.

Since Mr. Geppetto had given his instructions from the North's Share shop, Rosaelia walked in that direction and planned to follow said directions once she reached the shop.

She stayed within the forests this time, keeping the trail to her left so she didn't get lost within these woods. But she wanted to stay hidden. For no particular reason since she hadn't been threatened by anyone but Killian—and those men who'd been drunk on ale.

If she found Rowena today, should she go along with her original plans of ridding of the woman or should she wait until her meeting with Alana the next day? Rosaelia wasn't sure, especially because she feared now more than ever—now that it was a reality that it would be happening—that she wouldn't be able to kill her mother. The thought of taking a life wasn't an easy one to swallow.

Rosaelia decided she would remain hidden and simply observe. If the moment allowed for it, she would take action. She needed to remain of sound mind, couldn't afford to rashly jump into situations.

Once she made it to the shop, Rosaelia remained hidden within the trees so as not to grab Mr. Geppetto's attention, then moved around it to the back. From there, it would be a straight walk until the route broke out in two. He'd said the right would take her to the small homes lining the shore, and the left would take her toward the Bloody Fields.

She took the left, though the sounds of the waves crashing against the shore made the right route much more appealing, and stayed hidden as she followed that route. The next break had the Bloody Fields on the right and the route to the next town over to the left. Rosaelia followed the right silently.

Mr. Geppetto had been clear about the fact that most everyone avoided coming to these fields as along with the stains, the pollen was also heavy, so Rosaelia readied a piece of cloth around her face to cover her mouth and nose so she didn't go around sneezing and revealing she was about.

When this route ended, Rosaelia stayed hidden behind a large tree and followed the greenery with her gaze a few yards before it blossomed into a field of red. For miles surrounding her, there was red everywhere.

She pushed away from the tree and found one with branches she could climb, the nostalgia of doing so as a child with Sparrow, Miels, and Tristan flaming her memories. There was a bit of ice left on some of the branches from the night before, but it was an easy climb, nonetheless.

When she sat on the branch, she had a clear view of the fields, but remained completely hidden behind bushes of leaves.

But from this perspective, she caught sight of her mother. Rosaelia's breath caught at seeing the woman again. She wore the same frigid look about her features, though she looked frailer. Whatever that potion had been that Alana had thrown on her must've truly worked.

But Rosaelia could hardly focus on that.

Because Rowena wasn't alone, and Rosaelia was nearly ready to vomit all over these fields.

Rowena stood in the middle of a group of men and women, all of whom had darker skin tones than Islanders did. Not quite as dark as Gemma or James, the two Southerners part of her Posse back home, but almost like Rosaelia's coloring.

It made her waver on the question of whether or not they were Northerners when she heard the mutterings they were barely able to make out. "You are the rightful ruler of our lands. You are the rightful ruler of our lands. You are the rightful ruler..."

They were all half conscious, their blood seeping into the red fields around them and mixing in beautifully. Each one was gashed in so many places on their face, it was difficult to make who they once had been. If it hadn't been for the arms left unmarked, Rosaelia wouldn't be able to tell they were darker than the common Islander.

Rowena tipped her head back with arms held out into the air, blood seeping off her hands. She laughed. "Louder! Let the North hear you!"

It was clear the group of seven were muttering as loudly as they could. Two of them had barely intact faces, one of them had an eyeball hanging out, and three of them had one eye sewed shut. Around them, there were another five lying dead. From those five, one had a tongue sewed to the bottom of his chin.

Rosaelia silently vomited over the branches, emptying her stomach of any morsel of food. When she could no longer take it, she wiped her tongue with the handkerchief around her face.

Rosaelia wanted to turn and run from this. She couldn't imagine the horrors that had been done to them. She couldn't imagine how this had happened. Where had Rowena gotten Northerners? And if this was how she planned on making her way to the throne—by frightening the citizens into submission—Rosaelia felt a more dire need to put an end to it.

She needed to put an end to this.

But as she pulled her bow and arrow out, Rosaelia couldn't stop the shaking of her hands. She couldn't miss. One inclination that her life was in danger and Rowena would go running. And with the way Rosaelia's hand was shaking, she'd certainly miss her first try, end up hitting one of the seven.

But maybe that would be preferable. Maybe they needed this, needed to die already.

Rosaelia wanted to give it to them, but as she stared down the arrow and tried to calm her hands, she couldn't get herself to release.

Like a saving grace, the only one she'd given other than keeping Evony hidden two decades ago, Rowena pulled a sword from behind her and slashed it through the air. She took the lives of all of them in one pirouette. Graceful, elegant, queenlike.

Rosaelia tasted bile as she breathed a sigh of release. These Northerners needed the mercy—though Rosaelia was sure that wasn't the reason Rowena had done it—and she wasn't sure if she would've been able to do it. To take another life, an innocent life, even one in desperate need to be set free. It would haunt her for the rest of her days.

Rosaelia kept her weapons raised for a long time after that. So long, she'd gone numb before she was ready to drop down from the treetop.

Rowena was long gone by then, but the memory of what had happened here in the Bloody Fields would be with Rosaelia forever.

CHAPTER 10

ROSAELIA

Clearing her head of Rowena in those fields was difficult. The entire walk to the nonas' home, she fought the bile rolling up her throat.

She washed her mouth ten times over but still, Rosaelia felt sick.

Matters of Killian's savagery didn't help the hammering of her heart. She left one animal and was coming home to another.

When she stepped into the common space, after coming in front the bath and bathing, Killian was with his nonas, laughing and preparing the meal. He looked so handsome with that smile, genuine and large. It made Rosaelia want to smile too.

But then his gaze flashed to her, and his lips downturned, and Rosaelia's followed along. She was glad he hid that part of him from her. She didn't need to be growing a warm heart for the monster.

He was clean, having bathed before helping his nonas, and

though she logically knew to stay away from him, her cunt throbbed at how good he looked.

She didn't speak as she sat at the table and allowed for the chatter of Nona Tereza to fill the room. Killian joined the woman, and they spoke of matters Rosaelia wasn't familiar with, but she was glad to remain out of the conversation. With her mother still in her mind, Rosaelia wasn't in the mood to fake a smile.

But the entire time, she felt Killian's cruel stare on her like he was enjoying how uncomfortable being around him made her. She didn't allow him to see it though and stared back with a hard glare every time.

It was probably dumb to do so.

Now the nonas picked up the tension between them, and Rosaelia felt the stares of the two older women on her. They chatted on like nothing was the matter, but the entire time, Rosaelia felt their stares.

When she finished her meal, she moved for that spot in the nook of the living space and settled back, now lost in the memory of Killian telling her with a grin that he'd killed his entire family. Her stomach rolled at the idea.

It was astonishing—the variety of barbarian in this land. On the low end, there was Mr. Geppetto who may have been harsher in his younger years simply to survive but was now a sweet, happy old man. There were the nonas—technically Northern, but Island in their current mentality with the way they spoke of the publicness of relationships. Then there were savages like those men in the woods who may have tried to attack Rosaelia had she been alone. There were the men who fought and threw bets like those she saw in town square that first time.

And there was Killian—a man who had killed his entire family.

As the night came to an end, Killian seemed to drop his need to terrorize her, and moved to his room without a glance in her direction. Nona Tereza left quietly not long after, her stare burning until she was finally gone.

Nona Eleni wasn't looking at her, but as Rosaelia stared down at the small book in her hands, one she'd randomly grabbed to look busy, she felt a presence beside her. Nona Eleni sat on the arm of the chair, and when Rosaelia jumped at her presence, then tried to move over so the older woman could sit in the comfortable part of the chair, she smiled and patted Rosaelia's shoulder to stay her.

Nona Eleni played with her hair, then tipped Rosaelia's head back to meet her eyes. "What did he say to you, dove?"

"Nothi—"

"Do not lie to me, dove. What did he say?"

Rosaelia sighed. "He said he killed your entire family."

Nona Eleni gave her small nods as she analyzed Rosaelia's reactions, her thumb brushing at Rosaelia's cheek comfortingly. "I suppose that is all he said? He did not explain?"

Rosaelia's brows furrowed. "Explain?"

She gave a small smile. "He is trying to push you away, dove. He was trying to scare you thinking he killed them for fun. That he hurts people for fun."

"Why did he kill them then?"

Nona Eleni's thumb brushed her cheek again before she leaned down and kissed her temple. Then she sat back against the chair, and brought Rosaelia into her side, arm wrapped softly around her shoulders. "Tereza's husband was a bastard. Not at first, of course, but after a decade or so. It was when I married and our husbands met that they slowly began to turn worse and worse, like they brought it out of one another, but those first few years had been bliss." She spoke like she was in the memory of those first few years. Like she missed those short years.

"But eventually they got cruel. By then we already had children who were getting older. Tereza's oldest was about fifteen, youngest about six. I only had one, he was about ten. That's when things started getting really bad. It started with cheating. Lots and lots of serial cheating, wing manning one another to sleep with anyone but us. We were both far out of love by then, but we had a comfortable home here and no way to go back to the North, so we stayed as long as they didn't think they would also be sleeping with us as well. That lasted about five years before Tereza's husband, Marki, got another woman pregnant. When she told him, their oldest son didn't like that, so he beat the woman's stomach until the child within died. Marki only laughed when he heard of it and took his son to the whorehouse to celebrate." Nona Eleni played with Rosaelia's hair like that was keeping her grounded as she remembered her history. "Tereza and I had tried to keep the kids good, and for a while, half of them were. We were lucky, only half were like their fathers, but things changed. I believe the good ones got tired of always getting less than the others. I believe they got tired of being picked on. I believe, eventually, the savagery of their fathers and the others got to them. We tried, but the children were lost to us by then. I still do not know how we got lucky with our Killian."

"How many did Tereza have?"

"Five. Keegan was the oldest. Elin, that's Killian's mother, was her second. Helen was her third. Finn her fourth and Stella her last. Mine was Ewan."

So that was at least eight dead between the aunts and uncles and grandfathers.

"Over the next ten years after that, the children were between twenty-one to thirty, all of them with their own children and all of them with their own wicked spouses. We couldn't believe it, Tereza and I, how with all the good Islanders, every one of our children was wicked with their own wicked spouses and children. Killian was the fourth grandchild out of twenty-one and the only good one—at least, the only one to remain good."

Rosaelia wanted to argue she hardly thought him good, but then the memory of him throwing her against the tree to protect her, holding her into his side to keep her away from the men in the forest, came to mind, and she couldn't do so.

"For fourteen years he endured their ridicule when he didn't want to participate in beating up random poorer Islanders; when he didn't want to destroy people's livelihoods for fun; when he didn't want to go to the whorehouses. They smacked him around when he began jumping in front of me and Tereza when eventually our husbands and our own children began to hit us. Eventually, it was too much. Killian was out training because he's always been a strong man with hunting skills and always made sure to hone in his skills so he could take me and Tereza away from the monsters. When he returned home, he found the both of us naked and tied up with two of his cousins ready to..."

Rosaelia's heart stopped as she snapped her head to look at Nona Eleni, the woman off in space. Rosaelia remembered the fear she'd had when those men had cornered her in the alleyway before Evony had saved her. She couldn't imagine if she'd also been tied up and naked.

And by family!

"Most of the family was out, so when Killian walked in and found his uncle and four cousins in the room with us, laughing and uncaring that we were their grandmothers, he finally snapped. He only had a dagger in hand, and it was one against five, but Killian gutted each one of them. When he was done with them, they all had their guts shoved into their mouths. He got us untied and to the bathing chambers, made us tea while we dressed and made us stay in another room so we didn't have to see the mess. When our husbands came home, and Killian told them what happened, they got angry with *him*, said if his cousins wanted to fuck us, he should've let them. They ruffed him up, but Killian took it, and kept us away from them. We stayed hidden then—at the estate we were living, it was much simpler to hide—and Killian started planning. Because the rest of the family—his cousins and his aunts and uncles, their spouses—all of them were of one mind. Everyone thought it okay what his cousins had wanted to do to us, and every single one of them was killed because of it. He planned the killings out so he could get through all of them at once so he didn't have the others coming for us. Waited until they had a celebration that got them too drunk to stand, then went after them. He may not have had any chances going against them all at fourteen, but inebriated as they were, Killian took a few too many lives. The last to show up were his parents. By then, it had been weeks, and the bodies of the others were cleaned out and the house spotless, and we were happier than we had been in a long time with only our Killian. Then Elin and Ira, her husband, came home and smacked him around for what he'd done. Killian tried to have more respect since these were *his parents*, but when they turned on us, attacked us for allowing their *imbecile son* to do any of it. He snapped and killed them too."

He'd killed his entire family in the matter of a few weeks.

At only fourteen!

"We had thirty-four more relatives and Killian killed every single one of them to protect me and Tereza. He didn't care if he continued to get smacked around as long as we were safe.

He is the safest man to be with, dove. He would never touch you in any way you didn't want."

Rosaelia swallowed as she met Nona Eleni's warm gaze. "I was never afraid he'd hurt me, Nona." *I was simply afraid of the idea that he could so easily kill his entire family for fun.*

But now she understood completely why he'd done it.

Killian wasn't a monster. He was a protector.

CHAPTER 11

ROSAELIA

Going to bed on her own after Nona Eleni's story was hard when all she wanted to do was go back to Killian's room and cuddle into him. It was incredible to learn how soft and loving some Islanders were on the inside. They were meant to be the enemy, and Rosaelia knew some of them were—the ones who killed Sparrow's father came to mind—but Killian was far from the enemy.

Far from her enemy anyway.

But she went to her room anyway, then fell asleep to thoughts of going home to the palace where she could be surrounded by her family. She missed her father and Sparrow immensely.

In the morning, Rosaelia focused on the fact that she was seeing the Master Sorcerer again so they could begin planning out how to kill her mother and snuck out of the house before the others could see her. She didn't need their attentions on her as she carried her weapons out of the house.

They were to meet by the Black Tower, a large lighthouse building painted the deepest black Rosaelia had ever seen. It was much closer to the waters she had traveled to get to the Island Nation, so Rosaelia was filled with trepidation that a Northerner trading goods would see her and recognize the Princess of the Northern Lands. It was unlikely since many Northerners didn't recognize her, but it was still a very real fear.

When Rosaelia got there, bow and arrow at the ready the entire walk in order to protect herself, Alana was standing by the door to the lighthouse. She looked calm and smiled softly to passersby, looking completely unsuspecting. Rosaelia wouldn't be fooled by the niceties though. The fact was, she'd been teamed up with Rowena at some point. That meant she was just as greedy and dangerous as Rosaelia's own mother.

Rosaelia dropped her bow and placed her arrow back in her quiver so as not to draw attention to herself, then moved for the Master.

Alana gave a respectful bow of the head. "Princess."

"*Don't* call me that!" Rosaelia's head snapped to those a few yards out, hoping they hadn't heard a thing. And if they had, hoping they thought it the term of endearment rather than the title.

"As you wish." Alana turned for the lighthouse door. "Shall we head inside?"

Rosaelia rushed forward, loving the thought of being away from prying eyes, but hating that she couldn't know this wasn't a trap itself. Times like these, she wished she'd been trained as a spy like her brothers or that she had her sister's magic around to help her.

Rosaelia followed Alana up the dim, rounded stairways, the only lights coming from the burning candles every few yards. The fact that this staircase didn't have any handles proved to Rosaelia that maybe she did in fact have a fear of heights.

Alana moved with ease, clear that she had done this a thousand times over.

"Is this where you live?"

"In secret," the Sorcerer answered. "I never brought others up here so your mother won't know of it."

"You were partners yet you hid from her?"

Alana turned her head to look at Rosaelia while continuing to climb the spiral and smiled. It was impressive. "Our partnership did not mean I trusted her, Rosaelia."

When they reached the top of the tower, the stairs led to an expansive room with tables around the edges and a larger one in the middle. There were cauldrons and herbs and equipment and materials everywhere. It was fascinating to see, and a reminder that sorcerers were a physical profession, closer to that of a remedies maker, whereas magicians did everything mentally.

"Where do you sleep?" Rosaelia questioned.

Alana pointed to a door to the far edge of the room. "There is a small bedroom back there. I need nothing more than a bed and armoire. Everything else I require is out here."

Rosaelia moved for the table, slowly touching everything on it as she circled the room. "I saw Rowena yesterday." She met the Sorcerer's gaze. "She was in the Bloody Fields. I...didn't feel able to end her then."

Alana analyzed her before settling on her decision not to question Rosaelia about it. "I was unaware she frequented the Bloody Fields. I will look into it."

Rosaelia nodded. "I do not know her schedule, but I believe she prefers frequenting it in the mornings to early afternoons."

Alana nodded, then remained quiet.

"So where do we begin, Sorcerer?" Rosaelia filled the air as she tinkered with a mortar and pestle with a sparkling bit of herbs inside she knew had to be made by sorcerers.

Alana's lips quirked up. "I am not allowed to call you Princess, yet you can call me Sorcerer?"

"We are in the privacy of the tower. You may call me Princess if you wish."

Alana gave a soft nod, like she knew it was odd for Rosaelia to call her 'brother's' mother by her name, the woman who only a few weeks ago was aiding her own mother on a mission to kill her family. "We begin with the plan, Princess. What Rowena had wanted and what I had wanted in exchange. We begin with your learning what *was* happening to then see what *will* happen."

Rosaelia held her breath a moment before releasing it. She wanted to know this bit, more than anything, she wanted this explanation, but it still made her nervous. "Okay."

Alana stayed on the other side of the table, both of her hands clasped together at the edge as she watched Rosaelia explore. "Rowena came to me because she needed more than any simple potions. She needed aid in taking the Master Magician's power. She told me the Magician was her daughter and long ago, she had seen the power the girl held. When she learned of her daughter's existence nine years ago—because she knew the moment a Master Magician was announced, it was her daughter—she began planning. Rowena had thought her dead after she'd sent her men after her so she believed her plans were merely to take the throne from you and your father. When nine years later, she learned of the Magician's survival, she decided she had been hasty as the Queen, trying to kill her rather than take the power for herself. She wouldn't make that mistake again. She postponed her plans for years searching for the Magician, unable to find a trace. She tried to play it off as Evony hiding away meant she wouldn't be a problem, but I knew deep down, she needed to rid of the Magician. Six years ago, after three years of unsuccessful searches, she came to me asking for help in finding and taking the power from the Magician. I could not help with finding her, that is more a magician's job, but I could aid in taking her powers if she was before us."

"What did you get out of it?"

"Learning of the death of my husband and son had killed me, Princess. Learning only a few years after I'd disappeared, men had been sent out to kill them had ended the woman I was. So for years, I only made and sold potions, trying to find a way to get my vengeance. It was only recently that I learned that those men sent to kill them were barbarians rather than guards from the Northern King."

She thought King Edmund had killed her family? It was no wonder she had joined Rowena. Rosaelia herself would've joined for the chance at retribution. Especially if said retribution would also take the magical powers from the second heir to the Northern crown. "And that your son made it out alive," Rosaelia added.

"And that my son made it out alive. That he turned out to be the Master Assassin."

"How did you know it was him? You knew immediately."

"He looks exactly like his father had. They are copy and paste replicas. And his father had been a master—figuratively—with his work. He spoke of making Sparrow rings for his own matrimony, that he felt it in his soul that was what he had to do and he would know when the time was right to make them. I knew the moment I saw those rings that not only had Lazarus had the chance to make them, but that my Sparrow had found a mate who deserved to wear it. A mate I had agreed to kill. My son was alive and in love, and I had agreed to take that away from him. I knew the moment I saw him, the moment he wouldn't take his eyes off of that sword to Evony's neck, that I would do anything to protect the two of them."

Rosaelia was quiet a moment before asking, "Who sent the barbarians to kill them?"

She knew the answer, could guess it, but Rosaelia needed to hear it.

Alana gave a sad, close-lipped smile. "Queen Rowena. She didn't know who they were to the Master Sorcerer of course. All she knew was that Lazarus was the best sword maker for the crown, and she needed him gone if she was to take over the Northern crown."

"Why did you leave?"

Sadness filled her eyes. "I ask myself that daily, Princess."

Rosaelia didn't push for more of an answer. She would get it out of the Master. For Sparrow. Her brother deserved to know why his mother had abandoned him, and why she hadn't been around to protect his family with her potions when the men came to kill them.

"So what happened with the plans?" Rosaelia finally moved back to the story of her mother.

"For years, she continued on her search, but Evony was a splendid magician, exceptional at keeping herself hidden."

"She must've been. You do not understand how much it infuriated Sparrow to not be able to learn more of the Master Magician?" Rosaelia interrupted with a small smile at the memory of Sparrow's grumpiness each time he failed to learn more.

Alana smiled. "I suspect he is just like his father was so I can imagine it vividly." She was lost in her memory a moment before continuing her story. "After years, Rowena saw that the King's favor with the public was only growing. Her chances at a simple takeover were running thin. So she decided she would throw the search for the Magician out for the time being and attack the palace first. We were aware of the Master Assassin, of course, so we knew how trained the guards would be. She spent two years training men, then these last six months, began the rebellion." Alana smiled again as she said, "Then three months ago, the Master Magician was invited to the palace and Rowena had to pull all her plans. She knew with the Master Magician's aid, and with her familial ties to the throne there would be aid, any plans she had would be met with only failure. So she had to pull back. It made the rebels angry, anxious. They had been ready. But she knew she could manipulate your father into thinking Evony was the one after him. I cannot blame your father for being suspicious of everyone, and Rowena knew how to manipulate certain matters to make your sister look good for it."

Rosaelia thought back to that time a month ago. Her twin had been nothing but loyal, and both she and her father had been manipulated into believing her there for vengeance for being thrown out of the family. She had been as easily manipulated as her father because of their royal statuses making it difficult to trust anyone.

"She tried first with the Gwendolyn Powder during the explosion in the neighboring town to the palace. She thought if we could knock Evony out after wielding her powerless, then we would easily be able to take her magic. I agreed. But when that didn't work because Evony was too far from the powder, Rowena began to grow more antsy, especially with news that she had married the Master Assassin. Rowena was lucky to have raided the palace and settled that final bit of doubt into your father's mind when no one went for *their Queen*. The plan then was to take the Master Magician from that town. It hurt for me to be there, and I didn't stop to question how Rowena knew that is where she would be. Then she said she knew the Master Assassin would be coming for her. It would make things easier in revenge on the palace—to rid of both Masters together—so we waited.

"My vengeance was stronger being in that town than it had been before. It pained me to simply breath knowing the house we had lived in was so close. So when I got there and Sparrow was standing before me, I nearly crumbled. I didn't believe it a moment. I knew the Master Magician could not manipulate appearances, but I thought maybe I had heard incorrectly or she had lied. Somehow, the Magician knew of my family and was turning the Assassin into my late husband to distract me. I thought maybe the Gwendolyn Powder had faded faster on her or *something* had happened. That is why I needed to check their hands—even if they knew what my husband had looked like, they wouldn't know of the rings. It wasn't foolproof given Sparrow could've not found love or Lazarus could've been killed before having the chance to make them, but none of that happened. They wore their rings, there's an element Lazarus specifically had me make that made that clear as day. That loved one another. I needed to protect them. Sparrow, my son, and Evony, his entire reason for being."

"So that's why you betrayed Rowena?"

"And I would do so again, happily."

"So how do we get to Rowena?"

"There is a sorcerer in Ragon, it is a neighboring town. I would go myself but too many would recognize me. You need to go see him. He will have a list of Rowena's helpers here and a few vials that may help you in case I am not around."

"Why trust him?"

"When I found out Rowena had been the reason behind Lazarus's death and had been trying to kill Sparrow, I told him Rowena had killed his parents. It is the truth, but I hadn't mentioned it before. Now, he wants her dead as much as we do, but he is weaker, doesn't have much so he cannot do so himself. He will help you, Princess."

"Okay." Rosaelia nodded. Another ally in the Island

wouldn't be so bad. She was truly lacking in that department, not counting Killian's family.

And she certainly wouldn't involve them in this.

"You're a true Princess, Rosaelia. You are protecting your people and the Island's people. We will finish this and keep Sparrow safe. You will keep Killian safe."

Rosaelia stiffened. "What does this have to do with Killian?" *What did she know of Killian?*

"He is your mate, no? We take care of this, and your mother cannot harm him as she tried to do with Sparrow."

Rosaelia stuttered. "Killian isn't... we aren't... it's not the same thing."

Alana visibly didn't believe her, but she dropped it. "Well then, to keeping your family safe, Princess. To keeping my son and his beautiful wife safe. To keeping my future grandchildren safe."

Rosaelia nodded. To that much, she could agree wholeheartedly.

CHAPTER 12

ROSAELIA

When she returned home, the nonas were sitting at a small table in the back greens with blankets wrapped around them and tea before them. They both smiled at her but said nothing as she moved for the bathing chamber. She cleaned the day's sweat off, then moved for the room she'd been thinking about her entire walk home.

It was stupid, idiotic, moronic, but it was what she wanted. Needed.

A whole day of thinking of Rowena had earned her this escape. Had earned her a way to erase what she'd seen in the Bloody Fields.

After so much of her time spent planning out what to do about Rowena, she'd allowed herself the reprieve of thinking of Killian's body and everything she wanted him to do to her. She couldn't help how strong her desire was for him.

And she figured, while in the Island, there was no reason to fight it. They could enjoy one another for the duration of her stay.

She heard when he returned home, and knew he was in the

bathing chamber, cleaning the day's work off as she waited. This time, she was in only a soft robe that had been given to her against her protests. The nonas may be her favorite people to exist, truly.

It was black and skimmed the tops of her thighs and felt luxurious, even for the materials she knew of as a Princess.

Last time she had been waiting in his room, Rosaelia had been too nervous to do anything but stand in the middle. Though she'd noticed the way his gaze had raked her body before going to the room, that inexperienced part of her had urged her to not get cocky. He could still easily deny her request.

But that hadn't been the case. He'd accepted almost instantly, before she really even asked for it.

So Rosaelia felt more powerful now.

She moved for his bed, remembering the pleasure of being beneath him, the comfort of sleeping the night with him. So she sat in the middle of the bed, legs softly lounged to the side in proper Princess form and waited.

Which didn't take long. A few minutes after she'd settled, staring at the door, Killian walked in.

And paused like the last time.

He sighed and let the door close but didn't move toward her.

"What do you want now?" He sounded harsh, but his gaze raked over her body hungrily, and Rosaelia could see how quickly he was affected by her by the tightening of the towel that hung around his waist. She wondered why he'd forgone the sleeping trousers this time.

"You know what I want."

"No," he ground out and moved closer, more hunter than seducer, before pointing to the door. "Now get out."

She truly hadn't been expecting that. Throwing her down

and taking her, yes. Bending her over and taking her, yes. Pushing her into the wall and taking her, yes. But not a single part of her had expected a 'no.'

And most certainly not a 'get out.'

Rosaelia rose to her knees on the bed and crawled to the edge. "Why not?"

Those two scars were charming, especially around his shining eyes. Eyes that looked like they wanted to be cruel but were too filled with desire to do so. She knew he wanted her.

"What part of your spoiled little brain doesn't understand that you should fear the monster?"

"Your nona told me why you killed them. I don't fear you."

"But I am a monster."

"A handsome monster."

Killian tried to fight the amusement, but his lips tipped up with an airy laugh. Their faces were so close, Rosaelia felt his words hit her face as he switched tactics. "I don't go so soft, princess. I made an exception before. Don't get used to it."

"That's okay." The words left her before she could think them over. As if she truly understood the ramifications that came with them.

He quirked a brow, that smirk saying he didn't believe her.

"I..." She swallowed but refused to look anywhere but into his eyes. "I want to learn more."

"Well"—he pushed away and grabbed his towel from around his waist and began drying his hair—"I'm not interested."

Rosaelia's gaze snapped south, and she was hypnotized. It looked so beautiful, and she wanted nothing more than to taste it. Her cunt clenched at the thought of having him again. "I'd beg to differ."

He followed her gaze and laughed mockingly. "Don't play a

game you don't want, *princess*. How exactly would you feel if I left marks on you?"

Her cunt clenched again. Apparently, she would really enjoy the marks. "I told you the other night, *barbarian*, anything you want to do to me."

Something about that got his attention, and he finally just stared into her eyes. Then slowly down to her mouth, slightly parted and desperate for his, then lower, taking in her nipples peaked through the soft material and her thighs pressed together for any sort of friction.

"You're tempting a monster," he said, almost like a final warning to change her mind.

Again, Rosaelia didn't realize how much she loved the sound of that until it was in the air. "I want the monster. Give me him, Killian."

Stupid, idiotic, moronic, but she wanted him.

He watched her, still analyzing, as he moved to stand before her again, fully naked this time. Rosaelia wanted nothing more than to lick him everywhere.

But she remained still, allowed him the time to do as he pleased.

Killian took the ties to her robe and slowly pulled at them to open the robe up. Then he continued pulling until the silk belt was completely out of its loops and in his hands. He tugged on it a few times, as if determining whether it was strong enough for something, then caught her eyes with mischief behind his.

"Spread your legs, Sael, I want this room to smell like your desire."

She didn't hesitate a moment, wanting whatever he wanted. And more so, wanting him to touch her already.

He moaned as he licked his lips, his eyes raking her body. "Get rid of the robe."

She moved slowly, letting it slip off her shoulders, then to the side, but she didn't hesitate in listening to his command.

"What a good girl," he growled low as he pulled on the robe's belt in his hands, his cock visibly straining as he stood there.

"I want to please you." Rosaelia spoke the words that were all too true.

He laughed, dark and seductive. "Then fall back, princess. Hands above your head."

Rosaelia fell back until her head hit a pillow, then lifted her arms above her head. She didn't know what this was leading to, but she was growing wetter with the anticipation.

Killian crawled up her body, his tongue teasing her skin with the slightest of touches to her stomach, before moving straight up until they were face to face.

Then he kissed her, his tongue thrusting into her mouth and making her moan out before she remembered herself and the fact that the nonas were likely right upstairs by now. They'd have to be quiet this time.

But Rosaelia allowed herself to get lost in the kiss, loving the way Killian tasted and the way their bodies meshed together as she thrust her hips up and coated him in her juices.

"Good girls deserve rewards, princess." He kissed down her jaw and whispered in her ear, "Should my tongue give you a reward?"

"Please," she whispered back and moved her hands to his head.

Or tried to.

She pulled and pulled and realized then that her hands were tied to the wooden headboard.

Her gaze snapped to meet his, and he smirked. "Still want this, princess?"

"Anything you have for me, barbarian." She wasn't being

stubborn. Rosaelia genuinely found herself attracted to anything Killian wanted from her.

"Mm." He skimmed down her body. "That's my good little princess." He took her nipple into his mouth and sucked.

Her entire body jerked, and Rosaelia bit down on her lip to keep her voice muffled.

Killian released her nipple with a pop and continued down, rough hands pushing her legs apart. He shuddered as he breathed her in and it made Rosaelia wetter.

"If you're offering anything, princess"—his gaze snapped up to meet hers—"I want to taste you on my tongue every day."

"Deal," she whispered quickly, a whimper mixed with the plea to lick her already.

He smirked as he lowered himself. "Such a good fucking girl."

One swipe of his tongue had her body arching and her head falling to the side to muffle her moans into her arm. She let out whimpers with each lick and when he sucked on her clit, Rosaelia almost wasn't able to stop the scream before biting into her arm.

Then the attention to her cunt was gone, and she whimpered for an entirely different reason.

Killian kissed a few spots up her body before reaching her mouth and giving her a soft kiss. Then his lips were at her ear. "Why aren't you making a sound, princess?"

"Your nonas will hear!" she breathed out as her hips thrust up to meet his for any sort of friction, her arms tugging at the ties so she could reach for him, get on top and lick all of him.

He chuckled. "You didn't seem to have a problem with it before."

"I didn't know before!"

"Well." He chuckled against her skin, the sound like honey

to her ears. "I think it's important to let you know"—his fingertips softly grazed down her body until they met her clit—"that until I hear how much you're enjoying this," his fingers began rubbing circles, getting her closer and closer until she was about to finish. Then they were on her stomach, nowhere near where she wanted them. "I'm not going to let you finish."

"Killian, please," she whispered against his mouth.

He bit her lower lip before kissing back down her body. "I won't be able to hear that from down here. Matter of fact, your thighs may make it difficult to hear anything but your screams, princess."

His hands pushed her thighs as far as they would go, then licked her once and waited for her response.

She begged for him to continue.

And he did. With one lick. But never enough.

Then he watched her with that devious smirk and licked her only one more time.

After six solitary licks, Rosaelia couldn't take it any longer and cried out, begging for his mouth.

He chuckled darkly and finally latched around her clit, sucking it relentlessly as his fingers moved in and out of her until she was screaming his name with her release.

She thrashed, pulling on the ties around her hands to no avail, and he took every drop she had to offer.

When he lapped up all he could, he moved for her and sucked hard. Rosaelia hated herself for no longer caring whether the nonas heard, but she wanted to give Killian everything. And these sounds from their mouths somehow made the experience more. She absolutely loved the ones coming from him.

When he released her nipple, his lips moved to kiss her hard, almost bruising. Between that and the ties around her wrists and the pressure his hands had put into keeping her thighs spread, Rosaelia had no doubt she'd be left with marks.

He pulled away completely, and before she could beg him, he flipped her onto her stomach, her hands crossing as they remained tied to the headboard.

Killian licked her butt, biting down on one cheek hard enough that she knew she'd be marked as she cried out with pleasure. Then he licked up her spine, and every nerve ending in her body wanted him.

When he reached her ear, one hand shot into her hair to pull her head back. "Still want this, princess?"

"Please," she begged.

He chuckled as he kissed her, his tongue dominating hers before he pulled away again.

As she cried out her disappointment, his hands wrapped around her waist and hoisted her ass into the air.

"Such a pretty thing, princess. I must admit, I wonder what you do to keep it so round and luscious."

He smacked her before she could say a thing, and she cried out with the sting of his hand. He soothed it a moment before he smacked the other side. As he smoothed it, he laughed cruelly. "This ass is mine, princess. I hope the North won't mind."

His knees spread hers farther apart and without warning, he thrust into her. Hard.

She cried out, mixed with his deep groans, and lost herself in the pleasure. It was electric.

He held on to her hips as he pounded into her and he hadn't been kidding, this was much rougher than before.

But Rosaelia loved every second of it.

Then he spit on her ass and smacked the spit all over her cheek. Again. And again.

Then he mixed his spit with her arousal, and Rosaelia

yelped as a finger found its way to a hole she did not realize would be disturbed.

Rosaelia cried out with her release as his finger and cock entered her together.

It was a never-ending orgasm, and part of her wondered if she'd had multiple. Was that even possible?

His hips shuddered against her, then he pulled out and she felt the warmth on her back and butt. He'd come on her again.

She laughed into the pillow.

"Something funny, princess?" he growled.

"Am I still the prettiest princess if you finish on my butt?"

She could hear his amusement as he answered, "Definitely. Though I prefer it on your front. That way I get to see your eyes shine for me too."

She smiled into the pillow, then looked back at him as he slowly cleaned his mess from her skin. When she was clean, he hovered over her body and finally released her hands, but Rosaelia didn't move.

She laid flat on her stomach and left her arms high, though less strained now, as she snuggled into the pillow.

"You're in the middle, princess."

"Princesses get whatever they want, barbarian."

He chuckled, disbelieving, then got in beside her. His large size meant he needed to snuggle into her side in order to fit his whole form, but Rosaelia didn't care as she drifted to sleep.

CHAPTER 13

KILLIAN

It was now two mornings in a row where Sael had snuck out from beneath him and run off into the forests. The day before, Killian had only thought she was going out to eat and prepare with his nonas so he hadn't done a thing about it, but she hadn't been out there when he'd finally dragged himself away from the scent of her in his sheets.

His nonas had pointed toward the forests when asked where she was, and Killian hadn't been able to track her. It made him curiouser and curiouser about what she was doing in the Island Nation. He'd tried to fight his need to know in the days she'd been with them, but after getting another taste of her, it was impossible.

Today, he wouldn't be so foolish again.

If it happened that she truly was going to be with his nonas then he could simply go about his day without a worry. But if not, as he highly suspected, he wanted to be there and see what the hell the Northern Princess was after.

Rosaelia was out from beneath him early, before their twilight tryst where he made her come into his mouth as his first breakfast of the day. Killian was hypersensitive to her movements, so it was humorous that she thought he didn't wake with her each time.

He laid there pretending to sleep while she quietly dressed and left the room. Killian dressed quickly after her and was just as silent as he followed her out of the house and into the forests.

She was headed toward Ragon, the next town over toward the west, home of some of the best sorcerers.

But what could Princess Rosaelia of the North want with sorcerers? They were the ones who had banned the people from coming about their lands, the largest catalyst to the enemy barricade the North and Island now held for one another. The reason *she* was *his* enemy.

Killian kept his distance when he saw her come upon a sorcerer, although every part of his being wanted to storm over and peel her away from him. He was really more boy than man and it was obvious by Sael's lust for him that she was only into men, him specifically, but Killian hardly cared. His mind was already racing with all the ways he could kill the boy.

Not that he would, but oh the fantasies were enticing.

He didn't understand this possession. It wasn't simply because he'd fucked her. He'd fucked plenty of women before. But something in this pure, innocent one made the beast in him come alive.

He couldn't hear what they were saying but the two seemed to be in a deep, serious conversation before the *boy* took her hand and they moved into town. Killian saw red as he followed, every fiber of his being going toward *not* ripping the sorcerer's hand off completely.

Killian ground his teeth. He was going to fuck her so hard tonight, she wouldn't be able to move. He wasn't going to have her leaving him again, and especially not for a fucking boy! He would fuck her until she was only able to process breathing in and out, and if come morning she tried to get out of bed again, he'd pin her down and fuck her again, waking the entire house with her screams.

He was hard as a fucking rock thinking about the way she would beg him for more, the way she would scream his name over and over. Fuck, he wasn't sure if he'd be able to wait until they got home.

Killian followed them until he no longer could. He moved for a high window in the small shop they'd gone into but could hardly see what was happening. It was obviously the sorcerer's shop where he sold his potions to the public, but Killian couldn't understand what the two were doing together.

He could just catch them around the corner of the window and swore he could make out the sorcerer handing her some papers and vials. Was this the mission of the Northern Princess? Begin looking into sorcerers, maybe testing them to see if they could be trusted before they opened borders between the two nations? It would be a start. Especially considering the general public of the Island were far more dangerous than the sorcerers. Sorcerers normally made potions that truly helped the public, never truly caring for more power. If testing the sorcerers to see if opening borders would be safe was the plan, the Princess would need another reminder as to what the Island's *people* were like.

They headed back toward the forest together not long after, Sael's papers and vials hidden away. Killian assumed they'd gone into the sack for her arrows as there wasn't much else place to hide the things. It was clever too. Most wouldn't think to search there.

Killian followed them and continued to keep his distance as they said their farewells and had to force himself to remain still when the sorcerer touched her arm again, this time sliding his hand down until he took hers. He kissed her knuckles, then turned around to leave.

Killian didn't know how he managed to make himself follow Sael rather than turn around and kill that guy, but somehow he'd done it.

He followed silently to see if she was headed anywhere else, but when it was clear she was going home, Killian stepped closer. "My cock not enough for you, you needed a fucking *boy*."

She jumped, turning on him with her bow and arrow raised. At least she had some instinct to protect herself. She glared at him as she lowered the weapon. "Were you following me?"

"You put my house in danger by being there. I needed to see whether this thing you were sneaking off for would put my nonas at risk."

"Rest assured, I would never put your nonas at risk." The way she said it, with conviction, made him believe her instantly.

"So what was this then? Not getting enough cock?" He stepped closer.

Her hand flew through the air before he could register it and had his head flying with the smack. "I'm no whore, barbarian."

Killian licked his lips, fighting his arousal at her hit and meeting those emerald eyes. "No, you're not, princess. Which is why you are beneath me and me alone. You can run off all you'd like but we both know you'll be beneath me, screaming *my* name, every night. You belong to me!"

"I belong to no one!"

He threw her against the tree like their first meeting. And like their first meeting, she hissed as her sack of arrows bit into her back. "You are mine, Sael. I have you in my bed every night and have missed the taste of you on my tongue for two mornings now. You're bringing out the monster, princess."

"Fine. Next time I'll leave after you get your taste. Happy?"

He ground his jaw as a fist slammed into the tree by her head. "No, I'm not fucking happy, Sael! You are mine. You will not frolic around with other men!"

"I'm not frolicking around, you ass! You forget that I am on the Island for a reason. I won't let your tongue or your fingers or your cock let me forget that!"

He kissed her fast and rough, his tongue fighting between her lips until he was in her warm mouth. He thrust into that beautiful mouth until he felt her suck on the tip of his tongue. His entire body thrust into her then, unable to resist. "Will my kisses make you forget?"

She didn't open her eyes as she gave a dazed shake of her head.

He gave a cruel laugh and kissed her again, sucking on her bottom lip then taking extra care of her tongue until her moans had him about to come into his trousers. "You sure my kisses won't work, princess?"

Her hands clung around his neck as her leg hitched up to wrap around his waist, but she gave him a defiant look. "I need to do this for my family."

"What? Fuck me, princess?"

"Barbarian!"

He chuckled and gave her the kiss she wanted. He understood. Whatever she was in the Island for, she was doing it for her family. Whatever she had gone to that sorcerer for, she was doing it for her family. It was the one thing Killian could understand above all else.

Then he abruptly pulled away from her and reveled in her whimpers of protest.

He bit his bottom lip as he watched her. "You belong to me, Sael."

She dropped the sack from her back and pressed herself against the tree, hands skimming up her body. "Whatever you say, Killian. Just please!"

Killian laughed as he undid his trousers and let them hang around his waist as he moved for her again, two fingers dipping into her mouth. "Suck, princess. Show your barbarian how much you want him."

To his surprise, the lust in her eyes far overshadowed the shades of pink she blushed when speaking of sexual matters, and she sucked on his fingers like her life depended on it. Her hands played with her breasts and she gagged on his two fingers. *That* was how much she wanted him.

While her whimpers followed his fingers gone from her mouth, Killian quickly lowered his trousers and hiked her up so her legs wrapped around his waist. "You're mine, princess."

CHAPTER 14
ROSAELIA

Rosaelia hadn't meant to make it a big deal when she said she loved the Island's special cocoa brownies, but somehow, that comment had sent the nonas in an uproar. They were both excited as they moved from one corner to the next in the little kitchen space, preparing everything they would need in order to make them.

Rosaelia had tried to fight them that it wasn't necessary, but they seemed excited to do this with her. And that made her excited as well.

Her body was still sore from the way Killian treated it, but she tried to fight away the feeling so she could stand with the nonas when everything was set out and ready. It wasn't a difficult recipe as long as the cocoa needed was there. Without the specific powder, it merely tasted like any other brownie Rosaelia had in the North.

Rosaelia wanted to argue against making the delicacy when she remembered the use of butter and eggs—ingredients they traded meat for with a neighbor who owned cattle—but the nonas weren't listening to a single one of her complaints.

Eventually, Rosaelia knew it was fruitless to continue. They were just as excited to teach her as she was to learn.

Killian was out chopping more firewood for the colder nights here in the Island, so it left the three of them with all the time they desired to make anything they liked.

Rosaelia winced as she moved to the edge of the table to grab a spatula for her bowl as they were each making their own bowls—a wonder of how they were meant to finish this many brownies popping to mind—and the feeling made her think of Killian and how roughly he'd taken her against that tree in the woods. He'd always been savage, but there was a possession in the way he'd taken her that he hadn't had before, and Rosaelia couldn't argue how much she enjoyed it.

"Are you all right, deary?" Nona Tereza asked as Rosaelia got back to her bowl and began mixing.

"Perfectly." Rosaelia smiled knowing it wasn't a lie. Though her body was sore and she would have to make sure Killian was calmer next time they were together, she couldn't wait to recover to do it all over again.

The nonas' eyes glinted as they looked her over before Tereza smirked. "Are you sore, dear?"

Rosaelia's cheeks burned as they turned red. "Yes," she meekly replied, unable to look up at them.

Her brownie mix was coming together beautifully, the color a delightful rich brown, so she grabbed for the jar of honey and added a spoonful. She loved honey so she couldn't wait to taste it in the mix. She always added it over her Island-shipped brownies, so she was extra excited to get this new flavoring.

Both nonas laughed.

"Just don't forget to remind him that the softness is needed in between so you don't get too sore to the point you cannot be together any longer," Tereza advised.

"Okay," Rosaelia answered softly, still unable to look up at them.

"Do not be ashamed of your desires, dove," Eleni spoke softly, causing Rosaelia to look up. "We are taught in the North to be modest, but that does not mean you cannot like these things that are done to you."

It was always a shock to hear Eleni talk, but it was what she said that had Rosaelia asking, "Did you like... it too?"

The sisters looked to one another with bright eyes as Tereza placed a tray before each of them to pour their mixtures into. Then Tereza answered, "We liked it rough, yes, Rosaelia. We Northerners are not so different from the Island or South in the aspects of the body, deary. When you go home, ask your family, any woman in your life. They will tell you of some of the possessive things their men do that make them wetter."

Rosaelia's cheeks burned more at Nona Tereza's wording and the simple fact that she was having this conversation with the nonas. Her mixture was fully poured into her tray as she waited for the nonas to prepare the spots for them to be placed to bake over the fire.

While she waited, she thought of the women of her life. Before a couple of months ago, she hadn't had any. Now, she had Evony and Gemma. And possibly Atiana too if the tailor's assistant ever got comfortable with the idea of being friends with her Princess.

The nonas didn't know she had a sister, so she couldn't speak of Evony, and in turn Gemma. And she was not yet necessarily friends with Atiana to know where her relationship status held in regard to sex. Though her twin wouldn't mind not yet being friends and would bring the conversation up immediately, Rosaelia couldn't do such a thing.

But it made her think of those women who were so new to her life. Did they like it rough as well?

From the scenes she'd walked into with Gemma and James, and Etel and Miels, she knew they liked it against the walls—almost like the tree she'd been on—and their screams of pleasure felt the same as Rosaelia's had been. And she knew by the simple way Evony spoke of Sparrow that they enjoyed certain matters as well.

As Rosaelia watched the nonas place the brownies to bake, she smiled. Maybe they were right after all and all of the people from each land had the same desires to be possessed.

"It is why we thought ourselves so lucky when we married," Eleni started again. "Being with these men, these Islanders who had such a savage possession about them, was enticing."

Rosaelia smiled, then the memory of the type of men the nonas' husbands turned out to be came back to her, and that smile dropped. "It's enticing until the lure is dropped. Then they're just barbarians."

It's like they could read her thoughts perfectly because Tereza reached for her hand softly and explained, "Do not think it, Sael dear. This Island holds different types of barbarians—the ones who are savages to the people in their lives and those who are savages toward anyone who would hurt the people in their lives—and we all know which Killian is. He would never do anything to you that you did not beg for."

Rosaelia's cheeks burned some more. "I know."

She had no doubts of the type of man Killian was, but the memory of the nonas' husbands simply made her remember that all Island barbarians weren't like her barbarian. At least half of them were true monsters.

And maybe there was a deeper root to her grandfather closing borders than the sorcerers. After all, he hadn't closed borders with the South.

"In any case," Nona Tereza continued, "even after our

husbands were gone, dear. We found ourselves enticed by the possession these barbarians could give us."

Rosaelia's eyes widened. "You..."

"Our bodies continued to have desires. And after finally being done with the trauma that was our family, we were able to explore those desires once more," Tereza answered. "We never fell in love again, but there were explorations of the body that fill our dreams to this day."

Rosaelia gave a small smile because they deserved to be happy and if these men who were only used for their bodies were what made the nonas happy after everything they'd been through, she wouldn't judge them.

It didn't mean she didn't beat a brighter red though.

The nonas laughed at her reactions, and she finally decided to turn for the fire and watch their brownies bake. The smell was beginning to fill the space, nearly making Rosaelia's eyes roll back with how good they smelled. Something about this cocoa was simply superior.

"You know," Tereza started again as if she was playing a game to see how hot Rosaelia could burn with embarrassment. "I'm sure Kill has chopped enough for the week. If you're sore, go find him and have him lick the pain awa—"

Killian walked in at that moment, dirty and sweaty from his hard-laboring outdoors, and moved straight for where she stood. Rosaelia's cheeks burned some more at the thought of having him lick her soreness away.

His arms wrapped around her, and as they fondled her sides, he leaned in to kiss the crook of her shoulder. "How are my girls?"

Rosaelia was at a loss of how to feel about his sweetness as she leaned back into him because she loved the feel of his body. "The brownies are almost done."

She felt his smile on her neck. "Do yours have honey in them?"

Her head snapped. "How'd you know?"

"You put it on nearly all of your sweets. Every one of your teas."

Rosaelia blushed, surprised he'd paid so much attention to realize that much.

He kissed the crook of her shoulder again before he leaned up to whisper in her ear, "Come with me, princess. I have something to show you."

The thought of his tongue on her cunt being that something was too powerful to ignore.

Like he could read her thoughts as he pulled her body with his, he laughed. "It is nothing sexual, princess. Rest assured though, I will show you more of that later."

Rosaelia's cheeks would forever remain red. "Okay... just... slower tonight?"

He'd thrown their cloaks over their shoulders, and they were outside, the pile of logs high under the awning at the side of the house, when he turned for her abruptly. "Did I hurt you?"

His eyes, that perfect color of the honey she loved, looked so endearingly worried, so she smiled. "No. I liked it." She coughed as she said, "Rough."

He analyzed her before his lips turned up a little. "You're sore?"

She nodded without a sound.

He took her face between both of his and kissed her softly. "We'll go slow tonight. I need to get you healed up for all the other things I have planned for that delicious body."

She blushed but still smiled up at him. "Thank you."

His thumb played with her bottom lip as he stared down at her. "Tell me, Sael. Any time your body needs *anything*, whether that's to go slower or rougher or if it simply needs me to hold it, you tell me."

"Okay," she whispered, wanting his mouth on hers when his words reminded her—anything. "Kiss me."

He smirked, those scars lining his lips beautifully. "Ah, I see the Princess learns quickly."

"Very adaptable," she joked, still waiting for his mouth.

He laughed as he leaned into her, his kiss passionate and slow as his tongue explored her mouth.

He stayed there until they needed to pull away for breath. "Come now, princess. You're too desirable. You're going to make me forget what I wanted to show you."

She laughed as he tugged on her hand and pulled her through the forests around their house. They walked in silence for a few minutes when an explosion made Rosaelia jump and cling tighter to Killian's arm.

He only laughed.

Laughed?

"Wha—"

He tugged on her hand. "You'll love it, princess."

She was at a complete loss as to what he could be talking about when another explosion hit. Her heart raced. Was this part of some barbarian traditions? Explosions?

When they cleared the forests and were finally near the waterfront, Rosaelia realized what it had been that had Killian smiling so brightly. Not explosions, but...

"Are those..." She stepped forward, her eyes wide so as not to miss a moment as another explosion rang and the sky exploded in colors.

Killian's arms wrapped around her waist. "Fireworks. You do not have them in the North, but I knew you'd love to see them."

Fireworks.

They were extraordinary.

Another one shot through the sky. Then three in quick succession. Then another lone one.

Rosaelia couldn't take her eyes off of them.

Killian brought her closer into his chest, his arms tight around her. "I knew you'd love them. I love them."

"They're incredible," she said with awe.

His face fell into her neck. "Every few weeks they light up the sky. Many Islanders get bored of it, but it's never bored me. I come to see them every time."

When she turned to him, his eyes were closed as he breathed in, resting at the spot his face rested between her neck and shoulder. She smiled. "You're not even watching."

"This time's for you."

Her smile was wide, eating away at her features as she turned back to the sky. "I want to share it with you."

He kissed the side of her neck, and whispered so low, Rosaelia was sure she misheard, "I've found something more extraordinary."

She had half a mind to turn and ask him to repeat himself when six flew up at the same time, exploding in quick succession. It was enchanting the way more continued to fly up in different intervals. She could not imagine ever growing tired of this.

So she didn't fight him about watching too. If he wished to lay on her shoulder, then so be it. She would enjoy this night.

"There's this book," she started, not knowing why but wanting to share with him. "In a library in the southwest of the North. My family knows I love going to it often, to see what new books they have, but almost exclusively for this one book. They've tried to have it brought to the palace, but I think it's special—having to go there to read it. It means I must wait for it, anticipate it.

"It's a love story. One where they are forced to marry, but they hate one another. He's a complete ass, and even mean at times, ruins lives for fun. There're parts where they're sweet with one another and parts where they try to sabotage one another, but at the end of the day, they're married, and though they hate one another, no one else is allowed to so much as speak ill of the other without getting threatened. It's heart-warming and dark at times and funny and steamy..." Those books had been all the education she'd had on sexual matters, but none had ever been too descriptive, so she'd still wondered.

He laughed. "Why am I not surprised that you would love a story with a bad man in it?"

She smiled to herself. "He is not all bad once you get into his head. In fact, he's quite swoon worthy."

"Ah," he mocked. "Shall I be jealous, princess?"

"Quite," she teased.

He kissed her shoulder. "I love that you get engrossed in books. It is not so often that I find people proudly lost in those stories. Maybe I shall have you read one to me."

"Oh, if only you had that one from the library. Even you would love it! Though maybe a shop or library here may have it. It's an older story, one where the people weren't separated into the Island, North, and South, and fireworks took place all over. There's only one scene in the whole book with fireworks, but every time I read it, it makes me smile. I cannot have fathomed them to look like this. It is better than all of my imaginings. This is extraordinary."

"Give me the name. If it exists on the Island, I'll find it. But you have to promise you'll read it to me."

Rosaelia honestly didn't think he'd be able to find it, but she wanted him to so she could read it to him. She wanted especially to read the firework scene to him, where the husband held his wife for the first time because he truly wanted to.

She fell deeper into his arms, her own resting over the ones that held her, and she glowed as she said, "Thank you so much for this, my barbarian."

His kiss at her neck was the only thing that told her he heard her.

CHAPTER 15

ROSAELIA

Rosaelia suffered from a case of crimson cheek anytime she was around the nonas. They never spoke of what they heard at night—or in the early twilight mornings—but Rosaelia could see the shine in their eyes when they looked between her and Killian. Especially after their talk the night before.

It was excruciatingly embarrassing.

Especially when Killian didn't seem to mind the looks and would sometimes quietly step behind Rosaelia and kiss or lick up her neck. She'd squirm, wanting nothing more than to fall into him and let him take her—but definitely not in front of his nonas. It was always amusing to him, the ass.

The day before had been one of the best nights of her life. After watching the fireworks until they ended, Killian had walked her home and straight to bed where he'd been so soft with her, she wasn't sure how her heart withstood any of that treatment.

This morning, too, had been slow and soft, yet somehow,

130

Killian still managed to make her moan loud enough for the nonas to give her those looks.

She didn't know how much redder she could grow before the look became permanent.

Now, Killian was seated at the table by the hearth helping Nona Eleni de-skin a load of potatoes while the older woman prepared the vegetables. It was such a domestic look on the monster and somehow made Rosaelia escape into a vision exactly like this with a child running throu—

She snapped herself out of it and continued sweeping the floors, even though they were as clean as they were going to get. She felt herself needing to always do a little extra because of this family's generosity.

And she had a feeling she could lure Killian to the bathing chamber to help her wash off the muck from her face and body later tonight when he could be a little rougher with her.

Rosaelia turned away and finished off the final bit of her sweeping as Nona Tereza continued her ramble about the things she could make with the skins Killian had hunted a couple of days prior. The woman was definitely the talkative one of the family, Rosaelia herself falling more in with Eleni and remaining quiet and observant. She could imagine Evony and Tereza would make fast friends.

While she spoke, Rosaelia made sure to keep her back to them so they didn't see how affected she was at the image of Killian hunting for his family.

She had just turned with the broom in hand as her balance stick when the back door opened and a woman maybe an inch or two taller than her walked in like she owned the place. By the way nobody reacted to her, Rosaelia assumed she was friend, not foe, in this savage nation.

But who was she?

Rosaelia's eyes shot to Killian as the girl smiled his way and began talking. "Kill! I need to hear this from your lips because I believe even my own ears have deceived me."

Rosaelia's gaze shot between the two as they smiled at one another, and her heart thundered in her chest. She had no right to be jealous, she and Killian were only enjoying one another's bodies, but she couldn't help it. Especially with a girl so pretty.

"Did I or did I not pass by the house last night and hear the pleasures of rutting?" She continued on, still not noticing Rosaelia in the corner. "Because I swear that's what it was, and I had half a mind to believe it to be one of the nonas, but I swear I heard your name moaned out, Kill, and—"

Killian's gaze latched onto Rosaelia's, then shimmered as he realized her fury in the moment. And he smirked. The barbarian bastard was enjoying her reaction!

The girl cut herself off, and followed Killian's line of sight to Rosaelia, and she visibly froze. "Holy fuck."

Rosaelia swallowed as she caught the eye of the girl and tried to be civil even though every part of her wanted to throw the girl out of the house and lay her claim on Killian. She was damn near ready to piss around him like an animal to stake her claim. This nation was truly starting to get to her head.

Rosaelia gave her a smile only a lifetime as the Princess made possible. "Hi."

The girl turned back to Killian, completely ignoring her. "So it's true! Killian, since when?"

Rosaelia held on to the broom and brought her Princess training to the forefront of her mind. She would not react to this woman. Nor the savagery passing through her chest that she could only blame this barbarian nation on.

Killian smirked. "Only a few days, Nor, calm down."

"Is she claimed?" the girl asked, a sparkle in her eyes.

Before Killian could answer, the nonas did in unison. "Yes."

A squeal came out of the girl as she clasped her hands together and finally turned back to Rosaelia. "I'm sorry, I'm being rude." She moved until she was right before Rosaelia. "I'm Norya. Call me an adopted sister."

"Sister..." Rosaelia's gaze continued to shoot between the two of them, unable to hold back her need to know.

Norya's beautiful browns widened as she realized Rosaelia's position. "Oh no! No, no, no, no, no! Sister. That's it! I would never touch... ugh. Kill is just a brother. And trust me, any of the women he had touched before are long dead so you have nothing to be jealous over, not that you should anyway. You're claimed. That obviously means you have nothing to worry about!"

Another flame sparked within her at the mention of the other women he'd touched. It was ridiculous since Rosaelia knew he'd been with other women, could tell it the moment she laid eyes on him. But still, her heart raged.

Then calmed a bit knowing they were all dead.

And Killian had taken on celibacy.

She had to find out what the hell had happened.

"Yes, Sael," Killian teased. "Do not worry about my tongue. It'll always find its way back to you."

Rosaelia's cheeks burned. He had to stop saying things like that in front of the nonas!

She was sure her reaction was the only reason Nona Tereza interrupted, to give her a reprieve from her grandson's teasing, "Nor, dear, why the visit? Just curiosity about our boy?"

"Partially." Norya turned back for the table and sat across from Killian. "But I've also been kicked out again."

Rosaelia leaned the broom against the wall and moved for the small washbasin at the end of the room to clean her hands.

She knew Nona Tereza was speaking to her by the explanation. "Norya lives in a No Known Housing. It's a place people with no family live in, whether they're a grandparent or a child left with no one."

"Though she's been offered permanent stay here multiple times and refuses to take it," Killian swiped in.

Rosaelia kept her civil expression as she moved for the table, taking one of the only two seats left open. It was beside Killian, but she tried not to sit too close. She was being ridiculous with this jealousy considering he wasn't hers.

"Well." Norya took a few cut up carrots as snack. "I was going to ask for that permanent spot now, though as I speak, I realize I do not recognize Sael here from this or neighboring towns so I'm coming to the conclusion the room is no longer empty."

Rosaelia's gaze shot between them all, and that feeling of taking too much came back to her. "Oh, no! Take the room. I do not mind sleeping out here. I wasn't meant to stay here anyway."

She smirked. "Don't be ridiculous. It's your room. I go back and forth to the home all the time. I'll just hunt them some things they can't refuse, and I'll be back. I just like making them beg for it sometimes."

"No, no, Nor, Sael's right. You will take her room," Nona Tereza said at the same moment it looked like Killian was going to say something. And from the looks of his small nods, it was the same thing as his nona.

Rosaelia knew she'd been the one to offer it, but it still stung to be cast out so quickly. She was being unreasonable, of course, this girl was like family. Rosaelia was just a Princess from another place and a lifetime ago for them.

Norya went to argue again—at least she was on Rosaelia's side—when Killian interrupted, "Sael's been sleeping with me anyway, Nor." Slightly shocked brows shot up on the girl as Killian continued, "It won't be much to take her few pieces of clothing to my room. It won't be a problem. You're staying here."

Rosaelia's breath caught as both nonas smiled like that had been their thought as well. She knew she should argue but couldn't find it within her. It was true. She'd spent only a few nights in that room since she'd been living with them this past week—her first night and when Killian had tried to scare her with mentions of killing his entire family.

Norya leaned back like she was happy with that answer, a small smirk forming on her lips as her gaze jumped from Killian to Rosaelia and back again. "So, claimed, huh?"

Rosaelia really needed to find out what that meant.

Killian grabbed the edge of Rosaelia's seat and brought her flush against his side. "Not truly, Nor, no."

Killian's hand dropped between Rosaelia's legs and he kneaded at her thigh like he knew she was tense and he wanted to aid. That twinkle in his eyes said he also did so because he knew how wet she'd grow with his touch on her and the ass enjoyed making her blush crimson in front of his family.

All of the women stared between them as Norya's smirk grew. "Sure."

Norya was going out to hunt even though she didn't need the catch for her No Known Housing. She simply wanted to and could aid in the family's stores even though Killian looked to have the stores full already.

It gave Rosaelia the excuse to go on a hunt in the savage lands. Especially when she noticed the girl's bow and arrow. Some training was definitely needed.

Trailing after her to ask for the company, Rosaelia took in her appearance. The girl had dark brown hair that ended in layers in the middle of her back, though most of it was braided together. She was extremely fit. Rosaelia imagined most Islanders were more fit than the average Northern or Southerner because of the savagery of the land, but a part of her knew Norya also simply enjoyed to train. Part of her wondered if the girl would be able to take on her friends back home. She wagered Miels and Tristan's competitive streaks would require they battle the girl, and Rosaelia could imagine Norya kicking their asses. It made her smile.

"You planning on following me, Princess?"

Rosaelia froze for a moment but sped up after a moment. "I did not realize they told you who I was."

Norya smiled down at her. From this close, she looked a few inches taller. "I was shown the drawings of the nonas' friend through the years. You look like your grandmother."

"So I've been told."

Norya's smile was wide as she continued into the forest and eyed the bow and arrow at Rosaelia's back. "You hunt, Princess?"

"Please stop calling me that." The last thing she needed was any more Islanders learning her true identity. "Sael is good."

The girl laughed, and she was so beautiful as she did so. "Okay, Sael. So, are you coming hunting?"

"As long as you don't mind a far inadequate partner."

The girl smiled. "You're Kill's woman. I'd love nothing more than to spend time with you. I was worried you wouldn't want to degrade yourself." *Because you're a spoiled, better than everyone Princess.*

Rosaelia tried not to let it affect her. Most people thought wrongly about her in her own nation, she surely didn't expect the savage nation to think any better.

"What does that mean? Killian's woman? Everyone keeps saying it with such significance, but I don't understand. We are only sharing a bed." Rosaelia tried to fight the blush, but it was there.

Norya sent her a quirked brow as she came to a stop in a small clearing in the forest, looked around, then went to stop behind some thick branches.

Rosaelia followed. "You know what I mean." Rutting. The word itself sounded savage.

"May I ask you something, Sael?" Norya raised her bow and arrow into the clearing and stared off at nothing, effectively ignoring the question apparently no one wanted to answer.

"Of course." *Please don't be about Killian, please don't be about Killian...*

"Does he not scare you? Kill?"

Rosaelia didn't understand the question until she remembered the two massive scars running down his face. They made him a monster, but she found that she craved that more than she cared to admit. "Not at all. Don't most people on this nation have scars? Why would that scare any of the women?"

Norya shot the arrow, and watched it disappear into the thick of the branches as she calmly said, "The women here aren't afraid of his scars, they're afraid of his history. Not to mention, Kill isn't interested in any of them so it wouldn't matter. I ask *you*, Sael, because you are not from here, not used to these scars on males."

"Oh." She swallowed and remembered that her brother was

an assassin and his two best friends spies and assassins as well. She knew not to be afraid of men who caused death, though she knew her friends didn't kill with the same savagery they did here. Her family weren't barbarians. "No. His scars do not scare me."

"Do they turn you on?" She shot another arrow into the bushes, and Rosaelia wondered if she was merely wasting her arrows or if this was training for her.

She blushed but tried to channel her twin's disregard for talk of sexual matters. "They do."

Just the thought of him now. Dark eyes, dark blonde hair, that scar that raged from hairline to jaw on his right side and the one that raged from bottom of his eye to jaw on his left side. His strong shoulders and the veins lining his arms to those calloused, hard-working hands. She was growing hot thinking about him, her breath becoming shallow as she heated for his fingers, tongue, or cock.

When she snapped out her reverie, Norya was smirking down at her. "Are you thinking about fucking him right now?"

Rosaelia blushed. "If you don't mind, I would actually like to ask for some more training on the bow and arrow. I had some back home, but I know I'm not so perfect." *And it seems I won't be getting an answer about claiming from you.*

Norya gave her a warm smile. "I've been shooting my entire life, Sael. I needed to do so to survive. I wouldn't expect you, or most people, to be like me. But I would love to train you."

Rosaelia gave that genuine, soft smile that normally only made an appearance around her family. "Thank you."

Norya had her raise her weapons and began assessing her stance and hold on the bow and arrow. There were a few tweaks she made, but for the most part, she seemed impressed with Rosaelia. That made her feel amazing, better than her Posse being proud of her.

Then she wanted to see Rosaelia's shots—toward a large tree—in order to know a starting point for training. It was in staring at the bark that Rosaelia remembered her mother—the dead Queen of the Northern Lands. Alive.

And set out to kill her daughters and late husband for the throne.

It made her sick but sent the arrow flying beautifully. It wasn't a perfect hit, but a pretty good one, hitting the edge of the tree.

"Not bad at all, Sael. You're better than Killian. He's more hands-on, dagger-wielding. Not as great with a bow and arrow."

Now that made Rosaelia feel on top of the world. She knew her wide smile said as much.

They spent the better part of an hour going through drills and shots, grabbing the arrows from the tree bark and starting again. All the while, Rosaelia's pride in her abilities and her anger with her mother grew. Two warring feelings demanding attention.

Her mother got more of it. Rosaelia needed to figure out how to kill the woman and not involve these four incredible people she'd met—two nonas, a beautiful warrioress, and a barbarian that sent her breaths into a frenzy.

After a while, a large cat slowly moved through the other side of the small clearing, making its way to the bushes Norya had been shooting into. Apparently, Rosaelia would be getting a live target now too.

"Steady your breathing and shoot him."

Rosaelia did just that and got him in the hind leg. It wasn't a kill shot, but it felt invigorating. But also terrifying because now the large cat was coming in their direction.

Norya laughed, and pulled her own bow, shooting the large cat in between the eyes. "Good job, Princess."

She moved for the bushes first, coming back out with two rabbits with arrows through them. It struck Rosaelia then that Norya was such a good shot, she'd killed those animals through the thick of the bushes, then waited for a larger prey to be attracted by the smell of blood. She was amazing. The Posse would adore her.

CHAPTER 16
KILLIAN

"I like her," Norya said with a soft smile on her lips.

"Good for you." Killian kept his face hard so Norya didn't think he was pleased to hear that bit of news.

"You don't need to act so tough, Killian. She's your woman!"

"She is not claimed, Nor. The nonas are jumping to conclusions. They have fantasies of my future they wish to force upon us."

"Mr. Celibate Killian is fucking a woman and you expect us not to jump to conclusions? I spoke with your nonas, Kill. They said the way you stood with her that first night was one of a protective mate. They said you didn't even hesitate to sleep with her, Mr. Been Celibate For Seven Years And Not A Single Soul Interested You In All This Time."

"How exactly would they know whether I hesitated to sleep with her? Maybe I put up a fight."

Norya quirked a brow. "But you didn't, Kill. You jumped on her the second she spread her legs for you. We all know it."

Killian ignored the way his body tensed at the phrasing. It

was all true—the Princess had spread her legs for him, and he hadn't hesitated to devour her.

While he thought of said Princess, his mind wandered to her current whereabouts. She had kept her promise and was there in the morning when they awoke to get in another round, but she was gone after breakfast. Now, in the afternoon air, Killian was beginning to wonder if he should go look for her.

If he found her with another one of those boys, he was going to burn the fucking nation down.

"I see the way you look at her, Kill." Norya continued being a nuisance as he cleaned another one of the small fishes he'd gotten out of the waters for dinner that night. "I see the way your body reacts even now at just the thought of her. What were you just thinking about, Kill? Your body tensed. Were you thinking about her with another male?"

Involuntarily, his body tensed again, but Killian only threw her an annoyed look. "I'm thinking about how very annoying you are."

"Don't lie to me, brother." She threw her arm around his shoulders as she sat on the log beside him. "You *love* her." She elongated the 'o' in love to annoy him even more.

"I love my nonas. I love you, sister. I fuck Sael. There's a difference."

She rolled her eyes. "She's affected by the thought of you too, you know. When we were training together, she was thinking of you, and I could *see* her growing hot for you."

Killian narrowed his eyes on his sister. She was trying to bait him into admitting something he refused to by saying Sael was thinking of him when he wasn't around. He didn't care what she thought of when he wasn't around.

Norya's smirk told him she didn't buy the bullshit his narrowed gaze was trying to sell. Thankfully, though, she slightly changed the subject. "What is she here for anyway? What brought the Northern Princess to your bed?"

"She wanted to taste a monster, sister."

Norya pulled her arm off and punched him. "I'm serious, Kill."

Killian threw the last small fish into the bucket, all of them cleaned and ready for the nonas to pack more flavor into and cook. "I don't know, Nor. She hasn't told us a thing, and my nonas try to kill me every time I bring up asking her about it."

"Maybe she's hiding it to protect you and your nonas."

He shrugged. He hated not knowing what she was after, not being able to protect her from whatever danger he knew the Princess was attracting. He hated that she felt the need to do this on her own. Hated that little inkling in the back of his mind that wondered whether whatever she was doing would ultimately betray his family. "She's doing it for her family. Whatever she's here for. It's to protect them. That is all I know."

Norya's head fell onto his shoulder, and she smiled warmly. "She is more like you that I thought."

He wanted to fight her, but the memory of sending her back to his nonas after she helped him get loose from being tied to that pole came to mind. The memory of needing to protect his family on his own came to mind. Maybe he was more like the Princess than he'd thought. Did that make him more regal or her more barbarian?

"Yes, it's quite annoying," Killian begrudged.

Norya laughed. "I know. I've had to deal with *you* all this time. But we'll find out why she's here. We'll protect her, brother. You won't lose your woman. I won't allow it."

"She isn't my woman, Nor."

She didn't argue, simply stared up into his eyes. She watched him for long minutes before smiling. "You guys are going to make such cute babies, Killian. Your barbarian blood in them will scare everyone in the palace. I'm already entertained simply thinking of it."

Killian rolled his eyes, not bothering to argue any longer. And not because the thought of his barbarian children in the Northern palace also amused him.

He rose from the log and took the bucket of fish as he moved for the back door to his house. "Keep dreaming, sister."

AFTER ANOTHER HOUR, Killian was tired of waiting to see when she would show up. He didn't know where to start his search for her, but the basket of skins his nonas wanted traded for herbs and colorings would be his excuse to go out. Which meant he would start with the town square.

He highly doubted she was there. Even if she was, he was almost certain she hadn't been there all day.

Norya's knowing smirk as he passed her with the small basket in hand told him she knew exactly what his true purpose was behind going. Killian ground his jaw at the attention but ignored it. He needed to find Sael.

He was down the trail from his house to the market when he felt eyes on him from multiple angles, then Keir himself stepped out and each of the lackeys with him surrounded Killian as if they could truly harm him. All this did was ensure Killian didn't end Keir. It was why Keir always had men with him. He feared Killian more than most because he, unlike the morons who followed him, understood Killian's true power.

"Is it my birthday, friend?" Killian opened with a cocky smirk. "Are we celebrating? I believe for my present I would like your head on a spike."

Keir laughed. "I believe your birthday is still a few months away."

"So I must wait a few months before you deliver your head on a spike for me?" Killian feigned sadness when in reality he was annoyed they were blocking him from finding Sael.

"Come, Killian." Keir raised his hands as if accepting him into the fold. "I merely wished to congratulate you on that pretty little thing of yours."

Sael instantly came to mind, and Killian's eyes narrowed to slits. There was no way he would've seen Killian with Sael and not attacked. It would be the one moment to find Killian well and truly distracted.

Then doubly so because of his need to protect Sael.

Keir laughed. "You cannot fuck her in the woods if you wished not to be seen. But from what I hear from Valen and Cornor, she was quite the pretty thing."

Valen and Cornor. No wonder Killian hadn't been attacked while he was balls deep. No wonder they hadn't tried a single thing, not even stepping close enough to be detected. They were the weaker of Keir's men and would never try to challenge him on their own.

"I hear she was quite the loud thing too." Keir grinned like he was imaging Sael beneath *him*, screaming for *him*. "Then you definitely cannot wish it to be a secret."

Killian's fists were turning white with how hard he had them fisted, the basket handle in his left hand on the brink of cracking in half. He ground his jaw to relax before he said fuck it and took his blades out. He was on the precipice of risking fighting through all these men in order to finish Keir off. Not because of what he did to Killian, but because of how he was thinking of Sael.

"You know, dear Killian." Keir's eyes said he knew he was having an effect on Killian and he wanted to see how far he could take it. "If she truly enjoys this"—he pointed at the scars on Killian's face—"then I believe a thank you is in order for making you just to your woman's likings."

Only the mental image of Keir's slow death was keeping Killian sane at the moment.

"Are you done wasting our time now?" Killian took a step forward, staring at the man like he was better than him—because he was—and indicated he was prepared to leave their little group.

"Only one more question."

The twinkle in his eyes already told Killian to lock his body in place because this was going to be a baiting question and every fiber in him knew it was going to be about Sael.

"Do you mind sharing your pretty thing? If she is as pretty and loud as I hear, then I'd like a taste myself."

Thank the lords he'd locked himself into his stance already. But the basket in his hand could no longer take the pressure and the handle cracked in his fist, sending the entire thing to the ground.

"I hear she played with herself and gagged on your fingers, mate. If I'm to have that much fun with her then I can handle some added scars if that is what she likes."

The only thing she liked was Killian. Killian's body, his kisses, and most certainly only his scars. No one else would touch her.

Keir stepped forward so they were only a foot apart. "So what do you say? Share her?"

Killian stared him down. "If you touch her, I will torture you for the rest of your worthless life."

Keir gave that cruel chuckle. "But she is not claimed?"

Killian stepped so close, they shared breath as he bared his teeth. "She is my woman. You touch her, your existence is over. You so much as think of her, and I'll skewer you."

Keir knew not to be afraid with so many of his lackeys around. "But she is not claimed. If she wishes for my attentions, I believe I will gladly give it to her." He licked his lips. "Maybe she'll wish for me to claim her."

Killian's hands locked around his throat. "Say that again, Keir." Hands fisted into his shirt to tug him off but none were strong enough against Killian's rage. "I dare you."

He wouldn't show it to his men, but fear filled his eyes as Killian held him. He tugged on the hands around his throat, and the only reason Killian released was so the others didn't try to attack him. He was a great fighter, much better than seven years ago, but there were still too many around them.

Keir coughed up for air but didn't bait him any longer. He stepped back to allow Killian space to leave, but his eyes threatened how much he hated Killian.

Killian picked up the basket by the bottom since the handle was now broken and stormed off toward the market. He needed Sael now more than ever.

CHAPTER 17

ROSAELIA

Her wrists were bruised with the same small marks as her ankles, and Rosaelia was momentarily thrust back to the night before when Killian tied each of her wrists to the corresponding ankle and had her spread out on the bed for his tasting. Her cunt clenched at the memory. At every memory of being with him.

She knocked herself out of the fantasies as she followed the three women with her gaze. Each one looked like they could handle themselves around the brutes on Rosaelia's list, but she needed to pick the right one. One who was cunning enough to do more than simply distract them with flirtations in order to drug them. Rosaelia needed one who could get them talking.

She was in the town of Lagon, farther away from Killian's hometown than she'd thought but close enough that leaving early morning gave her hours still until she needed to get home.

Until then, Rosaelia was getting started on the list the boy had given her of Rowena's known helpers. After what she'd seen in the Bloody Fields, Rosaelia knew she needed a way to get Rowena unsuspecting. And she was especially coming to the conclusion that maybe asking for help didn't make her a damsel, it simply made her smart. She was certainly glad for Alana's help and knew she would need the Master to distract her mother if they were to rid of her.

For now, she watched as one of the women giggled at a barbarian as he convinced her to fuck him. The other two watched on with bored expressions, but it was all Rosaelia needed. The giggling one was too gullible to do Rosaelia any good. The girl to her left watched them walk away with sadness in her eyes, as if she'd wanted to be the one chosen. Rosaelia couldn't have someone who wished to please so much. She needed someone who wouldn't be swayed.

The final girl, one with long dark hair, dark eyes, and a scar across her jaw was the perfect match. She watched those two walk away as if the girl was a moron to give her services away for free.

Rosaelia moved to them before she could talk herself out of it. "Hello." She met the dark-eyed one. "May I speak with you, please."

She looked annoyed but motioned her friend away. "What?"

"I have a job that I think you would do especially well with." She held up a small bag of coin. It was a portion of the money she'd brought with her from the North and would definitely pay for this. Rosaelia wanted to cross off the names on the list on her own, but she knew she wouldn't be able to flirt with these brutes.

The girl's eyes shined. "What do you need?"

"What's your name?"

"Aster."

"Aster. I have two brutes I need information from." She held up a vial. "I need this dropped evenly between their drinks, and for them to finish their cups. For extra coin, I need any information you can get out of them about a Queen, Rowena, or Queen Rowena. I'll be sitting beside you lot to listen."

"Simple." She held out her hand for the first half of payment. "Which brutes?"

Rosaelia walked her to the pub she'd seen them move to, and discreetly pointed. She moved them to take the booth beside theirs, then a moment later, Aster was before their table.

"Well, well, well, boys, that's a mighty big booth to have no females within it."

The two smiled at one another, and the one Rosaelia could see was missing two teeth. "Why don't you join us then?"

Aster gave a seductive smile as she straddled one in order to get to the middle. The men eyed one another with the move, and it was simple to read what they thought—this woman would be an easy one to lay. Bingo. Aster was in.

The list Rosaelia had been given had recorded the two as Rowena's personal assassins, so she'd found it necessary to stop them first with the potions that would weaken their limbs to points they wouldn't be able to do much more than pick up utensils.

"You boys mind if I play with myself?" She teased her breasts.

One tsked. "That's our job."

Aster laughed as she dropped her hands and played with one of the coins Rosaelia's had given her. Then she met Rosaelia's gaze as she let it drop to the floor beneath her table. "Oh no," she teased to the men. "Which of you will be a gentleman and retrieve that for me? I'd be so thankful, I'd need to taste your cock then."

Both men jumped, bending under the table to retrieve her

coin. It gave Aster the perfect opportunity to douse both of their brand-new drinks with the vial.

The one with the missing teeth came up with the coin. "Got it!"

Aster giggled. "Good job. Now, why don't you two finish eating, then we can see if you two want to fuck me."

They grinned at one another like animals.

"I got the coin. I come in you first," the man said.

"Deal." Aster giggled. "Now eat. Fill your energy, boys."

They shoved their faces like true barbarian brutes.

"While I wait, why don't you tell me what you two do. Big men like you have to have powerful jobs. You didn't steal my coin, so I know you have money."

"We work for a Queen," the one closer to Rosaelia, whose face she couldn't see, answered cockily.

"Oh, yeah." The girl ran her fingers along the man's arm. "And how did you get started with such a big client?"

Aster probably thought Queen simply meant a powerful woman because she wasn't questioning it.

Missing Teeth gave her a wicked grin. "She needed a sword maker taken care of in the North. Two decades we've been working with the woman, and she'd never stiffed us."

Rosaelia's heart stopped. Sparrow's father had been killed nearly two decades ago, and he'd been the best sword maker. She couldn't believe these men were part of the group that had gone—though he failed to tell Aster that they backed down before getting the job done since Sparrow had killed all of the men who'd come after his father. These assassins were cheats, taking others' work and getting paid for it. Either way, Rosaelia was glad they'd be basically paralyzed after today.

"Oh." She smiled. "And what do you do now?"

The one closer to Rosaelia answered, "We just got rid of

two sorcerers trying to help with a plague in the North. Those fuckers in the North are better off dead."

"Lucky me to have chosen such strong men," Aster teased, and Rosaelia was especially glad to have given the job to her. If Rosaelia had tried to do it herself, she would've failed miserably.

Missing Teeth, whose cup was only about a quarter through, began undoing his trousers, and Rosaelia tried to hide deeper within the shadows so her widening eyes didn't draw attention.

Her gaze shot to Aster. She didn't want the woman to do anything physical to get this information.

But Aster didn't look perturbed at all. In fact, she licked her lips and her eyes swayed with desire. It shouldn't have been shocking that she may like this type of man, and the chance to fuck them might actually be a delightful one.

Rosaelia hoped so because she didn't want to be the reason Aster did something she was uncomfortable with.

His cock sprang free, and it was so large, Rosaelia could see it over the table.

"Why don't you get started while we finish." He licked his lips.

Aster didn't hesitate, taking his cock in her mouth and bobbing over it. Rosaelia wanted to look away, but she couldn't.

The men laughed as they continued on talk of new things they wished to buy with their coin. They were about halfway through their cups when the man groaned out, and Rosaelia knew he was coming. It was nothing like when Killian came. It made Rosaelia want to crawl deeper into the shadows whereas Killian made her want to take him again.

"Mm," she hummed, swiping cum off her chin. "Finish your drink so I can fuck you properly."

He gulped the thing quickly, and Rosaelia was relieved to finally have one taken care of.

He grabbed Aster, placed her on his lap, and they moaned in unison. He moved from the booth then, and past Rosaelia's table where Aster's hand shot out for the rest of her coin. Rosaelia quickly handed the bag and watched them leave right as the second brute emptied his cup and followed after them.

Rosaelia stayed seated for a while, trying to remind herself over and over that she was in barbarian nation and these things were common in the land.

Finally, she reminded herself the potion would take a day to set in place, and these brutes would be the first two names taken off the list. She smiled then and forced herself out of the pub. She had one more person in Lagon she wanted to get to before making the two hour walk home.

She was headed for the edge of the town where she'd been told Dustin would be. The man was Rowena's supply of work-ers. He held the lists of men who could and would work for Rowena. According to what Rosaelia had been told, the lists were so special that Dustin hadn't allowed copies in case anyone tried to take his business. It made Rosaelia's job simpler.

Once she got to the right cabin, Rosaelia pulled at her cloak to cover herself completely, then pulled out the light blue vial needed. This potion would make the words on any page disap-pear within minutes. All Rosaelia needed to do was get to the correct papers, so she decided she'd throw it over everything.

She breathed to ready herself, then readied her bow and arrow. She shot an arrow into the door, knowing the spiked edge would alert Dustin to an attack, and he would storm out to protect his place. Rosaelia had been told there was always someone who tried to fight him for the pages. Except she wouldn't fight him. She'd simply destroy the lists.

Dustin stormed out moments later looking huge and frightening. He took about five large steps away from his door and started glaring around for the culprit to the arrow. It gave Rosaelia the moment she needed to run within. She held her thumb over the vial in order to sprinkle the contents over the pages so it would be enough for everything. She ran as quickly as she could over the files on the table but knew instinctively that he'd have the papers in a drawer, so she pulled at all of them and sprayed.

"What the fuck!"

The voice made Rosaelia jump in her spot, then run as Dustin came for her. She narrowly made it out of the way with the final contents of the vial, and knew she succeeded when instead of chasing after her, he moved for his drawers, and roared.

Rosaelia ran quickly before he could chase after her.

She ran for as long as her body could handle, then slowed to a walk for the rest of the way home. All the while, she wore a large grin. That's three off the list.

She spent much of the walk looking over the list of names left uncrossed, and the map of the Island to see which towns they were in and how far those towns were. She paid extra attention to the more important matters—what they did for Rowena.

Next to the two brutes' names were the simple words *Lagon, Personal Assassin.*

Next to Dustin's name was *Lagon, Muscle.*

As Rosaelia scoured the list, she stopped on a woman. *Britt, Harmon, Health Sorceress.*

Health sorceress. Of course Rowena would have a sorcerer other than Alana on her team. And especially most important, one who could heal her. After what Alana had done to her with that powder, this Britt woman would be Rowena's most important ally.

Harmon didn't look too far away on the map, but Rosaelia wasn't too sure about going on her own. She knew now more than ever than she was no damsel, but she also wasn't stupid. To get to Harmon, she would need to pass through a large mass of forests, and she knew the wild animals and barbaric men would make that quite impossible. She knew even going with Killian would be dangerous.

And she didn't want to add Killian to any of this mess.

As she stared at the list, she realized nothing short of the Master Assassin's strength would feel safest, but she wanted this done before her family got to her.

Before long, Rosaelia was back in the town square she recognized from almost daily visits. It was cold out, and town would soon begin closing down for the night. With the twilight air around them indicating the end of the day approaching, Rosaelia made her way through the square in order to make it to the other side so she could take the trail that led home.

She was shocked to see Killian by a booth as she moved.

She smiled to herself. She would go to him and take his arm so they could walk back together.

CHAPTER 18

KILLIAN

He was still angry from Kier's earlier words, but more than anything his dick was hard. He'd searched for her through town, leaving the basket of skins with Gia to pick up the herbs later, then gone out to search two of the closest neighboring towns.

He hadn't found her or any evidence of her presence—not that evidence would be easy to find—but the time had allowed for his anger to subside. He still planned on killing Keir, more harshly now because of his comments about Sael, but it wasn't time for that yet.

He was now back in town square in order to pick up the herbs and colorings from Gia, but he couldn't ignore that all this time searching for her—thinking of her—had made his cock extremely hard.

Though it was almost unbearable, Killian refused to relieve himself without his princess. He wanted his cum to coat her and couldn't fathom ever wasting another drop on anything else. The thought scared him. This wasn't going to last, he would need to relieve himself on his own when Sael left.

But he didn't want to think about that. It made a deathly cool wash over him any time he did.

Soon he'd be back home, away from the townsfolk he didn't like, and back to the woman he wanted to shove his cock into. Hopefully she was home already and that was the reason Killian couldn't find her because he couldn't bear the thought of having to wait for her when he returned home. Especially with how late the day was growing, ice would begin to form along the trees soon. He needed her home for her safety as much as for his release.

His mouth watered at the memory of tasting her. Her skin, from hip bone to ear, slick with his tongue's long route up. Her nipples peaked and red from his assault on them. Her cunt dripping and tasting like the sweetest delicacy to exist.

His cock was harder now, and it was growing unbearable. He needed to finish here and get home immediately.

At the booth for the herbs and colorings his nonas wanted, Killian waited for Gia, the Garmez nona, to bring out his six medium-sized pouches of herbs and four vials of colorings. In the meantime, her grandson, Marco, leaned over the booth to him with a smirk. "I've passed by your house recently, mate."

His house was surrounded by woods so it wasn't often people came by, but Killian knew when they did it was to get to the harbors as it made for a shorter route.

Killian narrowed his gaze on the man but didn't entertain him with conversation. What was with all these men wanting to start conversation with him? They all knew he wasn't a friendly, talkative sort.

Marco had a teasing grin about him. "There were rumors you'd stopped rutting, but I knew a feral bastard like you wouldn't give that up. You got a loud one on yuh, huh, mate? I heard the bitch from a few yards out."

Killian growled so loud, other booths looked their way as

his hand shot out and grabbed the man by the throat. His hand cut off Marco's oxygen as he brought the man in close, and whispered deathly calm, "Call her a bitch again, and I'll cut off your cock and shove it up your ass before feeding you your fingers." The man was growing blue as he nodded ferociously. "Think about her inappropriately, and I'll skewer you alive. Matter of fact, allow your mind to drift to anything regarding her and your entire family's dead."

Killian was fucking sick of men thinking they could comment on *his* princess.

The man clawed at Killian's arm as he nodded his understanding, and finally, Killian pushed him away with disgust. His eyes turned toward Gia who'd come back with his pouches and vials, and he held his hand out. The woman looked terrified as she handed over the bag of products.

Killian could already hear whispers around him wondering what woman he was speaking of. Everyone would know now not to mess with her. But they needed to know who she was first. Killian needed to bring her into town on his arm, properly claim her as his.

As he left town square, the startling realization cut through him that he needed to claim her as his woman. He needed everyone to be clear on the matter. Because even in this savage nation, no one went after a claimed woman. Even Keir wouldn't dare go after his claimed woman.

Killian hurried his steps for home, needing now more than ever to be buried deep inside her.

He was only a dozen or so steps out of town square when a hand landed on his arm. He turned harshly, then paused abruptly when he saw his princess's beautiful emerald-greens staring up at him. "Sael," he breathed out, then stepped closer, his tone growing lethal. "Where the fuck have you been all day?"

"I told you the other day, barbarian, I'm here for a reason. I was out for said reason."

He gave an annoyed laugh. "And I'm still not worthy enough to know it, am I, *Princess?*"

She narrowed those stunning eyes. "This has nothing to do with worthiness, Killian. Your family wasn't meant to be involved, and I will do what I can to make sure you are not."

Killian wanted to fight her over the matter but his cock was growing intolerable. So instead, he roughly took her arm and turned them toward home.

About halfway down, Sael muttered, "You know, this wasn't exactly the walk home I was expecting. When Sparrow walks Evony to the dining hall, she always has a soft hand wrapped around his arm, not bruises from being dragged along."

Killian didn't respond. He couldn't because as they walked the path home, the memory of Keir came back to him. The memory of that horror of a man touching his Sael came to mind.

He needed to touch her.

But more importantly, he needed her to touch him.

WHEN THEY MADE IT HOME, Killian threw the bag of products onto the table, shoved Sael before him, and had both hands on her hips as he led her through the house and toward their room. He ignored his nonas and Norya as they all watched them, knowing smiles about their faces.

When they made it to the room, Sael didn't question him. She simply stripped out of her clothes and made her way to the bed like a good little fucking princess. In any other circumstance, he'd reward her thoroughly for it, but tonight, he needed her touch.

"Move," he ordered as he stripped out of his clothes.

She gave a confused look but moved to the edge of the bed, waiting for more instruction. He loved that about her—she was always ready and eager to learn more, to do whatever he demanded of her.

Killian took her spot in the middle of the bed and laid flat out, hands clasped behind his head so it was propped up to watch. "I want *you* to touch *me*, princess. Do whatever you wish to me."

Her eyes widened, but desire was filled within them as she slowly crawled between his legs.

She made a tentative touch to the small scars on his shins while watching for his reaction. He couldn't blame her. Up until this point, her hands hadn't gone lower than his shoulders and arms, and she was a smart little thing, she knew it was because he couldn't bear having people touch him.

When all he did was lick his lips, Sael grew more confident and positioned herself between his legs. She bent down to kiss a small scar he had on his knee, all the while staring into his eyes. As she moved to kiss a scar just above the inside of his other knee, her hands skimmed up his shins to his thighs, through the coarse hairs to his hips. Then those nails caressed back down his thighs and she gave a proud smirk as his cock bobbed against his stomach. He was leaking precum as she slowly made her way up his body, kissing small scar after small scar on his legs.

Her long, black locks were just as teasing as the hairs touched the sensitive spots her lips had just been. Killian had to pull on his own hair to keep from reaching out for her and turning them so he could fuck her.

Instead, he watched as she ignored his cock, and slowly

kissed up his chest, the scars on his chest even fewer and smaller, until she made it to his lips. She licked the outline of his lips, but ignored him when he opened his mouth to invite her in. Instead, she continued her tongue's trail down his jaw to his ear and sucked on his lobe like he'd done to her a million times this past week. His groan of appreciation made her smile so he did so again because he liked seeing her lips upturned for him.

Then she slowly kissed her way back down until her lips grazed his cock's head. She let the precum touch her mouth, then pulled back enough to lick her lips. "Mm, you taste so good, barbarian."

Then she blushed crimson like she hadn't meant to say those words aloud.

He chuckled at her reaction. "I'm glad you like it, princess. I love the feel of your lips on me." He couldn't remember a time when he loved the feel of anything on his skin half as much as this.

Then her pretty little mouth opened up for him and she had his tip in her mouth, softly hollowing out her cheeks as she sucked him. Her tongue lapped circles around his tip before she pulled away and looked at it. Killian didn't want to interrupt her exploration. He was hypnotized by watching her learn how to take a cock in her mouth, how to take *his* cock in her mouth.

When she took him in again, she swallowed more of him while her hand held him at the base. Her gaze latched onto his with a question.

"You're doing fucking perfect, princess." He moved one hand to take hers and squeezed. "You can hold me harder," he groaned as her fingers squeezed tighter, and she sucked a little deeper.

She popped him out of her mouth, and slowly stroked him

with that same pressure. His hand flew back to the back of his head, and he gripped into the short pieces of his hair to keep still and allow her to continue. He didn't want to come too fast so she had time to explore him, but with how hard he'd been all day, he wouldn't be able to control it.

When she flicked her wrist at the tip, his hips raised off the bed, and she gave him a wicked, proud little grin.

"Don't be a minx, princess."

She leaned in again, and took him as far back as she could, then slowly fucked him out of her mouth to the tip then back again, a little deeper. She did so a few times until she gagged on his cock, drool slipping out of her mouth and soaking his thighs.

She continued to suck and gag on his cock as her free hand played with the drool on his thighs and moved it to his balls, using that spit to play with his sac. Her shining eyes on his as she played ended it all.

He shot into the back of her throat without so much as a warning as he moaned so loud, people would be commenting on that rather than the moans Sael made on a nightly.

When he finished coming, and met her eyes again, there was a happy look in them as she swallowed his seed, then licked his cock for some more. She cleaned her face with her hands then licked her fingers clean before kissing back up his chest until she reached his neck. She stopped at the crook of his shoulder and sucked him until he'd be marked.

Killian laughed to himself. Maybe Sael was more like him than he thought. The one time he told her to do whatever she wished to him, and she was marking him like he had her.

"What's so funny?" She narrowed her beautiful eyes at him, which only made him laugh more.

He needed to stop before she thought he was laughing at her.

He finally released the hold he had at the back of his head, bits of his own hair falling out of his hands and cradled her face. "I simply cannot believe you blush so much when these are the things you dream of doing to me. You're just as dirty as your barbarian, aren't you, princess?"

She blushed even now, but her lips still tugged up.

Then she was straddled over his waist, and she held herself up with one hand on his chest as the other reached between her legs and led his semi-hard cock to her entrance.

As she sank down, Killian was transported to the last time a woman rode him, and bile rode up his throat. Then Sael whimpered his name as her ass hit balls and Killian was back, here in this moment with his princess above him.

The look of her head thrown back in bliss was enough to make every torture he'd been through worth it if only to get to this moment.

Then she leaned over him so her breasts grazed his chest, and caged him in. Her lips brushed his as she moaned, "I can feel you getting bigger inside me."

He grabbed her hips to help lead her and smiled against her lips. "Now you feel what you truly do to me."

She was so wet, she was dripping down his legs as she slammed down on him with the help of his lead. She took his mouth with hers, and sucked on his tongue, pulling all the pleasures out of his body.

The next time she came down, he raised his hips to meet her halfway, and they both moaned out in ecstasy.

She pushed back up and balanced her hands on his chest as she pumped up and down on his cock. Killian was hypnotized once more, this memory of her riding him forever overtaking any other woman. No other memory but every moment he was with Sael would come up when he thought of sex now. She was all his body understood any longer.

When her head flew back this time, the moans growing higher until all she could do was scream and cry out his name, he knew she was coming, milking his cock in all of her juices.

He pulled her down until their lips brushed so every time he moaned her name, she felt it. She was strangling his cock in the last two pumps he mustered before pulling out and coming all over her ass.

He held her there, her arms caging him, for minutes as they both caught their breaths before he forced her head down so he could kiss her long and hard. When they pulled away, she smiled down at him, then slowly lifted herself off the bed to make her way to the edge of the room where he kept a small tub of water with washcloths.

Killian placed his hands behind his head once more and enjoyed the show as she wet the cloth and cleaned her ass and legs, standing with her behind to him so he got the full view. After she finished, he groaned as she bent over to wet the cloth again and moved for him. She cleaned the mess around his legs and cock.

When she made to turn away, Killian's hand flew fast, grabbing at the back of her neck and forcing her down to him. "Thank you, princess," he said against those luscious lips.

She gave him a small peck. "You're welcome, barbarian." Then she walked back to dump the cloth by the tub, giving him a delicious view of that ass.

Killian took that moment to switch to his stomach and rest his head to the side so he could watch her turn and move back for him. She looked confused, but it was obvious she was chalking it to his wanting to sleep on his stomach as she got into bed beside him.

"You didn't get to explore my back."

She gasped, that slight part of her lips enticing. "Are you sure?"

His back was the worst sight. It was blemished all over with scars, and the most gruesome part of his body. He understood why she wouldn't want to. "If you'd like."

She moved to straddle his bare ass in seconds, and it made something beat extra hard in his chest that she wanted to touch all of him, even the messed-up parts.

Her hands were soft as they traced the raised skin, and they made him relax and close his eyes. He hadn't felt this serene in a long time. Matter of fact, he couldn't remember ever feeling this at peace.

Then his eyes shot open when he felt soft lips in the middle of his spine, over one of those scars.

"I'm sorry!" she immediately apologized. "That was too far. I didn't mean to startl—"

"You didn't," he interrupted. "Not in a bad way. I liked it."

She gave a soft sigh, and leaned in again, this time kissing a scar on his right shoulder blade. Then another on his left side and again and again.

Killian closed his eyes, losing himself in the feel of her soft touches and gentle kisses. He could tell her how he got these scars.

He should tell her.

He should.

But he wouldn't.

CHAPTER 19
ROSAELIA

Rosaelia growled at his cheeky smiles as she chased him around the room. She'd woken in the middle of the night from restlessness, and when she'd tried to snuggle closer into Killian's side, she'd realized why. He wasn't sleeping beside her.

Instead, he was sat up on the bed with a candle flickering beside him as he flipped through a book.

It had been on closer inspection that she'd realized he hadn't been reading. Rather, he had her sketchbook—one she'd bought from town on her third day in the Island—and was flipping through her sketches.

She'd been annoyed, and quickly chastised him while she reached to take the thing away, when he realized she was awake. He'd only been a few pages in, so she'd known he hadn't gotten to any embarrassing drawings yet.

Though, they were all embarrassing as they gave him insight to her thoughts, and he really didn't need those.

But the ass had only smirked and pushed the book out of

reach. When she'd sat up, the blanket falling from her chest and revealing her breasts to him, he'd been momentarily distracted, but not for long enough for Rosaelia to reach for the sketchbook.

Now, they were out of bed, Killian still naked compared to the robe Rosaelia had thrown on, and she was chasing him for the book.

He laughed. "What exactly don't you wish for me to see in here, princess?"

"My drawings are personal, barbarian!"

He laughed, the sound endearing and beautiful, as he ran from her. "Do you have drawings of my cock in here, Sael?"

"Killian!"

He stopped before her, his arm stretched too high up for her to reach. "What, love? There's no personal with me. I've been in every personal inch of you. I hardly think looking at your drawings is too much."

"It is too much!"

"Whyever so, Princess Rosaelia?" he teased.

She ground her jaw. "Because those are the matters of my mind, not my body. They're private."

His eyes shined down at her for a long minute before he moved for his dresser, the sketchbook still out of Rosaelia's reach. He pulled out a sheet of paper and turned to her. "Is that what this was then, princess? Your private thoughts?"

He showed her the first drawing she'd created when she got to the Island—one of him as the savage monster. He still looked enticing in it. It reminded Rosaelia of those first moments of seeing him, of desiring him.

Rosaelia took the drawing, her fingers tracing over Killian's form in it. "Yes." Her angry gaze shot up at her. "And like the animal you are, you took it from me."

He smirked. "I cherish it. I love getting into that little head of yours. And it seems your drawings are the only way for me to do so."

"Killian," she begged.

She knew what he was probably thinking—there were dirty images in there about him that he wished to see. And while that was the case and she had plenty of images of him, that wasn't all. If it were, though it would be mortifying to allow him to see them, she wouldn't mind. But mixed into all of his drawings were others. Ones of the Posse, of family she hadn't yet shared with him. Ones of her mother, her current problem she didn't wish to get this family involved in. And most private of all, ones of men.

Big, small, muscled, lanky, hairy, bald, every sort of man.

Ones of them surrounding her, of them holding her down as she cried out. The horrors that would've come about had it not been for her sister in the North.

And him in the Island.

She'd only drawn two of those thus far, but she didn't want him seeing those in particular.

"Please," she begged.

There must've been something on her face that made his arm fall because his eyes softened on her as his free hand moved to cradle her face. "I would never hurt you, Sael."

"I kno—"

"And if looking through this hurts you that much," he interrupted as he handed the book over. "Then I won't look through it."

Rosaelia swallowed as she took the book. Glancing up at Killian, he didn't look at her with anything but the protective darkness in his eyes—he could tell there was something deeper than their intimate moments in there.

Her heart swarmed with warmth at the look. He was right. He'd never hurt her. She knew that much.

In fact, he would protect her if she needed it. If she allowed for him to be in a situation where he could get hurt. If that were the case, she could tell him about Rowena, and ask for his protection.

But she wouldn't do that to him. He didn't need to be involved in this mess.

But she trusted him.

And maybe it was time she shared with him a part of her mind no one else knew.

She couldn't share her drawings as those were too close of the depictions of her fears, but she could talk to him. She could speak the fears and maybe that would help them dissipate a little.

She swallowed, never having spoken of the matter aloud. "I know you wouldn't hurt me, Killian. I... I trust you, like I trust the men in my family. It's..." She held the sketchbook to her chest as her gaze fell to his chest. "A couple of months ago, I had been that naive girl. I had finally gotten the chance to go into the closest town without guards, and I had been so stupid, I truly thought no one would hurt me."

His fists clenched at his side like he could guess where she was going with this. Tonight wasn't the night she would share her drawings of that night, but he could hear of them.

"I went into the neighboring town uncovered because I didn't think they'd wish harm on their Princess," she repeated, her voice weak because of how stupid this story made her feel. "I ended up cornered in an alley by four men. I was lucky I was being followed. They were taken care of." She swallowed. "It was after that night that I knew I was a spoiled damsel. I started basic training after that, and while my family were all busy in other matters, I found the bow and arrow and started training myself. Then I asked friends if they could teach me the basics, and they promised not to talk of it outside of helping me. I mostly trained on my own, but they helped with learning how to hold and shoot and handle the weapon."

"Did they touch you, Sael?" he said lowly like he was trying to control his reactions before her.

She shook her head softly. "You're the only one who's touched me."

He cradled her jaw, soft and loving. "Good, princess. And I intend on being the only one to ever touch you."

Such a wild declaration from a man she wouldn't see in a few weeks.

"I intend the same, barbarian."

A wild, wild declaration.

He kissed her softly. "I want to kill them."

"Too late," she tried to joke.

"I would never allow anything to happen to you, Sael."

She bit on his bottom lip, tugged on it because she didn't want to break their contact.

Finally, she pulled away, and flipped through the sketchbook. "I'm not ready to share everything..." She stopped on a page she'd drawn after witnessing him chopping wood for the first time. "But there are some that I know you would like to see."

He eyed her curiously as she turned the book to show him *that* drawing. The darkness in his gaze slowly faded until the honey orbs were alight with amusement. His lips tipped up, and his eyes shined. "Wow, princess. I cannot even work for my family without your mind running through the Rivorbant Waters."

The Rivorbant Waters—the filthiest place in the lands.

Her cheeks burned. "We'd been together at this point, and I saw you working and my mind... sometimes I need to draw to get things to stop running through my mind. To give myself a bit of a reprieve."

Killian's tongue dipped out to lick his lips as he took the book into his hands to analyze the drawing. His cock was hard in his still undressed form.

The drawing was one of him outside with chopped up logs all around him and an axe blade down in a tree. He was dirty and sweaty from the work, his muscles straining, and the determination in his eyes strong.

Oh, and he was naked.

Fully, stark naked.

And hard.

Very, very hard.

He stood in the drawing like he was watching her, waiting for her to go to him and get on her knees. Waiting for her to suck him off so he could get back to work.

She had gotten so wet imagining the scene that she'd needed to draw it in order to appease herself a bit.

Killian smirked up at her. "So what you did to me a few hours ago was only the tip of the iceberg, princess? What else do you fantasize about?"

Rosaelia swallowed away her nervousness—especially considering he'd done every imaginable thing to her body already—and took the book back. She flipped to another image, one she'd drawn only the day before as she'd been waiting for the brutes to get to the pub at their usual hour.

She turned it for him to take a look.

His eyes bugged wide before a devious grin took over his features. "Truly, Sael?"

She shrugged. "I understand if you wouldn't want to."

The drawing depicted *him* tied to the bed, arms and legs straining as they pulled the same way hers normally did. *His* head thrown back in ecstasy with his mouth open in a moan. *He* was experiencing the delight of being tied up while her fingers scraped at his chest and her mouth licked him, low on the cock. Maybe she'd known instinctively to pay attention to his balls before ever experiencing tasting him because the image looked like she was licking them rather than his cock.

"With you alone, princess, I wouldn't mind it."

Her blush deepened. "In the future." She was quite sure she wasn't ready for that control yet.

"Whenever you wish for it."

Her smile was soft as she took the book again and flipped it to a final drawing she wished to show him.

When she turned the book around, his smile was soft and genuine.

This one was of them taking a walk in the gardens of the palace with the nonas on either side of them. She was wrapped around his arm in the same way Evony wrapped around Sparrow's, and the four of them were laughing.

His fingers moved slowly as they traced the image. "I believe this is my favorite one."

"This is my favorite one too," she whispered.

Getting out of Killian's death grip around her waist had been a feat this morning. Not one Rosaelia won, but a feat in any case.

His hold on her was always strong but there was a possessiveness to it this morning that normally wasn't there. Maybe it was the vulnerability of what he allowed for the night before —touching every single one of his scars, even those gruesome ones on his back. Or maybe it was the vulnerability she'd shown him with the drawings that gave him a look into her mind, the vulnerability of the story she'd told him.

Either way, Rosaelia tried to gently get out from under him

even though she'd promised not to leave in the mornings until he got his taste, but it was of no use.

She'd wanted to be out of the house so he didn't question where she was going. It was obvious he was beginning to get very frustrated with the fact that she hadn't yet told them why she was in the Island Nation.

Rosaelia still had no plans on telling him or anyone in his family.

But because of that death grip, Killian awoke with her and ravished her body until she screamed so loud, it hurt to speak now. The memory of that morning, walking out to see the nonas and Norya, still turned Rosaelia beet red. She really needed to control what noises she made around them.

And because they'd woken together, then likely woken the entire house with their noise, all members of the family were up and curious as to her whereabouts for the day. Rosaelia hated not telling them, but she cared more about keeping them safe than if they were frustrated with her.

She also hated that as skilled of hunters as they were, Norya or Killian could follow her if they pleased. They hadn't so far, but that didn't mean they wouldn't.

Rosaelia met Alana in the woods this time where they would discuss what could be done before heading to the Black Tower to get the final bits required. Things were moving swiftly, but the moment Rosaelia had mentioned Sparrow would be coming for her soon, Alana had been more adamant than Rosaelia herself that they finish Rowena off before the Posse got there.

Now, they were back in the Black Tower as Alana moved around her workstation, preparing a potion for when they got to Rowena in 'two days time.' She insisted she knew how to get Rowena out here, that that bit had never been the problem, and needed to do so before her son arrived. She insisted that though Rowena wasn't in her normal home, Alana knew she was already on her way back.

It made Rosaelia wonder about the Sorcerer. She'd dropped it before, but now, Rosaelia wanted to know. And as her barbarian put it, Princesses always got whatever they wanted.

"You still haven't told me why you left Sparrow and his father."

Alana glanced up from the other end of the workstation table, peeking that Rosaelia was patiently sitting on a stool, then went back to her work.

Rosaelia understood that patience was always key so she said nothing else as she continued staring on.

Eventually, after glancing back up at her a handful of times, Alana said, "I was selfish, Princess. That is why I left them. I would blame it on being young, but you are younger now than I was when I had Sparrow so I cannot. I was simply selfish."

"How old was Sparrow when you left?"

"Eight months." Another bout of patient silence. "I loved Sparrow's father, so when I found out I was pregnant, it was exciting that we would have a child together, but I was never actually excited about becoming a mother. You find, Princess, that some women simply do not wish to be mothers. I knew that before falling pregnant, but I ignored it. I felt wrong. I know now, with time and experience, that it wasn't wrong. It was wrong, on the other hand, to have him and leave him."

She was right on that bit. There was nothing wrong with not wanting to be a mother. Rosaelia herself wanted to be one, but she would never wish it on anyone who did not see that future for themselves.

But the sorcerer was also correct in that she was wrong for leaving her son and husband without a word.

"I fell pregnant even when I knew I did not want it. I let the pregnancy pass the allotted time before I could make a potion for it. I carried through and gave birth. I spent those first few months breastfeeding. But none of it changed me. I didn't want to be a mother."

Rosaelia always forgot that sorcerers had potions that could terminate a pregnancy at the beginning stages. It was something that was lost to the North and South since sorcerers weren't allowed and that pained Rosaelia. To think, the amount of women who may've had a choice.

"Eventually, I couldn't take it any longer. I loved Sparrow and his father, loved the bond they had that matched no other, but I felt like a visiting aunt rather than a mother. I did not want to keep him, so I left. I was selfish, Princess. I may not have wanted to be a mother, but I already was one, there was no changing that. I should've spoken to my husband, found a routine that fit us. I could've gone to live elsewhere but still visited, still somehow protected the house they lived in. But I didn't. I left. Like a coward.

"I came to the Island because I knew that would make it harder for me to turn around. You have to understand, Princess, I still loved them"—she now met Rosaelia's eyes as she swirled the potion in her cauldron—"I missed them constantly. But there was freedom to being here. So I planned to enjoy my life and get to practice the potions I wished to practice, then with time, I would go visit with them. But... time passed, Princess. Eventually Sparrow was eight instead of eight months, and I got the message that they'd been killed. It broke me. I resented myself for never going back, for not being there for the two I actually loved in this life. I became resentful of the palace because I believed it the King's fault. I... it was my fault. Had I not been so selfish. Had I merely visited from time to time, things could've been different. I could've left potions for them."

Rosaelia didn't have anything to say to her ally. She could comfort the woman, but she wouldn't. She'd left Sparrow, and she deserved to hate herself for it. They both knew that.

"He looks exactly like his father now," Alana opened again. "It's unfathomable how alike they look. I suspect the genes strong enough that Sparrow and Evony's sons will look just like him. If they wish for children that is."

"They do." Rosaelia smiled at the memory of Sparrow saying he wanted a litter of his and Evony's children. The memory of what happened in that meeting—of accusing Evony of being the rebellion's leader—aside, it was a happy thought.

Alana quirked a brow like she was unaffected by the news but simply curious. "One or…?"

"A whole litter, whatever number that amounts to."

A small smile lifted on Alana's face before she fought it away. She would likely think of matters later but didn't wish to show Rosaelia. Understandable. She had left her son, why should she reap the benefits of said son's children?

Alana finally moved the liquid from the cauldron to a vial the size of Rosaelia's hand, then corked it before coming to stand beside the Princess. "This is a poison that will seep through the bloodstream and kill, so even if Rowena somehow gets away, her bloodstream will be infected and she will die. You will dip the tip of your arrow into it, Princess. She gets hit and either way, she will die."

Rosaelia swallowed at the thought of killing anyone, even if done by this poison and not a strike to the chest. This meant Rosaelia only had to hit her mother on the body, get the spiked bit of her arrow into any part of Rowena's bloodstream. One look in Alana's eyes said she read the hesitancy there.

Rosaelia took the vial quickly and put it in the small pouch she carried that held the list of Rowena's allies and a couple of other vials Alana had given her. "Okay. What else?"

Alana stared at her a moment before moving to her bedroom, then coming back with a small, handcrafted box. "Sparrow's father made this. Everything inside belonged to them. These were my memorabilia of them while I was away." She handed it over. "Give it to Sparrow when you see him next, Princess."

Rosaelia slowly took the box and ran a delicate finger over the designs. "It's beautiful."

She gave a warm smile. "My husband wasn't only the best sword crafter, Princess."

Rosaelia put it aside safely and met the Sorcerer's eyes again. "I'll make sure Sparrow gets it."

"Thank you, Princess. Now, as for your mother…"

CHAPTER 20

KILLIAN

Killian was a breath away from turning the dagger on himself. That was how frustrated he was with himself.

He should've followed her.

He knew it the moment she left the house without telling them where she was headed—again—but had pushed the desire aside on account of trusting her. On account of her *not* being his claimed woman.

But this had nothing to do with trusting her. This had everything to do with her safety in a foreign land.

By the time that part of his brain won out, she had already disappeared, and Killian had no way of guessing where to start looking for her since he hadn't the slightest clue what she was doing in the Island to begin with.

So he was bloody frustrated.

Killian was growling his way through the forest, kicking at rocks even though none of it was helping his aggression. He was so far gone, he didn't even care when he heard the winces of people getting hit by the rocks he'd kicked far and wide.

"When I find you, Sael," he grumbled to himself, "I'm going to fucking bend you over, and turn your fucking ass red."

He hacked at branches hanging low, hoping whatever direction he'd randomly chosen to walk would lead him to his princess.

"Fucking menace you are, Sael," he mumbled. "Did my life truly seem so calm before that you needed to be sent to bring in the chaos?"

As he stomped his way through the grounds, he heard a bout of laughter from his left that made him more irritated. Nothing was worse than a group of males making jokes in the forest. It meant they were either drunk or making crude comments.

"She's such a pretty thing."

The comment caught Killian's attention. At first because it meant a woman not meant to be in the forests was surrounded.

But then because he recognized that voice.

As one of Keir's lackeys.

Killian didn't think as he turned for that direction.

He was in the clearing within seconds. Surrounding the space was a whole group of men from Keir's estate.

And his princess in the middle, edging back like she was trying to get away from them. Her gaze shot from side-to-side, and there was a shake about her, so slight it wouldn't be recognizable to anyone who hadn't memorized her body, that notified Killian of how terrified she was.

Her bow and arrow lay on the ground, and she was left defenseless to a group of twenty fuckers.

As Killian stepped into the clearing, her gaze shot to his, and she visibly relaxed, though her body remained tense.

As it should be.

"What the fuck does he want?" one of the men cried out like a fucking child.

"How about you tell me what is going on here?" Killian found Keir in the group, standing back against a tree, and asked him directly.

"I hope you don't mind, dear friend Killian," Keir mocked him, but didn't step any closer. "We were talking with the pretty thing here."

He was smart enough to stay back from Sael. He knew, even though Sael wasn't yet claimed, he knew not to mess with a claimed—or almost claimed—female. He'd let his lackeys play because they were morons and he didn't care for them, but Keir was too smart to touch, or even get near, Sael.

Killian wondered if he knew that didn't matter. Allowing his morons to touch Sael was as good as touching her himself. He'd be a dead man.

Sael wasn't paying any mind to him, most of her focus on the two still standing too close for comfort. Her brows were furrowed, and Killian knew all of her fears were coming true.

With Keir around, it would've been impossible for her to get away even if she'd been able to. He would've made sure to torture her before ending her only because she was Killian's girl. Though Sael wouldn't know that part.

"What could you possibly be talking of?" Killian asked without too much interest as he inched closer to where Sael was standing, making sure not to make it obvious that he wanted to get to her. As an unclaimed woman, she was still fair game to all these other men, and he couldn't give them the satisfaction of hurting her because they knew Killian wanted her.

Keir leaned back with a smirk as one of his morons standing in the group answered, "We wanted to know if she liked bouncing on cocks as much as Mara had. You remember Mara, right, Kill?"

Mara was long dead after what she'd done to him. Bouncing on cocks had made him sick up until the night before.

"We wanted to know which ale she preferred," another moron baited. "You do not drink anymore so the poor woman can't get her tastes covered with you."

"I hardly drank to begin with." Killian slowly eyed all of them, his hand twitched to reach for the dagger tucked into his trouser.

"I seem to remember you drinking with Keir, what, seven years ago?" Another smirked. "Yes, must've been. What were you two joking of? Who would get Mara for the night?"

That night had been a culmination of every part of his past that disgusted him. The fact that he used to drink—though nowhere near how other Island men drank. The fact that he'd shared Keir's fuck buddy—because the man had joked about how well Mara rode cocks and Killian had wanted a taste. The fact that he hadn't questioned Keir in the slightest because they had been friendly—never friends, but friendly.

They'd grown up near one another, Keir had been to Killian's estate often, had every access to the place, so his desire to take over had been strong.

And Killian had been moron enough not to suspect him.

"Mara's dead, her worthless body hopefully thrown out in the Rivorbant Waters," Killian answered as he took another step toward Sael.

She backed slowly at the same time, but it seemed most of the morons could now see not to go after her, that Killian was moving for her.

"Ah," another moaned. "Are you taking away our prize?

Keir promised we could do whatever we wished with her if we got all the coin he wished for. Highest amount gets her first." He finally finished moaning, walking closer toward them as his anger grew instead, "I got the highest!"

Eran was a sick fucker who delighted in taking women against their will. He was smart to always stay within Keir's group so Killian could never properly get to him to kill the fucker, but he'd taken at least a half dozen girls like that.

He was a fucking beast when he did so too, hacking at their skin and biting hard so they'd never forget the encounter. He was possibly Keir's best man when it came to getting information from women. They knew to fear the things Eran might do to them.

Killian's gaze shot from Eran to Keir still standing too far back to get to. The fucker had offered Sael to this animal? Had known what Eran would want to do, and had dangled Sael as the fucking prize?

As Killian's jaw ground, knowing when he finally killed Keir, it'd be more savage than he'd been planning the past seven years, Eran started speaking again. "She is my prize." He stomped closer. "If you still want her when I'm done, you can take your turn then." He grabbed her arm.

Killian's vision turned red.

His blood turned ice cold.

The dagger was in his hand, the tip through Eran's forearm in the blink of an eye.

The man roared and released Sael. Killian didn't think of the consequences. He simply attacked, finally getting to end Eran for all the women he'd hurt in the past, but especially for trying to get to his princess.

His dagger struck into the man's dick, then was out and twisted into his heart too quickly for Eran to fight back.

Killian slumped him to the ground, wiped his dagger on his

trousers, then glanced around to see if anyone else was going to try anything. Some of them looked ready to bolt, others looked like they wanted to attack, but a clear shake of the head from Keir said not to touch him.

The fucker had known all along what would happen. Either Eran would get his way with Sael, and Killian would be tortured with the knowledge of what had been done to his—not yet officially claimed—woman or Killian would somehow interrupt them, and Keir would still enjoy getting this reaction out of him.

The fucker really underestimated Killian's rage. He hadn't been the one to touch Sael, probably had no intentions to ever touch her, but allowing Eran, or any of his lackeys, to do so was just as deathly of a sentence.

"You're quite territorial over an unclaimed woman," Keir mocked with a smirk as he nodded back, so the group would leave.

They were gone in the next minute, leaving Eran's body to rot in the forest.

Killian turned to Sael whose gaze was latched on to Eran's body. She probably hadn't heard of the types of things he liked to do but was running wild with her imaginings. Killian hardly thought her imagination was wild enough.

But it was clear—his death didn't frighten her. The thought of what he would've done frightened her.

As her wide eyes met Killian's, he couldn't help the thought that blared in his mind—what was she doing with Keir? Had this been a coincidental meeting? Had she been working with him? Had she been meeting with him only to find him betraying her by allowing Eran to have his way?

He didn't know the answers to those, but he tried to convince himself that she wouldn't do that to his nonas. Wouldn't do that to him.

He was more angry with Keir than anyone else, and he knew it may have been inevitable that Keir would go for her while she remained unclaimed, but still, his anger raged at the Princess. She'd come out without him. Again.

"Start walking," he growled toward her. "Now!"

CHAPTER 21

KILLIAN

"I'm not going to ask you again, Sael. Where. Were. You?"

"And I'm not going to tell you again, barbarian. None. Of. Your. Concern." Rosaelia tried to push past him to make her way into the house.

He grabbed her roughly, the dark laugh making him sound more barbarian. "None of my concern? Might I remind you, Princess, that this is my house you are living in."

"Might I remind *you*, barbarian, that I would never bring problems to anyone within this house. Might I remind *you* that I wanted to leave that first night, and *you* didn't let me."

"The moment you were caged against that tree with those men around us, you became my property. Now tell me what I fucking want to know! I am tired of watching you traipse around the nation. I understand that in your lands, all is safe and you can chase rainbows, but here things aren't so picturesque."

A look of sadness entered her eyes, like she was lost in memory, and Killian hated himself as he remembered she'd been surrounded by men even in her nation. He wanted to apologize, but before he could, defiance made its way back into her eyes. "Rest assured, I know that nothing is picturesque here or in the North. I am not so stupid as to go out unprotected."

His anger bubbled back up, and he gave another cruel laugh. "Really? Your little bow and arrow are going to help you against a group of men? If more than one gets you cornered, what exactly will the Princess of the Northern Lands do? Tell them your station? It will make them want to fuck you even more. Scream for help? Islanders hardly ever get involved in each other's businesses. You are naive, and it makes me sick the way your little family raised such a spoiled heir."

He was being cruel, but she needed a reality check.

Those green eyes dulled slightly. "It makes me sick that you speak to me in such a way."

"Why?" He got in her face. "Why, Princess? Because as royalty I should respect you? Cower at your feet? You're no royalty to me."

"No!" She pushed at him, eyes watering a moment before it was gone and pain and hatred filled her green orbs instead. "No, not because of my station, but because of what we've done."

"What we've done?" Killian paced the yard, circled back toward her, then turned again to punch the tree to get some of his frustration out. The hit hurt his hand like a fucker, but it was a good pain. He paced back toward her. "We've fucked, Sael. I used your body the same way you used mine."

"Stop it!" She pushed at him even though he didn't budge. "You stopped your celibacy to be with me. You let me touch you! Do not try to save face by denying what we had."

He collared her, pushed her little complacent body against the tree. His hand still ached from when he'd punched the tree, but fuck did his body love when he had his hand around her throat. "Fine, princess. I'll not save face as long as you tell me where you were."

"I already told you. None of your concern."

His gaze narrowed. "Where you *with* Keir?"

Her brows furrowed. "What? Who the hell is Keir?"

The only reason Killian had any inkling to believe her was because she'd just cursed and the good little Princess never cursed. He'd give her this benefit of the doubt that she hadn't sought Keir out herself before all the other men surrounded her. The scared way she'd watched them when they were in that clearing also made Killian believed she hadn't even been paying attention to know who Keir was, she'd simply been trying to stay away from them. But he couldn't shake the feeling that he needed to know what she was up to. "What are you playing at, Rosaelia?"

"I've told you before, and I'll tell you again. I'm here to protect my family as I'm sure you've done in the past. Let it be at that."

"I cannot!" His hand tightened. "I am protecting my family. Always. And if I cannot trust you, then you are not welcome near them."

"Then release me, barbarian!" she growled. "I told you before I did not wish to stay here, so if you're finally ready to allow me to leave, release me and I'll be gone!"

Killian was about to do it. Whatever she was here for, she wasn't telling him, and it made bile rise that it could possibly be because she was working with Keir. Any thought of her betrayal made him sick, and as the spoiled little naive Princess, Killian was sure that was the case.

"No." Nona Tereza's voice canceled the white noise around them, the one blocking anything but the sound of Sael's voice. "You are not going anywhere, child."

Killian released her, and took a step back, watched closely as Sael took a large breath in like she was preparing herself, then faced Nona Tereza. "Thank you for your hospitality, Nona, but truly, I was not meant to stay here anyway. I can find—"

"I do not care what high horse my grandson has found himself on, Rosaelia. We trust you. You will come home as you do every day, and Killian will apologize for making you feel unwelcome."

Sael met his honey orbs but she knew as well as him that he didn't intend on apologizing. He'd meant what he'd said— he didn't trust her.

So instead, she walked past him into the house for her bath. Nona Tereza closed the door before he could follow her indoors and stepped up to him. "You listen to me, boy. That is a good girl you have, and you will not mess it up. You know as well as I do that she is trustworthy. Whatever she is here for, she does not tell us for *our* safety. She is not naive. We've spoken plenty with her without your intimidations and maybe at one point she was, she admits that, but not any longer and you will not continue to call her so. And she is most certainly not spoiled. Would a spoiled Princess be doing all she is now? Would a spoiled Princess allow *you* to degrade her sexually, then allow others to know of it? A barbarian? Grow up, Killian."

It'd been a long, *long* time since he'd been chastised by his nonas. He couldn't believe the girl made it happen again.

Killian moved to walk around his nona for the house when her hand landed on his arm. "You will not go into the bath with her, Killian." Before he could argue the point they both knew he was going to make, she added, "I do not care if you've seen every inch of her. I do not care that you have tasted every inch of her and she you. She wants to be alone. You could read the hurt in her eyes as well as I could. She needs to be alone, and you will give that to her."

Killian didn't say another word but ground his jaw and moved into the house.

It was like all three women were ready to throw him out and keep Sael the way they gave him dirty looks. He assumed they'd all heard his argument with the Princess before Nona Tereza had come out, or that they'd discussed it while he'd bathed after Sael. Either way, all three of them sent him dirty looks.

Surprisingly, Sael wasn't hidden away in Norya or the nonas' room as he'd expected. She was in her usual spot on the comfortable armchair in the corner of the living space, a book in hand as she focused all her attention on those pages. Killian would wonder if she were acting if he couldn't tell how engrossed in the story she was. That little spark in her eyes and the small quirks of her lips either up or down told him she was reacting to every sentence. It made that soft side of him want to go in search of that book she said she loved so much.

"Look at the way you look at her," Norya whisper-seethed beside him at the table. "You cannot take your eyes off her as she simply reads a book, you know you were never going to allow her to leave."

Killian didn't respond to his sister. He completely ignored the game of cards he was playing with the three women as he thought about his princess. The way she'd looked at him—the way her body had winced—when he'd mentioned being caged in by those men, was what truly made him sick. She'd trusted him with that story only the night before, and he'd basically thrown it in her face. He was thankful to whoever had killed those men for her, but Killian hated that it meant he couldn't.

But it also told him as his nona had—she wasn't spoiled or naive any longer. She'd admitted to being so even a couple of months ago, but no longer.

The real question was whether or not he could trust her. Since the moment she'd come around, she'd stared up at him with defiance in her eyes, didn't take any of his shit, spoke to him in a way that no one else ever did.

Now, she had her legs tucked high into her chest with barely any space to hold her book. She was making herself small, invisible. He had done this to her. His strong, feral princess didn't want to make herself seen, and it killed him not to see her as she always was.

Because of him.

He'd been so fucking stupid. Of course they could trust her. He saw the way she looked at his nonas, at Norya. He knew she would never hurt them. Knew, instinctively, she would never hurt him. Never work with Keir.

Which also meant he knew whatever she was hiding was truly to make sure nothing happened to them. Because she hadn't planned on them when she'd come to the Island, so whatever she was dealing with was dangerous and she was trying to keep them out of it. He couldn't believe he'd made her feel wrong for doing so.

He also hated that whatever this dangerous matter was, he couldn't help her with it.

But he'd had enough of this.

Killian turned to his nonas and spoke calmly so Sael wouldn't be able to hear, but not quite whispering, "Tell me about the North."

All three women around the table eyed one another before, to Killian's shock, Nona Eleni answered, "The North is beautiful. Cool, but not as cold as the Island, and never as warm as the South. Like the other lands, it's filled with forests, so hunters never tire of their locations. But there's something more calming about the forests in the North. There're beasts, sure, but not in the same way they are here. I used to love taking walks through the forests—never too deep, but always within the trees. It is the thing I miss the most."

"They have no whorehouses, and alcohol isn't widely consumed. The only people I've heard drinking in the North are the criminals that hurt women and children, maybe thieves," Nona Tereza continued. "Though I love the wide acceptance of sex in the Island, there's something special about the reservations of it in the North. There is no difference in the type of sex—both peoples have the same fantasies—but sometimes there's something enticing about only sharing those moments with the one you're with rather than widely as is here."

"We've been here for decades so surely things have changed, but they were kind people then," Eleni continues. "Not so inviting as Southerners, but nowhere near as hostile as Islanders. The perfect in between."

The glint in both of their eyes stung Killian because everything they said were things he'd voiced in the past—wanting a calming walk through the forests; his hatred for alcohol and whorehouses; his desire to be civil even though the Island had raised him on the deep end of hostile. Maybe that Northern bit of him was stronger than the Island.

He turned back for the reason behind his recent curiosity of the middle nation. She was still lost in her novel, looking so beautiful, he didn't wish to interrupt her. But he needed to. He may have been an Island monster, but the North didn't sound bad after all.

Killian had needed to be sure he could stomach the land before he made her his. Based on the bits he'd learned, he didn't think he'd mind the middle nation all that much.

Killian pushed out from the table, dropped his cards, and ignored the others around him as he moved for her spot in the corner of the living space.

She visibly stiffened as her gaze shot up at him, but she didn't change her fetal position. She was hiding from him, that defiant look that was always in her eyes softer now. He had done this to her.

And now he was the monster prowling to her, double her size and looming over his little princess. Thankfully, she didn't look afraid. She was hurt and he despised himself for being the reason behind that feeling, but she wasn't afraid of him. Never had been.

He dropped to his knees before her and slowly took the book from her hands. She didn't try to fight him, but she also didn't turn her body toward him.

Killian dropped the book, and slowly reached for each of her ankles, turning her from that side position she had on the chair so she was facing him, then pulled on her ankles so her legs dropped and she was no longer hiding from him.

That move sent the defiant look flying back to her eyes. "What do you want?"

"You, princess."

"Why?" she spit, her eyes watering even though he knew she was trying to hide that bit. "I'm only a spoiled brat, remember? The stupid Princess, naive and untrustworthy."

Killian's hands moved up her calves, delighting in the shivers that ran up her body even while she hated him. When he reached her knees, he grasped her and pulled again so her body flew to the edge of the chair. With her legs caging his body into her, Killian leaned in, and cradled her face. "You're my princess, Sael. I'm sorry... for ever hurting you. Trust me, princess, if I've learned anything in your time here, it is how very unspoiled you are."

Her eyes closed as she leaned into him, a single tear slipping down her cheek. "I'm sorry for causing your family problems."

He kissed that tear away. "You don't, Sael. You've brought nothing but happiness since you've been here. Maybe too much if I'm honest." He got a small laugh out of her with that comment, and that made his heart jump. "Look at me, princess."

She opened her eyes and transfixed him with her gaze.

"I'm sorry."

"I know."

"You belong to me, princess. I won't fight that any longer. That's why it's truly killing me that you won't tell me what you're doing here. I need to protect you. You are mine."

She nodded as she sucked that bottom lip in thought. "I guess I am, barbarian."

"I need everyone to know, Sael."

She only nodded, giving him all the answer he needed— she would be claimed come morning. He wasn't going to wait any longer.

CHAPTER 22
KILLIAN

She'd woken him with her lips wrapped around his cock, then jumped out of bed before he'd finished. The vixen was in trouble for it, but he couldn't do anything while she helped his family ready the load to take into town square. They were savage people in the Island Nation so neither nona would bat an eyelash if he pushed Rosaelia around the corner and bent her over, but he enjoyed watching her with his nonas, especially after the night before.

After apologizing to his girl, he'd turned with her in his arms, and met the eyes of all three women in his family and saw their pride there. They'd been angry with him for hurting her and it was obvious they loved that he'd realized his mistake quickly rather than allowing his pride to keep their argument up.

Most important about their travel into town this morning was everyone knowing with finality that she was claimed. He needed to show her, and the others, who she belonged to.

The nonas normally took their basket of small blankets made of the leftover skins of the animals Killian hunted to the

No Known Housing unit themselves, but Rosaelia wanted to do it, and they'd both been too giddy to give the two of them this opportunity. It was evident with one look in Nona Tereza's direction that she was excited for the whole of the town to see them together. What she didn't know was that Killian never intended to leave Rosaelia alone in that town square again. At least, not until everyone knew it'd be a warrant for their death if they even looked in her direction too long.

Killian was carrying the basket, and they were on their way in a matter of moments. They were only a minute into their walk when Sael's hand softly wrapped around his bicep, and his heart stuttered. It was such an innocent touch, but he loved it. Was this what she had been speaking of the other day of how Sparrow walked Evony—whoever she was—to the dining halls? If so, he loved it.

"Will I know what claiming is now, barbarian?"

His lips quirked up involuntarily. "It's a way of telling everyone you are taken. It's one of our most respected laws."

"So... like marriage?"

"No, princess. Marriage can be done between unclaimed couples. Not everyone claims the person they are with."

"Why not?"

Her lips touched his tricep as she softly leaned into him, and he damn near dropped the basket with how badly he wanted to take her already.

"In the Island, marriage is a union, not necessarily a promise. Sometimes people simply need the protection or help, so they marry to get the benefits they require. Claiming is more instinctual. Once you know the person is yours, they're yours, and you need everyone to know that you are both taken. It's a promise to one another, as well as everyone else, that you are only for one another."

Sael was quiet for a while as they walked, and Killian knew

she was thinking about what that meant about them if he intended on claiming her. Killian also had a lot to think about in regard to that matter, but he wasn't sure he was ready to speak of it yet.

"So when a couple is claimed, do they not marry?" She finally broke her silence.

"When a claimed couple marries, it is more of what I assume the North and South marriages are like—a legal, soulful promise to one another. That is the difference in marriages in the Island—if you are claimed before, then it is a marriage in the way you know marriages to be. If you are not claimed, it is a union, more transactional."

"Your nonas weren't claimed, right?"

His lips downturned. "No. Tereza didn't know of it when they married and Eleni's husband convinced her it didn't matter, that she was taking it out of proportion. The difference was, they both knew the significance and they both knew they had no intentions of claiming my nonas. Claimed couples never step out, never hurt one another, never allow anything to happen to the other. It is an unspoken law here and taken very seriously. They knew from the beginning, even if subconsciously, that they couldn't make that promise because they fully intended on doing all of that and more."

Sael's hand held him a little tighter around the bicep, and she laid a soft kiss to the back of his arm. "Were any of your family claimed?"

"My parents. And my uncle and his wife. The rest were transactional unions and they were plenty okay with it. Those two couples were claimed. They never hurt one another, couldn't fathom it if they wished." He swallowed back the bile of remembering them. "But that didn't make them good people, Sael. They only claimed one another, promised not to hurt one another. They were still awful people."

She only nodded, still lost in thought as they neared the No Known Housing which was only a short walk from town square.

Before they could get too close, she tugged on his arm so he'd turn his head to face her but never released her hold of his arm. "How does it work? Claiming?"

Killian stared into her emerald eyes, lost in their beauty. His gaze traveled down her face to those plump lips, then lower still until they landed on her hand around his arm. "Like that."

She was adorable the way her brows furrowed as she followed his gaze, then met his honey browns. "But I'm only holding your arm."

He smirked. "In the Island, the only reason to show any ownership of a person is if they are claimed to you. We do not show affections with any randoms."

"But I've seen *many* people in town... enjoying one another."

He laughed at her blush. Still his innocent little princess. "Some of them are claimed, some simply do not care if the town sees their random fuck."

"So how do you tell the difference?"

"Depends. Once the claim has been established, everyone is expecting to see them together, touching one another, so those are the simplest to tell apart. Making the claim when others do not yet know come in different ways. Sometimes they're prefaced with touches, like these"—his eyes snapped down to that hold she had on him—"before they are announced. Other times, they are simply announced as they're fucking. People fuck randomly in public often, so simply having sex wouldn't be enough. Those are fucking touches, not intimate ones. In any case, once a claiming is taking place, the male tends to make sure everyone understands whose female she is. There's a possessive nature to him that even if he doesn't specifically say 'she's a claimed woman,' everyone understands."

"What if they do not... rut in public?"

She was adorable the way she wouldn't say fuck.

Her question brought a smirk to his features. Did she think they would not be fucking in public? "That hardly happens with a claimed couple, but that's why moments like these"—his gaze shot back down to that hand still around his arm—"are even more important. Fucking in public isn't the most telling sign of a claimship since people randomly fuck out there. It merely adds to it, helps solidify it. The most important are moments like these. Where the innocent touches, the territorial looks, the possessive stances tell everyone who you belong to. The male normally has his ways of making it known."

Her blush told Killian all he needed to know about the way she felt about the fact that she had inadvertently walked through town square to get to the No Known Housing claiming him.

He leaned in and brushed a soft kiss to her lips. "Let's go drop these off, princess." *Then I have something for you.*

Killian wanted more than anything to simply drop off the basket and leave, take Rosaelia to stake his claim. But his princess had other plans. The girl wore that sweet smile as they reached the older women who ran the housing unit, introducing herself and pushing Killian to give them the 'gift from the nonas.'

When he growled about her longer stay, she merely looked him up and down with an air about her and muttered, "Behave, barbarian."

It made Killian want to bend her over right there in front of the No Known Housing keepers.

But he'd remained the gentleman—or as much of a gentleman a barbarian could be—and waited off to the side as Sael spoke to the keepers and got to know a couple of the residents, as she was sweet on the children who ran on her foot as they chased each other—a fact that would've gotten a stormed rage from most Islanders, Killian included—and as she promised the keepers to return soon.

It annoyed Killian how enchanted the keepers were with her. They were old women, older than his nonas, and were as sweet as his nonas—meaning they knew some carnage and savagery was required on their land but they didn't commit any of it—but still, he wanted all of Sael's attentions for himself.

When they finally moved into town, Killian felt antsy with his need to be with his princess when he was stopped to discuss a future trade for a large beast, a business transaction Killian took on from time to time when families needed beasts for large parties. Sael walked off to allow them the moment to speak.

When he turned back for her after finishing his conversation with Amar, she stood by the wooded pillars at the edge of town while she waited, people watching and blushing crimson anytime her gaze wavered over to the man grunting in pleasure as two women kneed for him, sucking at his cock and balls. It definitely was a different sight. Normally when anything public took place, clothing was pushed aside rather than completely discarded as those man's trousers were. That, and the fact that there were two women, gave away that neither of those women were his claim. Claimed couples never shared and they would never get naked in public as their partners body were for their pleasure alone.

Those three were the only ones showing any displays that afternoon and as evident as it was that it was too much for

Sael's purer mind, her gaze's constant tug to watch them gave away that she was intrigued. Understandably so since she'd tasted him only two nights prior and had been doing so again that morning before he'd awoken and she'd grown too nervous to continue until he finished.

It'd be a lesson for another day—the enthusiastic, drooling way those women pleased the man.

Or maybe a lesson for that night.

But right now, her pleasure mattered more to Killian.

And that everyone understands who she was.

He silently stopped behind her, wrapping his hands slowly around her waist, and taking pleasure in how easily she fell into his chest when he grunted 'princess' against her ear. He grinned as he kissed her open neck, and again, loved how she tilted her head to give him better access.

He kissed up her neck before stopping at her ear and nibbling on it. "My pretty little princess."

Her eyes fought to remain open as she clutched at his arms around her waist. "I think I need some of your... cum to be very pretty." She still beat red when she spoke of anything past propriety, but it was invigorating.

Killian growled and bit down on her neck. "Only I get to see you that pretty."

She whimpered and clutched at his arm as he slipped one free and pulled up her dress so his fingers could dance beneath the skirts.

"Killian." Her voice shook. "What are you doing?"

His fingers skimmed the inside of her thigh as they continued upward. "Playing with what belongs to me."

"Killian." Now she had a reprimand and some worry to her breathlessness. "People might see."

He chuckled into her ear and loved the shivers that ran down her body. "Oh, they'll definitely see." She blanched, her breathing accelerating as his fingers found their way to her cunt but didn't touch her. "You're in barbarian nation, princess, they must know who you belong to."

His fingers slipped through her folds before she could argue and that beautiful little gasp between her lips made his cock twitch at her back.

"Let's give everyone a show they'll truly enjoy." He held her tight around the torso with one arm as the other hand softly played with her, teasing out those soft gasps and whimpers, building up for the show the townsfolk needed to see.

He wouldn't need to say a thing. The mere sight of them together would be telling enough for the whole town to know she was now claimed.

He knew on regular occasion, most of the folk would notice a couple, then go about their day, uncaring about what was being done in public, like that of the male and two females across the square. But he knew everyone was curious about his woman, curious about the woman he had grown angry for two days ago and had been seen holding him only an hour before, so they would be paying attention. They wouldn't be turning away as if it didn't matter, rather watching from the corner of their eyes. Attempting, as horribly as they did, to make it seem like they weren't paying attention when all they could do was watch Killian and his woman. His, now very obviously, claimed woman.

He groaned into her ear, loving knowing that she was his. "You're claimed, Sael. Mine."

She nodded vigorously as she bit her bottom lip to attempt to keep her whimpers in, her hips rocking against his hand. He slipped a second finger inside her and licked her neck as he reveled in the sounds of her pleasure, as the entire town watched with blatant intrigue as she got off on his hand.

His thumb finally moved to rub on her clit as those two

fingers pumped in and out of her and she finally let out that strangled moan he'd been waiting for. That loss of control.

On her moan, her head fell forward as if to hide from anyone watching them. A growl passed Killian as his free hand snapped up and roughly lifted her head to rest on his shoulder. He held her jaw in place as his other hand continued its ministrations, slick with her juices as he teased that nub and finger fucked her. "You will not hide, *Princess*." He threw extra mockery into that last word. "Show the people how I make you feel. Let them hear it."

"Killian, please, don—" She shook her head but couldn't form the words to tell him to stop. He loved that he knew as embarrassed as her Northern blood was at this show, she wouldn't stop him.

She wouldn't stop her nails from digging into his forearms or her hips from thrusting against his hand. She wouldn't stop the moans that left her lips—though nowhere near as loud as those she let out in their bedroom or in the forest—and she wouldn't stop from calling out his name like a prayer.

His cock strained against her back, and Killian turned Rosaelia's face toward him for a rough kiss. He needed some sort of distraction from coming in his pants, but the feeling of her tongue against his was too good to be considered so. He was too close when he pulled her jaw away, and nibbled at her ear, loving that this was being witnessed, that all would know not to go near her.

"Come, princess. Let that cream puddle at your feet. Come, Sael, all over my fingers. When the town sees my hand, it better be coated, dripping with evidence of your ownership."

CHAPTER 23

ROSAELIA

Sneaking out of the bed when Killian's body was half over hers was more difficult than Rosaelia would have liked, but she'd managed it. Slowly.

She hated that she would be leaving the bed, breaking her promise to always remain until after they'd had their morning fun, but she had to do this. She was this close to seeing out her plans of ridding her mother before her family arrived to the Island, so she couldn't wait any longer.

Rosaelia woke earlier than was required but she was too anxious for the way events might play out to hide in sleep any longer. She stared at Killian's beautiful scarred face in the dim room for a long while before it was time to go.

She traced the scars on his face softly, and loved when he cuddled deeper into her, taking comfort in her touch. But she knew the moment could not last.

Eventually, Rosaelia took the vial of sleeping potion turned to a serum that Alana had given her, and quietly uncorked it, taking a small amount onto a handkerchief and softly drawing

203

a cross over Killian's forehead to make sure he didn't wake after her.

Then, before she could convince herself to stay any longer, Rosaelia jumped out of bed and readied for her meeting with the Master Sorcerer who would be bringing her mother out. They would be ending this on their grounds.

It felt surreal that less than two weeks after arriving to the Island, Rosaelia would be seeing her plans through.

It felt surreal that it had only been a fortnight.

It also felt bittersweet because this meant after today, Rosaelia would have no reason to stay with Killian or his family. She hadn't allowed herself to think about leaving them, hated how quick things were coming to an end. But Alana had insisted that they could make quick work of ridding of Rowena when she heard of the time in the Bloody Fields—a story Rosaelia had finally told her in their last visit—and that it was very likely Sparrow was already on his way to find Rosaelia. She had no doubt they'd found her note at this point and were traveling for her.

Alana hadn't liked the sound of that. She didn't want the Queen to hurt her son in any way. For a woman who had left him as a babe, she showed more care for Sparrow than Rowena did for the two daughters she'd raised for their first two years —though as Rosaelia thought of it, she knew her father had raised her and the nursemaid Vitti had raised Evony.

They were to meet on the outskirts of the Black Tower. Alana had insisted she could get Rowena to come to her with the promise of helping her reverse the potion she'd fallen under when in the church's throne room quicker than any healing sorcerer she may have. Rosaelia truly hoped Rowena fell for it.

She took her bow and arrow and strapped them to her back where they lay perfectly. Rosaelia was especially thankful for the soft dress the nonas had given her that didn't twist around her legs too much. It made moments like these where she would need to sneak around the forests and fight a deranged woman easier. Though the former was much less of a concern now that Killian had made a show to the whole town that she was claimed. The skirts also made running, if need be, easier.

She hoped the frigid air the Island Nation experienced during its nights wouldn't be too bad in this twilight morning air because as comfortable and warm as the cloaks they had in the Island were, she was not yet used to wearing them and having to pull for a weapon. And the nonas had taken her cloak when she'd started living with them since it was a dead give-away from its most luxurious fabric—even though it was the one Rosaelia had worn specifically not to stick out—that she wasn't from around town, so she didn't have time to search for it.

Not to mention, Rosaelia wasn't sure exactly how long the serum would last on her barbarian and she couldn't have him waking to find her with intentions to go off and kill her mother. She wouldn't tell him where she was headed which would lead to another fight and make Rosaelia late for the meeting, so avoiding such a matter was key. Plus, she had no doubt Killian would follow her and her whole objective here was not to get him involved.

She was going to handle this and finally prove to him and everyone else that simply being the Princess of the Northern Lands didn't make her as weak as they imagined her to be. She was capable, not a damsel.

She especially hated that had it not been for her twin entering her life a couple of months ago, she *would* be that weak Princess everyone thought her to be. She was no heroine, she had always been a damsel.

Coming to this nation on her own and killing Rowena

would show everyone, and most importantly herself, that she wasn't the same weak Princess as before. She'd be a Princess more like her twin, though Evony refused to accept the title.

Moving through the forests on her own felt frightening, but Rosaelia had a feeling that had more to do with what would happen at her final destination than the probability of any male harming her. Again, she had Killian's claim to thank for that last bit. A claim she still blushed at when she thought about. A claim she had made when she took his arm even when she hadn't known it.

A claim she had no regrets about. She wanted to be his claim.

She wanted to be wrapped in his warm arms rather than out in this cold morning. The ice from the night before was only slightly melting away now that the sun was beginning to rise. By the time most everyone in the nation woke for their days, the ice would be gone and back to the normal early summer temperatures. It was the one anomaly of the nation Rosaelia had the most difficult time coming to terms with—how cold their nights were even in the warmer seasons.

At the edge of the Black Tower, Rosaelia spotted both women—her mother and her brother's mother. One, there to help her. The other, there to kill her.

Rowena had dark hair like both her and Evony, but that was where the similarities really ended. Understandable since Rosaelia apparently looked like her grandmother on her father's side.

The fake memories Rosaelia had made growing up came flooding back—ones of a mother who loved and cherished her —but she tried to fight them as she watched the two women. She didn't need the conflicting false feelings of a loving mother to scatter her very real knowledge that Rowena was an awful woman.

As she stood there now, behind a canopy of trees to watch from a distance, Rosaelia realized her naiveté again. They could both be there to kill Rosaelia and be rid of one Princess already. They'd never intended on killing her because of her uselessness, but maybe showing up alone with her own mission had shown the women differently.

She was a complete fool to have believed any of this would have happened so quickly. She should retreat, move back to Killian's cottage and wait to have this opportunity on her own.

As she took that delicate step back, her mother's words from the throne room came back to her. *I'd kill you too if you weren't so useless.*

Her sister's words came back to her. *You will not be the damsel!*

Her own promises came back to her. *You will show everyone that you are not the weak Princess.*

And with the decision that could more than likely get her killed, Rosaelia stepped forward silently, reminding herself of the way Alana had spoken of her family, of her son, and convincing herself that she wouldn't betray Rosaelia because in her own ways, the sorceress loved Sparrow.

Rosaelia moved slowly around the edge of the trees that opened to the clearing for the Black Tower as had been her original plan with Alana. If, by any small miracle, she hadn't been lying about being an ally, Rosaelia needed to stick to their plans.

When she was close enough to hear the two, but not yet be seen, Rosaelia listened in on their conversation. This would be her final chance to see if she needed to run because as much of a damsel as she may no longer be, she was not fool enough to challenge them if they were both waiting to kill her either.

"Do you believe me a fool, Sorcerer?" Rowena had a brow

quirked at the woman, her body unmoving beneath her warm cloak.

Alana hardly looked anywhere but at Rowena, but the way her fingers tapped at her leg caught Rosaelia's attention—she knew the Princess was among them. "Why would you believe so, Rowena?"

"You expect me to believe that you wish to help me? I am not in the market of trusting anyone, particularly not those who have proved themselves a liability."

Rosaelia moved slowly so as not to alert them to her presence. She picked an arrow, dropped a bit of the poison from the vial Alana had given her onto it, then slid it through her bow, pulling and aiming as she stood there. If either one was to turn on her—though she believed more as each second passed that Alana was a true ally—she would be ready.

"Then why would you have come, Rowena? Why risk anything by meeting with me?"

"Call me a curious Queen, Sorcerer."

Rosaelia's brows furrowed, wondering why her mother continued to not use Alana's name. There was no way she didn't know it. It made her wonder if it was the same reason she hadn't used any of their names in that church—naming made them people and that was too high a pedestal for *the* Queen Rowena to give to any of them. Rosaelia wondered what she called common folk who didn't have titles like Master or Princess.

"Answer me this, Rowena"—Alana's insistence to continue calling Rowena by her name rather than her title, the Queen, was obviously grating on Rowena's nerves as she silently huffed—"why have I invited you to meet with me?"

Rowena eyed her with suspicion before her back straightened to unimaginable amounts, and she turned to meet the point of Rosaelia's arrow. She stepped back quickly, but neither Rosaelia nor Alana moved for her.

"Ask me again, Rowena." Alana smirked as she caught Rosaelia's gaze, a kindness and sorrow within them. "Are you a fool?"

Rowena had two daggers out, one in each hand, as she watched the both of them.

"I think us all on this planet fools of our own making," Alana said with a small smile toward Rosaelia, one that was hardly noticed by Rowena now that she'd noticed her own daughter in the mix.

But it made Rosaelia wonder about the sorrow in Alana's eyes. Was it because she knew Rosaelia couldn't do this? Couldn't kill her own mother? Couldn't kill?

Then her mother moved. Quicker than trackable by the human eye, Alana was before Rowena, blocking the woman from killing her firstborn.

Rowena's dagger moved so quickly that Rosaelia didn't have time to process the Master Sorcerer—Sparrow's mother —getting pierced through the heart. She hardly saw it happen.

But one moment she was there—a companion—and the next, she was on her knees, falling to her back.

Rosaelia gasped, unable to hide her shock. This wasn't supposed to have happened. Alana wasn't supposed to be the one dying.

Yet, she looked to Rosaelia without worry, like she knew relying on Rosaelia would've led to this and she was all right with that decision. She whispered her final words as blood slipped from her lips. "Tell Sparrow I loved him, my girl. Tell him the best thing that happened to him was Evony."

"No." Rosaelia shook as she stared down her arrow once more toward her mother. She had to release, but in that moment, knowing she was the reason behind Sparrow's mother's death, she couldn't move. "No."

Rowena watched her with wide eyes, the second dagger ready in her hand. "*You*? What are you doing on the Island? I was sure if anyone would come for me, it would be your sister and her husband."

Because you're useless. Rosaelia still heard the words clear as day.

Her hand shook as she held the bow and arrow up, a tear slipping down her cheeks at the thought of Alana gone. "I'm still trying to figure out how you could raise two daughters, then try to kill them."

She scoffed. "Oh, grow up. I didn't raise you. In fact, I tried to stay as far from either of you as possible. You were disgusting, annoying things. I only had you, only had that portrait taken of both of you on my lap, so no one would be able to refute that I was the rightful holder of the throne once the rest of the line was gone."

"So you felt *nothing*? You grew us for nine months. Pushed us out. Watched us grow from infant to toddler, and no part of your womanly heart thought you could be Queen with us?"

Rowena laughed. "Deplorable child. I will not share my crown with anyone." She played with the dagger in her hand. "Honestly, it is amusing that you believed at all that you could do anything to me. Though I guess I can now take care of you. An easy hurdle to be over."

Before Rosaelia could argue, say anything, think to release her arrow, the dagger in Rowena's hand went flying through the air, straight for Rosaelia's forehead.

"Sael!" A roar crashed through the silence of the forests. "Sael! Duck! Sael!"

His voice was so sharp and demanding, Rosaelia's body

followed his instructions without question. Her arrow shot through the air, but Rowena easily ducked out of the way.

Rosaelia lay on the dirt ground, the vial of potion spilling out beside her as her blurry gaze tracked up into the eyes of her mother as she pulled the dagger from Alana's chest, and readied to throw it.

Then Killian was there, standing before her body as the monster ready to shed bodies apart. Rowena paled at his presence, the scars making him look more frightening, as he stalked toward her, his own daggers flipping around in his hands.

Trained.

Skilled.

Poised to kill.

Like his name indicated.

Rowena was smart though. Before running off, she threw her dagger in Rosaelia's direction, enough of a distraction for Killian to turn to Rosaelia rather than run after her.

With Killian by her side, Rosaelia cried out a final plea as her mother ran off. "No!"

CHAPTER 24
KILLIAN

This woman was sent by the devils to play with him for all the destruction he'd caused to the lands. She had to be.

Because why else would she have slipped out from beneath him in their bed, run off into the forests, and stood there as a woman threw a dagger in her direction.

Killian had been content with the way her fingers traced the scars on his face. They were as gentle as they had been on his back and made him simply desire to lose days laid in bed with her.

Then she opened a vial, and the scent had hit him immediately. Killian had done everything in his power to make sure his body didn't react to knowing Sael had a sleeping tonic in hand. When he felt the wetness of the serum on his forehead, he knew whatever she was running off to would be dangerous, and she was trying to keep him away.

So the second she'd turned her back to get dressed, Killian had pulled the sheets up and wiped the serum off his forehead before it could take effect and truly knock him out. Whatever the reason behind her journey to the Island, this would surely be an important meeting if she felt the need to put him to sleep, and he wasn't going to miss it. It was time he found out what the fuck was happening with his princess.

So he'd waited until she'd been dressed and out of the house before quickly throwing on his clothes and following her trail. Every second of putting on his trousers, top, and boots felt like a millennium as he feared losing her trail.

He'd followed silently, not disturbing even when he saw Sael pull out her bow and arrow—which had instinctively made him pull out his daggers—in order to find out her true purpose for being in the Island Nation. So far, he'd watched the Master Sorcerer be murdered and the Princess of the Northern Lands almost follow in her footsteps but had learned nothing of Sael's purpose for being there.

In fact, he was more confused now than ever.

He dragged Sael up and made her follow him as he carried the Master—by Sael's instruction—to their home, readying her for burial in a spot of land up the hill by his house. Sael had been especially emotional with needing her to be buried somewhere safe, though Killian couldn't figure out as to why.

And how the Princess of the Northern Lands and the Master Sorcerer had teamed up at all. Why?

He laid the Master down in his back shed which he'd cleaned only the day before, and pushed Sael to the main house, promising to do a burial once he got all he wanted out of her.

Thankfully, she didn't argue. Though with her frozen wide eyes, Killian doubted she could. The girl wasn't used to the savagery with which citizens killed one another in this nation.

When they entered the house, both nonas and Norya were seated at the table readying breakfast, and all Killian wanted to do was take Sael to the bathing room, slip her dress off, and wash her trauma away.

But he needed to know first. Needed to know what the Princess had gotten herself into and why.

"Sit down," he growled at her, attempting to sound kind to ease her but failing miserably.

She listened, swallowing her nerves as she seemed to come out of her shock.

"What's happened, Kill?" Nona Tereza eyed the two of them with worry, eyed the blood dried on him from carrying the Master.

Killian took the chair beside Sael, needing to be close to her after watching that woman throw two daggers in her direction, even though he was angry with her. "That is what Sael will be telling us right now."

Now Sael met his gaze, a striking defiance about her emerald eyes. They were ridiculously beautiful. Hypnotizing, if he was a poet prone to such pretty words.

Her gaze narrowed like she would not be taking orders from him.

"Rosaelia," he growled out slowly, controlling his need to push her against a wall and fuck the answers out of her. Hard, rough, with a touch more pain than normal.

Still, she watched him without a word out of that pretty little mouth.

"Sael, dove?" Nona Eleni asked, and Sael finally breathed out, and turned to meet the women's gazes.

She sighed as she fidgeted with her fingers. "The reason I came to the Island Nation was to find my mother, the long dead Queen."

"But she's dead..." Norya stated with a hint of question.

"As we all believed," Sael answered. "Only a few weeks ago, she showed her presence again, wanting to rid of us on the

Northern crown and take her rightful place without sharing or being second best to any of us. She had the aid of the Master Sorcerer."

"But..." Killian began, thinking back to that retreating woman. That would mean that had been Sael's mother.

"Alana, the Master Sorcerer ended up betraying my mother when it came down to it because, as we also came to find out, she's Sparrow's mother. The Master Assassin, my brother."

Hearing another male's name off her lips froze Killian, his blood boiling with the need to beat the man even though he knew of their relationship. His blood only cooled with the addition of 'my brother' like he needed Sael to acknowledge it.

Sael swallowed, but continued talking, her green eyes on her fingers now. "I came to the Island Nation because this is where she's been hiding for eighteen years. I needed to get to her, kill her before she killed my family. Because though she'd been betrayed, she would not give up her chase for the crown." She swallowed again. "Two days after arriving here, Alana found me. She wanted to help me in order to keep Sparrow safe from my mother. We were supposed to finish it all today."

"But?" A low growl left Killian now, hating what any of this meant for Sael, but needing to know the rest.

She shrugged. "You saw the rest. Rowena killed Alana, and I was too much of *a bitch* to kill her. *I froze!* The sole purpose of my journey and when the opportunity presented itself, I couldn't do it."

There was so much self-hatred in her voice that Killian didn't think before pulling her out of her chair and into his lap. He held her close. "She's lived in the barbarian nation for two decades, princess, you shouldn't have been able to do it as easily as her."

Her head shook as she stared at her hands still clasped in her lap.

Killian cupped her cheeks and forced her to meet his gaze. "I vow to you, Sael, I will help you kill her. I promise."

She stared back, confusion and hope in her beautiful green eyes.

"As long as you vow to talk to me, to keep yourself out of harm's way, to keep me by your side." The last statement was meant to signify as regards to killing Queen Rowena alone, but Killian couldn't help but want more than that, to want to be kept by her side for all matters.

There was more hope than confusion now, but the latter still lingered in her eyes. One glance around the table showed the rest of the room was less confused and more delighted. Of course they were, they annoyingly wanted Killian truly claimed and content in a woman.

Killian ignored them as he pushed off his chair, settling Sael to her feet, and softly took her hand. He led her to their room, and closed the door, then released her and moved for a dresser off to the side.

He rummaged through it a moment before finding the small dagger between a few other weapons. He turned back to find Sael in the same spot, watching him curiously but quietly.

He smirked and moved for her, raising the dagger. "I will make a thigh sheath for you today. I intend to feel this beneath your dresses from now on."

She looked excited, but remained calm as she said, "I was barely taught how to use one, barbarian."

His smirk turned into a soft, small grin. "I'll teach you, *princess.*" His hand slipped beneath her dress in a flash, gliding over the soft flesh of her calf to her thigh. "But I intend on feeling it here every day, Sael. I intend on being the *only* one to take it off you every night. Understood?"

She swallowed again, this time with pure excitement and hunger. "Understood."

Leaving Sael after making the leather sheath for her dagger had been difficult, but the air was a more bitter cold that day and his family was running out of wood for their flames. He'd been surprised since he'd only chopped some the other day, but he knew his nonas' kinder hearts would've offered some to the local elders to keep warm.

He didn't mind working for them though, so he never complained when they did such things.

While Norya was around, it gave Killian the peace of mind to chop for more as he got lost in his thoughts, not needing to keep as much of an eye out for his family as usual. It was one of the many reasons he had always insisted Norya move in with them—she was as trained as Killian, she could keep them as safe as he could.

At the same time, it was more dangerous now that he did not have to worry about the family. It meant all of his thoughts could run back to the Princess who had infiltrated his life and that was a very precarious place to be.

But he could not help it any more than his cock couldn't help growing hard at the mere look at her, the mere sound of her name or her voice, the mere thought of her. Princess Rosaelia of the Northern Lands. His princess.

And she was in trouble.

Surprisingly so, not because of an Islander. But because of one of her own kind. One of her own blood.

It wasn't as shocking of a predicament for Killian to consider as it might've been for the common folk since both of his parents were worthless and would have no problem hurting him for their own gain, but Killian also knew his nonas, and had been raised on their love. He couldn't imagine one of them turning on him for power or greed.

He wondered which of the two relationships Sael's mirrored when it came to her mother—was it one where the woman was always hated and therefore this wasn't as shocking, or, and if Killian had to guess would be the case, was it one where Sael had always thought her mother a good woman?

Piercing pain shot through his chest at the thought of Sael in any sort of danger, and Killian had to growl at himself to get back to chopping at the wood. He could not allow himself to grow too warm toward the girl, no matter how pretty she looked covered in his cum.

Killian swung his axe down, forcing his thoughts to blank. He succeeded for the count of four logs before Sael came back to his mind—the look of her poised with the bow and arrow aimed at her mother. She'd looked ethereal and enchanting, like a goddess. If it took all of him, Killian would teach her not to freeze up next time. Though, as he had that thought, Killian didn't know if that promise could be fulfilled.

He didn't know if Sael had it in her to kill, and not because she was a damselled Princess, but because she was inherently a good girl. A very good girl, and he loved that about her.

Loved that she was pure yet she did not judge him for his murders or the disgusting scars across his body. Loved that she seemed to love the scars and his savagery even when she called him a barbarian. Loved that being a monstery barbarian made her wet for him in a way no other could. Loved that she still blushed that pretty shade of pink when things got a little too risqué.

He loved her pretty little mouth every time she was getting mad at him or smiling up at him. Loved those soft hands when they glided down his body or when she simply took his hand. Loved that crinkle her nose made when she was annoyed with the way he said something. Loved her long black locks when they fanned over his bed or when they fell over her eyes as she did simple tasks around the house. Loved the way those lashes fanned her eyes when she simply looked at him, but especially when she glanced through them while they were in those risqué positions.

Most especially, he loved her eyes. Her emerald-green, breathtaking eyes.

And he hated himself for all of those feelings. Hated what it could mean for him. Hated that it meant he was opening up to her in a way he had promised himself he would never do, even before the scars. Hated that he had never, not once, hesitated to let her into his life. Hated that he knew he trusted her, that he wanted her to know all of him almost as desperately as he needed to know all of her.

But most of all, he hated that he didn't know where their relationship might go. Would he be allowed to the North to be by his princess's side? If Rosaelia said he was, he hardly thought anyone would fight her. Especially if the stories she'd told him about her father being wrapped around her finger were true.

But what would a move to the North be like?

From the men he'd seen at the docks, not all Northerners were the soft things he'd heard of. Some of the sailors were soft, sure, but a good amount of them were roughened through the years and their labor. They were still nowhere near the harder lives of Islanders, but they were men Killian had liked on the couple of times he'd spoken to them.

From what he'd heard—through the years and through Sael's stories—the North was more proper, more reserved, less savage. They didn't walk around trying to look scary whereas in the Island if a man didn't look scary, they were likely to become prey.

They were more formal with one another, only those closest to them getting to see the real them. That part didn't bother Killian.

They didn't publicly entertain their relationships, which made Killian a bit sad to think of. How depressing to never be able to fuck whenever they wished simply because they were in public.

But if that was his only real problem, then Killian could certainly deal with it. He could make a life with his princess in the North, his nonas could go back home.

And though small aspects of growing up on the Island would be missed, Killian couldn't say he'd be upset to leave any of it behind. He didn't need this savage life.

The real question at the end of the day was whether Princess Rosaelia of the Northern Lands wanted him for the rest of her life? The answer scared him. She didn't even want to share her mission with him now, would she want to share her life?

Killian hacked at more wood, finishing the last few pieces before it would be time to start taking the cut logs into the storage doors by the house.

"Sael, Sael, Rosaelia, Sael," he muttered to himself after the final swing of the axe as he stared at the pile of logs. "What am I to do with you, my princess?"

CHAPTER 25

ROSAELIA

Those beautiful dark hazel eyes stared down at her as his hips thrust into hers. It was enchanting.

"I almost lost you yesterday, Sael." His voice was filled with heat and a passion that sounded like more than sex. "That can't happen. Ever. I can't lose you."

Rosaelia didn't know what to do with that information. Mostly because she felt the same way, but there stood the problem of her station as the Northern Princess and his being an Island barbarian.

His thrusts were slow as he held on to your curves, her thighs, kissed up her neck and over her lips. "You're my woman, princess."

"And you're mine, barbarian." Her nails scratched down his sides as those slow, deep thrusts sent her closer to the edge, and she lost her breath. "You're not going to lose me. I'm sorry for…" She moaned out as the thrusts went deeper and his body rubbed her clit. "Killian!"

"You're sorry for what, princess?" He grit his teeth to control his reactions to her ecstasy.

"For... Killian, please."

"Tell me, and I'll let you come."

Her legs clung to his waist, and her nails raked into his shoulders. "For scaring you yester— I'm so close."

He took her lips into a scorching kiss, held on to her curves, and made finishing thrusts that had her moaning into his mouth.

When her cunt finally released his cock from the tight grip of her orgasm, those aftershocks played with him until he needed to pull out.

His cum covered her belly and upper thighs before he fell over her, forehead resting over hers as he stayed there. "My pretty fucking princess, Rosaelia."

She smiled up at him earning her a chaste kiss before he pulled away, grabbed for the shirt he had sitting at the end of the bed, and cleaned her with it. Then he dropped beside her in bed.

The early mornings of twilight may turn to Rosaelia's favorite time of the day. At least as she lay awake at Killian's side after she'd awoken from a toe-curling dream and woken him to take care of matters.

They lay, catching their breaths now, waiting for the sun to rise and melt away the ice outdoors as they stared at one another, both with satisfied grins and glazed eyes.

"Wake me with such matters every day if you please, Princess." Killian spoke with formality, making fun of her status.

"I intend on using you any time I need it, barbarian."

His returning grin, seductive and cocky, made the spot between her legs tingle with the need to have him inside her again. To distract herself, Rosaelia lifted a hand, her pointer finger moving to trace the scars on his face, hating whatever had happened to create them but loving them all the same.

This was her monster and the scars were part of him. "I know I should hate them for the pain they signify you've been through, but every time I look at your scars—all of them, but especially these two—I fall for you, Killian. It's a dangerous predicament I find myself in."

He kissed her finger softly, not saying anything as he allowed her to trace the two scars—one sliding from eye to jaw, and the other sliding down his entire face, barely jumping over his eye so as not to cause damage. They framed his dark lashes, and even darker hazel eyes beautifully.

"If I could come up with what perfect looked like, Killian, you'd be it."

She met his gaze as he analyzed her a moment before he silently turned away, giving his back full of scars to her.

"Killian, I didn't mean to—"

"Touch the scars, Sael," he interrupted. "Make them feel as soft as you do for the ones on my face."

Rosaelia swallowed, thankful to realize he wasn't turning away from her confession but giving more of himself to her. She moved slowly, not knowing where to start with his back as covered as it was with raised skin.

They lay for a couple of minutes in the silence of the twilight air before Killian began speaking, low but strong. "The scars on my face are part of the reason I was celibate before you, princess."

Rosaelia froze, her breath hitching as she realized he was finally going to tell her about his past without her needing to ask for it. It scared her how thankful she twas that she could be this person for him, and how much she wanted him to be that person for her.

She realized then that her finger had stopped tracing his scars, and in turn, he'd stopped talking, so she continued.

And so did he. "The way this nation works is you kill, or

fight, for your spot. I have always been powerful without truly trying. I didn't kill or fight for my spots, I merely had them because it had been my family's before, and others feared challenging me for them, but I didn't care for them. There's a man, Keir, he's the one who led the group that had you surrounded the other day. He wanted to be where I was—he wanted my estate so to say. It was the only real indicator of where we stood. You kill or chase off the residents here in the Island, and the place becomes yours, no questions asked. Keir wanted me gone essentially, but he knew one on one he could not take me. He was smart, I'll give him that. He's lost his edge in the years, but back when he was fighting for that spot, he thought it all out, especially when I wasn't looking for what he had planned. He took his time, and had the entire thing—the people required, the items, all of it—arranged before acting." He sounded calm as he spoke, as if the tracing of his scars numbed the pain of remembering what had happened. "I have never claimed a woman, obviously as we only really get one and I've claimed you, but at the time I had long-term lovers. My last lover was killed along with her family for their place, so I was on the search for a new fuck when Keir told me about one he had, Mara. His stories were enticing. I wanted a taste. Mara was the last one I ever had, and the reason behind these two on my face."

Rosaelia's jaw involuntarily ground together, her finger pausing as she listened to his final statement.

Killian only laughed, obviously picking up her irritation without having to see her. "She was only a fuck, Sael. I have never touched her, or any other woman, the way I have you."

She knew he meant like they were worth anything to him, but she still didn't like the thought of him with anyone else even though she'd always known he wasn't a virgin.

"I don't care," she forced out.

He laughed harder now before sobering to continue his tale. "I was with her that night. She was riding—"

"I don't need the specifics," Rosaelia growled out.

He gave a breathy chuckle before sobering again. "I don't either. I hate thinking of her. But her positioning is important, love."

His use of that small term eased Rosaelia so much, she leaned in to kiss the spot between his shoulder blades, letting him know without words that she was there for him.

"She was on top, and while she rode me, she pulled a dagger from beneath a pillow. The bigger one is from her first swing. I threw her off immediately, but she'd already gone for a second swing and that's where the second scar came from. I killed her the second I had her off me, but that was only phase one. Keir knew it was highly unlikely that whore would be able to kill me so phase two was waiting outside the doors courtesy of that bitch.

"I dressed in only my trousers before moving for the door to clean up the mess on my face and there, I found ten men waiting for me. I killed six of them before they got enough of a handle on me to drag me out to the stand in the middle of town square—the way to establish the power to the degree of the estate I had is to show the whole town of your takeover. I had bruises and cuts from the fights, but nothing substantial. I was at her house that night so the trek to the square wasn't long either.

"They tied me to the pole, hands around the front so my back was exposed. Keir did the rest. If he allowed any of his men to touch me anymore, the townsfolk wouldn't regard him as anything but a coward. He had to be the one to do it. So he did. He carved in my back with multiple daggers—some duller, some sharper, some thicker, some longer. I bled out, but as cold as our land gets, especially in late winter, it kept me from bleeding out as quickly.

"Then he threw a bucket of sorcerer-salted water over my wounds," he said that final bit with remembered pain, like he still felt that sting. "It's the reason my scars have remained as prominently as they have. Sorcerer salts are for preservation, they did their job. If I, by some miracle, survived and got to my nonas to make me a salve for them, I still would've scarred but nowhere near as badly. The salt meant nothing could be done for them. Then Keir announced to the town he would be taking the house—which thankfully both nonas had been with Norya and out in a different village at the time—and left me there. I was left to freeze that night, but when my family made it back into town that night, Norya heard about what had happened and sent the nonas to the No Known Housing, then came for me. When she untied me, I made her go back to the nonas."

"Why?" Rosaelia gasped, barely focused enough to continue tracing his scars as she listened.

He held his breath like he was nervous for the next part. "I needed to find us a house."

It took a moment, but Rosaelia figured out what he meant —he had to kill or chase off another family. She stopped tracing the scars, and in the moment it took to reach for his shoulder, she saw him stiffen like he was scared she hated him now. She tugged on his shoulder so he turned back to her.

When he finally faced her again, the light streaming in through the mostly closed drapes showed Rosaelia his every feature. She traced the smaller scar on his face again before simply cradling his jaw. "I don't care about what you've done to survive, Killian. I'm simply glad you survived."

He'd survived.

He'd survived basically being gutted from the back. He'd survived the piercing pain of that salted water on his wounds.

He'd survived the frigid temperatures the night brought in the Island Nation, especially in the winter. He'd survived.

He moved slowly then, like he was giving her time to back out, and kissed her. She returned the soft press of his lips before pulling away for the one thing nagging at her mind. "Did you end up killing any of them?"

He kept his face cradled in her hands as he answered with a small shake of his head. "On their own, I could and have killed many. But Keir is never on his own when he comes out, as you saw, and he knows if he sends his men that they need to be in packs. But slowly, one by one, I've been getting my revenge."

Rage raced through her. "I want to kill them for you." More than she wanted to kill her mother.

That was a thought for another day.

He gave a small chuckle, not to tease her but because he liked the sound of her words. "Okay, princess." He said that term so differently now. There was no snark to it anymore, hadn't been for some time. He said it like she was a jewel in his eyes.

"Can I ask you one more thing?" Her thumb caressed his chin and bottom lip as she stared into those eyes she was falling helplessly for.

"Always."

"Why celibacy? If you didn't have anything else for them, why stop?" She was glad to be his only one for the last seven years, but it made her wonder.

"I couldn't bear the thought of any of them touching me again. Couldn't bear the thought of *anyone* touching me."

"But you've always let me touch you." It'd been less at the beginning, needing to remain above the neck, but that rule had quickly disappeared.

He shrugged. "Your innocence has always called to me. Something about how good you are made my scars feel safe."

Rosaelia only gave him a small smile as they continued staring at one another. Then he fell to his back and opened his arm for her to lay her head on his chest.

When she did, her leg falling over his hips to half lie on top of him, his hand wound into her hair, playing with it as the other traced soft lines up and down her thigh.

She took the time to think about what she and Killian had done a few days prior. He'd taken her to town and publicly claimed her as his woman.

As a part of the Island customs, Rosaelia loved it.

As a Northerner, she wasn't entirely sure how to feel about it.

As Northerners, they were more reserved with their relationships, choosing to stay away from public displays. They were much more quiet about the physicalities of their relationships where Southerners were quite carefree with theirs. It was how Evony brought Sparrow out of his grumpy shell to show her all the affection she desired—she was a born Northerner, but a raised Southerner. And Sparrow would do anything for her.

Islanders were more like Southerners in this regard, except they were far more explicit with the things they cared about letting be known. If the North found out she'd been claimed, which any relationship with an Islander would make that a known fact, how would they feel? How would her father feel about it?

Rosaelia's finger traced over Killian's chest, small scars from daily life in the Island running under her fingertip.

She loved that she was claimed. It made her blush a deep crimson, but she wanted the North to know about it. They would never get the same show Islanders got, but she was proud of this Island custom, and didn't want to hide it.

If Killian were to come back to the North with her, there

would be a lot of whispering. But Rosaelia found she didn't care in this instance. She was a claimed woman, and she was proud of that. Her father, her brothers, Northerners would all learn to deal with what it meant to be with an Islander.

Her lips tipped up at the picture of Northerners scurrying away when a big, scarred, scary looking Island monster was walking through the palace corridors. They would surely think her insane.

"What's so funny, love?"

"Northerners and Islanders."

He gave an airy chuckle. "We're quite different."

Rosaelia kissed his chest and continued tracing at his scars. They were different, but she loved that about them.

Nothing else was said as they lay there in silence, and the sun rose to greet the day.

CHAPTER 26

KILLIAN

She was holding that dagger like she was ready to throw her arm back and thrust it down to end him with it. It was fucking sexy as hell, and Killian's cock was already hard watching her stand there simply holding the weapon.

He gave her a small smile. "While I appreciate the readiness, princess, let's start you off with the simple outward position first."

She looked down at the hand holding the dagger. "What position is this?"

"The chambered or reverse grip."

"Okay, so what's the outward?"

Killian took his own dagger out and held it the way she was so he could demonstrate while he spoke to her. "The way you're holding it now, you have four fingers behind the handle and your thumb before it. You're going to take those three bottom fingers and move them to the front too, so the dagger is balancing between your middle and index. Good job. Now use those two—your middle and index—to flip it up into position, then grab it with your thumb again, four fingers going behind it again. Now you're in a forward hand grip, the outward."

She was a quick study as she followed his instruction, then did so again on her own thrice more before moving on. It shouldn't have surprised Killian that she could quickly pick up on instruction. As the Princess, he was sure she'd had to pick up a lot of things rather quickly.

"Let's have you learn how to go back into your favored chamber position, princess. That way you know how to handle both and you'll always have your hand on the dagger in case you need to switch from one to the other."

She eyed him with a spark in her green orbs that said he better be careful around her. The vixen was ten minutes into her first lesson and already threatening him. He couldn't believe he'd ever believed her to be a brat. At least in the negative sense of the word.

Because she was a brat, that spark in her eyes told Killian that much. But she was a sexy fucking brat who'd be getting a spanking later and he couldn't wait to deliver such punishment to his princess.

"You're holding in your outward position, four fingers behind, thumb in front." He started to distract himself from said thoughts, demonstrating as he went along. "You're going to move your index in front this time, releasing those bottom two so it's balanced between your index and middle again and flip it down. Balance it with the thumb and put the other three behind again. Now you're back to the chambered position."

Again, she executed beautifully, then did so again three times without his demonstration.

"Good job, princess. Eventually you'll get advanced enough to switch between them quickly." He demonstrated again, the dagger basically flying in his hand with the speed it moved from outward to chamber position, then back again.

"Thank you." She gave a soft smile, and those eyes looked down. Killian was flabbergasted at seeing this shy woman come out. He definitely wasn't used to this look on her. She always met his gaze, either with a challenge or defiance. This shier one was rather sexy too.

He was coming to find anything regarding her was sexy.

"You have a shorter dagger, but it will work the same way as any other. This size simply works best for you." When she nodded and met his gaze again, he held up his dagger to explain a few things. "I wanted you to be able to hold it first in those basic handles in case of an emergency where you need to use the dagger. You now know how it'll work. Now, for the anatomy of a dagger. There's the spine and the true edge. The true edge"—he swiped his finger down the one edge of the spine—"is the sharpened bit. The spine"—he swiped his finger down the opposite edge—"is sharpened at the very top, that's called the false edge, but most of it is blunted. That blunted edge will come in handy in matters that don't involve fighting. Especially in the Island Nation, we need to be able to use our weapons for many purposes."

That little spark was back in her eyes, and when Killian grinned because of it, the vixen in her seemed to come alive as she bit her bottom lip, and said, "You're really sexy like this, barbarian."

Killian took a large breath in, and stepped back, dropping his dagger as he moved to relax against the tree. "I won't over-whelm you with too much now. You got the basics of the holds. Take your time and try switching between them and wielding the dagger in each position as if you're getting attacked. Take your time. Go slow. Move at your own pace."

She was so beautiful as she nodded and did as she was told. He loved that she listened when he ordered her around, loved that she did not shy away from making mistakes in front of him. Loved the pace she set for herself, definitely slow, but obvious that she was taking this training seriously.

It gave Killian the time to think about her and this predicament they'd found themselves in. Both the one where the Northern Princess was in the Island Nation to kill her mother, which he would be helping her with and the one where he'd claimed her as his.

The latter was something he hated thinking about because he didn't know where this went after they handled the business of her mother. Were they to simply break up? Killian had never heard of claimed couples separating in any way other than death. He couldn't fathom it happening.

So he wouldn't be thinking of it.

Instead, he thought of Sael's mother and how the crazed woman was trying to kill her daughter. He still had the image of that woman throwing the daggers toward Sael ingrained in the forefront of his memory. It made him more protective and territorial of her. The thought of losing her pained him, destroyed him, killed the very beat of his heart.

He needed Sael to talk to him so that he could figure out a way to take care of the woman before she tried hurting his princess again. It baffled him that anyone would want to hurt her. She was all pure goodness and soft smiles.

His thoughts only angered him more so he forced himself to stop and pay attention to Sael's movements. She wasn't bad. Most of what she practiced looked good which he knew was because of her brother, the Master Assassin. Even never being trained by the man, Killian was sure she'd watched him enough times to have subconsciously picked up a few things.

He finally moved for her again and watched the tantalizing rise and fall of her chest as she paused and waited for him. "Good job, princess. Now, let's get into specifics."

KILLIAN COULDN'T LIE, he was ecstatic to have had Sael to himself the entire day. From waking and telling her how he'd gotten the scars to having breakfast together to spending the day training her dagger, then a bit in training up her archery skills and the snacking bits in between, to now walking back home for dinner. She'd been his all day and he was obsessed with keeping her all to himself.

Now, as they slowly walked back home, he wanted to know her.

"Where did you learn archery? Is that what your family taught you instead of the dagger?" he asked mostly because he wanted to learn everything about her, but also because she didn't feel advanced enough to have been doing this her entire life. He needed to know when she'd started, if *something* had triggered her need to defend herself.

She shook her head. "I only started learning a couple of months ago. And the Posse—that's what we're called in the North—didn't teach me. I kind of picked it up on my own then asked Gemma and James, Evony's best friends, to help me a bit."

He nodded, anger bubbling within him knowing with certainty now why she'd picked up the weaponry. "And Evony is your brother's wife?"

"And my twin," she added slowly, softly.

Killian froze. "What?"

As he met her gaze, there was a look in her eyes, like she'd made a decision to trust him completely now, so she would be sharing her most treasured thoughts—those of her family.

She gave a small, almost sad, smile. "We only found out a

few months ago. Apparently said mother whom I'm after now had twins and didn't tell my father because the King Edmund of two decades ago would've killed a magician heir."

His brows shot up. "She's a magician?"

Her gaze latched onto his, and he could see an unbearable amount of trust in them. "The Master."

Killian froze again. "You're telling me your 'brother' is the Master Assassin and your *twin sister* is the Master Magician? And they're married? And *his* mother was the Master Sorcerer? How did the King find himself so many Masters?"

She gave that adorable little laugh. "Well, none of us knew of Alana until recently. And we didn't know of Evony until a few months ago. And my father adopted Sparrow before he was recognized as a Master. So, my father hadn't exactly been trying."

"So your Posse consists of you, your father, the two Masters, and her best friends?"

"And Tristan and Miels."

His heart stopped at the two male names. "Who're Tristan and Miels?"

"They're Sparrow's best friends, like brothers to him. They're his seconds and some of the best spies we have."

"So." Killian tried to control his extreme reaction that was definitely trying to overreact. "Essentially you have three brothers?"

She gave a soft shrug. "Not really. They're more like Sparrow's brothers and really great friends to me. Tristan, I *might* call a brother, but not Miels."

His heart banged rapidly. "Why not?"

Her cheeks blushed deep crimson. "You don't crush on your brothers. I crushed pretty hard, and I'm pretty sure everyone knew about it."

"And what did he do about that *pretty hard crush?*" he grit out.

She didn't seem to notice his reaction as she stared ahead, in her head about her family and friends in the North. "Nothing. He always acted like he didn't know of it, they all did. He acted like everything was normal until it was. Now, he has Etel and I love seeing the way he turns from this big bad spy into this puddle at her feet."

"Etel?" He breathed hard.

"She's the Remedies Expert and a shy girl, but they're incredible together. It makes me smile thinking of them so happy. Almost as happy as I feel when I think of Sparrow and Evony together. That's two of my men down. Now there's Tristan left to fall in love which he seems very opposed to, and my father who has pretty much never shown interest so fat chance at that happening."

"Right," Killian responded, but all he could think about was that *pretty hard crush* she had on this Miels guy.

"So, yeah, that's the Posse. My father, me, Sparrow, Evony, James, Gemma, Tristan, Miels, and Etel now too, even though she feels really awkward about being included."

Killian swallowed back his annoyance at any time she said Miels's name and asked her the question he wished to know the answer to, even though the memory of being trapped in an alley with four men made him sure he knew it. "Is there a reason you decided to pick up weaponry?"

Sael sighed, in deep thought for long moments, before answering, "Before a few months ago, it was only me and my four men. They all love me and always excelled at protecting me. I think they didn't realize they'd sort of turned me into a damsel until..."

"Until?"

"It was like two weeks after Evony and her friends had

arrived. I figured now that the men were distracted with them, and especially Sparrow with Evony, that I could finally use this opportunity to go out into town without *my bodyguards*. I was stupid, *naive*." She said that last word with disgust, and Killian hated himself for ever calling her the word and bringing up these feelings. "You know the rest. Evony had been the one following me, hidden behind her magic."

Killian's heart raged as they neared the house. He took Sael's arm, moved her for the log off to the side, and sat her down so they could continue this private conversation.

"We're very different." Sael continued letting him know about this new twin of hers. "She grew up in the forests, grew up protecting herself. Even without her magic, she's an exceptional fighter. She didn't even use her magic as she killed all four of them and took me back home. She yelled at me for not having any training and I'm sure she nailed the guy's one even worse. She insisted I would be no damsel before we got back to the palace. And after experiencing that for myself, I decided the same. That's part of the stupid reason I came here by myself—partly because my family wasn't in as much of a hurry as I was, but also because I felt this need to prove myself. I don't think the stupidity of being on the Island on my own hit until I was on the ship coming here, but by then there was nothing I could do, so I convinced myself I'd be fine."

Killian leaned in close to kiss her temple. "And look at you now. You're more than fine. You've basically become a barbarian with public claiming and hunting and dealing with others on the land."

Sael gave him an amused eye roll.

He kissed her again. "You've done much better than I can imagine doing in the North. Even without the scars, I don't think I could blend in quite like you have here."

"Yes, I don't think your presence is ignorable. You take up

space when you're around, and people instantly feel a need to pay attention to you."

"Fight or flight, princess. Their bodies are preparing them for the monster in their midst."

She smirked. "Possibly."

He pushed a lock of hair behind her ear. "How do you think an Islander would be accepted in the North?" *How would I be accepted?*

She shrugged. "It's difficult to say. I think even if a Northerner didn't like it, they'd be less likely to do something about it because of the more savage way an Islander might take care of a situation. That's part of the reason opening borders would be difficult—there're the sorcerers, but also the people here. It might be too easy for them to take advantage of the Northern people simply out of fear."

"You guys have thought about opening borders?"

"My father's been working on it for years. He's tried to especially give everyone the same resources so when borders do open, all Northerners might be able to stand against an Islander, maybe not in battle but in wits or some other sense. It's a slow process."

"You think introducing a couple of Islanders at a time might help?" He tried to mask his desperation to know the answer.

She smiled warmly as she met his honey browns. "I think it would be a shock, but once they see their Princess is with an Islander—a tactical choice, of course, no other reason that would be possible—then I think the people would see that though they're different, they actually make quite great friends. Like the men at the docks."

He leaned in for a kiss. "I'd love to be your tactical choice, Princess."

CHAPTER 27
KILLIAN

If he intended on leaving with his woman when this was over, he needed to finish off Keir's men. He would start with only one for the night.

Getting one of their attentions wouldn't be difficult. Any time he walked by the whorehouse on the other end of town—the one and only whorehouse on this side of the island—the men circled him like vultures. It made it all too easy to kill Keir's men.

But Killian only went there when he was in an especially vulgar mood. He didn't need to give away that he knew Keir's men were disgusting oafs who needed to pay for a fuck. This little easy chase was saved for when Killian needed it most.

Like today.

As Killian strolled through the dense expanse of trees toward the smell of the whorehouse—smoke and vile pleasures mixed together in a nauseating collection—he wondered if his desire for this death was something more than just finishing off his mission before he needed to go with his woman. If it was something more instinctual. That's how it felt.

He felt the need to protect, to stand before Sael and take a million lashings so she remained pristine. So to calm that storm raging within him, Killian moved for the whorehouse where he would find multiple of Keir's men, and be able to get rid of them, clear this world of anyone who might try to hurt his princess.

At the edge of the trees that lined the whorehouse, blocking it from the casual passerby, Killian stood and watched on as men traipsed drunkenly after naked women, as men chased giddily after naked men, as they all snorted and got drunker and more obscene with their acts. Even as a barbarian himself, Killian had never understood the pleasures of a whorehouse. Maybe it was because he had always been able to easily get a lover when he wanted one.

Or maybe it was that distant Northerner blood in him.

Killian watched two men he recognized that liked to stalk around town when they saw him but never tried to confront him. He hadn't decided if that made them smart or cowards.

They were both mostly naked as a whore slipped between them, sucking one's cock and letting the other fuck her ass.

Beside them was a man seated back with his cock in a whore as she bounced up and down on him while another sucked at his balls, beads of his cum already dripping out as they continued to fuck. He had his hands spread beside him, one hand in another whore's cunt, making her squirt all over them, and the other holding a pitcher of ale.

He was the one Killian wanted tonight.

He was one of Keir's higher-ups and one of the four men Killian hadn't been able to kill the night he'd been dragged to the pole in the middle of town square. It had been a slow process to finish those four off, but now there only stood two more—Von, and the man across from Killian now, Brayd.

It made Killian especially annoyed and ruthless that he would need to wait for Brayd to be finished here. If he made a show of going to grab him now, too many would see him and some of Keir's men would likely try to jump in, and Killian really wanted to have his slow fun that evening before returning to Sael and delighting in the taste of her cunt all night.

It was another hour before the man finally pulled himself to the outdoor showers at the edge of the whorehouse—put in for the visitors who needed to clean off before heading home. Not ten minutes later, Brayd was dressed in his simple trousers and loose shirt and making his way back to Keir's residence.

Killian followed him, a large bull of a man, until they were far enough away from the whorehouse and yet still too far from Keir for anyone to make anything out of some distant cries. At this distance, no one would be able to tell it was Brayd meaning no one would interrupt.

Because in the Island Nation, people did not intertwine themselves with matters that did not pertain to them.

Killian whipped his dagger around in his hand as his head tilted, thinking about what he wanted to do to the man. Part of him wished he had a sword, though the weapon was far less common in the Island Nation.

Instead, he pulled a whip from where it was rounded at the back of his trousers and sent it flying until it beat around Brayd's legs, searing off some skin as the man went tumbling down. His drunken state would make things all too easy for Killian, but he didn't particularly care at the moment.

Brayd tried to move quickly, but in his state, he was sluggish as he pulled himself back up. Killian only whipped out again, hitting Brayd in the back now, and delighted as the man face-planted into the side of a tree before completely falling to the ground.

"What the bloody fuck..." Brayd growled, his bull-like muscles struggling to pick him off the ground.

"Hello, old friend." Killian grinned down at him with a look so sinister, the man looked to shiver in his spot. "Miss me?"

Before he could answer, Killian swung his arm around, landing the dagger into the spot that interlocked the man's arm and shoulder. He pulled the dagger back out, watching him bleed.

"Let's have some fun tonight, Brayd."

He swung again, this time sticking the dagger into the back of the man's kneecap and loving the way the man growled and roared at once.

"And to think, you had three others helping you drag me away, friend." Another swing, this time hitting his ankle. "Your bulk of a size couldn't handle me yourself?" Another strike to the wrist this time. "Though, I suspect, if this here is any indication, you're not much of a fighter, huh? Prefer to use your size to tackle." Another strike to his thigh. "Too bad you inebriated yourself too much to tackle now, buddy." Another strike into the second wrist. "You should know not to lose your senses in a place as dangerous as the Island Nation." Another strike to the back of a kneecap. "Or did you think no one would try because of your size?" Another to the other shoulder-arm joint.

Brayd was bleeding out, but none of it was to a point where he'd die instantly. If Killian left him there to bleed out, it would take all night.

But that wasn't the plan. Killian intended to see him dead before leaving. He was merely having some fun first.

Killian flipped the bloodied dagger in his hands a moment before swinging hard, landing the blade in the man's ass, and listening to the loudest roar yet. It made Killian giddy with laughter.

He hardly gave the man any time before pulling it out and kicking him to turn onto his back. Killian pulled at the man's trousers, then caught his scared gaze and winked before crouching and castrating him. As vile as it was to touch the man's cock, it felt amazing listening to him cry out for it.

With his cock in hand, Killian kicked him again so he rolled over to his side, too weak to fight much, and jammed Brayd's own cock up his ass. "There you are, friend, nice and tucked in for you."

Then he stepped back and leaned against a tree, crossing his arms before his chest while he enjoyed his handiwork. He leaned there a long time, thinking about Keir's men finding Brayd; thinking about what he would do to Keir when the chance came; thinking about how he didn't seem to care as much about any of this as he once had, as he had only a couple of weeks ago. Now, his thoughts wavered on and on to the beautiful black-haired, green-eyed defiant pretty little princess who waited for him in their bed.

In *their* bed.

His claimed woman in their shared bed.

His claimed woman whom Killian could not imagine losing, could not imagine letting go of.

At last, Killian moved again and kicked Brayd so he was lying on his back once more, bleeding out and hardly able to keep his eyes open as he begged Killian for mercy.

It made Killian sick—an Islander begging for mercy. Islanders knew of no such thing.

For his final strike, Killian thought of Brayd forcing Rosaelia down. He thought of Brayd forcing her to touch him, suck him, fuck him, and he saw pure unadulterated red.

Killian sent the whip in his hand flying so hard and fast

against Brayd's neck, his entire head snapped from his body, spurting blood everywhere.

As the head rolled to Killian's feet, he looked down at it, the wide eyes still open, and felt a relieved ease fill him that the man could not hurt Sael even if he had wanted to. All he truly felt was an ease that he had done one more thing to protect his woman.

And the desperate need to get back to her.

CHAPTER 28
ROSAELIA

It had been a few days since Killian found out about her purpose for being in the Island Nation, a few days since Alana's death. She still hated herself every time she remembered that she could've released her arrow and been done with her mother. *Before* Alana's death.

Killian had been wonderful after it all. He'd spent the night reminding her that she was a naturally good person, and there was something special about hearing the words from him. They made her feel proud to be a good girl.

They also made her finally accept what she'd always known—it was unlikely she would kill anyone, better yet her own mother, no matter how vile of a woman she'd been.

It was more likely that whatever happened, either Killian, who now insisted he was part of the plans, or Sparrow would end up killing Rowena. Both had merit. Sparrow, because she'd gone after his wife and had eventually killed his mother. And Killian because of her. Because he wouldn't let that woman hurt her again.

She'd accepted that now which meant she could move on

with the plans. If she was no longer trying to fool herself into thinking she could take a life, Rosaelia could focus on other matters—like dwindling down that list the sorcerer had given her.

Out of the original seventeen names, she still had fourteen left. A few of which, like the healing sorceress in Harmon, would have to be left until later. For now, she could focus on those she knew she could get to on her own, even though it still annoyed Killian that she wanted to do anything on her own. Apparently being his woman meant he was glued to her side. But just because she'd accepted she couldn't kill didn't mean she needed someone's help with all matters of her plans.

It hadn't been too difficult to sneak off once she'd told the nonas Killian had been mean to her, and they went to reprimand him. He'd been so adorably confused, but Rosaelia hadn't been able to stick around to take it in for long. She needed to leave before he realized her ruse.

That had been this morning.

Now, she had two more names taken off the list.

And she was on her way to taking off another two.

Those first two had been men who worked at the docks closest to Killian's home. They were how Rowena so easily got things shipped to the North, how she so easily traversed the two nations.

They'd been a simple fix. She'd simply planted a cherished possession she'd stolen from two sailors—a pocket watch from one and a necklace from another, both taken off so they weren't broken and placed on a safekeeping table—on them and been all too worried when she ran to the group of men to report those two rummaging through their belongings.

The group had been furious and gone to check themselves to find their possessions taken. Rosaelia hadn't stayed to watch them get beaten, but she had heard that they were terminated from working by the docks—as trust their things wouldn't be taken was a large factor of the brotherhood—and showing back up would get them thrown into the deep waters.

Now she had these other two who were also quite close enough to deal with.

She was at the whorehouse on the other side of town and her nose crinkled as she tried to keep the bile down. It smelled awful as she traveled hidden through the forests that protected the whorehouse from the outside world.

Killian would be furious to learn of her being there. She already knew it was dangerous given anyone seeing her may think she wanted to participate, but she had her bow and arrow, and her lovely new dagger, ready if that were the case. Though she knew she wouldn't be able to kill anyone, or truly injure them, with her weapons, she could scare them enough to give her time to run away.

These two men owned the whorehouse, but they ran other businesses as well. One of which, Rowena took full advantage of—the transportation of common Northerners for Rowena to play with. These men were how Rowena got her hands on those she tortured in the Bloody Fields.

From talk she'd heard from the drugged-up participants of the whorehouse, the two owners liked to play cards in the back greens of the lodgings. Rosaelia found them quickly then.

Just the two of them playing a round of cards.

Their little consequence for helping her mother would be similar to that of the brutes that woman had taken care of for her. There was a potion she needed them to ingest. Except this one would have to be on her since the women at the whorehouse worked for them, so Rosaelia wouldn't be able to convince or trust them.

Rosaelia swallowed back her anxiety, trying to remember the way Aster had worked the brutes, but unable to bring up the same seduction, and moved for the men. "Mind if I join in?"

Both men, who were likely in their fifties with little ale bellies, eyed her with savage intent before that look turned to lust. It was vile. Even over the layers of clothes—her dress and cloak covering all of her, even her weapons—she felt like ripping off her skin at such looks.

"Darling, darling, darling," one answered with a glint in his eyes as his hand motioned for her to come forward. "Please, join us. Though I must say, we do not wear so much here."

Rosaelia fought her body's need to recoil at his insinuations. "I am as dressed as you are."

Both men smirked at one another as one began pulling at the noose around his collar. "That can be amended."

"Don't be so hasty, men," Rosaelia cooed even though she wanted to throw up. She was trying to be more like her twin—cool, in control, and a savage when the time was right. "We were to play cards, no?"

"Darling," the original one drawled. "We play a game only done here in this whorehouse. Would you know it?"

She smirked. "I'm a fast study."

She needed to be a faster thinker because she didn't know if she could sit here while they eyed her like so and spoke to her in such manners for long.

The second one pushed his seat closer to Rosaelia as the other leaned back in his chair, hands reaching for his trousers. Closer as he was now, the second one leaned in, and whispered, "Why don't you go sit on his cock? Then we'd be happy to teach you."

Rosaelia swallowed as her gaze flickered to the other man who now had his penis out and was pumping himself. Bile was hanging around her throat, ready to pour out at any given second.

She was proud of herself for being able to speak to them thus far, but she really shouldn't have done *this one* alone.

Before she could answer, Killian's storming voice boomed over them. "Get the fuck away from my woman."

Both men jumped up, the one finally putting his penis away, as Rosaelia turned to see a furious barbarian coming for them, a teenager at his side.

They eyed her, then him, then her again as the first man asked, "You're claimed? What kind of claimed bitch comes to a whorehouse?"

Both men had their weapons out, obviously knowing they wouldn't be able to reason with a claimed woman's male.

"That's a great question," Killian growled.

"They're helping my mother, Killian," was all she said.

That seemed to make him angrier, so she wasn't sure if it was necessarily the right thing to say, but he needed to know why she was there—not that he would ever believe her at a whorehouse for the pleasures.

Killian swung at them with a dagger in each hand, but both seemed to be well-trained. They fought back and far too well for Rosaelia to ever have been able to protect herself against them.

But still, they were attacking Killian. She couldn't let them hurt him.

As she moved for them, a hand pulled her back. She looked into the young eyes of that teenage boy. "Who're you?"

"I'm from the No Known Housing," he ground out, pushing her behind him. "I figured your mate would've liked to know his woman was coming to the whorehouse."

Ah, so that's how Killian had found her.

The fight between the three men was never-ending. Every time Rosaelia was relieved to see Killian strike one of them, the other struck him back. She couldn't stand around and watch it, but she also couldn't do a thing about it. If she drew her weapons, there was a higher likelihood she'd hit Killian by mistake than not.

When a dagger impaled Killian's thigh, Rosaelia could no longer take it. "No!" she screamed as she pushed the teenage boy aside and ran for them, dagger unstrapped from her thigh and at the ready.

She had successfully hurt one—though the blade didn't go as deep into him as she would've liked—before she felt the sting of something on her thigh. She looked down as the man pulled his dagger back, and a whole new stinging sensation hit her. Blood was seeping out onto her dress, but it was all clouded by Killian's roar.

Rosaelia had never seen someone so feral.

He was a true monster now.

He hacked at the two men with renewed anger, getting strikes and cuts along the way, but in a matter of moments, he had them both dead. It wasn't the potion making them both useless she had planned, but it was one way of keeping them from helping her mother ever again.

As she processed the deaths, Killian pulled her away and shoved her back into the seat she'd been in. He was furious.

"What the fuck are you doing here?" he roared at her.

She swallowed back the shock of what he'd done to those bodies, then all her attention was on him sitting in front of her now. He pulled up her dress to see the injury to her thigh— which was absolutely nothing compared to all of his, especially the one on his thigh.

She tugged on his trousers to rip the bit around his wound. "There's a list of people helping Rowena. I'm slowly stopping them."

"And you figured coming to a whorehouse on your own was a genius plan?" he growled as he grabbed the clean rag and alcohol from the boy from the No Known Housing who'd helped them.

"No." She had his thigh open for her viewing, and the wound looked deeper than she'd thought. "But I figured it was a plan." She pushed at him. "Now stop and let me clean you."

His hand was rough as he grabbed her wrist. "Don't even think about it, Sael. You're my woman. I'll clean you."

"Mine is hardly a cut, Kill. Yours is deep. Not to mention, you have multiple injuries!"

He shoved her away, and she finally relented only so he could finish sooner and she could tend to his injuries. "Things would've gone smoother if you'd included me like you said you would."

"Rowena's not exactly here," she huffed. "And killing them wasn't exactly in the plans." *Plus, I never* agreed *to include you.*

He eyed her with a truly crazed glint in his eyes, then went back to his work.

Rosaelia winced at the sting of the alcohol on her thigh as he cleaned her, then wrapped her with gauze the boy had found from who knew where.

When he had the gauze wrapped around her thigh, he tried to stand. "Let's go home."

She pushed him back in his own chair. "You're far more hurt, Killian. Don't argue with me."

He ground his jaw but allowed her to take a look at him. His shirt was torn up from all the hits he'd taken, and the tear in the thigh of his trousers was smeared in red from all the blood loss from the deeper wound. It scared Rosaelia to see him so injured.

She quickly took another clean rag from the pile the boy had brought and tipped the alcohol bottle so more than a bit fell over his thigh. He roared with the sting of it as he clutched for the arms of his chair, and though she was worried for him, the reaction made Rosaelia's lips tip up involuntarily.

"When I get you home, Sael…" he threatened through gritted teeth, fists still clutched in the chair's arms.

After cleaning the wound, she wanted to apply salve to it, but knew she'd have to wait until they got home to do so, so instead, she ripped the rest of the trouser leg to give herself space to wrap his thigh with gauze.

When she finished, she met his gaze with a small upturn of her lips. "Take that sad excuse for a shirt off."

The thing was so torn, it was hardly covering any of him anyway.

Killian ripped it off his body with no effort and allowed her to clean the rest of his injuries. "What the fuck were you thinking, Sael?"

She sighed. "I wasn't apparently. I realized I should've come with you, should've let you handle this one, but I was already here and with them, so I had to make do."

At least she knew for certain now that seductions were not in her powerhouse.

His jaw ground together, gaze searching the property like he couldn't stand to look at her at the moment.

Her gaze saddened as she softly cleaned him. "I know it was stupid, Kill. I-I'm sorry. I guess I'm not used to the idea of help yet. I came here with the goal to do this on my own, without getting your family hurt, and I guess it's difficult to pull myself from that. I cannot stand the thought of putting you in danger."

"Then you can understand what it does to me when you put yourself in danger!" he roared.

She flinched, so unused to his yelling. "Killia—"

He pushed her hands away, which was fine since he was

basically cleaned now, and got in her face. "You promised me, Sael!"

She gently played with the scars on his face because she knew it calmed him, and it calmed her too. She hadn't promised him anything. He'd stated it, she hadn't agreed. But she wouldn't say that because he'd make her promise now, and that wasn't a thing she could do. "I'm sorry. I won't do any of it on my own again." *Because the Posse was likely to be close at this point. I'll still do anything I can to keep you and your family safe.*

He sighed and leaned his forehead against hers. "I won't lose you, princess."

She kissed him softly, then leaned back. As her gaze traveled down his form, now with more injuries, her desire for him grew. Then her eyes stopped on the wrapped thigh starting to turn red again, and her lips turned down.

"I'm a barbarian. I'm meant to get hurt," he said before she could comment on his injury. "*You're* not."

She stifled the eye roll as she glanced from her thigh to his. She met his honey browns with a soft smile. "We have matching wounds now."

He growled as he pulled her to slowly walk home and properly clean these wounds. The boy, whose name was Clark, would surely be thanked in a way he couldn't fathom from the look Killian gave him as they left.

CHAPTER 29

ROSAELIA

Rosaelia was glad Norya had convinced them—which had taken almost no effort in Rosaelia's regard—to go to the adjoining village which consisted of people Killian didn't absolutely hate. Not that any of that meant he was thrilled about going out. He insisted that he'd rather spend the night staying in which the twinkle in his eyes didn't hide meant 'between her thighs.'

It was a look Rosaelia knew the others picked up on which made her blush, only seeming to invigorate Killian's sex drive.

It was difficult to turn his insinuations down when simply thinking of him sent her body on a race, but Rosaelia was curious about tavern nights in the Island. She hadn't experienced tavern nights anywhere, but it was more likely in the future that she would in the North or South rather than actually coming back to the Island.

All she had to do was give Killian a small pout, and he'd been putty at her feet, agreeing to do whatever made her happy. It was a new sort of invigorating to have *that* power over him.

And it was clear all three women picked up just how much power Rosaelia held over him by the grins they gave that made Killian growl with annoyance. The nonas moved about their business after that, choosing to leave him be, but the entire walk to the next village, Norya teased him about how easily Rosaelia controlled him.

Then the eye-opening revelation about her barbarian came when they got to the tavern, and Rosaelia got to watch Killian interact with people he *didn't* want to rip apart. He held her hand the entire time telling everyone there they were both claimed, but he didn't seem as testy as he was in his own village. Rosaelia couldn't believe she'd actually seen him smile at anyone who wasn't his family or her.

It was absolutely fascinating to see him joke with other barbarians while he clutched at her hand. Then, when they all moved indoors toward the tall tables by the far walls and Norya was lost to them, flirting with a huge barbarian, Rosaelia got to experience the tavern.

She remained by Killian's side, her hands playing with the arm that remained before her chest, as she paid attention to the goings-on around the establishment.

Since she'd never been to a tavern, she couldn't necessarily decide what was Islander customs and what was inherently tavern customs. But she had a feeling the six couples she caught rutting was definitely the former. She knew that even the more vile of Northerners found privacy, or some semblance of it before they did anything.

The tavern was made entirely of wood and dark within even with all the lights placed around the walls and on every few tables. It wasn't necessarily dirty, but it was definitely not spotless with drink stains and crumbs and other bits Rosaelia didn't wish to pay too close attention to.

There was a lot of drunken laughter, a lot of flirting and

dancing, a lot of betting. But none of it felt savage. Barbarian, mostly because of the rutting, yes, but not savage.

Then her gaze was on the couples again. Two of the six were a bit more discreet than the others—though still very obvious—as the men sat back in their chairs with their women bouncing on top of them, the dresses covering anything from sight.

One of the other couples had the woman laid out on the table with her man under her dress, between her legs like she was his meal. Rosaelia blushed at the sight, and the reminder that she had been Killian's meal one too many times.

Another two couples had the woman's dresses hiked up so much more was visible, though they faced the walls so it was more butt than anything else being seen. One of the men from those couples had his trousers all the way dropped so his butt was also in plain view. Though not inherently obvious, because Rosaelia found herself paying attention, she could see his cock coming out a few inches then thrusting into her again and again.

The final couple, the woman was on her knees before the seated male. It was obvious his trousers were undone and his cock out, but because of the woman, Rosaelia couldn't see much else. She could see, though, that the woman's dress was down around her bodice and she could make out that she was stroking him between her breasts. That was something she hadn't experienced yet.

She supposed this was what Killian meant when he said claimed couples don't like showing their partners to anybody else. They were all rutting, but none of them were entirely visible to the masses.

"You like what you see, sweet girl?" one of the men speaking with Killian asked with a smirk and a glimmer in his eyes.

Killian's hand tightened in hers, and Rosaelia knew that she should be more annoyed with this whole claiming nonsense, but she loved the ownership it gave Killian. Loved the savagery of his growl toward the man.

Rosaelia didn't answer as she snuggled closer into Killian.

"If he doesn't come on her tits, that'll definitely end in a facial. Oh, what a lucky man," another one of the men said as he eyed the last couple Rosaelia had been watching.

"Oh, absolutely. You think he'll turn her around to show his mark?" the original one who called her 'sweet girl' asked. "I've heard some claimed men love to show their mark on their women."

A third man turned to Killian. "Is that true? Would you turn your woman for all to see."

"Not with a facial, no," Killian barked. "I prefer bruises and bite marks." As evident by the bite mark on Rosaelia's neck still fading.

"Ah, but still possessive." A woman leaning into one of the men laughed.

They all continued with their jokes and laughing, but Rosaelia stopped paying attention again as she clung to Killian's arm and rose to the tips of her toes so she could whisper into his ear. "What's a facial?"

His dark gaze turned down on her, and he gave a wicked grin that she recognized from their many nights and mornings together. "Would you like me to tell you or show you?"

Her fingers dug into his arm involuntarily as her heart made a giddy jump. She tried to bite down on her bottom lip to hide the excited smile, but she knew he caught it. "Show please."

His grin turned up like he was pleased with her answer, then pushed the others out of the way as he pulled Rosaelia after him. His large body pushed more people out of the way until they were at the other end of the tavern and he was pulling her behind the stairs to a private hallway. They moved until they turned a final corner and stopped at a door there, hidden away from everyone. Killian hadn't been lying when he said he didn't want others to see them bared.

Rosalia could see through the small window of the door into the room and it looked to be an office space. When Killian pushed it open, and they were inside, she took in the desk in one corner with a chair behind it, a couch in the other corner, and not much else.

Killian grabbed a pillow off the couch, then stopped by the desk, and dropped her hand. He cradled her face lovingly and kissed her gently. "You're my woman, you know that, right, princess?"

She nodded.

He smirked, and his voice turned dark. "Good. Now get on your knees."

He threw the pillow down before his feet and watched closely as she did as she was told.

"Take my cock out, princess."

Rosaelia's hands moved immediately for his trousers, opening them and letting them drop to his feet so his cock sprang free. Was a facial simply tasting him? She'd done that already, so she doubted it.

She kneed there patiently, not touching him, as she waited for instruction. She grew wet as he took his cock in hand and stroked himself. "This is your cock, princess."

She nodded as she subconsciously licked her lips. It was her cock. All of him was hers.

He stroked himself again and moved the tip to glide over her lips. "So suck it, Sael."

Her mouth moved immediately, taking him in and tasting him. She'd only tasted him a couple of times so far compared to the daily tastings he's had of her, but she knew she was obsessed. He tasted like nothing she could ever imagine.

Her mouth salivated with how much she wanted this, and she felt it drool down her chin. She pulled away, embarrassed of the mess, and tried to swipe the drool away when he tugged her hand down. "Don't you dare, Sael. Get messy. Get wet for my cock, princess. I'm fucking your mouth like I fuck your cunt. I want the mess."

Her cunt clenched at his words, and she listened, leaning back in for his cock and letting her spit mix with his precum and coat down her chin and onto her dress.

She licked, sucked, and let him fuck her mouth. She felt him at the back of her throat, close to gagging, before he popped his cock out and did so again. It was cruel and unusual punishment how much she wanted him in her mouth and how much he played with her instead of giving her what she wished for.

When he popped out a third time, she stroked his cock instead of taking him into her mouth again and instead moved for his balls. She was curious about them like she was curious about all of him so she licked his balls and loved the hiss he made at the contact. As she stroked his cock, she continued sucking on his balls until so much precum was sliding down her hands, she needed to have him in her mouth again.

"Fuck, Sael. You're such a good fucking girl."

She sucked on his cock again, letting him hit the back of her throat with hard thrusts as more drool and cum slid down her face, then he pulled out and pumped thimself.

"Close your eyes, princess. Now!"

She did as she was told then felt the hot spurts of liquid hit her face. It hit her cheek and sprayed up her eyes over her forehead before another pump had it falling lower. She opened her mouth in the hopes that she'd catch a taste of any of it.

When his grunting subsided, Rosaelia swiped at her eyes, then opened them to stare up at him. His gaze was hazy from his orgasm but there was obvious delight and pride there.

With all the cum covering her face, Rosaelia understood fully where the act got its name. She also realized she may desperately want these facials often.

Rosaelia licked at her lips to get the taste of him, then licked her hands for the cum she'd swiped off her eyes. "I love the taste of you, barbarian."

He held her jaw in his hand, breathes still coming in hard, as his thumb brushed over her drool and cum covered bottom lip. "Such a pretty. Fucking. Princess."

CHAPTER 30

ROSAELIA

Norya came into the house with two large sacks. She grumbled as she dropped them to the floor. "I don't know what the fuck is going on out there. Did the sorcerers say they were closing off areas?"

"No," Nona Tereza answered. "Why? What area was closed off?"

"None, I guess," Norya answered. "I just couldn't walk through my normal shortcut to get here from the neighboring village. I kept trying and it felt like as much as I knew to walk that way, my body wouldn't listen."

Rosaelia froze. She knew sorcerers were plenty in the Island Nation, and they could manipulate body or mind, but that needed to be done by a potion. There was only one kind of person who could do all that without the use of anything.

A magician. And there were no magicians in the Island.

"Was..." She almost held her breath. "Was it a small clearing?"

"No!" Norya sounded exasperated. "I had to walk all the way around into town, then back up this way. No matter what

I did, I could not get myself to walk through the clearing. It's never happened before!"

A Master would be needed to hold down a large area.

It was time.

They'd come.

Nearly three weeks since she left the library, and they were here.

Rosaelia tried to contain her reaction as the excitement of seeing her family once more exploded within her. She hadn't realized quite how badly she'd missed them. A shaky hand pointed to the back of the house. "Back there?"

Norya looked confused, they all did, but she answered slowly anyway. "Yes. Back the way of the tavern we went to last night."

"Sael." Kill stepped before her. "Why are you—"

Rosaelia didn't stick around to listen to his question. She turned and ran in the direction Norya had been indicating, knowing it was her twin sister holding up the shield and that she would allow Rosaelia entry.

So she ran.

Ran hard and fast because as much as she's enjoyed her time in the Island Nation—specifically with this family—and wanted to be there to show she wasn't a damsel, she'd missed her family. She'd especially missed her brother.

So she ran, listening to Killian's footsteps following her as he gave up calling for her.

It took almost a mile, but eventually the shield loosened around them and there, in the short distance, Rosaelia caught sight of a group of friends and family, of Sparrow.

She gave a giddy laugh which he matched with a wide grin as he moved forward and caught her in his arms the moment she jumped for him. She hadn't realized until that moment how much she would miss her brother in the time apart. It had never been something she'd considered—being away from him for long spurts of time—since his relationship with Evony had kept him close, either at the palace or his childhood home which was less than a day away. She could not imagine not living by her family for the rest of her life.

"I've missed you, sister," he muttered into her hair.

"I've missed you too, brother."

With a final sigh, Sparrow pulled away enough to catch her eye. "You're still in trouble, you know that right? For running out and coming *here*!"

She laughed. "I know."

He hugged her tightly again, then released her. She didn't have time to think before she got pulled into Tristan's arms, holding her tight, before moving into Miels's arms. The two men she was closest to and loved most outside her father and Sparrow.

Then she turned to her twin and was surprised when Evony pulled her in for a hug. "There you go, running off on your own again." When she pulled away, she looked more proud than annoyed or angry.

Rosaelia smiled at her before turning to the final two in the group—Ashtyn, the best healer at the palace, and Gabriel, a stable hand. She didn't want to sound rude asking what they were doing there, but Ashtyn seemed to read it in her eyes.

She smirked, not an ounce of affront about her. "We're in barbarian nation, Emerald. I had to be here to heal them when they inevitably got hurt."

Rosaelia understood that, and respected her more for it, before glancing at Gabriel. He didn't offer an explanation, but the way he stood close to Ashtyn was answer enough—he was not going to allow her to come up on her own.

She turned back to Evony. "Where are Gemma and James? I'm surprised they allowed you to come without them."

She laughed. "They would be here, but they've recently found out some news"—she patted her stomach—"and there was no way James would allow Gem in danger or leave her side." She shrugged to Miels. "Etel stayed behind to watch over them as the Remedies Expert."

An even wider smile broadened Rosaelia's lips. She'd never been particularly close to any of them, but the thought of Gemma and James becoming parents was an exhilarating one. From the simple way they showed patience and kindness to her while teaching her archery the two times she'd asked, she knew they'd be great parents.

As she turned back to her brother, Rosaelia followed his now hard gaze—and those of the other three men—to a spot behind her.

She turned to see Killian standing at the edge of the clearing, the two scars on his face making him look more the monster than ever. It almost reminded her of their first meeting, out in the forests where this beautiful monster threw her against a tree to protect her.

She kept the smile because she could see the jealousy in his eyes and it invigorated her as she moved for his side. Her hands clasped around his arm as she pulled him forward a few feet so they stood before the Posse. "Killian, this is my family. That's Gabriel and Ashtyn. Tristan, Miels, Sparrow, and I'm sure you could guess this part, my twin, Evony." Their giving features were still their choice of trousers and vest against dress, their eye colors, and Evony's slightly darker skin tone from growing up in the Southern Lands.

Killian watched all of them closely before his gaze landed on one. "You're Miels."

Everyone looked shocked by Killian's choice of first words, but it only made Rosaelia giggle into the back of his arm. He'd laughed the other night when she'd been jealous of his ex-lover, he deserved this.

But wicked grins slowly came up on everyone's face as they glanced between the two of them before landing back on Killian. Miels turned his cocky tone on, but he sounded sincere as he said, "It was only a childhood crush. Nothing ever came of it."

Killian knew that. Rosaelia had told him it had been an unrequited crush that she was completely over now. She'd told him Miels had never tried anything with her.

But it seemed meeting him made all that disappear as he eyed Miels like he needed to pummel him to the ground.

"Why don't we go home, and talk about what you all are doing here?" Rosaelia knew why they were there—for her—but tugged on Killian's arm so he broke his death glare anyway.

When he looked down to her, his eyes softened, and he nodded.

Evony caught Rosaelia's gaze with a nod, telling her they would remain cloaked in magic until they got to the house.

Norya was standing with her arms crossed before her chest, bow and arrow at her side—her quick reaction could have them strung and aimed in the matter of seconds—as she waited for them to return. She looked both annoyed and curious as she stared out in their direction, Evony's magic obviously making it impossible for Norya to see they were only a few yards out.

"You can drop it, Evony. She's a friend," Rosaelia said softly, knowing her twin would not completely drop it until they were indoors, but wanting Norya to see them so she didn't try to fight.

She knew when Evony pulled back the shield because Norya's eyes widened from not seeing them one moment to seeing a group coming at her the next, her brother at the front.

"What…" she started.

"Inside," Killian ground out and followed her in, waiting for everyone to shuffle in before closing the door and moving for the windows.

Both nonas turned from where they were cleaning a window and stood frozen to their spots. Then their gazes jumped from Evony to Rosaelia and back again.

"Wow," Nona Tereza mumbled.

Rosaelia herself remembered the shock of seeing her likeness for the first time. It was discombobulating, especially when the whole of the world thought there to be only one Princess of the Northern Lands. They still did since Evony refused to take the title.

She smiled as she moved between the two groups. "Nona Tereza, Nona Eleni, Norya, this is part of my family. My twin, Evony—who hates being called a Princess so don't do it because she is the Master Magician and will hurt you—and her husband, Sparrow. Our best friends, Miels and Tristan, and some newer, but just as great friends, Gabriel and Ashtyn." She turned back to her friends. "Guys. These are Nona Eleni and Nona Tereza, Killian's nonas and Northerners. They were friends with my grandmother before moving here. This is Norya, Killian's sister like Sparrow is to me. And… Killian you already sort of met."

Evony smirked with a teasing grin. "Hm, no, I don't think you introduced us to *Killian*. Who is he to you?"

Sparrow laughed into her hair as he pulled her before his chest, arms wrapping around her waist and holding on tight.

Rosaelia blushed deep, but a simple look in Killian's direction showed he was also waiting for an answer to that question—who was he to her? Was she claimed in the Island alone or would she let her family know of their relationship?

Who was he?

He was everything.

But she couldn't tell him that. Not yet, and especially not for the first time in front of everyone.

"He's..." A small smirk grew on her lips as she met his dark hazel eyes. "The man who claimed me. I think that makes him my claimed male as I'm his claimed female."

His gaze heated, darkening as a small grin lifted the corners of his lips. His voice was rough as he said, "That's exactly what it makes me."

"Claimed?" Tristan asked. "That's quite barbarian of you, Ro."

Killian's jaw ground like he was annoyed they weren't alone at that very moment, and Rosaelia couldn't argue, she sort of was too. Before Killian could turn to tell him something cruel or dark, Rosaelia answered, "I like being claimed. I like that everyone in town *knows* about us." She didn't have to tell them exactly how they knew.

She especially didn't have to tell them how much she had enjoyed being watched by the town. She hadn't even told Killian, knowing he would take her out to do so again the moment he found out, and as much as she'd enjoyed it, it was too crude, too barbarian, for her.

But as Rosaelia turned back to her friends, she saw in their looks that they knew exactly what being claimed meant. Or, at least, what was normally done to claim a woman, the type of show that wasn't needed to be done, but almost always was— public displays.

They may not have known much else as Rosaelia hadn't, but as most of them were spies, they would know that much.

Rosaelia's cheeks burned as her friends looked between the two of them, her three favorite men quirking a questioning brow at her. Her blazing cheeks definitely gave away that they had done *stuff* publicly.

"Why don't you all sit, children." Nona Tereza jumped out of her shock and started pulling out chairs. "Sit, sit, we'll grab drinks. You must be starved!"

She didn't leave room for argument as she began pulling for cups and plates Rosaelia believed to be hardly used since this family didn't get many visitors. She, along with Nona Eleni, giddily pulled for more chairs and bowls, and they readied small meals for everyone.

Rosaelia nodded to the table, telling them it would be useless to fight the women. As they all moved, Killian's arms wrapped around her waist, and his breath hit her ear. "You *like* that the town *knows*, Sael?"

There was a seductive undertone to the way he asked the question and Rosaelia knew that he knew what she had meant. She burned crimson but nodded slowly, her head brushing his chin and making her want to push him to their room rather than sit with her family.

Killian chuckled in her ear. "You should have told me, princess. I'll bend you over next time, let them hear your screams."

She gasped, shaking her head no, as she pushed her body closer into him.

He laughed at her ear, dark and seductive. "You like the sound of that, don't you, princess? You want me to take you like the barbarian I am."

She wanted to say no, but her head nodded instead as her chest rose and fell heavily.

"Okay, princess. I'll take you back into the square and have my way with you."

My way.

It *was* what she'd wanted from him—*I want you to do whatever you'd like to me. With me.*

She should say no, especially with her friends now here, but she couldn't find it in herself. And she knew he wouldn't do anything in front of them, not out of respect for them, but out of respect for her.

Instead, she tilted her head back so she could meet his gaze. She was sure her eyes were as heated as his, but neither of them moved to do anything about it. Hopefully, Evony would use her magic to shield whatever noises were made that night from her friends. It would be more mortifying if they heard than when the nonas did.

"Anything you want to do to me, barbarian."

He smirked and leaned in for a soft kiss before reluctantly leading her to the table to join the others.

CHAPTER 31
KILLIAN

"Your father's especially angry with you, Ro," Miels, the fucker with the cocky grin, spoke from his spot on the side of the table.

Killian had taken his seat at the head of the table with Sael at his side, putting himself between her and that pretty spy. He knew he was being irrational being jealous since Sael said she didn't feel anything for him any longer—hadn't for a while—and he had his own mate so he had absolutely no interest in her, but Killian couldn't help it.

"I imagined either he or Sparrow would be," Rosaelia answered with a small smile, her hand resting on Killian's leg and stroking softly at the inside of his thigh.

Distractingly so. Little vixen.

Her friends ate greedily from their plates, no doubt starved from their travels to get to Sael, as they smiled at her.

Sparrow growled through his own smile. "Sparrow *is* especially angry."

Sael stuck her tongue out at him, teasing him in the same way Norya loved to tease Killian. Though he hadn't loved watching her jump into another man's arms, it had been a relief to learn it had been her brother. Had she jumped like that to either Tristan or Miels, especially the latter, Killian would've seen red. He'd been close to completely losing it before he found out it was Sparrow who held her tightly.

Evony, who looked so similar to his princess it was a bit jarring, laughed at her husband. "I'm proud."

Sparrow growled at her, a lightness in his eyes as they landed on the second heir to the Northern Lands. "Of course you are."

Tristan smirked at them, a gleam passing his eyes as they traced over Norya to get to Sael. "Why don't you inform us of your reasoning for coming here *without* any of us."

Sael gave a large sigh, leaning into Killian's side as his arm tightened around her waist. For such a good girl, she seemed to constantly be getting reprimanded—first by him, then her friends. "You guys were there. You saw my mother. She needs to be stopped."

"So you thought you'd stop her on your own, Ro?" Her brother sounded annoyed, like he was extra protective of her.

"I'm not weak, Spar!" She said it like she was ashamed that he was angry with her, and that made Killian want to rip the man apart.

Sparrow rolled his eyes. "I know that, Ro. And I also don't care how strong you are. You think I would've allowed any of you to come here on your own? You think Evony would've been allowed here on her own?"

Sael's gaze dipped. "That's not the same, Spar, you know that. You're in love with Evony."

The man looked extra agitated now. "The only difference that indicates is I would've required that I be the one by her side. I wouldn't have let Miels or Tristan come here on their own either. I wouldn't send anyone against your mother on their own, especially to a foreign land. Even without the Master Sorcerer, she could—and most likely does—have others at her aid."

She definitely did, the fucking stint at the whorehouse had shown Killian that much.

As he watched them eat, Killian wondered about the man's thoughts on knowing the Master Sorcerer was his mother. The way he spoke of her indicated no familiarity. Killian was the same. When he spoke of his own parents, it was never with familiarity, never with any emotion.

"I'm sorry, Spar." Sael met his gaze. "I really am. I just wanted to show you, me, *her* that I wasn't just *the spoiled little Princess,* and I couldn't get it out of my head that she wanted to hurt you through Evony!"

Killian swallowed, knowing he had thrown those exact words at her countless times when she'd arrived to the Island Nation. In his defense, they'd been enemies—an Island barbarian and the Northern Princess. It would've been preposterous for him to think of her as anything but a spoiled brat.

When Sparrow went to argue, Evony's hand landed on his arm, immediately stopping him. She pulled at him to open up so she could move into his lap now that they were finished with their meals. "It's okay, Rosaelia." She spoke for her husband. "You're unhurt, and you've found friends. You've found a man, I'm particularly interested in that!"

"Of course you are," both Miels and Tristan mumbled.

It caused a growl to pass through Killian toward the man to his right. Miels's gaze narrowed on him, but he didn't say anything about the growl.

Sael was too busy blushing to notice. Instead, she ignored Evony's teasing looks and met her brother's. "You're here now, Spar. We can take care of Rowena, and she won't be a problem for Father any longer. Or for Evony's magic."

The man's arms tightened around the Magician. "I'll gut her alive, Ro."

He was the Master Assassin, so Killian had no doubt about that. Any way he had previously killed would likely be child's play to Sparrow, though Sael had mentioned he normally didn't play as much with his victims.

Sael nodded. "We need to find her first."

Evony smirked. "Don't worry. The moment she knows I'm here, she'll run for us."

Sparrow ground his jaw. "Not happening, Magician."

"Ooo," Miels teased them, and their entire Posse laughed, both nonas alongside them. "Someone's in trouble."

Sael laughed at the man, her eyes shining and her smile wide. Killian's savage upbringing couldn't handle it as he stiffened and another low growl passed through him.

Miels looked especially annoyed when he met Killian's gaze. "Calm down, mate. I have a woman. Not to mention, Ro is obviously interested in you now."

Now. Killian hated that Sael had been interested in him at all.

His glower remained as they all turned back to their conversation, Sael's hand more insistent on his leg as she leaned up to kiss his jawline, right where one of the scars ended.

"Have you seen her at all since you've been here?" Ashtyn asked.

Sael nodded down at the hand in his lap. "I froze when I had the chance to kill her."

"Ro—" Tristan started for comfort before she interrupted with a shake of her head.

The man was only trying to comfort Sael, reminding her that most people could not kill on demand, and for that Killian appreciated him. He knew they all believed that, knew it to be a fact. Even most Islanders could not so easily kill. It was why some people were in power and others weren't.

It was Miels's caring look, though, that got to Killian. It was irrational because he shared the same concern and comfort as his lookalike, but it was Miels who irritated Killian. He didn't growl this time, but his look was dark as he stared at the pretty spy.

"Oh, would you stop it!" Miels looked especially irritated now. "She's gonna end up sucking your cock at the end of the night, *Killian*."

Killian couldn't even pay attention to the annoyed emphasis on his name. Before anything could be processed, he was out of his seat with the spy thrown against the wall, a dagger at his neck. "The only reason this isn't already in your chest is because I don't feel like arguing with her tonight."

Miels gave him a snickered laugh as he met Killian's dark look with one of his own.

The only thing that brought Killian back was the soft hand on his bicep, running up and down before it moved slowly up his arm to the dagger held against Miels's throat, and pulled it away.

Sael held the dagger facing down in one hand as she pulled on his shirt with the other to put enough space between him and Miels so she could step in. She gave him a soft, shy smile that turned cocky as their gazes met, and she shrugged. "Don't be angry with him, Kill. It *is* true."

Killian's nose flared with his shock at her less than proper admission around her friends. Then, finally, he stepped off, away from her friend.

Killian dragged Sael's body into him as he moved back to the table, not apologizing to the man but seeing in Miels's eyes that he didn't need to. Thankfully, the man had his own woman and would understand this possession that Killian wasn't accustomed to. It was a good thing because Killian had no intention of apologizing.

When he sat back down, Killian pulled Sael into his lap rather than allowing her to take her seat beside him again. He much preferred this and had been jealous when he saw Sparrow doing it with his wife.

Sael's cheeks were still pink as everyone calmed back into their seats and Kill knew it was both from what she'd just admitted to and from the attention sitting on his lap brought them.

"So, friends." Tristan looked specifically to Norya as he spoke. "Back to business?"

The way they looked at each other made Killian grind his jaw. The last thing he needed was his sister with one of Sael's whore friends, even knowing his sister would only be looking for a fuck and nothing more.

He wasn't as angry with the fact that Miels, Sael's old unrequited love, was around, but the emotion still lingered in him. It had only been a few hours, so Killian was impressed with his restraint.

But if he wanted to keep from attacking the man again, Killian needed to be away from him for some time. He needed to expend his energy doing something else so hunting it was.

He moved through the forest with only a dagger in his hand, a second one strapped to his belt, and a third to his boot. He wanted to feel the life of whatever beast with his hands, needed it to calm the storm within him, so he didn't require any other weapon.

Killian moved slowly through the forests, breathing focused on the ice of the air as he listened for anything around.

He heard it then. A soft crunch coming from behind him. He smirked, ready to attack whatever it was and feel the blood race down his hands.

He turned, dagger ready in hand, and paused right before he was going to run for it.

It was only Rosaelia.

"Where are your bow and arrow? You do not come out here without a weapon, Sael," he growled at her as she slowly moved toward him.

She gave a seductive smirk as her hand slowly lifted her dress. "I have a weapon. Remember, barbarian? *You* made me promise you'd be the only one to take it off me."

The dress hiked up to show the strapped dagger and a hint of her cunt, and Killian's savagery clicked into place. "Do not play with me, Sael. I am not in the mood."

That cunt looked delicious as she swayed the dress another moment before allowing it to fall back down. He wanted a taste, but he needed to get this adrenaline out first.

"Go home, Sael. I need to..." He shook his hands at his sides. "I can't hurt you."

She gave a knowing smile. "You won't."

"Walk back, Sael," he demanded. "*Do not* run. You'll ignite a chase." The words were meant to scare her, to show her he was as much the beast as any of the animals in these forests, and if she went running, he wasn't sure he could control himself from chasing after her like when the savage animals of these forests went after their prey.

Instead of being frightened and turning to slowly leave him, Sael's lips twitched into a wicked grin before she stepped in the opposite direction to their home. She took another slow step in the wrong direction, and Killian caught on to what she was doing.

"Sael." It took too much control out of him to mutter the word. "*Don't.*"

That tongue dipped to lick her bottom lip before she took it between her teeth and nibbled, enticing him. When his heated gaze met hers, she turned and ran.

Every fiber in him gave chase that very moment. Not only to catch her but to protect her as well. These were still dangerous forests. Though at that moment, he was the most frightening thing in it.

He caught her quickly, tackling her and turning in time to take the fall. He twisted with her in his arms immediately, holding her on the dirt ground and staring down at her with need. Her dress was hiked as she bent both knees, opening to make room for his body, and he got a delicious view of that dagger strapped to her thigh and her wet cunt, ready for him.

As much as he wanted to eat her until he gorged himself, Killian moved for his trousers, untying them only enough to get his cock out and roughly thrust into her.

He collared her throat and brought one of her knees up to hold on to as he fucked her hard and fast.

"Fuck, Killian," she moaned, the curse coming harsh off her tongue and making the monster in him lose control. His good little princess was cursing.

His fingers would leave bruises to the sides of her neck, but that only invigorated him more. He'd told the men at the tavern last night that he preferred bruises and bite marks, and he'd meant it. So to emphasize that he leaned in and bit her hard, leaving the mark of an animal as he thrust savagely into her.

He growled as he teethed the top of her dress down to suck

on a nipple, biting at it to add pain to her pleasure. "You'll be marked, princess. *My fucking woman.*"

He placed her leg at his shoulder to keep her opened for him as he forced her dress down so he could attack her breasts with his mouth. He licked, sucked, and bit at them until they were bruised and red all the while her moans grew incomprehensible as she came around his cock, squirting him in her juices.

"That's my fucking girl. Drench me. Let them know what I've done to you. That's a good." His breath left him harshly. "Fucking," he grunted. "Girl."

The praise sent her beautiful green eyes flying to the back of her head as she came again, soaking him and strangling his cock inside her.

His fingers dug into the sides of her throat, holding her jaw in place as he kissed her violently, then leaned up to watch her ecstasy as he reached his end.

Killian didn't even think to pull out as he came inside her, filling her with his cum. He growled against her lips, his monster knowing they'd only just started this game, "This pussy"—he rubbed at her clit, making her cunt strangle his still hard cock inside her—"is going to be full of my cum every day from now on, princess."

"But I want to be a very pretty princess, barbarian," she got out before her words became strangled, and her body shook with another orgasm, all the while milking him for another climax.

When the orgasms subsided, but she still shook a little, Killian rose to his knees and pulled out of her, watching as his cum dripped out, her cunt too full to take any more. "You're still covered in my cum, princess."

She gave him a barely awake, happily sated grin. "Good."

CHAPTER 32
ROSAELIA

Sparrow was on his feet, eyes dark in that Master Assassin way of his, as he stalked toward her and Killian as they came from their bedroom the next morning. Rosaelia paled instantly, knowing Evony had promised to shield any noise from the night before—not that any of them were allowed to judge her. Especially not Sparrow with the sounds that came from his and Evony's suite at home. From the noises that would've come had magic not been shielding it here.

But Sparrow wasn't the only angry one. Tristan and Miels were behind him, growls vibrating out of them. Gabriel, for his part, stood straighter but remained calm as he threw dirty looks at Killian.

All the while, Rosaelia stood frozen with all those eyes on them, Killian at her back, growling in return. Of course he wouldn't be afraid of the *Master* Assassin's threat, the fool.

A quick glance to the women showed... amusement?

Then Evony was before her husband, a strong hand on his

chest, and Norya was before the boys, stopping both of them as she pressed herself into Tristan.

"Calm down, my love," Evony teased.

"I'm going to kill him," Sparrow growled, and again, Rosaelia wondered what could have changed his mood so suddenly.

Evony only laughed. "Trust me when I say, she wanted those, my love. Be a good assassin and I'll let you give me some."

Sparrow's nostrils flared, and he turned away from Rosaelia in disgust before his dark eyes landed on his wife with hunger. What the hell were they talking about?

"You heard her, boys," Norya teased. "Do not be so upset. You are in barbarian nation. We like it rough here." There was an extra glint in her eyes as she said those words, Tristan catching her gaze and mirroring the look.

Rosaelia was about to question them again when her glance landed on Gabriel for a moment, and she saw him play with his neck as if telling her that's the root of the chaos in the house.

Her neck?

Rosaelia's eyes widened as she remembered Killian's hold on her last night. She'd loved his possession and hadn't thought about how it would look come morning.

Her hands flew to her neck immediately as she turned on Killian, hissing, "Why didn't you say anything?"

His annoyance with the boys was still there, but when he caught her gaze, a satisfied smirk replaced it. "What's to tell, princess? You're marked. I intend on doing so again the moment those disappear."

"Killian," she hissed. "They're my brothers!"

"And you're my mate," he whispered against her lips before kissing her in front of everyone. Then he pulled away and moved for the back door, holding out his hand for assistance. "Nona Eleni, the herb garden is ready for picking."

Rosaelia smiled at the sweet way the old woman took his arm and left the house with him. Nona Tereza followed with a basket for the picking.

It was sweet of them to give her time with her friends. Even though it was the very last thing she wanted at that moment. She was sure her cheeks would burn right off.

"Gem is going to be mad she wasn't here to witness all of this," Ashtyn teased as she took a seat beside the one Gabriel relaxed into to start carving a piece of wood with a small, sharpened dagger.

Evony snort-laughed as Miels said, "James would've been on our side."

"And Gem would've stopped his ass the way Sapphire did the Assassin." Ashtyn looked to be enjoying the moment too much as she turned to Rosaelia. "Oh, calm down, Emerald. So you were fucking your man. We all knew that's what would be happening when Sapphire's magic enveloped the place."

Rosaelia took her seat at the table, confused at the way Ashtyn spoke with her considering she *was* the Princess, but liking it all the same. She liked that the healer wasn't afraid to speak her mind, didn't act differently specifically for her. It made her feel included.

"Doesn't mean we want to see it," Sparrow growled from where he stood with his brothers.

Evony laughed as she moved for the basket of fabrics the nonas kept in the opposite corner of the room. "Oh, please, Assassin, you mark me all the time. And we both love it! Why should they be any different?"

Sparrow only narrowed his gaze on his wife before turning back to his brothers to whisper about whatever they were talking of. Gabriel took that moment to leave the house for the back greens. Rosaelia had a feeling he needed to be outdoors. As the stable hand, it was pretty much all he ever did.

Rosaelia left Ashtyn at the table with Norya to look over different remedy recipes the nonas had as she moved for her twin in the corner. "Thank you," she whispered when she got to her.

Evony smirked. "For what? I'm only speaking the truth."

Rosaelia blushed. "Still. Thank you."

Evony's smirk grew more wicked. "Anytime. But if you'd really like to thank me, you can tell me *how* Killian dearest *claimed* you." *In front of everyone.*

She didn't need to say those final words for Rosaelia to hear them. Her blush deepened as she took particular interest in the fabrics within the basket. "With his hands."

Evony laughed. "I think I'll take Sparrow into town and try it. Sounds like it can be exhilarating. But maybe another town. We don't need these townsfolk thinking Sparrow's touching another man's claimed woman."

Rosaelia's heated face was almost unbearable. "Alright. That's enough about me!"

Evony giggled before her features turned serious. "I'm truly glad you're more than okay, Twin."

A sweet smile replaced the embarrassed one on Rosaelia's face. "Thank you. I'm glad you—"

Before Rosaelia could finish the sentence, Evony was out the front door, both quickly and not at all so as not to draw Sparrow's attention. Rosaelia followed her, jogging the moment they were out of the house to catch up to Evony's sprint to the thick of forest trees.

They were only a few yards from the house so Rosaelia wasn't worried as she stopped at her twin's back, the magician bent over, vomiting the morning away.

Rosaelia moved back for the house, picking up a glass of

water and moving back to her twin slowly so she didn't catch anyone's attention. She had a feeling the fact that Evony hadn't wanted to alert her husband when she left meant she wanted him to remain ignorant.

When she got back, Evony was wiping at her mouth, and gladly took the water from Rosaelia. As she sipped a little to gurgle into her mouth and spit out, Rosaelia waited patiently at her side. She couldn't see why her twin would hide a sickness from Sparrow.

She remained silent as Evony drank half the cup before saying, "If you're sick, he should know."

Evony gave a small, humorless laugh as she shook her head, taking her final drink of the water. "I am not sick, Twin."

Evony said nothing more as the glass held loosely in one hand, the other moved to massage her stomach. It took a moment longer than she would've liked, but Rosaelia's eyes widened. "You didn't tell him so you could come?"

Evony's eyes were softer, less guarded than they normally were with her twin. "No. No, I would never. I would've never hidden it from him. I just found out yesterday."

"So why hide it now?"

"I'm already here. If he finds out now with me here, it'll make it more dangerous for him. He'll be hyper-focused on me and not at all on himself. I can't risk being that distraction to him right now."

"Evony, he needs to know—"

"And he'll find out soon. Let's just finish off our mother first." Evony moved to stand before her twin. "Please don't say anything. I need to be the one to tell him."

Rosaelia searched her twin's deep blue eyes, finding nothing but love for her brother there. "He's your husband, Eve. I would never take that from you."

A small smile lifted her lips. "Thank you."

BEING in the house with Sparrow and Evony and knowing her brother didn't know about his wife was difficult. But the news made Rosaelia extra protective of her twin, so she could only imagine the amount of overbearing Sparrow would be.

She felt awful for hiding it, but Evony was probably right to keep it from him. For now.

And if it felt this horrible for Rosaelia, she could only imagine how badly her twin felt every time she met her husband's gaze. But their love was strong, and Rosaelia knew her brother was going to be overjoyed when he found out.

Until then, he needed to remain safe and alive.

And he needed to hear about his mother.

Rosaelia hated to be the one to tell him, hated that she was a large part of the reason Alana had been killed.

Rosaelia found the handcrafted box underneath Killian's clothes in the drawer she'd placed it for safekeeping, then moved for her brother. She took Sparrow's hand wordlessly and tugged him to the comfortable armchair in the living space. They sat—Sparrow in the seat and Rosaelia on the arm—and watched the others around the table in the open living space.

Rosaelia's hand wrapped around Sparrow's shoulder as she sat an inch taller than him because of the higher spot of her seat. "I need to tell you something, brother."

Sparrow's gaze was hard, searching, as he turned on her. "You don't sound happy, Ro."

Evony watched from across the room but didn't move for them. Her worry that Rosaelia would break her promise evident, but she didn't try to stop her. Rosaelia knew it was her twin's way of putting faith in their relationship and her promise.

And Rosaelia had no thoughts of breaking said promise. Especially not since she had been the reason so much doubt had plagued her twin only about a month ago. She had some making up to do, and this would be part of it.

"Rowena... she isn't working with the Master Sorcerer. Hasn't been since she was betrayed in the North."

"How do you know?"

Rosaelia swallowed. "Because I was working with her when I got here."

"You... were?"

"Alana. She... found me. She knew, I don't know how, but she knew I was here for Rowena. She said she needed to help me. For you."

"For me?"

"She knew Rowena wouldn't stop until she got her spot on the throne and along with it, Evony's magic. She knew you would die before allowing anything to happen to Evony. She needed to protect you."

"So she was helping you?" Sparrow looked to be staring into space, but in actuality, his gaze followed his wife as she moved around the others, laughing and teasing. "Did she betray you like she did your mother?"

"Never," Rosaelia whispered. "She would never betray you, brother."

He turned to meet her eyes.

"Rowena came to her as was planned, and when it came down to it, Alana sacrificed her safety to keep Rowena's attention off of me long enough for me to shoot."

Sparrow turned back to find Evony like she calmed whatever storm he was feeling. "She's dead?"

"I'm sorry, Sparrow."

"For what? You didn't kill her. And she was never truly a parent to me anyway."

"I'm sorry because when Rowena killed her, I froze, Spar. I couldn't release the arrow. If it weren't for Killian, I'd be dead now too."

Sparrow's eyes closed as he took in the news. "I guess I should be thankful to the man then, rather than tear him apart for your neck."

Rosaelia's blush felt permanent now. "Sparrow, *I'm* sorry."

Sparrow took her hand, his attention nagging to the box in her lap, then to their intertwined fingers. "Do not be, sister. I always believed her dead, now she is. Knowing for a few weeks that she wasn't didn't change a thing. It felt worse, actually."

She knew exactly what he meant. Because she'd *chosen* to leave him. "She told me why she left. It is no excuse, Spar. She knew it, I know it, everyone does, but when you wish to hear it, I can tell you."

He nodded. "I think I'd like to, Ro. Eventually."

Rosaelia held him for some time before finally releasing her hand from his and reaching for the box. "She said this was made by your father, and it holds the few things she took to remember you guys by. Sparrow..." She felt this next bit imperative, especially given she hadn't been able to kill her mother when the time called for it. "She did love you, in her own ways. When she was dying, the last thing she wanted was for me to tell you that she loved you. That Evony was the best thing that ever happened to you."

Sparrow peeled his gaze from the box to find Evony again before meeting Rosaelia's green orbs. His lips quirked into a smile that juxtaposed the sad look in his eyes. "She is."

Rosaelia kissed the top of his head. "I didn't open it. That is for you, and maybe your wife, to do on your own time."

Sparrow brought Rosaelia down for a kiss on the cheek.

"Thank you, Ro. I—when we get home, Evony and I will open it at our house. Maybe look toward a future for a family of our own."

Our house. The one his father had been killed in and he now considered his and Evony's permanent residence even though they spent far more time at the palace.

Then there was that next bit—*a family of our own.* Rosaelia's heart raced knowing the secret her brother did not yet.

She kissed his crown again. "I cannot wait to see you as a father, Spar. You're going to be overbearing and amazing."

A deep chuckle left him as his gaze latched to his wife again, love flooding over. "I cannot wait either, Ro. She's going to look stunning carrying my child. She's going to be powerful, pushing our child out. I cannot wait to hold her in one arm and our child in the other, Ro."

"Child? One?" Rosaelia asked, unsure why but loving the way her brother spoke of his magician. From a man who never wished to find love, it was all Rosaelia had ever wanted for him.

He shrugged, dark browns never leaving Evony. "The bloodline does indicate twins a high likelihood. But if you're asking how many I want with her, I want as many as she'll give me. A whole team if she's willing."

Rosaelia laughed into his hair, imagining it now—Sparrow chasing after some blue-eyed, dark-haired kids while Evony fed a brown-eyed one in her arms. "I believe she'd be willing to give you far more than her body could take. Etel will have to force serums into her drinks to prevent any more."

Sparrow laughed now, catching his wife's attention. "Etel should heed her own advice. Miels was speaking of switching out her serums with placebos to get her pregnant the entire trip here. He's jealous of James apparently."

Rosaelia laughed now as Evony turned to watch them. "Your wife is watching, Assassin. I think she is a bit obsessed with you."

He smirked. "The way your barbarian is you?"

Rosaelia's blush erupted as her gaze shot to find Killian watching them from the other end of the room. She smiled as their eyes met, and part of her was thankful for her mother.

For being the reason she came to the Island.

"I think it might be my turn to thank you, Spar," she said before moving her gaze from the scarred monster to her brother. "For putting it in the air for me too. For Killian."

His smile was warm. "I'm glad you have someone, Ro. I couldn't have known before Eve how magical it would be."

"Yes, well, being the Magician can put you in some spells."

He rolled his eyes before they stopped on her neck. "Spells? Like the ones that the barbarian put on you? I think he needs to put in more practice"—he tapped her neck—"your spells are showing."

They were both laughing, Sparrow with humor and Rosaelia with embarrassment, when Evony moved for them, taking her seat on her husband's lap. "What's so funny, my love?"

"Brother-sister conversations. You wouldn't understand," he teased her with a wink in Rosaelia's direction.

Evony only rolled her eyes and leaned in to kiss him. It was Rosaelia's cue to leave them.

As she moved for the others, Killian's arms opened for her as he continued his heated argument with Norya about finding sorcerers. Rosaelia didn't particularly care for their conversation, she simply felt safe and at home in his tight embrace. It scared and invigorated her all at once.

CHAPTER 33

KILLIAN

She still didn't look fully at health, but Rowena was getting better. A glance her way from across town square solidified that much for Killian.

She was bold, showing herself with the entire Posse now in the Island. Even if she didn't know of their presence, which Killian seriously concluded was true, she was bold enough to come out after she'd tried to hurt Sael right in front of him. She'd been a claimed woman when that dagger had flown for her.

Even had Killian not yet claimed her, he'd be feral seeing Rowena.

But she had been claimed.

And all Islanders understood what it meant to go after a claimed woman.

Rowena wasn't a born Islander, but she'd been there nearly two decades. She knew the rules as well as any true Islander.

"What's got you so growly again?" Miels's annoyed question came from his right.

The moron twins had somehow enlisted the Master Assassin to bother him on his 'quick' trip into town, and now Killian was glad for it. Killian was sure he could kill the woman himself but having the Master Assassin by his side definitely helped odds.

Especially considering it was the Master Assassin's wife who was the true prey for the late Queen of the Northern Lands.

"Don't react," he demanded, which got all three of their attentions on him. "Up ahead, eleven o'clock."

All three men followed his instruction to the woman who still hadn't clocked them.

Killian's focus was on Rowena, but he felt the others stiffen around him when they caught sight of her.

All four of them remained close so they could whisper to one another as they slowly made their way around town square. He normally got too much attention because of his past to go straight through undetected. And there was something about Sparrow's presence that captured attention, his Mastery taking up space.

"She looks better than I was expecting," Miels said.

"She has a healing sorcerer helping her," Killian answered, remembering that one from the list Sael had.

"Perfect," Sparrow grumbled as they circled the square, never losing their sight of her.

"There's a list of Islanders Rowena has helping her. Our girl has dealt with a few of them on her own," Killian mumbled, the thought still annoying him.

Tristan scoffed. "She's turning out to be more like Evony than I thought. Stubborn little thing."

"They get it from their father," Miels added as they closed in on her stance at this end of town square.

In that moment, Rowena leisurely turned and caught sight

of the four of them moving for her. Her eyes widened as they landed on the Master.

She turned without a thought and ran.

Sparrow was fast, too fast, as he chased after her.

The three of them followed, and by the time they reached the clearing, the two were in, Sparrow had her.

His arms were wrapped so tightly around her throat her eyes were rolling back after only being held for two seconds. He was going to kill her.

Finally.

Killian should've never doubted her desire to reach her goals; should've never doubted she wouldn't go down without a fight; should've never doubted she would have something on her person to protect herself.

Whatever was in the needle she injected into the Master's arm must've stung worse than was imaginable because he released her immediately. He covered the affected area as Rowena moved quickly, grabbing a child passing through the forest walkway toward the No Known Housing.

She was too quick. If Killian threw his dagger now, he wasn't sure he wouldn't hurt the kid.

Killian tracked her progression backward, the child before her with a dagger to his throat, as Miels moved quickly for Sparrow, handing him a vial of what must've been preventatives against anything Rowena could harm them with. Being mated to a remedy's expert made him annoying the amount he spoke of the things she's taught him to make.

The child in Rowena's arms remained quiet, ever the Islander, though his eyes showed his fear as Rowena moved back toward the Housing with Killian and his princess's brothers following. They took cautious steps as the dagger was already making the kid bleed.

Rowena looked poised, yet frightened even though she

tried to hide the latter reaction. Her throat was already bruising a deep purple, and she had constant coughs rack up her body like her lungs were still asking for air. Another second in the Master's arms would've surely ended her.

"Release the kid, Rowena," Sparrow demanded, shaking out his arm as the vial Miels had worked its way through him.

"Why? He is the only thing keeping you from touching me. Isn't that backward, Master? Aren't you supposed to save women from being touched by monsters?"

"Women can be monsters too." He didn't break his cold stare.

It looked terrifying the way his dark browns shined. Killian couldn't imagine being on the receiving end of such a look. Even as a hardened Islander, it frightened him.

"Release the kid, Rowena," Miels repeated.

"Release him, Rowena," Tristan called.

"Release"—Killian flipped the dagger in his hand, preparing to run for her the second he had a chance, he wanted to feel her life leaving her—"him."

Instead of listening, she continued back until her back hit the No Known Housing building. It wasn't the most structured of buildings and was made entirely of wood as many of the places close to town square were, but it was perfect for the needs of those without family.

"You're not getting away, Rowena," Sparrow continued. "I won't let you touch my wife."

"She's a magician!" Rowena barked as she lowered to reach for something behind her, the dagger still pressed into the boy's throat. "The Master Assassin hates magicians!"

"The Master Assassin hates you," he roared in such a calming tone it unnerved Killian.

Rowena handed the boy a piece of wood. "Hold that."

His hands shook as he reached for the wood.

Then they all watched as she dropped a small vial of potion to moisten it, and Killian's eyes widened as he realized what she was about to do. "Stop!"

Rowena dropped the piece of flint over the moistened bit, and the entire thing went up in flames. She took the piece from the boy and then threw him aside as she hovered the wood beside the home. "They're unwanted, but will you ignore them to come after me?"

"Kill?" Tristan asked, and Killian understood the unvoiced question—was there reason to worry?

It was four in the afternoon—the children's lessons started half an hour ago. Meaning every child currently living in the No Known Housing—and most of them were children—was upstairs in their lessons.

Every

single

child

would

burn.

"Yes," he answered as his gaze latched on to that raging fire so close to the home.

"Don't you da—" Sparrow started but was interrupted when Rowena dropped the flame, and the place caught fire like a firework explosion, beautifully and all at once.

He needed to go after her because of her threat to Rosaelia.

Sparrow needed to go after her because of her threat to Evony.

They all needed to get those kids out.

Rowena ran through the forests toward the direction that would lead her north, into the forests and toward the other Island towns and villages.

And all four of them let her go as they raced into the building, screams filling the air with how quickly the fire enveloped the house. Sorcerer flames were always far more dangerous.

Sparrow was fast as he raced ahead of everyone and straight up the stairs. Tristan remained downstairs, and as Killian realized Miels was helping Sparrow upstairs, he knew why. If the stairs burned, they needed a way out for the kids.

So he remained by Tristan's side, ready to catch each out.

Then quickly, right after one another, kids came flying down.

There were two adults holding two infants each in their arms as they raced down the stairs.

"Get out," Killian demanded as he placed another child on the ground. "All of you. Run!"

The flames were eating away too quickly. They needed a way to stop this otherwise the kids would burn and all four of them would go down with them.

Then, by some miracle, Sael and Norya were in the house.

"Sael, get out of here!" Killian demanded as Norya got beside them and started catching kids to release on the ground floor, right as the stairs crumbled.

Sael ignored him as she took the hands of the kids he, Tristan, and Norya were releasing and ran them outside.

"How'd you guys know?" he questioned his sister.

"The Masters can speak to each other in their minds. The Assassin informed the Magician when she lit the flame. We came running. She's outside, using her magic to slow down the process so everyone can get out."

Sael was back by their sides, taking more hands with an Islander who had likely run in when the smoke filled the air.

There was a crash beside them as more kids came down, and Killian knew the structure didn't have long.

"That's all!" Miels called as he jumped down to search the ground floor with Tristan at the same moment Sparrow yelled, "I'm checking the rest of the floor."

Killian took that moment to pull Sael and Norya out of the building.

They coughed, the smoke having filled their lungs as they ran away from the building, toward the group of No Known Housing residents watching their only shelter burn to the ground.

Another crash and the side of the Housing exploded in flames.

Tristan and Miels ran out in the next moment as the rest of the place exploded.

"NO!" Evony's voice filled the air as a force Killian only concluded could be magic hit him. She was running for the flames as Miels caught her around the waist, and both he and Tristan tried to hold her back. "NO!"

Sparrow had been on the top floor.

"No," Sael cried and moved like she was going to reach for the flames. Killian caught her as the tears bubbled out, and she screamed, "No!"

Tristan and Miels were barely holding the Magician back when a black mirage came from behind the flames.

He was covered in smoke and debris, and in his arms was a limp elder man, but he demanded attention like the air around him bowed down to such a presence.

"Sparrow!" Evony's cry was enigmatic as she wrenched out from the boys' holds and ran straight for her husband. There were already two others taking the man from his arms, so he caught her the second she jumped for him.

Sael was shaking in his arms as she cried her relief. Killian only held her and let her heart settle.

That force he'd felt before was still in the air, but it wasn't as stifling any longer. Evony shook in her husband's arms as her snot and tears littered the crook of his neck, and she kissed him like they were the only people on this world.

Rowena almost took the Assassin away from the Magician. She would surely pay for that.

CHAPTER 34

KILLIAN

His woman was safely knackered out in their bed. After the trauma of almost losing her brother, she'd needed his distractions. So Killian had pleased her, clouded her mind until all she could think of was him.

He hadn't been able to control himself from tasting her over and over until she'd come four times on his face. He'd wanted to continue, but she'd been crying as she begged for his cock so he'd given her another two orgasms with it before he'd made her a very pretty princess, finishing inside her as he promised he'd always do, then wiping the excess across her thighs and stomach.

She'd pulled him to cover her like a blanket afterward, finding comfort in his weight, before immediately falling asleep.

It had been after an hour of lying on top of her, thinking about life with her forever by his side, that Killian knew he needed to leave the house. He needed to find Von—after Keir, he was the only real person Killian needed dead.

And there had been word that Von made rounds every few

nights. Killian was merely lucky that the night he felt the need to finish him was one of the nights he was meant to be on rounds.

He moved quietly through their room, getting dressed and picking up his weapons—whip and dagger again—then turned back to the bed.

Killian kissed Sael softly on the lips before he placed another gentle kiss to the spot below her ear and listened to her sigh his name. It made him more determined to finish Von and get back to her.

He was out of the room before he convinced himself to get between her legs again.

Killian was silent as he traversed through his now full house and was in the back greens in no time. Then he was around the house and on his way toward Keir's estate where a half mile out, Von would be making rounds.

He'd only been walking a few minutes when he felt eyes on the back of his neck, tracking him.

Killian slowed his trek but didn't stop and didn't turn as he called, "Go back inside." He didn't know which one was following him and didn't particularly care.

"Our Princess cares for you, barbarian," Tristan called. "It means you cannot go and get yourself killed. Where're you going anyway?"

"If I was going to get myself killed, I wouldn't last long on the Island Nation. You should heed your own advice," Killian called back.

"You going to answer where you're headed?" Miels's voice came.

Killian ground his jaw as they continued following him. "Don't worry about it. Just head back."

"Who're you trying to kill?" Miels called instead, sounding understanding rather than judgmental.

"I am not *trying* to kill anyone," Killian answered only because he hoped the answers would make them leave him alone.

"Fine," Tristan huffed. "Who are you going to kill?"

"None of your concern."

"You are Ro's concern which makes you our concern, barbarian," Miels called. "Is it blasphemous on this goddamned island to just be reasonable once in a while?"

Killian twisted in his spot so fast both men took a step back even from the distance they followed. "If you must know, I am going after the final man who delivered me to the one who did this!" He pointed to his face, hoping they finally understood to leave him be.

Their gazes held no pity, but they hardened like they truly understood.

Killian didn't wait around for them to back down and finally turn back. He simply continued on his route, his annoyance adding to the violence he would impede on Von.

Not a minute into his trek, he heard them again, felt their stares. "What part of 'leave me be' do you two morons not understand?"

"We're not leaving you, barbarian," Tristan answered.

"You're not stopping me either."

"We don't plan on it," Miels said. "We won't get involved either. But we'll be there in case it's needed."

Logically, if Von had others with him or if they were heard, having the moron spies with him wouldn't be a bad idea. It wasn't something Killian would admit, but he stopped arguing with them.

"If you die and Sael gets angry with me, I'll bring you both back to kill you myself."

Chuckles came from behind him as both muttered, "Deal."

In the following silence, Killian was able to think about

Von. The man was much smaller than Brayd, but that only made him faster. In the past, that would've made Killian excited. The opportunity to chase him, then gut him. Now, he simply wanted to make it painful, then make it back to his princess.

If he wasn't so bound to her, Killian would ridicule himself for the thoughts. But nothing about being with her made him uncomfortable or ashamed. She was everything good about him, and he was now realizing how much he craved that.

When they reached the spot Von was meant to be passing for his rounds, Killian stopped and waited. The twins behind him didn't make a noise as they stood and waited with him.

The whole half hour they stood there, none of them moved or made a single sound. The whole time Killian thought of Sael.

Then Von came strolling by the clearing Killian was watching, his form relaxed but alert enough that he'd be able to run if he heard Killian. And Killian truly wasn't in the mood for a chase at the moment. To be honest, he never wanted to chase again if it didn't end with his hands around Sael's throat and his cock shoved deep inside her.

"Sandwich him," Killian ordered silently. "I'm not in the mood for a game."

A satisfied chuckle came from behind him, no doubt because he had in fact ended up using their assistance before both men left. Thankfully, their spy backgrounds made them undetectable.

When enough time was given for the two to get into their positions, Killian moved, making noise so Von knew he was no longer alone. When the man turned, eyes wide at seeing Killian and knowing he had no backup, knowing what Killian had done to his friends, he stumbled back, then ran.

Killian walked after him and delighted in the way that man

flew back when Miels's arm strut out of nowhere and knocked his nose. Killian reached him as he stumbled on his hands, crawling backward and preparing to run.

Tristan's laugh behind him made the man freeze, true fear lighting his eyes. Hopefully this one wouldn't ask for mercy. The weakness of it sickened Killian.

"We meet again, friend." Killian gave him a wicked grin.

Von's gaze was quick as he shot from one side to the other, trying to find an opening to run off. With each of the moron twins standing around, allowing him to do his work, but ready in case, Von wouldn't get the slightest of chances.

"You don't want to hurt me," Von stuttered. "Something happens to me and Keir will go after that woman of yours."

The insinuation made Killian's body roar, but he remained calm and grinned wider. "He's not stupid enough."

And Keir truly wasn't. Nor did he care for any of his men enough to enact retribution.

"You're angry with him! Why come for me?"

Killian laughed and stalked forward. "I don't have time for games, friend. I have a woman I need to get home to."

Von continued stumbling as he crawled back, away from Killian. And neither Tristan nor Miels stopped him. Good. It wasn't a chase, but it was riling Killian up enough to make this brutal and fast.

Killian didn't reach for his daggers at all this time. His hand went, instead, straight to his whip.

He had the thing flying through the air so quickly Von didn't have time to flinch away from it as it wrapped around one of his hands. Then Killian pulled at it so fast and hard Von's entire wrist snapped, skin tearing off.

He roared, and it was music to Killian's ears.

"Cry, little baby, make all the noise," he sang as he whipped out once more, this time catching his thigh, captivated as half the limb tore away when he pulled the whip back.

"Killian's gonna fill you with so much worse," he continued, another whip around his torso, searing around his entire waist.

"And if that pain doesn't take your life…" He whipped again, wrapping the weapon around Von's ankle and pulling as his entire foot flew through the air. "Killian's gonna rip you limb from limb."

Von's cries were so loud there was no way Keir's men couldn't hear him. But Killian also knew none of them would come, especially not after seeing what had been done to the others when they were found alone by Killian.

The whip flew through the air again and wrapped itself tightly around the spot that connected Von's arm to his body. Killian pulled taut and watched the limb fly off, blood squirting everywhere.

It was obvious Von wasn't going to be able to hold out much longer so Killian finally dropped the whip and grabbed his dagger. He moved slowly until he was hovering over the man's body, blood seeping onto his boots. "Next time someone tries to threaten my woman, I hope they think of you."

He knew Rosaelia wasn't the reason he was out there or the reason behind how savage his killings were, but she was his entire reason for being so he found the threat apt.

Killian thrust down with the dagger, cutting the man's face in half until it hung from his skull. He gave a final spit at the disgusting excuse for a man and stepped away.

The moron twins allowed him to cool down for minutes before they joined at his sides.

"If that's what you do to your *friends*"—Miels stared at Von's limbs spread throughout the clearing and his unrecognizable face—"it's a good thing you hate us."

CHAPTER 35

ROSAELIA

Taking a bath on her own wasn't as fun as taking one with Killian, but with all her friends in the house, Rosaelia could not handle them knowing what they were doing in there. Even though they already knew she and Killian spent their nights—and mornings, and any time of the day they had a chance—having plenty of fun.

But she'd insisted he went first since he was covered in sweat from working outdoors all day, and she'd gone after him. Now, dressed in a simple dress that reached mid-calf, Rosaelia moved to Norya's room—the one that had been hers for all of a few nights when she'd first gotten to the Island Nation—to ask for the comb she'd given the girl earlier.

Rosaelia was so lost in her thoughts she didn't realize how timid her knock was or hear a command to come in when she opened the door.

And immediately froze in her spot because on the bed was Norya, naked with her face in the blankets, biting for dear life, as her hands fisted the sheets. Tristan was behind her, equally as naked as he held on to her hips and roughly pushed into her.

His jaw was grit tight as he tried to control the groans that left him, as they both tried to control any noise even though Evony's magic still blocked it with the door closed.

Rosaelia stood frozen, watching the sweat glisten on their skin as they truly *rutted*, for a couple of seconds that felt like years before closing the door behind herself, and hoping they hadn't noticed. The fact that they hadn't stopped or made any indication of having noticed the door open—which in their blissed states wasn't shocking—made her believe they hadn't seen her.

Thankfully.

She stood frozen in the hall, trying to reel back from what she'd seen. The animalistic way Tristan had been taking her. It reminded Rosaelia of the second time she'd ever been with Killian. Of when he'd tied her hands to his headboard, then turned her to her knees and made her back arch in that delicious position. She understood Norya's need to bite down on the blankets, but she still blushed at what she'd seen.

Rosaelia moved slowly then for the front living space where the others were gathered.

"What's happened?" Sparrow asked almost immediately when he saw her face.

She shook her head. "I-I was going to Norya to ask for the comb."

"And...?" Ashtyn asked.

Gabriel smirked. The man spoke so little, it was shocking he was the one to finish the thought. "And neither Norya nor Tristan are with us right now."

All heads snapped to her, and Evony laughed. "You've now caught Gem and James, Miels and Etel, and now Tristan too? I'm starting to believe you're doing it on purpose, Twin."

Rosaelia gasped as Killian's hands landed on her hips from behind. Her cheeks burned at the insinuation. "I would never!"

Miels smirked as he caught her gaze. "After what the two of you were doing in that tavern. *Now* you're shy?"

They'd heard about her being claimed—knowing it meant public displays—and had seen the marks around her throat, but still, he'd chosen *those* words. *What they'd done in the tavern.*

Rosaelia blanched. "What..."

"How do you think we found you, Ro? We saw you at that tavern. Watched you two go to that back room."

"You... saw us?" Rosaelia was ready to throw herself off the highest tree.

"Well," Ashtyn smirked. "We had to make sure you were all right. Had to check what you were going into that room for."

She gasped. "You *saw*."

They all looked over to Miels as he smirked. "Not all," Ashtyn teased.

Rosaelia met Miels's gaze, wide-eyed and horrified.

"Hey, you caught me and Etel, I caught you two. Lucky you, I did too. Sparrow would've torn that entire tavern apart had he been the one to see it."

Sparrow growled his assent, his eyes dark like he hadn't liked hearing about it either. Understandably so.

Rosaelia didn't know where to look. Her heart raced too fast. He'd *seen* them!

Rosaelia turned to Killian for comfort and found the proud glint in his eyes, the cocky way he watched Miels like he was glad they'd been caught.

"Killian," she growled low.

His gaze snapped to meet hers, and that smirk widened. "Princess?"

"*Do not* look proud!"

His hand snapped for her jaw, taking her roughly, and

forcing her in close so their lips brushed as he spoke. "Do not raise your voice at me, princess. We both know I own you."

Her cunt clenched and her clit throbbed with need, arousal pooling between her legs immediately. This was so not the time for that.

Rosaelia pushed away from him before her body took it upon itself to lean forward and kiss him, instantly giving Killian permission to carry her off to their room.

She turned on Miels. "*How much* did you see?"

"Don't worry, Ro, I didn't stick around. Once I saw how *happily* you were in that position, I had no reason to stay. In fact, I needed to make sure Sparrow didn't come around."

Rosaelia's hands moved to her beet-red face, hiding from the others. This was officially the worst day.

Killian's fingers enveloped her forearms and pushed her into the wall, prying her hands away once he was covering her body with his. When Rosaelia allowed him to move her hands so they rested on his chest and opened her eyes, he was all she saw. He was so big, she thankfully couldn't see the others behind him.

"I'm not going to apologize for being happy he saw, Sael. *He* especially needs to know who you belong to," he whispered against her lips.

Rosaelia rolled her eyes. "I belong to you, barbarian! That's been clear from the beginning! Now will you stop being annoying about it?"

He chuckled against her lips making her clit throb extra hard to have him inside her. "Anything for you, my princess."

Looking into his dark hazel eyes, her green ones softened. Her hands played at his chest as she stared at those beautiful eyes framed by those scars. "I love that you belong to me too, Killian. I cannot go back to a time where you didn't."

His lips pressed hers in a gentle kiss. "You won't."

CHAPTER 36

ROSAELIA

Evony was straddled on Sparrow's lap as they basked in the fields outside of Killian's house. Her arms were wrapped around his neck, and they smiled lovingly as they talked, eyes never leaving one another. Rosaelia loved seeing her brother so enamored.

The way his hands played with Evony's sides, his thumbs skimming her stomach, almost made it look like he knew of her condition. But his calm demeanor gave away that he didn't.

Rosaelia still couldn't believe her brother was going to be a father. She was going to be an aunt.

Rosaelia didn't want to interrupt their private moment, but she wanted to talk to them. She needed to ask them.

"Well, well, well, Spar"—she walked around them and plopped down so she was facing their sides—"I thought the big, bad Master Assassin would never fall in love. Look at you, so enraptured with the Magician, it's almost sickening."

They both laughed as Sparrow pulled his wife closer on his lap. "She's a magician, sister. I'm at her mercy."

Evony skimmed down his neck, whispering, "Yes. You. Are." And Rosaelia knew it was time she said what she was there for before the two got too distracted in one another.

"Okay, well." She clapped her hands together to get their attention again. "I'm actually *not* here to watch you two."

"You sure?" Evony smirked. "You seem to enjoy doing so, Twin."

Rosaelia's lips twisted down as her nose crinkled. "Even if I were—which I'm not!—I definitely wouldn't want to watch *my brother*!"

Sparrow laughed. "What's up, Ro? You guys find anything regarding Rowena?"

She shook her head. "I need your help with something else."

They both must've heard the seriousness in her tone because they straightened and searched her face for more information.

"I... the scars on Killian's body. They were put there by a man—Keir—when he wanted to take Killian's property."

Sparrow nodded. "I'm familiar with Island politics. And with where Miels and Tristan went with him the other night."

Killian had told her about that when he'd gotten home from killing Von. She'd awoken feeling him getting back into bed—after bathing—and he hadn't tried to hide what he'd done. Rosaelia loved that about him—he was always honest with her.

And every time, he'd stiffen like he was afraid she'd judge him or hate him for what he'd done, but it never bothered Rosaelia. With the Master Assassin as a brother, and justifiable reasons, Rosaelia had no reasons to care.

Rosaelia nodded at the two in front of her. "He's taken care of the four who delivered him to Keir and a bunch of randoms of Keir's men. We're too close now to finishing Rowena, and I cannot leave the Island without also finishing the rest of Keir's supporters, finishing Keir."

"Ro..." Sparrow started while Evony watched her like she understood.

"I need to, Spar. Every man that works for Keir needs to be taken care of. Keir needs to be taken care of. I love Killian's scars, but I need them dead for what they did to him."

"Rosaelia," he started slowly. "You're talking of killing all those men. There must be dozens in that house." *You're talking of killing, Ro. You couldn't do it when you had a clear shot of your mother.*

She heard that true argument even though he didn't make it aloud. And she understood his hesitations. But as angry as she was with her mother, it didn't compare to how she felt about Keir. Because killing anyone would be hard, but she had a true reason to kill Keir's men. The evidence of it was all over Killian's skin.

With her mother, on the other hand, Rosaelia had to continue reminding herself what she'd done—the Bloody Fields the biggest reminder—and fighting the false memories to get the anger up. It wasn't the same.

And it certainly didn't feel the same. She felt protective of herself and her family, but this feeling for Killian was so much more. She needed to do this for him. Because as savage as he was, he was still a good guy, one who only killed because it was required, not because he wanted to.

Rosaelia sat up straighter, poised. "Imagine if you weren't the Master Assassin, Sparrow. Imagine if you were a regular guy, and you had the chance with the men who gave Evony that scar."

He froze, gaze hardening. "If what you feel for him is what I feel for Evony?"

Rosaelia paused. She hadn't admitted to those feelings yet,

and the first time she said them wouldn't be to anyone but Killian, but she didn't need to say those words for Sparrow to understand. "I do."

He didn't look particularly happy, but his gaze cleared with acceptance now. "Then we have an estate to tear apart."

THE HOUSE WAS ENORMOUS, with a set of metal gates around the entirety of the property. It was less shocking now seeing the place that anyone would want to take it. Killian had known that, but he hadn't expected what had happened to him.

So now he was slowly getting his vengeance, and Rosaelia wouldn't stop until he got it.

"Okay, Twin," Evony started at her side. "My magic is around the property so no one will know what is happening inside, and no one will be able to make it out."

"We'll stop them from coming at you," Sparrow continued, always including his wife in the fights because he knew how capable she was. "These men are yours." He took her shoulder and forced her to meet his gaze. "If you need help, you tell us. Whether or not *you* kill them, they'll be gone because of you, Ro."

It was both a reminder that she didn't have to put on a brave face she didn't feel and that she still had time to back down if this was going to sit on her conscience for the rest of her life.

Rosaelia only nodded. "I know."

And she did. She knew every death that day would be on her shoulders, whether she personally took the life or not, and she was okay with that.

She also felt so much rage within her that she couldn't

fathom hesitating for even a moment. This wasn't the same as when she'd thought of her mother. All of those times, she knew she would hesitate. Killian said she was such a good girl, even those fake scenarios she'd made of her mother felt too real to easily fight off.

But she didn't have any of that with Keir's men. All she had were the scars on Killian's body and the trauma in his head.

Rosaelia turned back to the gates and watched as Evony's magic opened them slowly.

They moved quietly with Sparrow in the middle to make sure no one jumped out at them. To his left was his wife and to his right, Rosaelia with that dagger Killian had given her in hand.

She still wasn't entirely trained in using it, but she knew it was more practical than her bow and arrow. And Killian had been through enough with her in their second training the other day that she had a basic understanding. Sparrow and Evony would be around to make sure she wasn't hurt in the process.

The first two men to make an appearance were making rounds around the estate, so they were rounding back to the front from either side when they paused and gave conde-scending looks.

Then they were running for them.

Sparrow took a step back and whispered down to her without taking his eyes off of the men. "Ready, Ro?"

Rosaelia stepped up and took a large breath in. "Ready."

She knew Evony's magic must've slowed them down because by the time one of them got to her, Rosaelia had her dagger coming down into his chest. His eyes froze, and then blood bubbled out of his mouth when she pulled the dagger out.

He fell back, and Rosaelia was momentarily frozen at the sight of her first kill.

She felt a little sick but absolutely no remorse.

It made her smile as her gaze shot to the other one, and she swung her arm out, scraping through his chest before using those basic dagger switching techniques Killian had taught her to get the weapon in a forward position before depositing it into the man's gut.

She knew as the man fell that her sister's magic was the only thing making this possible. Knew that if Evony wasn't there then these men would be much faster and actually be able to make it out from under her. In the past, that would've made Rosaelia feel like a damsel. Useless.

But now, she understood that there was nothing wrong with asking for help. She was a very brand-new trainee and the good girl Killian always reminded her of, so doing this much was impressive enough.

They left the two bodies on the ground as they moved in.

Sparrow didn't try to push her back and protect her when they entered and multiple eyes shot their way. Rosaelia knew part of the reason was knowing his wife had her magic up, but she also knew that he trusted her to be able to take care of herself now that he'd seen that she hadn't hesitated with those men.

All four men rushed for them, and Rosaelia was aware of her brother and sister deadlocking two of them to give her the time she required with the other two, and she was thankful.

The men eyed her like they believed her adorable that she could hurt them. The same ridiculing look most people sent the *spoiled Princess*.

Rosaelia allowed them to get close before swiping her dagger in a full one-eighty so it cut straight through both men's abdomens.

Then she turned for the one Evony had. Her sister released the man and let him stumble out so Rosaelia could hook him with the dagger straight in the stomach. Blood started bubbling out of his mouth as he fell to his knees, but Rosaelia had learned one vital bit of information from her brother—don't leave them to die slowly, they could always find a way to survive that way.

So she kneed beside him and stabbed him in the heart. Then did the same with the other two.

When Rosaelia turned to Sparrow, the man was unconscious in his deadlock. She quirked her brow at her brother, and he merely gave an embarrassed shrug, like he hadn't realized he'd used so much strength because he truly wanted all of these kills to be hers.

"Drop him, Spar. It's okay. You forget the power you have."

With the man tumbled on the ground, Rosaelia kneed beside him and stabbed him through the heart.

On her feet, Sparrow stopped her with a touch to the shoulder. "How are we doing, Ro?"

"Good." Honestly. She didn't feel remorse for them or any ill will toward herself. She felt good for ridding them from hurting Killian, or any Islander, ever again.

Sparrow winked. "Good. Now let's get through this because it's taking too much of my control to allow my wife and sister around these animals without shredding them apart."

Rosaelia laughed as she met her sister's eyes. Maybe Evony had been extra right in not telling Sparrow yet. If he knew, he'd have destroyed this entire place without asking them their opinions simply to make sure his wife and child were safe. As much as Rosaelia appreciated his love for them, she needed to do these herself. She needed Killian to finish this himself.

So they moved.

From room to room, finding different men that either Sparrow or Evony held off on their own or knocked out so they couldn't rush at her and she could kill. Rosaelia had cleaned her dagger off on her dress three times now and was blood splattered from all the killings and yet, she felt nothing but excitement that they wouldn't be able to bother her male any longer.

Sparrow and Evony were blood splattered as well from the remnants of any flying spurts from her killings or from the sucker punches they themselves threw at the men.

It took a while, each room silenced with Evony's magic so as not to alert the estate until they made it through. She knew it would've taken a fraction of the time with only the two Masters taking care of matters, but she appreciated that they gave this to her.

After the mess they'd made of the estate, bodies littering the place, Rosaelia finally made it to the room Killian had told her about after having rehashed his past with Keir.

It was the estate's main office, and everyone knew the owner used it himself. Killian had done so before and Keir did so now.

And he'd told her exactly where it was, so Rosaelia knew where she was going to find the one man responsible for all of this.

She motioned for Sparrow and Evony not to follow her as she opened the door and stepped in.

Keir's head snapped up, a threat for interrupting him on his tongue when he noticed who was before him and the state she was in.

He was a handsome man, possibly her father's age, but there was greed and a cruelness in his eyes that took away any bit of attraction. His light skin balanced well with his dark hair and brows. His light hazel eyes would be inviting if his intentions weren't blatantly written within them.

He stood from behind his desk and showed Rosaelia that he was a tall man at possibly six-three or four. As tall as the men of her life, if leaner than said men.

"You're Killian's woman." He gave her a grin that didn't look pleasing in the least.

Rosaelia closed the door behind her. "I am."

"Yet you are here, darling." He stepped around his desk and stopped before it, leaning into it as he eyed her body. "Do you please to ask me for something, sweetheart? Maybe to show your body a good time?"

She gave a sweet smile. "Killian's taken care of my body plenty."

"Yet you still came to me."

Cocky son of a bitch. Rosaelia was shocked with herself for the language even in her mind, but she couldn't help it. That's what he was.

"Does it not bother you that I look like this?" Rosaelia changed the subject. "Do you not wonder how I must've gotten in this state?"

He eyed her a moment before his gaze shot to that door she'd come in from. From the light in his eyes, he picked up what must've happened. "There's no way you killed all of them."

She smirked. "Isn't there?"

He stood tall now. "You truly believe you can kill me, little girl?"

She wore that sweet smile again as she slowly shook her head. "I don't want to kill you."

His eyes widened with hope, and disturbingly, desire. "No?"

Her head shook tentatively. "That will be Kill's prize."

Keir's jaw ground together, and he looked to be thinking over his choices. Rosaelia wasn't sure if he'd come to the conclusion that hurting a claimed woman—Killian's claimed woman—would end him in a way nothing else could or if he'd realized she must be talented enough to get through all of his men without his hearing a sound.

Whichever it was, he seemed to settle on his decision. He turned for the door behind Rosaelia and moved for it. Rosaelia watched him go without moving.

When he opened the door, he skidded to a stop when Sparrow came out of nowhere, his size large and domineering. "Hello, friend."

"Who—who're you?" Keir stumbled back.

"You may call me Master." Sparrow grinned wickedly at the man.

Keir didn't wait around to ask questions, he merely turned to run in the opposite direction where Rosaelia saw the double doors to his balcony.

Then skirted to a stop when Evony grinned after he opened those doors. How she got there was a mystery, but Rosaelia figured it was all her magic's doing. "You may call me Master as well."

Keir's frantic gaze turned back to where Rosaelia stood analyzing him. "I'd like you to meet my brother and sister, Keir." Her smirk turned sinister. "You messed with the wrong person's mate."

CHAPTER 37
KILLIAN

Keir was on his knees at the front door to his house.

Beside him, a blood-splattered Sael.

Killian didn't know what to think as his gaze jumped from both Masters standing behind them to his woman to the man on his knees, both trembling in fear and glaring at him with utter hatred.

"Sael," he growled but forced his voice to remain calm. "Why are you covered in blood?"

His heart raced. If she had been hurt and he hadn't been there to help her...

Her lips gave a little smirk that made his cock jump. She was never cocky, but this look was definitely enthralling on his princess. "I told you last week that I would kill them for you."

His eyes widened, and his breath left him as realization dawned. "Sael."

"They were all her kills to take." Sparrow's deep voice came from beyond. "And she didn't hesitate, barbarian. When your life is on the line, she won't hesitate. We saw that today."

Killian stared at his princess with disbelief before his body pumped with too much adrenaline telling him she went to that house and killed all of them, put herself in harm's way, for him.

Then he was moving, rushing for her, and taking her face between his hands as his lips forced hers open. He had her pushed against a wall and kissed her savagely. Feeling her tongue against his was the only thing keeping him sane at the moment.

She could've been killed. *Sparrow wouldn't have allowed it,* his inner voice reminded him.

She could've gotten hurt. *Evony wouldn't have allowed it.*

She had to live with it for the rest of her life. *She was more powerful than any of them. That spark in her eyes said she was okay with that fact. She never minded hearing about your attacks on Keir's men.*

His breathing was ragged as he pulled away from the kiss only enough to speak, lips still brushing with the need to steal her air. His hands shook as they held her face between them. "You're okay?"

She nodded, staring up at him with those bright, proud eyes. "I brought him for you. I know you need to take care of him yourself."

His lips brushed hers as he breathed her in, eyes closing to take in this moment. "You're all I care about, Sael. *You're* all I need." *And you could've been hurt, you priceless little thing.*

He knew, in that moment, he was certain that as long as he had Sael by his side, he didn't care about what happened to Keir. It was a happy coincidence that she caught the man for him, but she was truly his beginning and end.

Her breathing hitched, chest hitting his with each inhalation, as her brows furrowed and those emerald-greens stared at him like he was everything. "Killian..."

Her lips moved to form words but nothing more came out.

She didn't need to say any more for Killian to hear the words. He felt them pierce through his chest.

He nodded. "I know, Sael. Me too."

THE MORON TWINS were coming in more useful than Killian cared to admit. They both rolled their eyes every time he ordered them to do something but did so without complaint. He knew it was partly just to be helpful because of the situation he was taking care of, but Killian also understood it was because of his position. As Sael's male, he was also their Princess's mate, meaning he outranked all of them.

Killian wasn't particularly fond of the status, but it was working for him at the moment.

They dragged Keir between them as the whole house moved for town square. Killian didn't care if they came or stayed behind, this was all for himself, but they seemed insistent to be there. His nonas, who understood how much he needed this more than anyone else would, clung to each of Norya's arms as they came.

Miels and Tristan moved for the pole Killian pointed to in the middle of the square, the townsfolk pausing and hushing as they realized what was happening—a vice versa of the same events of seven years ago.

Except Killian didn't want to use a dagger. Keir deserved something else.

And Killian had no thoughts of leaving Keir to bleed out. He would make sure the man was dead before stepping foot out of the square. He wouldn't make Keir's mistake.

Killian dropped the box he'd been carrying without letting go of Sael's hand which he held in his other. Her friends readied Keir for him, and he could hear the whispers all around the square. He could already imagine how much worse it would get when they learned that all of Keir's men were killed earlier and the entire estate was up for the taking.

When Keir was placed and everyone stepped away from the pole, Killian didn't move. Having Keir in the same position he'd been in seven years ago was therapeutic.

He still remembered the feel of the cold air hitting his torso and back as he waited against the pole for what Keir had planned. It was much warmer now that they were in summer but in the twilight air leading to dusk, the temperature would be dropping soon. Nowhere near how cold he'd bared it, but cool enough to send shivers through a man.

He remembered the way his heart had beat strapped there with no way to defend himself. It had been a true weakness he'd never experienced before, and a naiveté on his part.

Killian scoffed inwardly. He'd ridiculed his princess for being naive when she came to the Island, but he had been far more naive at her age. And like the men who attacked her in the alleyway—a fact that still sent Killian's blood boiling—had taught her, that incident with Keir seven years ago had taught him. They were no longer innocent in the ways they had been before.

Finally, Killian turned in his spot and released Sael's hand only to cradle her face in both of his. "This is going to be ugly, princess."

Those soft hands of hers traced his forearms until they circled his wrists. "And I'll be here for you the entire time."

"That doesn't mean you have to watch. I wouldn't blame you, be offended in any way if you need to—"

"I'm staying, Killian. I killed all of his men. I didn't enjoy it the same way you don't. They needed to die. So have this final retribution, and you can finally stop killing."

He could finally stop killing?

What made her think he wanted to? How did she *know*?

"Sael..."

She gave a tentative smile. "I'm the quieter twin. It also makes me the more observant one. Every story about your horrors has been you killing for retribution, Kill. And every time you tell me about them, you freeze in fear I'll hate you because you hate that you kill so much. Your family's gone, and Keir's line will be gone after today. You'll be free."

He gave an internal scoff at her perceptiveness as he shook his head, lips tipping up as he leaned down to kiss her. "Thank you, princess."

She kissed him softly. "You're welcome, barbarian."

Sael pulled away before he could try to convince her not to watch again and moved for their family where she stood between Sparrow and Nona Eleni.

Killian took in Keir as he stood against that pole. He didn't beg for Killian to spare him, and for that, Killian respected him. He hated when they cowered and begged for forgiveness. Killian himself had stood strong as Keir had bled him seven years prior.

After a long minute, Killian reached for the box he'd carried along with him. Inside was a flail. The edges of the spiked ball were sharp as he grabbed for the wooden handle and let the weapon dangle by the chain that held the ball.

Keir's eyes widened at the weapon, but he didn't cower. He knew, had always known, that eventually Killian would get to him. And he'd always been aware that it twould be an ugly way to go.

But as Killian stood there, the same anger didn't come up. He still hated Keir, but the tortures he'd dreamed of for seven years didn't matter any longer. It was more imperative to end

Keir now because he'd allowed Eran to go after Sael than because of what he'd done to Killian.

Killian made a slow walk around the man tied to the pole, the stares of everyone in town on him. After a full round, Killian stopped at the man's back and took a large breath in. He caught Sael's eyes for a moment and met the unconditional loyalty in her orbs—this won't scare her away, her emerald-greens said.

With his gaze back on the man's back, Killian swung the weapon and watched with delight as the spiked ball struck into his back. His roar was loud as multiple wounds opened.

Killian gave him a moment before striking again, the wounds opening in different areas, covering his entire back.

That had been for what had been done to him seven years prior.

Then again.

For the family he'd had to kill to get the house they lived in now.

Again.

For all of Keir's other victims.

Again.

For any threat—Eran especially—Keir ever made toward his woman.

Again.

For his sanity that was taken from him that day. To finally getting it back because of his princess.

Keir's back was gashed open and bleeding out so much, there was a likelihood he was already dead, but Killian needed this final part.

He moved around the pole until he was standing before the man, barely there breaths still escaping him as blood pooled out of his mouth.

Killian gripped his shoulder to steady him and leaned in

close so only he would hear. "This final one. This one's for the life I'll leave behind here. For the savagery that has no room in my princess's life."

He pulled the small knife from the back of his pants and pierced Keir's heart, the life leaving him immediately.

Blood smattered the ground around the pole, under every step Killian took back until he was simply looking at his handi-work. All was quiet as every person took in what this meant— the estate was his once again.

He let out a relieved sigh to finally be gone of the man and turned for the townsfolk. "Keir is gone. Every one of his lackeys are gone. The estate is mine now, and I have decided the No Known Housing will take up residence there. Try to argue, and you'll join Keir up here."

CHAPTER 38

KILLIAN

Killian hardly paid the others any mind as he held Sael's hand tight in his and led her to the back bathing chamber. She'd insisted since her friends showed up that they not bathe together—even though said friends knew exactly what they did when they were alone—but Killian couldn't heed that command any longer. And especially not after the day they'd had.

Sael was still blood matted, and he had a fresher set on his body. They both needed the wash, and Killian wanted nothing more than to be the one to clean his woman.

Thankfully, she didn't argue with him when he closed the door behind himself and locked them in the bathing chamber. Instead, she reached for the laces at the front of her dress.

"Don't," Killian commanded, delighted as her hands instantly froze. He moved for her and softly replaced her hands with his. "I will undress you, princess. I will wash you. I will take care of you."

She stared at him with more trust than Killian was accustomed to. "And I you, my barbarian."

He didn't react to her words, but he knew she could read it in his eyes, he wouldn't have been able to hide it even if he wanted to—thank you. Thank you for the gift you've given in delivering Keir. Thank you for looking at all of the scars and feeling nothing but affection. Thank you for staring the monster in the eyes and telling him he was everything you wanted. *Thank you for choosing me.*

Killian slipped her dress down her body, thankful that most of the blood was matted there and not on her skin.

He dropped to his knee when she was naked and reached for the strapped dagger that he'd been responsible for taking off every night since the moment she began wearing it. It was one of his favorite parts of the day, only beat by the taste of Sael on his tongue and the feel of her around his cock.

He pulled on the strap slowly, teasing her thigh with the brush of his fingertips and the slow slide of the leather off her leg. She didn't try to hide her heavy breathing, but she also didn't try to rush him. She simply watched him as he worked.

The dagger had been cleaned between her spree of killings and delivering Keir to him, but Killian would give it a thorough washing and a sharpening in the morning to make sure it was in top shape for his woman.

When she was completely bare in front of him, Killian rose to his feet and ogled his princess.

She allowed it for a moment before she stepped up to him, hands already untucking his shirt as she whispered against the skin at the opening to his shirt. "My turn."

Because of the bagginess of his shirt and the violence of the way he took Keir out, there was more blood on his skin than hers. His chest and arms were matted with it, but she didn't seem perturbed in the least.

Sael moved slowly, peeling his shirt away before dropping

to the ties of his trousers, all the while never breaking eye contact.

"I love your eyes," she whispered against his skin. "They're such a deep hazel. They make me think of honey. I've always loved honey."

"Yours make me think of freedom," he whispered back, voice hoarse and full of honesty.

The cute way she crinkled her nose made him smile.

"That green. It makes me think of the greens out in the forests and on the lands with nothing but grass in all directions. It's freeing—no expectations, no violence, nothing but your own thoughts and will."

She smiled at him with more emotion than Killian could put into words before she sighed and pointed to the bath. "Can I clean you first?"

"If you wish."

It only meant he could take more time on her since she wouldn't be insisting it was time he got clean too.

Sael tugged him to the bath where the water was full and steaming, Evony's magic on the place would no doubt keep it hot for far longer than was normal.

Sael stepped into the large tub, then tugged on his hand for him to follow along. Killian didn't say a word as he did as she wanted.

When they were both within, she pushed softly on his chest so he'd sit back, then dropped to her knees between his bent legs. She lathered her hands, then met his gaze again, never once breaking, as she started at his chest.

She made thorough work, moving from one collarbone to the next, down his chest, over each pectoral, down to his stomach. Over each ab, then up his sides to his shoulders. She moved softly around his neck, thumbs soothingly running circles as both hands circled his throat.

Her eyes glinted when she had him in that position causing a small smirk to grace Killian's lips. "I will always be at your mercy, princess."

She didn't say anything but leaned in to kiss his lips.

Then she continued to clean his body. Her hands slipped from his throat to one arm, starting at the shoulder and slowly making her way down to his hand, giving each finger its attention before kissing the tip of each one and allowing his hand to fall back to the side of the tub. She repeated the actions on his other arm until most of the blood was off of him, all the while staring into his eyes.

When she finished, she lathered her hands with more soap before they disappeared into the water.

She started with one foot, massaging at it before circling his ankle and slowly moving up, massaging and cleaning his calf, then the back of his knee, then his thigh. When she was so close to his cock, it bobbed and hit her, a small smirk quirked her lips and she switched to the other leg, starting again at his foot.

Killian was impressed with how well he kept himself together, but he enjoyed this view. He loved being taken care of by her.

When she reached the top of his thigh this time and his cock twitched against her arm, begging her for attention, she gave it to him. She took him in both hands and softly stroked him, not to get him off but to clean him—and tease him.

Then she had him drop his head into the water to clean his hair, and when he sat back up, she tipped her head back. It gave him a beautiful view of her breasts as she got the blood out of her hair.

When she was all done, she pulled on the pulley that would empty the tub, and when all the blood from their bodies was gone with the water, she replaced the pulley and pushed down the tab that would send more hot water into the tub. Then she redid her entire earlier dance, this time washing off the lathered soap on his body in the cleaner waters.

Once all the soap was off of him and he truly was clean, she gave him a warm smile and leaned in to kiss his throat, right where her hands had been holding him only minutes ago.

"My turn?" he asked but was in no rush. Her hands were like magic the way they soothed every part of him.

She nodded slowly. "Your turn, my love."

He swallowed before turning off the stream of water, then reached into the water, hands dragging up her thighs until they reached around, and pulled at her body until she was straddled over his hips.

With her hands featherlight on his shoulders, Killian reached around to lather his hands, then began his own slow exploration of her body. Most of the dried blood was already off, but he took his time, being more thorough than even she had been, as he cleaned her.

He started with her feet, moved up her ankles, massaged her calves to the backs of her knees, and lazed over her thighs. Her wiggle over his lap as he took his extra time there made a small smile rise on his lips.

Then his hands moved for her behind, cupping both cheeks and massaging them. The way her fingernails dug into his shoulders told Killian how hard she was trying not to move. He was enthralled as one hand continued kneading and the other slipped between the cheeks, a single digit entering her hole. Her gasp and back arch were involuntary then, but her eyes glinted with how much she enjoyed the intrusion as they continued to stare into his.

His finger moved slowly as it thrust into her, going a little deeper each time until his entire finger was filling her. She wiggled her hips like she wanted to slip his cock in—more restraint on her part than Killian would've given her credit for.

That's when he pulled his finger and reached for more soap to lather his hands. Sael was obviously frustrated, but she didn't stop him.

Once lathered, his hands landed on her hips and slowly kneading up, from her sides to her stomach, to her back, to her breasts—which got extra attention—until finally, his hands wrapped around her throat. He copied her soothing circles as he held her there and watched as she breathed hard.

"Killian, I'm gonna come. I... this is... I need to come."

He finally released her neck and let his hands skim down her body. "And you will, Sael." His hands clasped around her waist. "But first, we need to go to bed."

She looked like she wanted to argue, that defiant look blazing in her emerald-greens, but she didn't say a word as he washed her completely clean, then lifted her out of the bath and slung a towel around her form. Killian took his time drying her body before drying himself off as well.

"How come I can't dry you?" She pouted.

He took that sad bottom lip with his thumb and soothed it over. "I can only control myself so much, princess. The monster needs to be inside you."

That hungry look he was obsessed with took over the irritation in her green orbs, and she said nothing more as he wrapped them both in towels so they could move from the bathing chamber to their room without flashing anyone who may be in the halls.

He took her hand softly as they moved—undisturbed—to their room.

Killian had the door locked behind him the moment they were inside and dropped the towel from around his waist. He loved that she was already propped on her knees on the bed when he turned around, towel forgotten on the ground. It reminded him of their first couple of times together. His innocent, pretty little princess.

"Is the barbarian still allowed to do whatever he wishes to you, Princess?"

Her smile was wide, and her gaze heated. "Always."

CHAPTER 39

ROSAELIA

"Where are the nonas?" Ashtyn asked.

"They went with Norya to help with the members of the No Known Housing as they're figuring out the specifics of taking over Keir's estate now that he's gone."

"It's a lot of space. It'll be good for them. Rightful that they get such a large residence," Evony said from her spot on Sparrow's lap.

Gabriel gave his small smile, seated at the table while he carved at the wood in his hands. "Maybe Rowena burning down the place was a blessing in disguise."

They all scoffed, but Rosaelia couldn't argue, they all agreed with him. Had she not done that, Killian would've let the estate up for the taking of whichever Islander won out. This way, no one needed to fight for the spot, and those who truly required such space would take it.

"Ro," Tristan called. "He's out hunting. I doubt your standing by that window will make him come back any faster."

331

Rosaelia tried to ignore him as her cheeks pinked. She'd been waiting for Killian. She couldn't help it.

He was out hunting for a large beast for a family party one of the neighbors was having. They were paying him by trading delicacies that the nonas loved, so Killian had no intentions of denying their trade.

Rosaelia loved that about him—the fact that everything he did was for his nonas.

And he had no intentions of letting the Posse join him. He didn't say so, but Rosaelia knew this was also a break from her friends.

So she remained by the window as the others did their own things within the house. They'd taken care of Keir, who was Killian's biggest problem. Now they needed to finish with Rowena, then Rosaelia could speak with Killian about his moving to the North with her. She was sure the nonas would want to, but would he?

"I should head to the inn," Miels stated to the whole room.

"Why?" Rosaelia asked. Why would any of them stay at an inn?

He smiled. "It's where we stayed the night we first arrived. We paid for a week's visit and a little extra, so if there was any information about Rowena, we'd know."

"Plus, this way, if Rowena does try to look for us, she'll think we're staying there and not here," Sparrow added.

Clever.

Especially when dealing with Rowena. She would definitely look for their stay.

And if she got word that a group had checked in with bribes to keep quiet, she would know it was the Posse. And where the Posse went, Rosaelia would follow. Their entire group would be taken care of together.

It frightened her a bit. Would Rowena go after that inn just to end them? Would she burn it down like she did the No Known Housing? Would she—

A flicker of movement caught Rosaelia's attention through the window. She focused on it to make sure it wasn't Killian or Norya. Another second passed, and she saw it again.

It was a large male, his long blonde hair tied at his back. Rosaelia paid close attention to make sure he wasn't simply an Islander passing through when she caught sight of another male toward the other end of the house's front.

"Guys," she muttered as the two males took out machetes, then louder, "Guys!"

"What is it?" Tristan was at her side.

She tried to point with her chin in case they saw her. She didn't want to alert them that she was aware of their presence.

Tristan watched them for a moment, testing whether this was a threat.

Then Rosaelia knew it was because there she was.

Rowena, long lost Queen of the Northern Lands and her mother. She stood with a vial in hand and six more Islanders at her sides, then gone.

"Rowena!" Tristan called, then to the Magician. "She's got a vial, Eve."

Rosaelia felt Evony's magic with the force and speed it spread through the house only half a second before Rowena was back. She tossed the vial, and an explosion bombed only ten feet from the house. From the looks of it, Evony's shield was the only thing keeping any of it from nearing the house.

"Come get me!" Rowena mocked, then dropped another vial of the wild flames. Right where she was standing.

The two men beside her lit up in flames immediately, screaming—something that would be ignored out in the Island—but she was fine.

"Wherever she got these potions," Miels muttered. "She has the antidote. Probably doused in it before coming here."

Smart. In case the flames got out of hand and got to her. She'd be fine either way.

"Cover me, baby. I'm gonna get her," Sparrow mumbled to Evony.

"I can't," she spoke, and it was clear she was growing tired which was shocking. As a Master, she should be able to hold more magic than this. Was this an effect of her pregnancy? "I won't be able to hold this on both you and the house. It's a strong sorcerer's potion. If I had to guess, one she got from the Master before she was betrayed."

Sparkling flames were lighting her everywhere, beginning to catch onto the trees surrounding the area. If this continued much longer, this entire side of the Island would be alight with sorcerer fire.

"We need to stop it before the flames rea—"

"Come get me, *Killian!*" Rowena called out again. "Or are your nonas alone in there?"

Rosaelia's heart stopped.

"We're meant to be staying at the inn," Gabriel summarized.

"And Killian's family is meant to be here alone," Rosaelia finished.

Her heart stopped. Rowena had come for them. Wanted to burn them simply because Killian was hers.

"No," she barely got out. "No. They were meant to be here. She would've gotten them if Evony wasn't here. Because of me!"

Tristan's hands on her shoulders soothed her. "Calm down, Ro."

"What do we need to stop some of this?" Sparrow asked his wife.

"I need her to stop adding to it," Evony answered. "Then I'll be able to focus and control it."

He nodded. "Hopefully this'll stop her rather than ignite her anymore," he said as he stepped out of the house, and they all followed.

Evony stayed back on the threshold of the door as she focused on the flames. Rosaelia worried for her in her current condition, but at the moment, she was glad Sparrow didn't know about it.

From the look on Rowena's face, she definitely hadn't expected them to be there.

Before Rosaelia could question what Sparrow could possibly do trapped on this side of the shield, the Assassin picked up a more slender piece of log Killian had cut earlier in the week and threw it straight for the long-dead Queen. Because of his Masterhood, the thing moved so fast it was hard to keep track of it with the naked eye.

But Rowena still got out of the way.

Barely.

She cursed out as her shoulder started bleeding. Sparrow didn't delight in the sound. Instead, he already had another log flying at her and another in his hands, ready to go.

It was keeping Rowena distracted so Evony's magic was able to control the flames beating around the house, but Rosaelia wasn't sure how long this would last. They needed the deranged woman gone.

She needed to protect this beautiful Island family from her psychotic mother. She was the reason Rowena knew of them. She couldn't be their demise when all the nonas, Norya, and Killian have been was welcoming.

Rosaelia thought back to all that time she'd spent with Alana and ran back into the house. She'd kept a small bag of vials that Alana had given her by the box she'd kept for Sparrow. There were small labels on them. She couldn't remember what they were, but hopefully one helped.

From the bag, she pulled out a vial—for soothing burns—and another—for slowing the body down—and another and another. None of them seeming to be of use. She needed something that would hurt Rowena, not soothe her.

Then she came across another vial—for clearing potions. It was one used when the wrong potion was used. Almost like erasing words on a letter because they weren't the right ones.

She didn't think. Simply grabbed it and ran.

Outside, Rowena had taken cover but there was another bout of flames sparkling so Rosaelia knew the woman had thrown another. Sparrow—along with Miels, Tristan, and Gabriel—were throwing logs, keeping her distracted and busy. The men around Rowena were dead, either by the flames she'd caused or the logs, and it was only her left.

Rosaelia moved fast. She reached the edge of Evony's shield where she could feel the light breeze of the flames' heat and threw the vial at Rowena. If it worked like she thought, it would wipe away the antidote Rowena had coated herself in and she would be in danger against the flames as well.

Rosaelia held her breath as she waited, and nothing happened.

Then, to her relief, Rowena moved as if opening a clear shot to throw another bout of sorcerer's fire when she yelped with the heat coming off the fires around her. Her eyes widened, and she took cover behind a tree once more so she wasn't a live target for the boys.

She screamed again, and Rosaelia knew the fires were beginning to affect her. There was another loud noise, then the sound of Rowena running off.

It was clear the boys wanted to chase after her, but they all stopped at the edge of the shield. Until Evony could calm the fires down and douse them completely, the safest place for them was behind this shield. Plus, if Rowena had been caught by those flames, she would need to get herself back home and apply some remedy—one Rosaelia was certain the woman kept in stock in case of moments like this. Because Rowena was cocky, but she was also cautious. It's what made her so smart and able to come this far. She was always cautious.

They all breathed heavily, staring out into the distance around the house in case any movement was noticed. But there wouldn't be. Anyone attacking them was either dead or long gone by then.

This was what was best. When Killian's family came home, they didn't need to be met with resistance. They'd already have this carnage to come to.

Oh, what a mess she'd made of their lives.

CHAPTER 40
ROSAELIA

She'd been so close to telling him she loved him the other night.

When he'd kissed her after seeing Keir on his knees for the first time. In the bath with her hands wrapped around his throat, listening to his declaration. When he'd had his hands wrapped around her neck. When he'd taken her hand softly in his to lead her to their room—always her leader, her protector.

She wanted more than anything to do so, but she wanted even more so to keep him safe. So she was glad she hadn't said it. There would've been no way to keep him away if he knew how she truly felt for him.

She was going to keep him, and his nonas and Norya, safe. And that meant keeping him away from her mother and whatever problems may come with her. Maybe her mind had known that even when her heart hadn't wanted to.

Maybe that's what had stopped her every time she came close to saying the words. If she'd said them, there was no way Killian would believe anything about her not wanting him. The only way to keep him safe would be if he let her go, if he believed her the spoiled Princess he once had.

Her friends were out in the front yard by an apple tree that had somehow survived the carnage Rowena had done to the forest surrounding the home. The others were inside, Killian giving her time with her friends as his family planned what to do with the mess that was their yard now.

None of them had been angry when they got home to spot the tarnished mess Rowena's flames had left behind.

All of them had been worried. For the Posse's wellbeing only. They didn't care for the house.

Killian had been the last to arrive, and Rosaelia would have the image of him running into the house after seeing the carnage outside to spot her, to make sure she was unhurt, forever burned in her memory.

Now they were trying to deal with the aftermath of Rowena's destruction.

Sparrow held Evony on his shoulders while Ashtyn climbed the tree to pick some apples that still looked fresh for eating. The other three stood below, ready to catch if either one fell.

"Enjoying yourselves?" Rosaelia smirked at them. It was these little moments, when they could find amusement in the mess, that made them the close-knit Posse the North knew them to be.

Tristan grinned. "Extremely."

She watched them another few minutes before opening, humor gone, "We need to leave. Deal with Rowena. We need to take care of it without hurting this family."

They all froze and turned on her. Ashtyn slowly climbed down, Gabriel's hands lining her hips in case of a need to steady, and Evony slid down Sparrow's body.

"But Killian—" Evony started.

"Is safer without me. No Islander is stupid enough to go

after him, and I've already spoken with a sorcerer I know to line these lands with the antidote to any more flames. He's been paid well and instructed to check on the house and add more potions for its safety, every day. I trust him. He'll do it." That one sorcerer was probably the best thing that could've come out of her partnership with Alana.

And maybe finding out a little bit about why she'd left Sparrow and his father.

Rosaelia had gone to him early in the morning, somehow able to pull away from Killian without his realizing and was back in time for him to think she had merely been outside the entire time. She hated lying to him.

"He's been through enough," Rosaelia finalized. "I can't put him through any more."

"Don't you think leaving him will put him through worse than whatever got him those scars?" Miels asked, pain in his eyes, no doubt remembering the time Etel had refused him.

Rosaelia shook her head, partly to keep her tears from lining her eyes and partly to convince herself she was doing the right thing. "It's not only about Killian. There's Norya, and—"

"Norya's a warrior. She's the least of our worries in battle," Tristan defended.

Rosaelia caught his gaze and held it, wondering if it was more than just sex between them. They'd both told her plenty of times now how much they enjoyed one another's bodies but didn't need more. Rosaelia wasn't sure, as she searched his eyes, if that had changed within him.

Or maybe he truly saw her capabilities. Rosaelia knew if nothing else, they would make great friends.

"There're the nonas too." She decided not to poke on about Norya. "After everything they've done for me, everything they've been through in the past. I can't put them in more harm." She stood taller and forced her eyes to remain dry. With the memory of what their own family had done to them—stories her friends didn't know—she couldn't add to their struggles. She needed to protect them. "I am a Princess, and that comes with making difficult decisions. As hard as it might be, it will keep them safe. And off of Rowena's radar. If, for any reason, we can't kill her, I need them away from her. If she sees I'm no longer taking interest in them, maybe she'll stay away."

Hopefully. She was so tired of relying on hopefullys.

"Killian won't allow you to just walk away from him, Princess," Gabriel responded softly.

I will always be at your mercy, princess.

"Killian thinks I love him," she forced out. "I don't need to say the words for him to think it. When he hears that I do not, he will be forced to remember that I am nothing but the spoiled Princess who uses people and then throws them aside."

"But you do, Emerald," Ashtyn muttered. "Clear as day."

"And it will be my pain to bear as long as it keeps them safe."

"No, Ro," Miels argued but put no force into it. He sounded like he knew she'd made up her mind. "It will be his pain to bear as equally. Even worse if he believes you don't love him in return." It was clear in Miels's eyes as he stared at her—*I cannot imagine Etel not loving me back. It would kill me.*

"He has his family. He has more important people to love and care for."

"You know that's not true, sister," Sparrow whispered, just loud enough for them all to hear. "He loves you."

You're all I care about, Sael. You're all I need.

"I need to do this for them. For you, Spar. Then, if they allow me, I can come back to them, to him. But I need to do this."

"I know." He stepped out from behind his wife and cradled

Rosaelia's face in his hand. "But you also have to understand how much it's going to kill him."

Rosaelia held her breath, heart already broken at the pit of her stomach with the knowledge of the pain she was going to put her barbarian through. "I know."

CHAPTER 41

KILLIAN

Sael was outside with her friends giving Killian his only opportunity to be alone with his family. They'd spent the entire night making sure everyone had been all right after Rowena's attack and plenty of the morning speaking of the cost to get sorcerers to deal with the mess the land had taken from all those sparked flames.

They needed a break from speaking of so much gruesomeness, and Killian had the perfect distraction. He wanted to show the three other women of his life the rings he'd been playing with in his pocket for days now.

"Look at you, Kill," Nona Tereza teased. "When you brought her here that first time, you didn't want to accept her as your woman, and now you cannot keep your eyes off of her."

The glass doors that led to their back greens, where Sael and her friends now sat after having picked apples from the front, gave Killian a perfect view of her profile. She wasn't laughing, none of them were, but that didn't worry Killian. On top of the hunt to find and kill her mother, she was a Princess and there were probably political matters she was being reminded of.

Not to mention the very recent moments she'd had with her mother.

"She's so beautiful, Nona," he whispered, uncaring that the words made him sound weak. "I cannot stop. It feels physically impossible."

All three women laughed around the table, but it was Nona Eleni who spoke. "You have claimed her, Kill. From the moment you saw her, she has been yours. Do you intend to be marked too?"

So anyone who wasn't from their town, or knew of them, would know that he was taken. That she was taken if she agreed to the markings. To the claimed marital markings, not the simple marital markings.

The simple ones were for the couples who united for their own gains, not because they were claimed to one another.

"She is the Princess of the Northern Lands, Nona. I highly doubt she would mark her hand in Islander customs."

"But she has marked her body with an Islander," Norya teased.

Killian's gaze drifted to Rosaelia's neck where the fading lines of his fingers, and a fresher bite mark barely hidden by her dress, showed she was his.

"In any case"—Killian forced his gaze away from her, though it continued to fall back to her involuntarily as he turned to his family—"I am part Northern as well, so it would make sense to go with their customs."

"You will wear a ring? Like Sparrow has on his finger?" Nona Tereza asked, astonished.

"Proudly."

"Well, well, well, brother. Quite in love indeed."

Killian's lips twitched into a mix of a grin and a smirk.

"Shut up, Nor. If I get her forever, you get to keep riding that spy's cock for the rest of your life."

She sat up straighter. "Well, then, what are you waiting for? Mate the girl."

He shook his head as he laughed, muttering under his breath at her, "Horny fucking bastard."

She licked her lips and fell back into her seat, eyes glazing over like she was in memory. "Mm, but he tastes so good, Kill. I could never have enough. He had to beg me to stop the other night because he'd come in my mouth four times and his body couldn't take any more."

He smirked. "And how many times did you come in his mouth?"

Her grin was so proud, her eyes shined along. "Seven."

Both nonas shook their heads at them, laughing alongside them—a fact Northerners would probably be appalled to see but was normal on the Island—before Killian turned back to the matter at hand. He pulled the box that carried the two rings from his pocket and held it tight in his fist. "I intend on mating her, whether it be with the markings"—he opened his fist to reveal the box—"or not."

They all stared wide-eyed at the black cube as Nona Tereza asked, "You've already made rings?"

He nodded as he opened the thing to show them the two pieces of metal. "I intend to ask her tonight. I wanted to wait until this mess with her mother was over, but I cannot bear it any longer."

"She won't mate you without her father around," Norya breathed out, still staring at the rings in awe. Though she'd always insisted she never understood how anyone could desire someone else so much as to claim, she'd always been fascinated when people did.

After ridiculing them, she would study the couple to see

what it was that people desired so much. She'd been far more discreet with Killian's relationship, but he'd noticed her doing it with them too. She was happy for them, of course, especially knowing that deep down, it was what Killian wanted, but she couldn't understand it. Norya was the anomaly of the population—she didn't want a claiming. To her, the only things that made sense were unions and that was only if there was a good enough reason behind it.

For someone like Norya, a woman who could provide wholly for herself, there was never a good enough reason to tie herself to another.

But maybe if she ever found love, there could be. Killian couldn't imagine her falling in love ever, but maybe if she did, she could better understand him and every other claimed pairing, even ones like Sparrow and Evony who weren't claimed in exactly the same way as Islanders, but the theory was all the same.

Killian sighed. "I know. But at least I will know the moment we step into the palace, I can officially make her mine."

"So you hold no doubts then?" Nona Tereza asked. "You will move to the North with her?"

"I'd do anything for her," he answered without hesitation. "But I figured you three would come, that you two would want to go home."

Nona Eleni gave him a warm grin. "We would follow you anywhere, son."

Killian turned to Norya. "And you?"

Her hand landed on his forearm, and she caught his gaze. "I would follow you anywhere, brother."

He smiled wide at all three of them. "Then we will be moving to the North."

CHAPTER 42
ROSAELIA

He watched her differently that night. It still held the same affection he normally looked at her with, but there was something more to it. A happiness that wasn't normally there.

Rosaelia wasn't sure if she was merely imagining the look because she knew she was about to strip said happiness away or if there truly was something about him that night.

She wanted to ask him, to take him to their room and enjoy him one last time, to steal him away and live in a bubble where nothing else mattered. She wanted so much to love him the way Sparrow and Evony loved one another.

But he was currently in harm's way because of her, and Rosaelia would not be the reason he was thrust back into these messed up situations, constantly fighting and never seeing the light at the end.

Her friends, for their part, did well to keep the sadness off their faces. She knew it pained them to hurt the family in order to protect them. She knew it hurt them to leave said family, having grown to love them as strongly as Rosaelia did even in their short acquaintance. She knew as Tristan continued to find every excuse to touch Norya—currently massaging at her shoulders—that it pained him most out of all her friends to leave her behind. Even if it was merely a friends-with-benefits situation, they had a relationship, a friendship that was probably as dear to him as Miels's was, and Rosaelia wasn't giving Tristan the option to keep it.

At least, not until after they took care of Rowena, and she came back for this family. If they would have her.

She hated herself even more for that. Hated herself for the pain she would cause every person in the room.

Nona Eleni and Nona Tereza kept looking at her fondly, more so than in the weeks she'd been living there, and their smiles told Rosaelia how much they adored her. It all made her want to cry.

Forcing down the tears was almost as difficult as what she was about to do. She couldn't allow herself to feel the pain. Not yet.

Not now.

"My princess." Killian motioned for her to move for him with two fingers. She was currently leaning against the opposite wall, far from the others in the room. "Come here."

She swallowed, knowing this was her moment, and moved for him. He got up from his seat and stood before her, and the entire room grew silent. Her friends wore somber expressions, his family excited ones.

"Barbarian?" she barely got herself to mutter.

His smirk said he loved when she called him that as his hand fidgeted in his pocket.

"I was talking to my nonas earlier about the North, the palace in specific. I must admit, I'm more curious to see it now than I had been before." His eyes shined with their own little secret.

She wanted to know that little secret so desperately, but as she stared into those honey orbs, Rosaelia knew there were no more nice times ahead of them. This was it. This was when she'd break his heart and make it look like she was entitled to playing with people because of her status.

She hardened her gaze at him and made herself scowl. "Why would you go to the North at all, let alone the palace?" She wanted nothing more than to take him to the palace to introduce him to her father.

That shine disappeared, and a furrow dropped between his brows. "Sael... you're my woman."

Rosaelia hated herself more for the confused stutter he barely kept contained as he spoke. "I was your woman for as long as I was here, barbarian. For protection. I am the Princess. We're taught young how to use whatever is around for when we're in need, and I was in need of a stay. You were around."

She could tell by the look in his eyes he wasn't going to give her up that easily. As he went to argue, she forced a mocking laugh out. "It cannot be true. *You* truly thought I would choose you after I was done here? I thought those conversations were for jest."

"*You* came to *my* room, Sael." He still looked confused as the hurt began to fill those beautiful dark hazels.

Another hateful, cruel laugh. "For a fuck! My body reacted to you, barbarian, and it is very thankful for everything you've done to it. But that's all you've been—my use for protection, shelter, and a hot, skillful body."

"You spoke to me of the North, of the palace, of the things that happened, the things you thought I'd like to see," he argued.

"Because you're nobody in the North." Killian flinched, but Rosaelia forced herself to continue, "I could tell you things, spew out my thoughts, and not fear them getting out."

"You killed Keir's men. Brought him for me." The words were said through a gritted jaw as pain shone in his beautiful honey orbs.

"As payment! The crown does not favor staying in any debts." She shook her head in cruel disbelief. "You truly thought this would go past the Island? That I would take *you* to the North, anywhere near *my father*? A barbarian monster? You didn't strike me as a fool, Killian."

His gaze hardened now, the pain in his eyes moving over for fury. "Sael—"

"Oh, would you stop with that insufferable name," she interrupted.

She loved that name.

Especially off his tongue.

And she knew it pleased him to call her it. Knew this would be the final straw.

Because final straws were normally the small things, not the big ones. Killian would be able to look past her insinuations at using him, but that name had been meaningful. It'd been theirs. It was his.

And she was telling him she hated it.

"Take him to the North, to my father," she muttered under her breath as if she was in disbelief that he would ever come up with such a ridiculous plan. It was loud enough that she knew the others heard, saw the way the nonas flinched hearing it.

He was all fury now, standing taller and bigger, looking down at her as *the* monster and not *her* monster. She wasn't afraid though, her body reacted the same as it always had.

"*Princess,*" he seethed, his hands out of his pockets, gone with the fidgeting. Now they rested by his sides, fisted to keep himself controlled. "I apologize for assuming you more than the spoiled little palace doll. I guess I wanted to convince myself the woman I'd break celibacy for wasn't a complete moron." He stepped closer as if he could scare her when, in fact, she loved the monster in him. "Shall I assume this is your announcement that you will be leaving?"

Rosaelia forced her tears away the way she knew Killian was forcing his. He was angry now, but she knew deep down was the pained man who was finally done killing and wanted to live simply with his woman. "We can leave in the morni—"

"No," he interrupted. "You can leave now, Princess."

"But..." It got icy cold in the nights, and though it was still light out with the later days, it would begin to get cold soon.

He gave a cruel laugh this time. "I'm a barbarian monster, Princess, let's not forget that. You came to the Island on your own, figure out how to survive the night the same way. You have your lackeys here too. Steal a house with the Assassin or Magician. Frankly, I do not care. I want you out. Now."

As those words left him, Rosaelia had to pause. They'd told the family about the Masters. That was a dead giveaway that they were trusted and cherished.

But the Island didn't know much about the politics of the North and South. They probably thought this was public knowledge.

Not crying was hard. Not narrowing her eyes on him with annoyance and defiance was far more difficult than Rosaelia could've imagined. Even a lifetime of Princess training was nothing compared to this.

But she did so for him. Allowed him to hate her so he'd remain safe, growling in disgust if Rowena tried implying he had a relationship with the Princess. She could come back for him later. If he'd have her, ever trust her again.

Rosaelia turned to her friends and nodded toward the door. "Let's go."

They all stood, Tristan even playing it up with Norya and giving her a smug, 'you truly thought I would care for your lot' look before heading for the door. They'd come with nothing and would leave the same way, not needing to take anything from Killian's family.

"A final payment. For the shelter." Rosaelia dropped a bag of coin onto the table, knowing if she tried to hand it to any of them, it would cause more problems than it was worth, and turned to leave.

"Dove." Nona Eleni's soft voice stopped her. That soft, beautiful voice that was hardly ever heard.

With her back to them, Rosaelia swallowed to pull up that fake brave face, hardened her eyes, then faced the nonas, knowing they deserved that much. She made a small curtsey, then met their gazes. "Thank you for your hospitality."

She was out before either one could say a thing.

CHAPTER 43

KILLIAN

He was staring at the door where Sael had walked out ten minutes ago. He couldn't look away.

In the silence of the room, he could barely get his mind to catch up with what had just happened.

She left him.

Sael—no, Rosaelia—had left him. She wasn't Sael, probably never truly had been.

He scoffed inwardly. She played with him and deposited him. Ridiculed him for that name he'd given her, the one he wanted marked on his body. She laughed at him for truly growing attached.

Then walked away.

She left him.

The world came crashing down around him when Norya's soft voice interrupted the silence. "Kill..."

He growled, unable to hold himself together any longer. His hand found the box in his pocket and sent the thing flying through the room. It cracked against a window, but he didn't care.

"Killian," Nona Tereza said more forcefully but with sincerity all the same.

He ignored her and turned for the back doors, kicking the fallen box as he moved, and swung the doors open.

Nona Tereza's hand on his shoulder stopped him momentarily. "Another woman won't do anything for you."

A long growl left him. "*Do not* ever insinuate such a thing again, Nona. The thought of another woman disgusts me. I have a woman. Whether she wants me or not, my body is taken." *I am taken.* He shrugged out of her grasp and continued walking. "I'm going to hunt."

They didn't need any more kills with how full their stores were, and there was no need for more coin to trade the animals, but Killian didn't care. He needed to get bloodied and rip bodies apart.

With only the three daggers strapped to his body, Killian made his way into the forests, breathing in the fresh air. He could smell the ice that would come in soon, matting the greens of the summer trees in a small layer of snow, before it was all gone again come morning.

He was glad for the light covering that would come. It would shield away from all the green that now made him only think of *her*.

He couldn't believe how much of a fool he'd been. She was a Princess. She was *the* Princess.

He wanted to believe this wasn't what it seemed, but what else could it be? Now that she had her family, she didn't *need* his protection. And now that they were so close to that mother of hers, they wouldn't need to drag out any stay with him. That stint her mother pulled had probably been the catalyst to get them away, seeing to all the damage they had been responsible for. That bag of coin they'd left would cover whatever costs to fix the damages, but if they stayed any longer, they may have to provide them with far more. It was decided—it would be less costly to leave the family now that they didn't hold any real uses.

It made him sick.

A rabbit ran past a small bush to his right, and Killian snapped, jumping for it with his dagger and gutting the thing, thankful for the clearing it gave his mind. He left the dead thing on the dirt ground, allowing for another beast or hunter to find it. Either way, he didn't care. He was far enough from his home that no beast would be led back to his nonas.

He continued deeper into the forests, more of Rosaelia clashing around him. Her natural scent in every inch of his room. Her delicious scent when he was between her legs, smell always strong and pussy always soaking for him. At least he knew, if nothing else, he knew how much her body needed him. Even if her heart hadn't been affected, her body had needed him as much as his had needed her.

His cock still twitched at the memory of the way she'd looked up at him as if he was a sad fool. It broke his heart, but it was unbelievably sexy.

Killian breathed hard. He hadn't believed it. It was all a ruse to keep him away from knowing any more like how she'd kept secrets when she'd arrived to the Island. But when she'd ridiculed that sweet little nickname, his heart hadn't been able to take it.

A low growl came from his left, and Killian turned in time to see a large cat slowly prowling toward him. He laughed. As if the beast was the monster between them.

When the animal jumped for him, Killian swung two daggers out and crossed them before his chest so when the beast landed on him, his underbelly was completely ripped apart.

Blood soaked all over Killian as he pushed the beast off of

him and rose to his feet. He looked at it for only a moment before turning and continuing on his way, unsure where he was going but needing to continue.

Thoughts of Rosaelia were persistent, this time the memory of her running away from him coming back. How sinfully she'd grinned at him and how happy she'd been to get caught. How she'd soaked him in her juices. At least her body had always evidenced to him that she'd enjoyed his company, if only partly.

He hated himself for missing those juices, for wanting them in his mouth at that very moment.

He then thought of that twilight morning. The one where they'd laid together, and he'd told her how he'd received his scars. She'd been sincere as she'd listened, he knew that by the vengeance she'd taken on Keir's men. He knew it by the delivery of Keir to his front door.

Even if it wasn't love, she'd felt something for him.

That thought made him angrier. He didn't want her sympathy, or for the kills to have been some kind of payment for allowing her to live with him.

A snake slithered around a branch, its red eyes finding Killian, and its jaw opening with those poisonous fangs. Killian didn't even wait for it to attempt to attack. He simply threw one of his daggers at it and watched as it landed between the animal's eyes. The thing went limp instantly.

He didn't try to retrieve the dagger, knowing there may be some poison on it, and not having the patience to clean it properly at the moment.

Killian moved again, going back to only an hour ago when his woman had stared up at him with those beautiful emerald-green eyes and made him realize how great an actress the Princess of the Northern Lands was. She'd been so innocent her entire stay, and now Killian's brain was a mess trying to figure out which parts were true and which she'd put up as a show. It all made sense. If she truly had been innocent, there was no way the palace would've allowed her to come up to the Island. It had been their ingenious plan—the Princess acted innocent in order to get them to help her. Killian couldn't believe he'd fallen for it. The crown used its power, used people. Just like he knew they would.

Killian's steps through the forests made crunch, crunch, crunch over the leaves as his head wrestled with the knowledge that he'd been used while his heart and gut tried to convince him this was the act. That the Sael he'd know was the real one, and the Rosaelia she'd shown herself to be was faked for his protection. He had no idea which to listen to.

He scoffed. Of course he'd listen to his head. That's what kept his family alive. It was what had kept his family safe his entire life. It had been his head, not his heart, that knew it was right to kill his entire family, because although he'd hated them, his heart still thundered at the thought of murdering his blood. It had been his head that knew he needed to kill that family in order to take their house after Keir's incident seven years ago while his heart had cried out that he could find another way, a way that didn't kill a six-year-old boy. It had been his head to be wary of the Princess while his heart had warmed at the way she spent time with his nonas.

His head was always right. His head was what kept his family safe. His head was the reason he had a family.

Killian finally stopped to find himself standing in a small clearing. He didn't realize until he was standing there that he'd subconsciously walked to the clearing where he'd thrown Rosaelia against the tree for the first time. Their meeting spot.

His gaze moved over each spot until it landed on the tree. He moved for it slowly, his hand reaching for the spot Rosaelia had been when he'd caged her in. His fingers skimmed over the bark there, and finally, he could not hold it any longer, and a tear slipped from his eyes.

It made its slow descent down his cheek as he stared at the spot.

Then his other hand moved to meet it there, and he was caging in no one, hovering over the spot as if Rosaelia was beneath him. Another tear slipped free as he held himself there.

His princess was gone.

His Sael was gone.

CHAPTER 44
ROSAELIA

Tears strolled down her face the moment they were away from the house. Far enough that Rosaelia knew none of them would run after her. She kept her head held high, but she allowed those silent tears.

She appreciated, more than she could ever put into words, that none of her friends tried to comfort her. Rosaelia didn't want comfort. She wanted to feel this pain. She deserved to after what she did to that family, what she did to Killian. That pain in his eyes would forever haunt her.

He loved her. It was evident in the hurt and in the anger. It was evident in the fury it took to throw them out of the house, how much he loved her and how much her words hurt him. Evident that the life he'd envisioned for them was never going to happen.

She wondered, as she followed wherever Evony was leading them with her magic, what life Killian had envisioned. It was obvious by his opening before she'd ripped his heart in two that he'd planned on moving back to the palace with her. He was ready to upend his entire life to a nation who would look down on him for being a barbarian, who would run away out of fear from his scars.

For her.

Rosaelia wondered what else he had planned. Were they married in his dreams? Mated with the markings the Islanders used? Did they have children in that future? What did Killian do at the palace? Did he hunt to get the need to be in the forests out of his system? He hated Miels, and wasn't entirely fond of Tristan, but did he become friends with James, or perhaps one of the hunters?

There were so many questions, and Rosaelia wanted to know everything Killian had envisioned for them. She knew her dreams as if they were more real than her life.

They'd go back to the palace, the nonas able to finally go back home, and she'd introduce him to her father. The King would love him if only because she loved him, and because of how much Killian loved her. They would share her suite and get married. In her dreams, they waited a while to have children so that they could selfishly enjoy one another, but if it happened sooner, she wouldn't be angry. Sorcerer pregnancy concoctions worked better than remedy maker's, so Rosaelia wasn't sure how things would work in the North.

In her dreams, he eventually warmed up to Miels, and became close with the four—Sparrow, Miels, Tristan, and James—though she knew that may be a bit too perfect of a fantasy. She supposed their hate-love relationship was good too.

Most of all, in her envisioning, they were happy and together every night.

And every early twilight, they warmed each other with their natural body heat, even in the North where the cold was never as bad as in the Island Nation.

Rosaelia didn't know how or what route they'd taken, but

she was standing before a tiny shed. It looked like the entire thing held one whole room, and when they opened it, she'd been right. It was one big room with a large bed in the corner, a sofa in the other corner, and a small kitchenette area in the third corner. The final corner held a door that she supposed led to the bathing chamber.

"I didn't want to take anyone's home," Evony explained as they all shuffled inside, finding spots on the bed and couch and two extra chairs by the fire in the kitchenette. "This was empty. I suspect it's for travelers getting stuck in the weather."

"This is perfect," Gabriel said as he started on the fire by the kitchenette to warm the shack up from the Island's colder temperatures setting in. Then he took one of the chairs.

Evony smiled at him from her spot on Sparrow's lap as Sparrow found Rosaelia's gaze. "Sit, Ro."

Rosaelia was still standing by the door, but she numbly listened and moved for the spot beside him. With Ashtyn and Tristan on the edge of the bed, Miels took the final chair and they all sat silently.

She knew they were all hesitant about speaking because of her emotional state, so she opened because the very last thing she wanted was for them to sit in silence now. "I have six more people left on the list of Rowena's allies. One of them is the woman who continues to heal her every time we even come close to hurting her. Two messengers—it's how she gets anything done in the North. And the final three don't have the occupation, so I'm not entirely sure. We need to get to these six first. If we destroy any help she may have, we can actually finish this." Take away the possibility that those helping her would continue her mission.

"Can I see the list?" Miels asked.

Rosaelia pulled the folded paper out from the small pocket she'd sewn into her dress and handed it over. "The ones crossed off, I've taken care of, so they won't be of any help to Rowena any longer. I know there's no guarantee she doesn't have other help as well, but..."

"But it doesn't matter," Evony finished for her. "You have two Masters on your side. We'll finish her for sure this time. You've basically done all the work already, there really isn't all that much left for us to do. We'll end this, Twin, then you can go back to your man."

Rosaelia internally scoffed as her gaze shot down to her fingers fidgeting together. She knew she would go to him after, but she wasn't entirely certain he would allow her back in. Once trust was broken, it was broken. Even mended, the cracks would be visible. Rosaelia truly wasn't sure he would feel the same trust he had for her before.

Sparrow's large hand fell over her intertwined ones. "He'll more than take you back, Ro. He'll glue himself to your side. It's what I did to Evony." That got a chuckle out of everyone before he finished with, "He loves you, Ro."

Rosaelia swallowed to keep the emotions from overtaking her. The tears had stopped, and she really didn't want them coming back again. Not yet. "Can we just focus on Rowena?"

They needed to keep the crown safe from her.

They needed to keep the North safe from her.

They needed to keep the Island safe from her.

They needed to keep Killian safe from her.

CHAPTER 45
ROSAELIA

The plan was to head to Britt, Rowena's healer, and on the way, stop at each of the other five. Considering she was farther up north and the rest were in between Killian's town and Britt's, even if they couldn't mess with each one on the way, they could do so on the way back. It was the same plan Rosaelia had thought up before, except now she had others to traverse the Island forests with.

Gabriel, the horse whisperer of the group, found them a band of horses to make the journey north faster. How he'd found a perfect seven was a miracle, and when Rosaelia praised him for it, he only gave a light blush and a simple nod of the head. He was endearing. Cute. She understood the gossips she'd heard whispered between a couple of the servants at the palace about him.

They'd ridden the horses for maybe an hour before stopping in a town that held one of Rowena's helpers. They'd discussed how to go about all of these helpers the night before in the shack and had settled on allowing everyone their opportunities. This one, Miels and Tristan wanted to take care of. After everything Rosaelia had done, she was okay with allowing the Posse to handle these final few. After all, they were angry with her for coming up to the Island Nation without backup, so this made up for it. Slightly.

She couldn't believe how splendidly she'd made everyone she loved angry with her.

But at least the Posse would be easy to gain forgiveness from. Killian had been betrayed too harshly in the past for him to so easily give her the same treatment.

Because they had decided to break up who would be able to do each task, while Miels and Tristan strolled into town to find Logun, one of the individuals whose task they weren't sure of—thus making it more difficult to stop his aid to Rowena, which is why the boys wanted him—the rest of them waited, hidden within the trees of the forests.

Sparrow and Evony took this time to lean over one of the trees, kissing and whispering to one another with broad smiles. Rosaelia wondered if she was finally telling him about their big news. She doubted it as that would mean Sparrow would become insufferable, and this close to the end, Rosaelia didn't think Evony would risk his concentration.

Gabriel stood alone with the horses, brushing the mane of one as his gaze constantly hovered to the healer.

Ashtyn sat in the weeds by a large tree as she plucked at the greens. Rosaelia wasn't entirely sure if she was randomly doing so or if the healer in her saw useful ingredients, but Ashtyn's focus never wavered.

Rosaelia pushed off the tree she'd been leaning against and moved for the stable hand. She felt a stare on her as she moved and wondered if, in fact, Ashtyn was more perceptive than she was leading herself to look.

Rosaelia stopped on the other side of the horse Gabriel was

currently brushing—coincidently, Ashtyn's—and gave him a warm smile. He returned it before his gaze fell to the horse, then quickly snapped to Ashtyn as if he couldn't help himself.

"She's beautiful," Rosaelia commented.

Gabriel's cheeks flushed as he cleared his throat, head snapping back to the horse as he continued to brush her mane. "Yes. They all are."

Rosaelia tried not to laugh at his deflection but couldn't help the smile that lifted her lips. "The horses are, yes. But I meant the healer."

Gabriel met her eyes with sharp ones of his own. "She is."

Rosaelia brushed at the horse's side to give her hands something to do. "You do not seem to mind others knowing of your feelings?"

"Why should I?"

He was the complete opposite of Killian. He was soft boyish charm, whereas Killian was pure rough-honed barbarian. He was flushed cheeks, whereas Killian was wicked smirks. He was warm gazes and soft smiles, whereas Killian was hard stares and fury. He was kind, whereas Killian was mean. But they were both completely unperturbed of others knowing of their feelings.

Rosaelia knew most men in love were like that, but something in the way Killian acted was so different to the ways Sparrow and Miels had. She saw that now in Gabriel. He didn't care for propriety, he only cared for Ashtyn.

"Does she know?"

He gave an amused chuckle. "Of course she knows, Princess. She's quite perceptive. If the lot of you have figured it out, she most definitely has."

"Are the feelings not reciprocated?" By the feeling of the stare on her back, Rosaelia highly doubted that.

"They are." Gabriel's gaze snapped back to the healer's and

stayed there. "She's a lot like your brother, Princess. She fights her emotions in order to not feel them at all."

Killian fought his emotions too. And no wonder. Look what happened when he finally decided to give his heart to you.

"Your being here, your going with her when Sparrow was going after Evony. You're always following her. Much like Evony breaking down Sparrow's walls."

He reached into his pocket for a snack for the horse they were with, then forced his gaze to remain on the animal rather than the woman across the open forest grounds. "I am here for her protection. I wouldn't be able to live with myself if something happened to her, Princess."

"You're in love with her."

He swallowed, his eyes rolling up to meet hers before he stepped back and toward another horse. It was clear—he wouldn't be saying any more on the matter.

She followed him anyway, needing to talk and, for some reason, enjoying that he wasn't one of the men she grew up with. It made speaking her emotions easier somehow.

"May I ask your opinion?"

"Of course, Princess." He began brushing Evony's horse's mane.

"Well, first, stop calling me Princess. I think we've been through enough for you to call me Ro or Rosaelia."

"Not Sael?" He gave a cheeky little smirk with a light shimmering in his eyes.

The name struck her chest like a stab, but her lips twitched up at the teasing matter of the stable hand. "You're not a barbarian, so no."

"My opinion?"

Rosaelia petted the horse's muzzle as she asked, "Would you forgive her?" She met his gaze but kept her hands busy petting the horse. "If your entire life you stayed away from forming relationships because of all the betrayals you'd experienced and finally you allowed her into your heart, and she left you like this. Would you forgive her?"

He swallowed, his gaze snapping to Ashtyn and turned warm as they settled. He could try to avoid her statement from before all he wanted, but it was clear as day that he was in love with her.

"I cannot say, Prin— Rosaelia. It is easy to say I would, but I have never been in a situation where my faith in all people has diminished." He met her gaze again.

She gave a soft smile as her gaze saddened. "Thank you for your honesty."

Maybe that's why she wanted to speak with someone outside of the Posse. While they meant well, the Posse would convince her that nothing else mattered when she knew that wasn't the case.

"I cannot imagine saying no to her, Princess. I am too weak to watch her go off with another male. I am too weak to say no to her. But your barbarian has grown up with far worse than any of the rest of us. I may not know the specifics, but I imagine he's had to let go of his desires for the life he imagined in the past. He's stronger than the rest of us in a way. All Islanders are."

Rosaelia stepped up to him, holding on to his forearm to lift herself toward him. She kissed his cheek and whispered, "She's an idiot to deny you, Gabriel."

"Thank you, Princess."

Rosaelia stepped back to the horse's other side to pet, and as she turned, she noticed Ashtyn's sharp gaze on her. Her eyes looked darker than their normal hue, and her countenance more uninviting than her usual bitterness.

As Rosaelia turned back to the horse, she knew one thing

for certain—the healer would need to be snapped out of her denials for the stable hand.

"So, Gabriel," Rosaelia started in order to pass the time and clear her mind of her barbarian. "How did you find these seven?"

LOGUN TURNED out to be the weapon's maker for Rowena.

Miels and Tristan had especially loved their task then, breaking his hands and fingers so they'd never assemble the same again. So he'd never be able to supply for a war again.

It was a good thing they'd taken care of him and not Sparrow. His father had been a sword maker, and Rosaelia imagined it may be too close to his heart for him to break the man's hands.

They were only about an hour away from Britt's village, having stopped to find numbers four and five on the list.

Numbers two and three—one of the messengers and another unknown who turned out to be a supplier to the North, which gained them access to the supplies on the ships —were taken care of by Sparrow and Evony.

Gabriel opted out of causing harm. He was only there for Ashtyn's protections, and they were all aware of that. And this wasn't an initiation. No one would be forced to do something they didn't want to. Especially with four others giddily ready to take the task.

Ashtyn, too, chose to stay away from those matters. As the healer, it made sense. She was there to take care of people, not harm them.

So four and five were Miels and Tristan's again. They won the argument against the married duo only because "they needed some release and didn't have the luxuries of their females to be with." Apparently, that had been just the thing to say to shut both Sparrow and Evony up.

Four was the other messenger. Miels took care of him in a matter of moments—by breaking his legs to an unfixable degree, thus making it near impossible to do his job. Rosaelia realized rather quickly that they were much harsher than she was with their parts of taking care of the list.

Five was another unknown helper. Tristan had won out on getting him because "Miels had a woman to be inside when they got home, and since he didn't, he was obviously in need of more of a release."

The way they handled these matters was laughable, but at least the way they negotiated worked for them.

Number five turned out to be the supplier of women. Rosaelia's stomach roiled as she understood what that meant. With all those brutes working under her, Rowena would need to have a way to give them their pleasures. From the looks of some of the girls, the youngest couldn't be older than fifteen.

It was different than a whorehouse. Whorehouses were jobs where men and women chose to be there and kept all of their proceeds. This was slavery.

It made her sick to learn of these matters, but she also needed to be there. She needed to watch Tristan take care of this one.

It wasn't surprising that Miels, Sparrow, and Evony would also want to watch, probably dying to join, but it did shock Rosaelia to see Gabriel and Ashtyn watch. The violence here would be greater than any of the others.

"I am no barbarian," Tristan opened as he slammed the man, whose name was Alen, to the ground. "But my barbarian brother has shown me how to take care of matters here. And I must say, you deserve it more than his victims had."

My barbarian brother.

Rosaelia's breath caught at the phrasing. Being a brother to her meant Killian would become his brother as well if they married. To hear the acceptance so wholly nearly knocked Rosaelia back.

Tristan was savage as he severed Alen's penis from his body.

Rosaelia's instincts made her freeze at the sight, but when Miels tried to comfort her, she pulled away. Not only because she didn't want the comfort—no, she needed to see this, to not be naive to what happened in the lands—but also because she knew Killian would hate it. He already hated her enough. She wouldn't add cozying up with Miels to the list of reasons why.

Tristan tied Alen's hands above his head, then hung him from a tree as he bled out. He shoved the man's own penis into his mouth, then turned to the women of the brothel. "Would any of you like a chance at him?"

Rosaelia's heart melted at the sentiment because as much as the Posse hated the man for what he'd done, he hadn't done it to them. Tristan would give these girls, who had gone through all the horrors, the chance to end him.

One girl, probably the youngest of the lot, stepped up tentatively, like she was scared Tristan had only been joking. When Tristan only smiled and stepped aside, she let out a long sigh, then promptly sucker-punched Alen in the gut. With his own penis in his mouth, he could hardly react to the hit.

But that one girl seemed to be the ember to the others.

One by one, more stepped up to get their turn until too many of them were punching and kicking at him. It was clear not long after that he was dead.

He deserved it.

Tristan looked at them proudly as he said to their group,

"Let's find this final woman. Then Rowena." He turned to them. "Then let's go home."

Rosaelia's heart broke in two at the word home. She thought of the palace in the North and her father and meals with the Posse.

But she also thought of Killian.

He was her home.

CHAPTER 46

KILLIAN

It was twilight as Killian stepped for the door that would lead into the bathing chamber. Unable to sleep, he'd been working to distract himself all night. It was right about this time every morning that he woke Rosaelia, or she woke him, with the need to be together, to taste each other.

Killian hadn't realized how accustomed his body had become to it until the morning after she'd left and he didn't have her at his side, when his cock or tongue or fingers weren't buried deep inside of her for the first time since she promised to stay with him. In the days that had passed, Killian's body strummed with the withdrawals of still not having her every early morning.

He undressed and stepped into the bath quietly, remembering only a few nights prior when he'd brought Rosaelia into the tub to clean off. The way she'd touched him, stared into his eyes the entire time—how could she have faked that? When he'd placed her on his lap, legs straddled, as he cleaned her—how could she not have been affected? Was her heart that cold?

Gone was the sweat from his work outdoors, but Killian

didn't remember getting through his bath. He couldn't peel his mind away from Rosaelia no matter how much he tried. She was a part of every inch of his life—his home, his forests, his town, his body, his heart. This had been the torture he'd been living through for days, and each one that passed made him hate her more.

He dressed on autopilot, still thinking of her—now remembering every time he'd peeled her clothes off—then moved for the hall that would lead to his room. No longer their room.

Her speech that day was evidence enough that it had never been their room. She had merely been a guest in his room.

It made him sick.

He'd been her little plaything. *Fucking Princess Rosaelia.*

He paused on the way when he noticed his family sitting around the dining table as he passed the opening to the living space. He turned to them instead of heading to bed, not yet ready to sleep in sheets with her scent still clinging to them.

That also made him hate her more. How much he needed rid of that scent, but at the same time, how unable he was to do so. Every time he came close to peeling the sheets away to wash her scent off, his heart thundered too quickly.

"Why are you all up?"

They all stared at him wide-eyed and sad as he stopped before the table, but not the same sadness that had been in their eyes when Rosaelia left with her friends.

Nona Tereza rose to her feet and stopped before him. "She was smart. She put the note with the coins knowing we wouldn't care to open it right away." She handed him a folded piece of paper. "And if we hadn't been checking for the amount in order to tell the No Known Housing of the total they would be receiving—because there was no way we were keeping any of that coin—who knows how much longer before we found this. Hell, she may've been back by then."

Killian still didn't understand what she was on about, why they weren't more angry, as he reached for the note in his nona's hand. He swallowed hard, afraid to open it and read anything from *her*.

Nona Tereza moved back for her seat next to her sister and watched him silently.

Killian's hands shook slightly as he finally unfolded the note and read the words meant for all of them, but especially for him.

Nona Tereza,

Nona Eleni,

Norya,

My greatest monster,

At the start of the year, my life was filled with only four men—my father, Sparrow, Miels, and Tristan. Three months ago, I found out I had a twin who came with two best friends of her own. Two months ago, I knew I could trust her, that I needed to protect her. One month ago, I decided I would come to the Island Nation for my family, but also for myself. To prove to myself that I was more than a Princess.

You weren't in my plans. I was meant to be alone, to find and kill my mother, then return home. No attachments. I never expected to fall in love with a family. None of you were in my plans.

But especially not you, Killian.

I'd always wondered what love felt like. I always imagined it and desired it based off the books I get lost in. I truly witnessed it for the first time when Sparrow fell in love with Evony. Then those desires from the books weren't enough because I could see the way Sparrow had grown with Evony. It had been one thing to imagine love and an entirely other thing to witness it. I could not fathom—even though I wanted it so desperately—how it would feel to experience it.

Then you pushed me into that tree, Killian. The Monster.

My monster.

You allowed me to experience it, my barbarian. You allowed me into your life and opened up for me. You are more than I thought myself deserving. You are the one I would like to take home. To meet my father. To rule the North with me in decades time. To scare the servants and run the greens. You are the reason I close my eyes every night and picture markings on my hand, mirroring the ones on your own, proving us claimed forever. You are the only person I can ever fathom at my side, Killian.

You are the one who taught my body all about its desires.

You are the one who taught my mind all about its ability to love.

It is because of you that my heart beats any longer. It is because of you that I would never hesitate to kill—to protect you. It is because of you that I feel alive.

You're scarred, imperfect. A threat, frightening. A beating heart looking for its breath. And I'm so sorry for leaving. But it is because you are my definition of perfect that I cannot allow you to put yourself or your family in danger for me. Rowena proved she would not hesitate to kill any of you the way she didn't hesitate with Alana. I cannot risk that.

I cannot risk you. Any of you, but especially not you, Kill.

I intend on making my way back to you, my barbarian, but lest that not be possible, I need you to know that you are, and forever will be, my monster.

Always and forever yours,
Sael

I love you, Killian.

There were dried teardrops smearing a few of the words, and Killian could imagine her as she'd written it. Not Rosaelia, Princess of the Northern Lands, but Sael, his princess.

His own tears landed on the paper clutched in his hands as he stared at those final words.

Finally, his eyes closed, and his jaw ground as the letter

crashed into him. "I let her leave," he whispered to no one in particular, hating himself as he stood there. "I didn't fight. I..."

"You have never felt like this," Nona Eleni said with determination. "You were just as scared to trust your heart as she was to leave you, Kill. She knew that and used it to keep us safe. You will do no one any good blaming yourself now."

He opened his eyes and met her strong ones. She was so quiet normally that he tended to forget how *great* she was.

"You are not at fault, Kill. We all believed it, and she counted on that. Because of how much she loves us. We were hurt because of how much we love her. There is no blame. There is only finding her and protecting her."

Norya's hand landed on his back as she stood at his side, a soft smile on her face past those sad eyes. "Then you mark your hands. She *wants* your Island claim, Kill."

A relieved, disbelieving laugh left him as his head fell, and more tears strolled off his cheeks. "She loves me."

Norya's arms wrapped around him. "And you love her. So, let's find your woman."

Tears continued to stroll down his face as he forced himself to lift his head, and meet her gaze, then those of both his nonas before meeting Norya's again. "Let's find my woman."

Both nonas were by his side then, Nona Tereza reaching out to hand him a box.

The box.

The black box that held his rings.

He would mark his hand with her and wear the ring. As many ways as he could to show the world that he was claimed. Anything to show everyone how much he loved her.

CHAPTER 47
ROSAELIA

These rides through the towns, the villages, the forests were probably the worst. These moments where Rosaelia only had her mind to speak to. Hours where she thought of nothing but Killian. Every single moment they'd been together.

They were riding to Britt's town now, having left the brothel's women to a No Known Housing in that town, and Rosaelia needed out of her own mind. Needed out of thinking of that cozy armchair in the common area where Killian had kneeled before her to tell her she was his. Needed out of thinking of his smiles as he taught her how to use a dagger. Needed out of the memory of their bath where she knew inexplicably that she was in love with him, that he was in love with her.

Being that the men in this group were protectors, they rode on the outskirts of their group, so Rosaelia was stuck in the middle with Tristan to her left, Sparrow—with Evony to his side, which he wasn't fond of—before her, Miels to the right beside Ashtyn, and Gabriel behind them. It took away any privacy she may like, but as Rosaelia glanced toward Ashtyn, she figured riding close to her and keeping her voice down would have to do.

So she did just that. "You know, I've only had a couple of weeks with Killian. I'd do anything for more time with him."

Ashtyn's brows furrowed as she turned to her.

Rosaelia nodded her head as if pointing behind them. "You'll regret all this time you could've had with him simply because you're fighting your desire for him."

"Look, Emerald. I don't know what's gotten into you, but I don't need your matchmaking."

"He's a good guy."

"I know he's a good guy."

"Is that why you stay away? You think he's too good?"

"I do not think, Emerald. He is too good."

"And that means you do not deserve him?"

"That means mind your business, Emerald."

Rosaelia should be affronted by the way she was being spoken to, but instead, she was relieved by it. It was how the healer spoke to her twin. True and open, not faked simply because she was a Princess. "He's in love with you."

"He's infatuated. He'll get over it."

"You're saying you're not in love with him?"

Ashtyn huffed. "Is there a sign on my forehead asking for therapy? No? Then leave me be."

The healer's defenses only made Rosaelia smile—though she tried to hide it because she was a scary medic. "I'm sorry. I simply wanted to talk, and I figured Gabriel would make the most sense with you."

Ashtyn turned to watch her as they rode on.

Her stare made Rosaelia want to explain. "If you were Sparrow, I'd speak of Evony. And vice versa. If you were Miels, I'd speak of Etel. Tristan is a bit difficult, given he is not in love, and though Norya is an option, I do not wish to remember walking in on them. But I am not the best with opening random conversations, so the romance of my friends seem to be a simple measure."

Ashtyn's gaze softened. "Distractions work better if they are of a different subject, Princess. If you wish to distract your mind from your barbarian, then speaking of romance will only solidify the thoughts you are running from."

Rosaelia shrugged. "I suppose you are right."

After a minute of silence, Ashtyn said, "We can speak of the three gowns poor Atiana made you for when you came back from the library and how upset she was that you weren't there to try them on. Masterworks, she calls them."

Rosaelia smiled at her efforts. It made her remember that the girl was a healer, and that meant more than simply physical pains. She may be as grumpy as her assassin brother, but she was soft on the inside, always wanting to help others.

"I'm quite certain they are masterworks. Atiana has an eye for designs that no one else possesses. It is why I do not understand why my father would rather Odolf than her. She is clearly the best tailor. Even Odolf knows it. The only reason he hasn't given her his spot as head tailor is because she denies to take the position."

"Not being head means she has time for her own matters, like making you gowns that you are not there to try on."

Rosaelia laughed. "I suppose, yes. Have you seen them? Are they wonderful?"

"Stunning." Ashtyn smirked. "They fit like a glove too, Emerald."

"You tried them on?"

"Atiana made me promise not to tell."

"Yet you're telling?"

Ashtyn's grin was devious. "All I said was they fit like a glove. I said nothing about trying them on."

Rosaelia laughed, surprised that she was able to so freely with a heavy heart, but unsurprised that the healer was able to make her feel lighter. "I will make sure Atiana makes you one when we return."

"For what, Princess? I have no reason for a gown."

Rosaelia shrugged. "Why not? To wear and feel extra beautiful. I'll be sure to send Gabriel to you when it is done."

Ashtyn rolled her eyes. "Send him. Atiana's the most stunning woman at the palace. He can finally drop his infatuation and scurry after her."

"You underestimate his heart if you think his gaze would waver anywhere but after you."

Ashtyn stared ahead, but her lips tipped up. "Maybe you're worse at this not speaking of romance matter than I thought."

Rosaelia laughed. "My apologies." As she stared ahead to Sparrow and Evony in their own world of conversations, Rosaelia opened with, "Where were you before the palace?"

BRITT HAD a shop similar to Etel's workstation with a table in the middle for potion making and tables and shelves around every wall to hold vials and ingredients and materials.

She stood shell-shocked as their entire group filled her space, her gaze jumping from Rosaelia to Evony and back like she knew who they were. Her frightened look as she picked out Sparrow at Evony's side, his menacing presence as the Master Assassin said she knew exactly why they were there as well.

"My shop is closed," she stuttered as if that would deter them from their reason for being there.

"It is a good thing then that we do not need any of your potions," Tristan drawled.

She cleared her throat and stepped back, but with only the shelves behind her, she had nowhere to run. All three sides of the shop were littered with their group. And as Miels and Tristan closed in on either side of her, she seemed to realize there was no way out of there.

"Stop!" she pleaded. "I'll give you what you want. But please, no."

"Aw." Tristan smiled. "She's such a good girl." He gripped her arm and shoved her toward the other end of her shop where Sparrow had a chair ready for her. "Were you such a good girl for Rowena, *Britt*?"

The girl shook, frightened by what the three boys Rosaelia grew up with would do to her. Deservedly so. "I—"

"Remember, Britt," Evony interrupted her. "We don't like liars."

It was clear by the way the girl was looking them over that Rowena had been truthful with her about who they were. Britt knew Evony was the Master Magician as much as she knew Sparrow was the Master Assassin. Whatever deal she'd had with Rowena was hopefully worth going against them.

Though, she likely believed she'd never have to go against them.

"Now"—Sparrow leaned down to her ear but was loud enough for all to hear—"why don't you tell us why you helped dear old Rowena."

"I-I..." She swallowed, then squared her shoulders as her gaze shot to each of them. "I'm in love with her."

Snorts came from every corner of the room.

"That monster continues to surprise me," Miels said. "How exactly she made anyone love her is astounding."

"She's broken, but that's because she hasn't been loved. I go to her and mend her."

Gabriel cleared his throat from Ashtyn's side, and it was

clear he was keeping in whatever he wanted to say. Ashtyn met his gaze, then turned to Britt as if she would ask if he wouldn't. "Mending with potions or with your body?"

Rosaelia's lips tipped up. It was truly no wonder that girl was friends with Evony. They had no filters.

It did surprise Rosaelia, though, if that had been Gabriel's question whispered into Ashtyn's ear. If so, maybe that sweet, shy man had a filthier mind than she gave him credit. She shouldn't be surprised. She was also quiet, and apparently, she truly enjoyed some depraved things.

"That's personal."

"I'm a healer. Call me curious."

"You went to her?" Sparrow asked. "Where? And why when your work is here?"

She swallowed like she didn't want to answer, but eventually, her self-preservation won the battle. "I take vials with me. And ingredients. One bag filled with my things is all I ever need."

"But why go to her?" Tristan asked.

"It takes much longer to travel up here, then back down to the North's border. I go so she can remain close to her plans."

Sparrow leaned down to her ear again, his voice frightening all on its own. "So I ask again, Britt. Where?"

She swallowed again and shook her head. As her gaze snapped around the room, she realized there was only one way out of this. "In a cottage. By the waters. I travel south and through the forests. I know the area as I grew up here. I wouldn't know how to explain it."

"By the water?" Rosaelia questioned, then knew how she would need to be with Britt. If she was as condescending as the others in her group, the girl wouldn't want to give up any information. She would need some sentiment toward Rowena. "My mother enjoyed being by the ships so she was close to her people in the North? By the Black Tower, so she could look over the waters?"

Britt's eyes warmed on her. "Yes. She misses her people. That hut is close enough that she gets to see her people. It's a good place for her up here in the Island. With benches for her to sit, and look out at the waters, the flowers by her feet. I go there because the cottage, being by the North, heals her as much as I do."

"And you were okay with the woman you love going back to the North without you?"

"I was going with her. I am going with her."

Tristan gave a dark smirk as he leaned down to Britt's eye level. "The problem there, sweetheart, is Rowena isn't stepping foot back in the North."

"What?" she whispered, her eyes widening. "No. You cannot hurt her. She needs to be back with her people."

"It does not bother you then? The atrocities she's committed to take the throne? All the *men* she's sucked off to get to her place in life?" Ashtyn asked, disgust in her voice.

Because every single man they'd gone after on the list had told them about the things Rowena had allowed them to do to her body, the things she'd done to them.

Britt's gaze sharpened. "She's done what she needs to do."

And in that moment, any sympathy Rosaelia was feeling for the woman—a simple girl who'd fallen in love, something none of them in that shop could find fault with, and most of them could empathize with—was gone. It reminded Rosaelia —to love a monster, you must be a monster.

Sparrow crouched in front of the seated girl. "And we must do what we need to."

The girl narrowed her eyes. As a sorcerer, even one specialized to healing, it was not surprising that she believed whatever they did to her, she could not treat herself from.

"You know, Britt." Miels tinkered with some of the ingredients at the other end of the shop before turning with a mortar and pestle and setting everything on the worktable. "My wife is the Remedies Expert. It is not specifically potion making as the sorcerers do, but it is as close as a commoner can get. She's taught me a thing or two."

His wording made Rosaelia smile. Etel wasn't his wife yet, but she knew he was in desperate need to finish here and return to her, make her his officially the moment they were back together.

Then, to everyone's shock, he began working like his expert *wife*, completely in the zone and knowledgeable about all that he was doing. His interest in her, and thus in her life's work, was obvious in this moment.

Britt sputtered and shrugged in her seat, unable to get up, and Rosaelia realized it was Evony's magic keeping her down. She likely didn't want to believe he could cause her harm, but the thought of trainings with a Remedies Expert could not so easily be thrown under the rug.

When Miels finished ten minutes later, he held a vial of light purple liquid bubbling within. "This is used when too much healing concoctions are given in order to counteract the healing."

"I haven't taken a healing potion," Britt said with wide eyes, like she understood where he was going with this even if the rest of them didn't.

"No?" Miels smirked. "I wonder what it would do to you then?"

Britt's eyes widened with fear. "No!" She tried to fight off Tristan holding her to the chair, but it was no use. It took only another moment with Evony's magic forcing the girl's mouth open for Miels to slip the vial down her throat.

Evony's magic made her swallow as Miels explained, "If

taken in complete health, this works against the body, like a poison, especially if made by a sorcerers pre-made ingredients. Stuck on the chair and unable to make herself a counter potion in time, she'll grow weak and frail, foggy in mind, an elderly at her deathbed in a young woman's body."

"Please!" Britt shook her head. "The counter potion! Please! Please!"

"You mean these?" Ashtyn raised the bag of clinking vials emptied from the shelves. "I'm sure there are people all around this nation who would appreciate these. They thank you."

Gabriel had another bag filled with ingredients and one more with some materials. His cheeks pinked with all the attention as he said, "We don't want these wasted either."

Then Tristan pulled Britt outside of the shop, and Sparrow placed the chair before the hut but far enough away. They tied her to that chair as Evony's magic set flames to the shop, containing the fire to only that one space, as Britt watched.

It was a kindness they were showing her. For all the help she'd given Rowena, she deserved worse, but none of them wanted to kill her. She wasn't as bad as Alen—who they actually hadn't killed, simply allowed the women who deserved to cause him harm do so—and she was definitely no Rowena. She was simply a girl blinded by love.

As the flames contained themselves to that one shop, their group got on their horses and began the ride back to the bottom of the Island Nation where Rowena would be, and where they would end this.

And maybe where Rosaelia could run back to Killian's arms.

CHAPTER 48
ROSAELIA

They were giving the horses a break as they all stood around to eat their meals. Not a single one of them wanted to sit as their butts were too sore from the ride down.

No one complained, but it was clear they all needed this break.

Rosaelia leaned against a tree as she watched Miels on a branch at the top of a tree, staring out in the direction of the North, of his future wife. As she watched Evony and Sparrow stretch behind a few trees, teasing and laughing as they did so. As she watched Gabriel and Ashtyn by the horses, Gabriel smiling and excitedly explaining some part of the animal to her. She didn't show it as outwardly, but when Gabriel turned to grab for snacks for the animals or to pet or control one, her gaze latched on to him with the deepest warmth.

"I was hoping when we got here, I would have you on my side, but it seems I am the only one left not in love here." Tristan startled her as he spoke from right by her side.

Rosaelia gave him an apologetic smile. "Sorry. Has it been all that bad?"

He chuckled. "The entire boat ride here, Miels stared out toward the palace. He talks about her without realizing it. Sparrow does the same with Eve when, by some miracle, they actually separate from one another. And those two? They're... more reserved, but they stay together. I don't know what's going on with them, but it's quite clear there's something. Then we found you, and just when I was going to come at you with the largest of hugs for saving me away from all the lovey-doveyness, Miels comes out telling us how *enthusiastically* you were with your barbarian. It broke my heart, Ro. Because I knew you would only do that if you were in love, which meant I was all alone again."

Rosaelia didn't feel bad because she physically couldn't when thinking of her relationship with Killian, but she tried for a frown even though she wanted to laugh. "Aw." She leaned up to kiss his cheek. "I'm sorry, Tristan."

"No, you're not." He pushed her away, grinning widely.

She shrugged. "I am. You didn't seem all that bothered before."

"That's because I had a hot little barbarianette to play with before."

"You sure *you* were playing with *her*?"

He smirked down at her, eyes gleaming. "You tell me. Apparently, you were taking in the show."

Rosaelia's cheeks beamed red. "I wasn't *watching*. I didn't mean..."

"Yeah, yeah. Keep telling yourself that, Ro."

Rosaelia huffed, going back to watching her friends and eating her apple. Tristan allowed the silence between them until Rosaelia broke it once more. "I'm truly sorry, Tristan. I didn't even consider what this meant for you."

"What do you mean?"

"You and Norya."

"Norya and I were sleeping together, Ro. Was it an incredible experience to be with her? Did it feel different to the Northerners? Yes. But does that mean I cannot live without her?" A soft laugh passed through his nostrils. "No, Ro. I was never in love with her. We had fun, but we both knew it would end at some point."

Rosaelia nodded, then turned to him. "But if Killian were to come to the palace with me, she would most likely join. Would you not consider more then?"

Tristan gave her a sweet smile. "I thought I would when I was younger, sure. And there are moments when I see Miels and Sparrow gone for that I consider it. But, honestly, no, Ro. I don't *want* a relationship."

"You just want to screw random women for the rest of your life?"

"I didn't say that. I just don't think a relationship is in the cards for me. I see the way you all are, and as much as I love you all, that feeling, that possession that Sparrow and Miels have, that Killian showed with you, it's not in me. Women can do as they please, and it's never bothered me. So don't apologize to me, Ro. You didn't mess anything up for me and Nor. Plus, let's not forget that your barbarian isn't going to leave you behind. Even if he's angry with you, he's going to come to the palace. We all saw the way he possessed you. He won't give that up. So maybe I'll get my bed buddy back after all, and I truly won't need your apologies."

Rosaelia shook her head as the smile grew on her features. "You're kind of a pig, you know that, Tris?"

He winked.

When she turned back to take in what her friends were doing, she leaned into Tristan's side to take comfort. She missed Killian too much, wanted to be in his arms too dearly, to deny herself this moment with a brother. Killian had no problems with Tristan, so she felt completely fine doing so.

Then Tristan whistled and called out, "Hey! Where're you two going?"

Rosaelia's gaze shot to her twin's wicked smirk as she pulled on Sparrow's arm to go farther into the forest, and answered, "Mind your business, spy."

Rosaelia's cheeks pinked. "At least her magic will mean we won't hear it."

AFTER SPARROW and Evony's little escapade into the woods, they were back on the horses and riding down south to the cottage Rosaelia was almost certain she recognized. By Britt's description, she remembered one exactly fitting on her way to the Bloody Fields. She'd passed the hill that led to those cottages again when she was meeting Alana at the Black Tower, and they were all near the ports to the North.

When they made it to the hill that would lead toward the cottages, closer to the Bloody Fields than the Black Tower so they could remain hidden in the forests, Rosaelia tried to figure out which cottage they needed.

Evony stood beside her as the men started looking for the best way down. "I have my magic checking the houses. I need to go slower as I don't want to alert her that we're here."

"Good," Rosaelia muttered. "I can't believe I was living this close to her. I can't believe she would choose to live in such a small place."

Evony shrugged. "She probably wasn't there as often. Or

maybe she'd spent so much of her funds preparing and paying off others that it was all she could afford."

Rosaelia mocked a gasp as her hand flew to her heart. "Are you saying *the* Queen Rowena could have any trouble stealing the home?"

Evony laughed. "She's still a Northerner. And alone. Islander families would likely skewer her if she tried to go for them."

"Touché."

"Found it." Evony smiled toward the small green cottage second in the line of homes.

Before Rosaelia could say anything, Tristan called out, "Hey, spider-monkey, your assistance may be required."

They turned for him, and Evony's smile turned devious. "What may I help you with?"

They all moved into the small clearing surrounded by trees, before them, leading toward the cottages, a small cliff with weeds and branches everywhere.

"Climb up there"—he pointed up the tree above the cliff— "so you could get a better view of what's around. Then, we need your magic to set a path for us to get down. These branches aren't strong enough to hold our bigger sizes."

"She can't." The words flew from Rosaelia's mouth before she processed them.

Miels laughed. "She sure can. You didn't see the way she was swinging from trees years ago when she was running from us. She's only gotten better in her skill."

Evony laughed. "I'm glad you see my skills." She looked down at the nature-covered cliff, and there was a hint of worry behind her amusement.

Rosaelia racked her mind for another way down but realized this was it. The spring rains had likely messed with this path, and no one had been around to clean it again. She should've taken them through the longer path that would pass the Black Tower. She wanted this route since it was closer to where they were traveling from and completely hidden so they didn't need to worry about townsfolk, or Killian's family, seeing them; didn't have to worry about staying hidden deep in the forests.

"C'mon," Tristan started. "If your magic could find stones for us to walk on instead of these branches, that'd be great too."

"She can't do it," Rosaelia argued again.

Evony swallowed as her eyes narrowed on Rosaelia, warning her that any more worry would snap her husband's attention to her. Then she looked down at the cliff, and muttered, "I'll be fine—"

"No, Evony!" Rosaelia demanded. "It's dangerous enough for any of us to be over those branches, but *you* can't. We'll go through the Black Tower route."

That caught Sparrow's attention, and Evony's jaw gritted knowing she was finally caught.

"Why not?" Sparrow's sharp browns demanded of his wife. "What is she speaking of, Magician? Why can't *you*?"

Evony swallowed, her ocean-blues softening as they met her husband. "I only found out a couple of weeks ago. We were already here."

"What..."

It was fascinating watching Sparrow's mind work. With all of his attention on his wife, he didn't try to hide any of it, and Rosaelia could see the worry turn to anger turn to confusion, then that light shining in his eyes as he took her in from head to toe and paused at her stomach. His features gave away his shock, his excitement, then promptly led back to worry as he remembered where they currently were and anger as he realized she'd known and hadn't said a thing. "A couple of weeks?"

"Sparrow," she reasoned softly. "We're in barbarian nation. If you got too distracted with me, you could've been hurt. We needed my magic, and you would've fought me."

Sparrow breathed in slowly, then blew up. "We're in barbarian nation, Evony! You just said so yourself! We're. In. Barbarian. Nation. And you've been running around, into that fucking bastard's estate where anyone could've gotten to you, and you didn't think I should know?"

"You love me, Sparrow. You trust me as I am. You trust my abilities. What difference would this make to my ability to protect myself in that estate?"

"The difference is pregnancies affect every woman differently. What if your magic weakened because of the baby and I didn't know, Magician? What if something happened to you? You would've taken yourself *and* our child away from me!"

Tristan and Miels, as astonished as they were, stepped up as if they would get in the way if need be. They knew Sparrow would never harm Evony, but it was in their instincts to get in between when their sister was being attacked.

Tears sprang to Evony's eyes. "I couldn't risk something happening to you because you were too distracted with me, Sparrow. We both know you would've thrown caution to your own safety. It's exactly what you did when Rowena had me on my knees. I won't apologize for wanting to keep you safe, but trust me, it's killed me not to tell you. Every. Fucking. Day."

Sparrow's jaw clenched as he internally worked through his anger, staring into the eyes of the only person who could drop him to his knees.

Then, like magic—though Rosaelia knew Evony would never manipulate the situation—his anger was gone. He moved for his wife, cradling her face as tears sprang to his eyes as well. "We're having a baby."

She nodded as she stared up at him as if the rest of the world didn't exist. "You're going to be a dad."

A scared laugh passed his lips as he kissed her. "That's frightening."

She laughed against his lips. "I know."

Now Rosaelia was holding back her own tears. She knew she shouldn't have said anything, that she had promised she wouldn't, but she hadn't been in control as the words left her. The thought of anything happening to that baby had the words blurting out before she could stop herself.

She also knew that Evony wouldn't be angry with her. The girl didn't know how to hold a grudge.

And luckily, Sparrow's anger was there and gone quickly.

Like the moron twins they were, Tristan and Miels pulled the couple apart so they could attack Evony with their congratulations. Sparrow growled the entire time, but neither man cared as they laughed with her, then finally turned to bear hug Sparrow at the same time, tackling him to the ground.

It gave Ashtyn and Gabriel their moment to congratulate Evony before Rosaelia met her twin's eyes, and knew she wasn't in trouble.

Now, for them to make the journey around to the Black Tower and reach the cottage that Rosaelia could just about see from where she stood, Rowena's silhouette walking within clear.

CHAPTER 49

KILLIAN

That letter was like a thread hanging over him, teasing him with the fact that he'd let her leave.

She'd done it all on purpose, grown to know his family, but especially him, so well that she knew it would take time to open that coin pouch. That she knew he would send her off as he'd so nearly done before at the hint of betrayal. She'd used that fear of trusting anyone as the deepest of betrayals, and he'd fallen for it immediately.

He hated himself for it, and if anything happened to her because of his thoughtlessness, he would throw himself into the Rivorbant Waters and let the filth in the river swallow him whole.

He couldn't stand not knowing where she'd gone, but Killian was officially done with torturing himself with a way to find out. He still remembered the way to the boy's shop. He'd given her the list, and Killian was going to learn what he knew. If that little sorcerer was aiding Sael, he would be all Killian needed to find his princess.

It annoyed him even more that it took days for him to

remember this sorcerer. He could've been closer to finding his princess, could've already found her, taken away any chance that her mother may hurt her.

He couldn't walk to the neighboring town. He needed to run. There was too much adrenaline running through him to get to his princess that walking felt like he might explode into a firework show.

He made it to the boy's shop in record time. He knew that, yet it still felt like every minute dragged into the next day. When he reached the window he had eavesdropped through the last time, Killian took a peek inside to make sure he'd be clear to speak of his princess without the possibility of any harm coming to her. If this boy had any visitors, Killian wouldn't risk the chance that they may work with Rowena, thus informing her of the threats coming her way.

Killian was glad for the forethought because sneaking up to that window, he caught sight of two others within the shop. Jealous rage still swirled around Killian at the thought of this kid—who couldn't be more than eighteen—around his woman.

With the sorcerer were another boy and girl who looked to be about the same age. They smiled at one another, but it all felt more formal than familial. These were clients then. Most people in the Island bought from sorcerers, so it was not surprising to see the boy working to accomplish whichever elixir the couple required, likely a pregnancy one.

Still, though it killed him, Killian waited for the two to leave.

He was antsy in his spot, hopping on his toes in order to get the adrenaline out, but careful not to draw attention to the window he stood at.

It took ten minutes, twelve at most, and every second nearly sent Killian to his death.

When, finally, the couple left, Killian moved around the shop, and stormed into the space, shutting the door and turning the sign that told customers the boy was open for business. Until he told Killian what he needed to know, the boy would have no more sales.

One look at Killian had the blood drained from the boy's face. He was white as a ghost as he backed up, his gaze tracking the scars on Killian's face and the fists at his sides.

"You tell me what I need to know, and I won't touch you, kid," Killian opened in order to get the sorcerer to calm down enough to answer his questions.

"A-A-Anything. Sir."

Killian scoffed but moved closer. "A few weeks ago, my woman came to you, and you handed her a list and a few vials. I need to know why. Now."

"Y-Y-Your woman?"

"Princess Rosaelia." Killian hated having to give that information out, but he knew it was important in this case.

The sorcerer's eyes widened. "She's your woman? Claimed? I thought she wanted your protection as payment for protecting her."

"She is." Killian stepped closer, the table in the middle of the shop the only thing separating them now. "Now tell me what I wish to know or I'll break each of your bones one by one, kid."

He swallowed. "I-I-I gave her the list of her mother's helpers on the Island. The vials were elixirs to help her take care of a few of them so they would be of no use to Rowena any longer. She didn't wish to kill them, so she sabotaged their work."

Killian's heart beat quickly. His good little princess. Of course she wished them no harm. He internally shook his head at her—oh, how the good girl fell for the monster...

"Did you tell her where to find her mother?"

The kid shook his head. "I figured Alana would've done that."

"Alana's dead."

He stepped back again as if afraid Killian was going to end him next.

"I didn't kill her. Rowena did."

He bit his bottom lip. "Rowena lives in the little green cottage by the sea. The one by the Black Tower. It's close enough to the ships transporting to the North, but not so close that she may be caught or somehow recognized by any of them."

Killian had passed by the Black Tower plenty of times in his life, had seen the little cottages, each a different pastel color, that were spaced out by the sea below, but he'd never paid them any mind. It was an ingenious place to hide. He surely wouldn't have suspected someone after a throne—a whole palace—would spend her days in a tiny cottage.

"Why are you helping?" Killian asked in order to make sure this kid wouldn't be a threat.

"She killed my parents. I can't do anything to her myself, but I need her dead," he answered with soft vigor.

Killian looked him over. He was the opposite of a stereotypical Island male, and it took no genius to know he wouldn't be able to kill an animal, better yet another human being. There were plenty of these men in the Island, but they were so often overlooked by the barbarians.

For the first time in his life, Killian was truly thankful for some of these softer men. These were the types of men his nonas thought they were getting. Men who would be soft with them and kind to others.

Killian stepped back. "Thank you."

The kid nodded and took a sure step forward. "Please. Kill her."

Killian nodded. "I won't let her hurt my woman."

The kid nodded his understanding of the Island customs, then gave a soft smile like finally his prayers were being answered.

THERE WAS no one in the cottage when Killian arrived.

That wasn't the kid's fault. He hadn't said Rowena would be there at that very moment. He'd merely said it was where Rowena lived.

Killian thought he might stick around to surprise her but threw that idea out when he saw the footprints in the dirt leading toward the pubs by the port. They were closed now as no ships were about, but that didn't mean Rowena hadn't gone to one. The pub would be a perfect place to do her work while it was empty.

Killian followed the steps and along the way, saw more coming from the forest. He had to be thankful for the dirt on this side of the port that made the footprints stick to the ground. Now he had to determine whether these were the prints of Sael and her Posse or more of Rowena's followers.

The pub had only three windows, so Killian moved around the building to the side until he could see within. The things were made of a hard material so they were nearly impossible to break, but that made them less clear to look through too.

His heart skipped a beat at the slightly blurry sight of Sael again, magnetically beautiful and calling for him. He could hardly breathe from his desire to run in there and take her into his arms.

His gaze was forced away when darts flew through the air, and everyone moved quickly. His heart stopped.

Why wasn't Evony's magic protecting them?

Sael!

As he pushed away from the window for the door in front, Killian was only thankful he saw the moron twins jump for Sael's safety. As much as he hated Miels for Sael's past feelings for him, Killian was thankful for the man for blocking her from getting hit.

As he banged against the door that wouldn't open, Killian's heart hit the ground—Rowena could be hurting his woman at that very moment, and there was no other way into the pub.

CHAPTER 50
ROSAELIA

By the time they got close enough to the cottage, Rowena was already headed out. Rosaelia wasn't entirely sure if that was a positive yet. That cottage would've given them the privacy to finish this, and the small space would've made it nearly impossible for her to run.

Now, as they watched her move from her cottage to the pub the sailors used after trading delicacies—now empty as no ships had sailed that day—Rosaelia felt the crawling need to get this done and run back to Killian as fast as her body would take her.

"There's no one else in there," Evony said as her magic tested whether they should expect resistance going after Rowena.

Sparrow's hand laid over Evony's stomach like he was protecting his child, his entire focus on his wife rather than Rowena, and though it was the sweetest thing Rosaelia had ever seen her brother do, it made her realize just how dangerous it had been to tell him now, this close to Rowena.

Rosaelia knew he would not be moving from his wife's side

the entire time they went in, and that didn't bother her a bit. She loved seeing the protectiveness in her brother. Rosaelia only hoped he stayed in his own mind enough to not get himself hurt. Evony might kill all of them if that were to happen.

They followed Rowena into the pub, Evony's magic shielding them from being seen, and found her with a sword in hand, whipping it through the air skillfully.

So this was where she trained.

In the seconds they were inside, and it took for Rosaelia's senses to take in the sweetness around her, Evony coughed into Sparrow's arm. The Assassin froze with deathly cool as he stood before her, his arm holding on to his little family.

Gwendolyn Powder, the only thing that could wipe out a magician's powers for a limited time, was in the air. It was ingenious of Rowena to make sure she was covered now that she knew Evony was on the land, had proved with the use of her magic against the sorcerer fires to Killian's home how much of a nuisance she would be to Rowena.

But it also meant that the shield was now broken.

A fact solidified when Rowena's body stiffened in their direction.

As they all moved for her, Rowena swung her sword above her head in an arc, cutting a rope in half as she ducked, and releasing a dozen needles through the air. Because of the suddenness, the Posse hardly had time to move. Rosaelia was only thankful, as she dropped, that Sparrow had been fast enough to land on Evony before any made contact with her. They didn't know if whatever was in these needles would kill, but Rosaelia doubted it. She knew Rowena would want to kill the Masters herself, have a final chance at taking Evony's magic. These would immobilize, give her that chance.

But none of them knew what that could do to a baby.

Sparrow had a dart in either bicep.

When Rosaelia checked on the others, both Tristan and Miels had darts in their arm and leg each. They looked to be reaching for her, like they were covering anything from touching her. She loved them extra for that.

Another glance showed Gabriel over Ashtyn with a dart in his side.

Ashtyn's frantic pull on Gabriel showed her untouched, but Rosaelia imagined her feelings for Gabriel were about to show themselves if anything happened to him. She was a medic, not here to fight anyone but to heal them if something were to happen, so she could stay with the others.

This was Rosaelia's mission anyway. Rowena was hers to take care of.

In the seconds it took to check on everyone, Rowena was moving. She came running from the other side of the pub, so Rosaelia quickly rose to her feet in order to protect her family. She was probably one of the worst fighters, but she wouldn't let anything happen to them.

Every part of this frightened her. Killing for Killian's sake had been easy, but killing her own mother felt numbing, even though it was now partly for Killian's sake. She couldn't let anything happen to her family, who were only in the Island because of her.

She wouldn't exactly have a choice if Rowena killed her. With the way she swung that sword, Rosaelia doubted her own odds.

Her mother was coming for her. She was going to kill her, and the cold look in her eyes said she was very happy she could finally take Rosaelia out of this world.

Rosaelia's hands moved on their own as a banging came from the front door. Evony's magic had shut it behind them, but Rosaelia wasn't sure if it would be able to hold for long with her affected by the Gwendolyn Powder.

One moment, Rowena was coming at her defenseless form, and the next, Rosaelia had Sparrow's sword, which was much heavier than even her adrenaline was able to help her with. Rowena's sword banged against Rosaelia's, and they stood there, swords pressed together, teeth grit, cold stares on one another.

"Oh, drop it, weak girl," Rowena taunted. "You know you cannot harm me."

"You tried to hurt Killian's family," Rosaelia ground out as her arms shook from the pressure she put into the heavy weapon to hold Rowena back.

Another banging against the doors. Was that Rowena's helpers?

"Yes," she mocked. "And now you have a sorcerer protecting the defenseless little things, don't you? You are pathetic. You put a sorcerer up for the job because you're useless to protect them yourself." She pushed against the swords.

You are useless.

You are useless.

You are useless.

Rosaelia pushed back, her anger seething up. "I am not useless. I now know, I've learned to appreciate everyone's skills."

"Like mother, like daughter."

The thought made her sick as Rosaelia pushed against the swords once more. "Like father, like daughter actually."

Another banging against the doors.

How was she supposed to do this? Rowena was obviously a much better swordsman than she was, and the sword in her hand was already growing too heavy to keep lifted. The boys were all immobilized by the darts, and Evony and Ashtyn stuck beneath their males. Rosaelia needed to figure out a way around this.

Rowena laughed. "Your father is the definition of pathetic. He's useless, far more than you. I mean, look at him, sending children to do his bidding."

"My father"—Rosaelia pushed against her mother's sword, the bites at her father pushing her adrenaline—"is not"—she pushed her mother back another two steps—"useless."

"Your father's too kind!" Rowena blared.

Another bang.

"My father loves his people!"

Another bang.

"Your father"—she pushed on Rosaelia until the sword shook in the Princess's hand—"should've been killed. I should've worn that crown alone!" She pulled her sword back and swung at Rosaelia's, throwing the weapon from her hands.

The thing crashed along the ground, and Rosaelia was once again left defenseless.

Another bang.

Rowena swung that weapon around in her arms, eyeing all of them like she knew she'd won out over Rosaelia already, so she needed to decide who would die next.

That second's glance wasn't enough time for Rosaelia to come up with another plan. "What do you mean he should've been killed?"

Rowena gave her a look that said, 'oh, you pathetic child always thinking the best of people.' "You did not think I had those men sent to the palace to simply kill you and your sister? All three of you were meant to die. I had given them specific instructions. I would send your sister from the caves with my lady's maid. You and your father would be in his suite. They knew the way to traverse through the tunnels there too. Leave it to barbarians to mess up simple instructions."

Another bang. It must be Rowena's helpers. The second they got into the pub, the entire Posse would be gone.

Rosaelia took a minuscule step back as if she could throw her body over all of her family. "Why send them through at all if you wanted them dead?"

She laughed. "I could not risk others seeing of it. You know as well as I that servant gossip travels faster than anything else."

"And when that didn't work, you ran here!" Rosaelia was growing angry now rather than frightened about the fact that she was defenseless. "You came to ruin Islanders' lives."

"Oh, boohoo, look at the Princess caring about Islanders now. What? You got a cock in you, and now you think they're all worth saving? That boy was using you to get off." She scoffed. "Out of all the ones you could've chosen too. You chose *the most* messed up one."

All Islanders wore scars. The protective, masculine ones more than the others. Killian more than any of them.

Rosaelia loved those scars.

Her fists clenched at her sides. "Do not speak of him!"

Rowena swung her sword back, and Rosaelia knew she was done speaking. "You make me sick!"

She was coming at her, then her gaze shot to the side, and her smile turned more cruel as she turned the sword in her hand so it wasn't coming at Rosaelia after all.

As Rosaelia followed its path, her breath left her as it slashed down Killian's chest.

Killian's.

How? When...? She'd left him so this didn't happen. How...

As Killian fell to his knees, Rosaelia's mind blanked, and her hand moved on its own.

Every teaching.

Every instinct.

Every fiber of her being came to attention.

Her hand flew for the weapon strapped to her thigh—the one she'd forgotten about but had been there every day since the moment Killian gave it to her—and Rosaelia stared as the dagger flew through the air as if her cold gaze could dictate its movement. She watched as it latched into her mother's gut.

Rowena's astonished gaze—one that said '*you* did that'—was an added joy as Rosaelia moved slowly toward the late Queen of the Northern Lands, kicking the woman's sword aside.

She took the hilt of the dagger in hand and pushed on it, reveling in the cries of her mother. "That was for me." She twisted it. "That's for my father. And this, this is for Killian." Without hesitation, she moved the dagger up with all the force her body could muster so the sharp edge cut through her heart.

Rowena didn't have time to fight Rosaelia's grasp as the dagger met its mark, and her dead weight fell into Rosaelia's arms. Rosaelia didn't give her the nicety, and instantly dropped her body. As she stood over the dead body of her mother, Rosaelia feared the worst. Her entire being was afraid to turn for her mate.

This was what she'd been scared of. Her mother had been able to see Rosaelia's feelings for Killian and hurt him to get to her. She'd purposefully pulled away from killing Rosaelia to hurt her even more.

A tear slid down her cheek as her body shook, too afraid to turn but needing to more than anything else in the world.

When she finally faced him, he was on his knees, staring up at her with adoration as his hand reached from inside his pocket and pulled out a black box. He peeled it open as if he wasn't hurt. "Marry me, princess."

She broke down then, the tears falling in sobs as she rushed to her knees before him. The tears overwhelmed her as he softly took her face in his hands and kissed them away. "I love you, Sael."

Her hand shook on his chest, blood seeping out. Too much blood. "You're hurt. Kill, no, please. Ashtyn!"

She was busy with the others, but she needed to get out from beneath Gabriel, and take care of her barbarian.

He laughed as he forced her to meet his dark hazel eyes. "It's only a cut, princess."

"No, no! We need to clean you up. Ashtyn needs to look at you." Another sob broke out of her, and she fell into his chest as the tears fell. "Thank the lords Ashtyn's here. I can't lose you, Kill. No!"

He held her a moment before forcing her to look at him. "I'm okay, Sael. It's only a cut, a scar at best." He laughed. "Just another one to add to the collection. My favorite one."

She shook her head and couldn't stop the tears. "Killian..."

"I love you, princess. Marry me. Please."

She nodded vigorously. "Yes, yes, always. I'll marry you and mark my hand, Killian. Yes! I love you so fucking much."

She kissed him before he could comment on her curse, and she was finally able to breathe freely, feeling his lips on hers again. He kissed her back softly but hungrily.

CHAPTER 51

KILLIAN

Ashtyn did, in fact, end up looking at his chest after they'd pulled the men to lean against the walls, darts pulled out so the drug didn't continue to circulate into their systems. Sael insisted he get checked. She was so cute when she was determined like that, Killian couldn't refuse her demands.

The healer told him as he knew—it was only a cut. She said she could heal it so it didn't scar, but he hadn't let her. This was one scar he wanted. One he would love, the way Sael loved the ones on his face.

When they got home, and after the nonas fussed about their wellbeings, and Norya gave each of them bear hugs, having been upset not to be able to come along but knowing someone needed to stay with the nonas, they'd all sat for a meal.

The nonas handed them to the women, then pulled their arms back when Sparrow went to grab for one.

Nona Tereza answered his quirked brow. "It is customary

that on tough days or long travels, the claimed woman eats first, then her male takes his servings from her empty plate."

It would be his decision to make, and he didn't hesitate a moment. Sparrow backed away immediately and took his wife into his lap as she began her meal. Sael wouldn't let Killian place her on his lap, but she sat by his side, eating her meal out of the plate he would be using soon.

To no one's surprise, Gabriel remained back when the nonas tried to offer him a plate, and he stood behind Ashtyn's chair as she ate. The nonas nodded their understanding then. The girl hadn't heard the explanation—because they all knew she would argue with what it meant if Gabriel took her plate if she had—but she didn't question why the stable hand wasn't eating. She was usually a reserved girl, very in her head about matters.

The others followed along with their bowls then, Norya and each of the moron twins settled with their bowls of Eleni's chili before the nonas did.

They spent an hour speaking of the North—Evony, Miels, Tristan, Norya, and Nona Tereza doing most of the talking— and in that time, Eleni filled Evony's, Sael's, and Ashtyn's empty bowls and handed them to their men. Ashtyn had quirked a brow at the movement but hadn't questioned it— though her perceptive gaze said she caught that both of the mated males at the table were doing the same thing.

After their meals, everyone was sent one by one—or couple-by-couple in his and Sparrow's cases—to the baths to clean up, starting with the moron twins and ending with the married Masters.

Killian wanted to go last so they could take their time in there, but Sael had insisted if her twin went before them that they'd never get a moment in there, especially after the news Sparrow had found out earlier in the day. The fact that the two

Masters' had been in there for almost two hours made Killian trust Sael's words more than before.

It was early evening when they all sat around the living space and watched the nonas prepare to leave this home, and the Island Nation, behind.

Things would be easier for him and Norya because though this was the only home they'd ever known, neither one of them had accumulated much more than some clothes and weapons. Those of which they wished to take with them were already packed and ready.

The nonas, on the other hand, had far more things around the house they wanted to take with them. It would open this home up for someone else's taking, and for that, Sael was happy. She said it got both his family to go home with her and another family a home of their own. Killian had argued that point because he had no intentions of leaving the space open for the taking.

Clark would be getting this home.

Though the No Known Housing unit now held residence in Keir's estate, Killian knew if the members could have their own places, they would, so he knew Clark would love this home. Killian had every intention of making sure everyone knew this would be the boy's home. He knew Clark would take care of it.

He deserved this home. He'd saved Sael from the whorehouse fiends, he deserved far more than a house.

As Killian watched Sael from across the living space as she laughed with Norya, he got the overwhelming feeling that this was his life now—she was his life now.

Like she could feel his stare on her, Sael turned to meet his gaze, and gave him a warm smile of her own. Her eyes shined like *she* couldn't believe she'd gotten so lucky with him.

Killian smiled, warm and real, as he made his way to his

princess. He softly took Sael's hand in his and pulled her out of her seat. "Ready for your farewell to the Island Nation?"

Her brows furrowed, but she didn't question him as she nodded, ready to go along with whatever he had planned.

"That's my good little princess." He leaned into her ear, his breath tickling, and sending shivers down her body. "Now, let's go make you a very pretty princess."

Her breath hitched, and those green orbs heated as she nodded vigorously. Even as embarrassed as she always grew with each talk of sexual matters, it never failed to make her eager when he insinuated anything happening between them.

Killian laughed, knowing she didn't entirely understand yet what he had planned.

There was still another hour before the chill set in outside, and he intended on taking advantage of that time. He pulled away, her hand still in his, and led her to the front door. Before leaving, he turned to all the occupants of the house. "Do not go into town today."

CHAPTER 52
ROSAELIA

Being back in the Northern Lands truly felt revitalizing to Rosaelia. She hadn't realized how much she had missed her lands until she was back on it. A glance in the nonas' direction said they felt the same way—times tenfold. It had been nearly four decades since they'd been back.

Then there were the others. As they rode in their large carriage toward the palace, their bags carried in a wagon behind them, everyone silently thrummed with excitement. Rosaelia still couldn't believe they'd been able to fit this many people—including how large all the men were—into a carriage. She supposed her sister's magic may have had something to do with that as she sat on Sparrow's lap in the middle of one of the seats.

They'd given the Islanders the window seats so they could look out to their new home. Rosaelia sat in Killian's lap—per his request, and the need for space within the carriage—and looked out the window with him. He—like Norya across from them—looked to be taking in everything around them, a bit of excitement at the new location they could explore, as their gazes remained on the forests every time they passed by.

Her friends, on the other hand, looked like she felt. Like coming home.

Miels especially looked to be ripping his hair out in his urgency to get back to the palace. Especially when they stopped on two nights to rest—he had *not* liked that plan.

When they were close to the palace but still a ways away, Miels leaned over to Evony in front of him. "Call to her, please." He sounded so desperate, his eyes pleading, and it made them all feel for him.

Even Killian pulled her tighter into his lap, and it was evident he understood the pain of being separated from a mate. Finally, this would give Killian the evidence that Miels was entirely and wholly disinterested in her and entirely in Etel.

Evony took his hand softly in hers and smiled warmly. "She's already waiting for you, Miels."

A relieved laugh left him as his eyes misted over, and his leg jittered in his need to get closer to his Remedies Expert.

When they were on palace greens, Miels only allowed the carriage to carry him another few yards before he saw her in front of the palace, and his anticipation couldn't take it any longer. He fought his way through everyone's legs and out the door between Rosaelia and Norya.

Evony had the carriage safely stopped by then, and he was out, running for the girl at the front of the steps. Then the Remedies Expert was running for him.

They emptied out of the carriage farther away than planned, but Rosaelia didn't care as she laughed, elated at the way the two jumped for one another. The way Miels dropped to his knees, then his ass, with her wrapped around his waist.

It made her emotional and made her feel a bit selfish that she'd been the reason they'd had to be separated.

Then, beyond them, Rosaelia saw him. Her father.

Then she was the one running.

Right into her father's arms. His arms were tight around her, and a large relieved sigh left him as he held her again. "You cannot do that to your father, Ro. You cannot leave me like that. I didn't know what happened to you. Do you know what it does to a father to miss his daughter and not be able to go after her?"

Her eyes were wet now as she pulled away and met his gaze. Because he was King, he needed to stay in the North. She hadn't thought of the extra amount of pain not coming after her would've done to him, what sending all of his 'children' to barbarian nation would've done to him. "I'm so sorry, Father. But I needed to protect you. And I can't say I regret any of my decisions."

His gaze traveled past her to the four strangers—the one male stranger—before coming back to her. "Daughter?"

Rosaelia's cheeks burned, so unused to speaking of love with her father, as she pulled away from him, and stepped away until her back touched Killian's chest. She still held her father's hand as she turned to the nonas. "This is Nona Tereza and Nona Eleni. They're sisters and were once friends with your mother."

Edmund's brows shot up. "And you were in the Island?"

Nona Tereza smiled respectfully. "I had thought myself in love." She looked around at the couples around their small group, at Miels and Etel still on the ground. "I had no idea what I had been speaking of when I said love. But by the time I figured that out, we were stuck there."

Edmund's lips downturned with fault as he began to apologize. "I'm sorry for—"

"Don't be," Nona Tereza said. "I do not fault you, Eddie dear."

Rosaelia's smile grew at her father's blush. There were so few instances where he blushed that it made her giddy to have someone in her arsenal to make it happen so quickly.

Rosaelia turned to her newest friend. "This is Norya. Call her a sister the way Sparrow is a brother to me."

Edmund gave her a warm smile before turning back to his daughter. "And whose sister shall I call her?" His eyes were already on Killian behind her.

On the scarred man. The monster.

Rosaelia's blush was deep as she tilted her head to look at her love. "This is Killian, Nona Tereza's grandson, Norya's brother, and... my barbarian."

A small laugh broke from Killian's hard exterior as his hands reached for her waist, squeezing to tell her how much he loved the sound of that, how much he loved how red she got when speaking of matters of the heart.

Edmund watched them without saying a word until Rosaelia turned back to her father. "You love him?"

She knew, they all did, that his scars and hard exterior may cause some problems of acceptance in the North. "He's not as scary of a monster as he looks, Father. He's—"

"But do you love him?"

"With all my heart."

His gaze flickered to Killian. "And you?"

Killian's features were hard, serious, as he met Edmund's. "I'd throw my life down infinitely to protect her. She is my life. She is my only definition of love."

After a few minutes of staring at one another, Edmund finally met Rosaelia's gaze again. "Shall I expect two weddings then?"

Her breath hitched. "Two?"

He glanced down to Miels and Etel who were still wrapped together, kissing and whispering to one another.

Rosaelia laughed. "Yes, then. You should expect two."

His smile was wide as he turned from them to the couple on the ground to the couple embracing with Evony—Gemma and James. "Two more marriages and a child on the way. We shall have a festive year ahead of us."

Tristan scoffed good-humoredly. "Two children."

"Excuse me?" Edmund quirked a brow at him, then followed Tristan's smirk to Evony's belly.

Gemma's eyes widened then, smacking her best friend on the arm. "You're pregnant!"

Evony threw a death glare at Tristan. "I had planned on telling you inside."

Gemma screamed as Tristan laughed, and the girl threw herself into Evony's arms. "We're having babies together!"

Evony finally laughed with her. "We're having babies together!"

James's laugh filled with theirs, and the three embraced, back to the trio they had been only a few months ago.

Rosaelia's attention was only snagged from their happiness by Miels standing with Etel pressed to his side, a command on his tongue. "Everyone, head to the tailors."

Edmund's gaze hardened as they all spoke at once.

"What?"

"Why?"

"Now?"

Miels's hard glare quieted them all. "I am marrying Etel tomorrow. Prepare yourself because I will *not* be waiting any longer."

They all laughed as he didn't wait for another word before turning for the palace, tugging his woman with him as they no doubt rushed for their suite. Miels had weeks of exploring her body to make up for.

It was then that Edmund turned to Tristan and Sparrow. "My boys, your brother is a moron."

They laughed as the three embraced, and Sparrow said, "We're all morons in love, Ed."

Edmund quirked a brow at Norya. "Tristan too."

"No!" both Tristan and Norya barked as they chuckled at the insinuation of love between them.

They laughed, then turned for the palace, enjoying one another's company as everyone welcomed each other back.

THE TAILOR'S suite was on the second floor and was broken up between the main tailor, an old man by the name of Odolf, the tailor's assistant, Atiana, beneath him, and three more main tailors beneath her before all the tailor's maids came in.

Normally, they all worked out of the tailor's rooms which was a large suite with seven rooms within and a larger common area in the middle for people to stand before mirrors and for observers to get a look. Other times, the tailors took work to their own suites and worked from there, all of which lived in close quarters to this main tailor's area.

Atiana was Rosaelia's favorite and the best tailor. She was all of her friends' favorite tailor, and every time she saw them, a wide sweet smile would broaden her lips.

As they all walked in now, and Atiana turned to see the group, her eyes widened and shined. "Princess! You're back!"

Rosaelia laughed. "I am. And been summoned to the tailors immediately. Apparently I have a brother impatient to marry."

Atiana laughed. "Yes, I've seen many of Etel preparing her gown so she did not have to wait any longer than needed."

Rosaelia was happy to hear it as she turned to the newcomers and introduced them, and Atiana got excited with all she would have to get through. Their pre-made garbs would be the best fit for a last-minute occasion such as this one. The only thing needed would be to have everyone choose one to their body's requirements, then to tailor them to fit perfectly. Atiana was such a beautiful and quick worker, Rosaelia had no doubt she could get them all done in time.

As Atiana ushered them all to the room of garments, Edmund paused before her, his gaze hard. "I will find Odolf."

Atiana blushed, her gaze faltering. "Are you sure, Your Highness? I can take care of you without a problem."

Edmund's gaze looked to harden, nostrils flaring and jaw ticcing with annoyance. "Odolf will have plenty prepared for me. I will be in and out in no time. You, focus on the others."

Atiana's eyes saddened as she struggled to continue to meet Edmund's gaze, her cheeks burning as she gave a single nod. "As you wish, sir."

Atiana turned quickly, and Rosaelia's anger was already turned on her father. Edmund didn't allow her a moment for a lecture as he moved for Odolf, his gaze lethal the entire time.

Rosaelia ground her jaw as she moved for Atiana who stood at the edge of the garment room, watching everyone shuffle through the picks. She placed a soft hand to the girl's shoulder and gave a weak smile. "I'm sorry about him."

Atiana's eyes looked sadder than a mere hard word from the King would cause, but Rosaelia didn't know what it was. "Do not be, Princess. Please, have a look at that rack. Those are the gowns I'd made for you while you were gone. Pick one. I cannot wait to see how beautiful you look in them."

Rosaelia smiled. "Okay. As long as you call me Rosaelia or Ro. No more Princess. We are friends, Atiana."

There was hope in her eyes now, but sadness still filled them. "Thank you, Rosaelia. Now, please pick a gown so I can have everything prepared before Miels bites all of our heads off."

Rosaelia laughed and moved for Killian who was looking at dresses. "You'd like to wear a dress, barbarian?"

He smirked at her. "I'm thinking about which one of these I'd like to rip off of you tomorrow."

She laughed and shoved him. "Stop it, Kill. They work hard on these."

"And I work your body hard." He winked and continued searching for her dress.

She hip-knocked him. "These are Atiana's masterworks. You will not harm them."

He laughed as his arms circled her from behind. "Okay, princess. I won't harm your pretty dresses."

EPILOGUE
ROSAELIA

Their honeymoon was a trip to the Southwest Library. It gave Killian the opportunity to see more of the North, for the two of them to explore nature, but also to explore each others bodies in the privacy of the lands.

Privacy to be as loud as they wished, something Rosaelia was a bit more cautious about now that they were in the North where propriety was a matter of life.

They had the space to run around. To live.

And most importantly, they had the privacy for Rosaelia to read her most favored book to Killian.

"Gustav had spent so much of their relationship wanting to bash her head in that he hadn't taken the time to truly appreciate her beauty. And a beauty she was. Amoré would've been any male's desired wife, yet he'd hated every moment of being with her. 'I brought you here in the hopes I could get you close to the fireworks, wife. That way I could push you into them and be rid of you.'"

Killian's laugh a her ear made Rosaelia smile. They were sitting on the ground by a large window at twilight. Rosaelia leaned into his chest as she read the words aloud, cocooned in the safety of his arms.

"Amoré eyed him cautiously but with a hint of amusement. 'Yet you tell me about this plan.' Gustav's body moved forward like he had the urge to do something. But what?" Rosaelia continued reading. "As the first set of sparklers lit up the sky, Gustav stopped before her, so close it would take no effort at all to kiss her. But why would he want to do that? She was the bane of his existence. Then suddenly, she turned, mesmerized in the lights in the sky.

"Gustav stood there a moment, lost in her profile as she took in the sight around them. In the sky were thousands of sparklers of every color. They made a chorus of noise and called for the attention of anything alive. Gustav's favorite were the ones that changed color in the sky. As he stood there, taking in the beauty of lights in the sky, he felt the sudden urge to reach his hand out and take Amoré's. He couldn't do such a thing, she would ridicule him. Yet his hand reached out. If he touched her, he would be opening up their relationship and he was quite fine with where they stood now—hating one another. The back of his hand brushed hers, and everything in him noticed the way her body stiffened at the move. That was an odd realization—that with all this beauty around him, part of him was somehow still focused on her. His wife. His bane of existence wife. He didn't want anything more of their relationship, yet he took her hand anyway. Took it and let the warmth of her fingers intertwining with his travel through his body. Had his body ever known such...comfort?"

Rosaelia closed her eyes as she leaned back into Killian. This part of the book always made her smile. "I just love this book."

"I love all the voices you do when you read it to me."

She snorted, laughing at her husband.

Her eyes snapped open. Killian was her husband.

Her gaze traveled down to his hands wrapped around her waist, to his right hand where his ring sat and his left hand where the Island marking for a claimed marriage sat.

Then she was focused on her own hands. Her own right which wore the ring and her own left which held that marking. She didn't understand why everyone thought it so shocking that she would agree to it. Rings could be taken off, stolen. There was nothing that could be done to take away her markings.

She turned abruptly in her spot between Killian's legs so she could face him, dropping the book to the side as she took his face between her hands.

"Aren't you going to continue reading, princess?"

She shrugged. "Later. Right now, I want to be in the real world. Spend time with my husband."

He smirked. "I love when you call me that, Sael."

She pulled him in for a chaste kiss. "Would you like to go for a walk? Before it gets too cold and we're stuck indoors the rest of the night."

She couldn't help the mischievous glint in her eyes as she said those words. A large part of their honeymoon had been spent indoors, doing activities Northerners didn't openly speak of.

But they'd also spent the time doing a lot of other things. She'd shown him the expanse of the Library, taking him to her favorite parts. She'd been slowly reading this book to him. She'd taken him out to the greens where they could explore the fields around the Library—all lush green, giving Killian that freedom he'd always been searching for.

In the suite they were in, the one Rosaelia always took when she traveled to the Southwest Library, they danced and played games—her favorite a Northern one called nardi—and whispered stories in the dark. And of course, consummated their marriage over and over and over...

In the other parts of the library, they enjoyed living together. In the kitchen, they laughed as they made of mess of their meals. In the common space, they put on shows, creating a stage and improvising their roles.

Rosaelia was lucky. The keepers of this library adored her and were great at keeping any of her secrets. They'd been more than happy to give the two of them the privacy for their honeymoon. Even though as the Princess she could've forced them gone, Rosaelia loved that they had such a sweet relationship. She cherished it with all three keepers—Alí, Amí, and Agí.

The flash of the last week faded away and Rosaelia was back with her barbarian. "So what do you say? A walk?"

"I'd love nothing more, my wife, than to cherish this freedom with you."

He lifted her as he stood up causing giggles to roll out of her. "Good. And when we're back, we can light some candles—"

"I like where your mind is headed," Killian mumbled into her neck.

"And play a few rounds of nardi. I think I can definitely beat you majority stake." He'd been surprisingly great at the game.

Killian grumbled against her skin. "I don't like where your mind is headed."

She laughed, still wrapped in his arms, clinging to his neck with no desire to let go. "Then, after I win, we can spend the whole night doing what your mind is imagining."

He smirked. "Then I think—"

"You cannot let me win, Killian!"

"Oh, wife, wife, wife, you're no fun." He carried her to the doors where their cloaks sat on a chair.

"Oh, husband, husband, husband, you're such a barbarian."

They laughed as he threw her cloak over her shoulders and pulled on the hood to cover her face. Her sparkling green eyes caught his honey-colored ones, and Rosaelia couldn't believe her luck at having found her monster to love for the rest of her life.

NELLY ALIKYAN

WITH THE STORMS CATCHING DUSK

NORYA

Her back arched as his tongue slipped up her spine, ending with a bite to her shoulder.

He'd taken a tube of lube from the Remedies Expert, and had two fingers slick with the gooey stuff as they entered her ass, curling to hit the perfect spot as his cock thrust into her.

Tristan was rough as he pounded into her, guttural in the sounds he made. They made no attempts to quiet themselves. They were in the Northern palace where the walls were thicker, and in a room far enough away from civilization to care.

And she was an Islander. She surely didn't care if they were heard.

Norya gripped the comforter of the bed they were on as her climax hit, and she screamed, voice cracking as Tristan laughed behind her.

"That's three, little warrior," he teased. "I think you bet I couldn't make you come nine times before I came once?"

His fingers rubbed over her clit so ferociously, Norya's eyes rolled back, and she bit into the comforter, his other hand still fucking her ass. She wanted to fight her orgasm so he wouldn't have the satisfaction of winning this bet, but as his cock pounded into her, she couldn't fight it. Tristan's dick slipped out as she squirted all over the sheets, the liquid coming out of her in puddles before he was able to put his cock back in her.

"That's a good fucking girl," he ground out as the door opened to the room, and both of them turned to find the Princess of the Northern Lands standing there with a look of shocked fright.

By the sounds of her screams, Rosaelia had probably thought her in danger and come for some aid. The crimson of her cheeks said she now realized how very mistaken she'd been.

Sael muttered an apology, and slammed the door shut behind her.

It made both Tristan and Norya laugh as he flipped her onto her back. Tristan leaned down to kiss her as they shared this moment laughing at the Princess.

"My poor Princess has quite the habit," he teased.

"Your poor Princess may be traumatized."

He scoffed. "Please. She fucks your brother."

She bit his bottom lip. "Very true, spy. Now, are you done? Only four?"

He gripped both of her ankles and brought them up beside her face, spreading her wide. "Not even close. Now hold your ankles."

She smirked. "I'm not helping you win."

His fingers scraped down her calves as he gave her a teasing grin, and slithered down her body, holding her legs open as he took her soaking clit into his mouth.

Norya's hands fell into his hair and she pulled at it, lost in the talented daze his tongue had the power to put her in.

Tristan pushed her legs even more so her ass lifted off the bed, and he slipped lower to lick her puckered hole. He ate her ass as he dropped one of her legs to play with her pussy, fucking her then rubbing her clit, then fucking her again.

It was so fucking good, Norya didn't care if he won, she held onto her ankles to keep herself open for him. Tristan only laughed at her defeat as he now had both hands free to fuck her and tease her as he ate her ass.

She came hard, squirting onto his face as he licked up her slit to suck at her clit again, to get any taste of her.

He bit the inside of her thigh. "Five."

He licked back up her body, and while she kept her legs spread by the ankles, he collared her and held her down, grinning at her from above while his face dripped with her arousal. "You ready to give up yet?"

She smirked, needing him to continue. "You're not going to win, spy. You still have halfway to go, and there's no way your cock won't explode before then."

Lies. She knew how amazing his stamina was, but she needed him riled up with the need to prove himself so he'd be rough with her the way she wanted.

His hands tightened around her neck as he lowered to kiss her. She tasted herself on his face, his tongue, every inch of him, and damn near came again. He laughed like he knew what he did to her.

Then he peeled away and got off the bed.

Just like that.

She growled. "Spy! Get your ass back over here!"

He laughed again as he stood to the side of the bed, and reached over to take a fistful of her hair. He dragged her toward himself so her head fell over the edge, and his hands teased her mouth. "Open that mouth, little whore."

She was overjoyed at the prospect of getting his cock in her mouth as he tapped it over her lips, then slipped it into her waiting mouth. She moaned at the taste of their herself on his cock as his hands slid down her body, one taking a breast while the other slipped down until he had three fingers inside her.

"Suck, little warrior whore."

She laughed as drool slipped out of her mouth, but she did as she was told. Maybe she could get him to come before he hit six.

He didn't fuck her mouth like she wanted, merely stood there and let her suck him off while his fingers pounded into her, so wet with her arousal, the room sounded like a whirlpool storm was amidst them.

Then he leaned down to suck and bite at her nipples.

She didn't want to come. Didn't want to give him that satisfaction.

But with his mouth on her nipples, his fingers in her pussy, and his cock shoved down her throat, there was no stopping it. She came, spraying all over while her moans gagged on his cock.

He didn't stop fucking her pussy until her orgasm—which lasted an eternity—ended.

Then he quickly pulled his cock from her mouth with a loud groan.

"No!" she fought, reaching for his dick again.

He grabbed both of her wrists and forced them away. "No, no, darling. We're only at six."

"Cheater!" she yelled.

He collared her to force up to her knees, her withered body barely able to do as he wanted. "I never said I wouldn't cheat, little barbarionette."

She growled, and bit his bottom lip, making it bleed.

"Give me three more little orgasms, then you can tell me whether you want my come in your mouth, your pussy, or your ass."

"What if I want it on me?"

"Not an option tonight," he growled as he bit her shoulder.

She laughed at his sounds, knowing he wanted to come desperately, and started pumping his cock.

He pushed her hands away, and forced her onto all fours. "No touching me, whore."

She shoved her ass back. "You're no fun, Northerner."

He bit, kissed, and licked at her ass as he reached for the tube of lube once more, drenching his cock and fingers with it. His soaked fingers reached for her puckered hole, playing with and teasing it. "I think you talk too much, Islander."

He placed his cock at her ass and impaled her before she could respond, making her scream out. Her eyes rolled back as he pulled on her hair to keep her upright, his other hand moving for her clit. He knew how much she loved him in her ass, and she knew he would hardly be able to last while in there.

As he stuck his fingers in her pussy, she came again.

"Seven," he laughed through his grunts.

He pulled his cock out and dropped to his knees, sucking on her clit for only a few seconds before she was squirting again.

"Eight," he teased.

"You're not gonna win," she argued, barely able to get the word out.

He sucked her clit again before raising to his feet and sticking his cock in her ass again. "You're gonna come again, whore. You know you want me to win."

He fucked her ass hard, one hand fucking her pussy while the other pinched at her clit.

He was gonna win.

He was gonna win.

She couldn't let him win.

But she needed to come.

She needed—

Needed—

"Where do you want it? Mouth, pussy, or ass?"

She couldn't let him win.

Couldn't—

Couldn't...

"Answer me!" he growled.

The sheer power in his voice paired with what he was doing to her had her screaming with number nine.

She was still in the middle of the orgasm when he growled, "Answer me!"

"Mouth," she cried. "I want you in my mouth!"

He pulled out of her quickly, turning her so she sat on the bed before him, and shoved his cock into her mouth. He only pumped once before he came inside her mouth, cum dripping down her chin as he continued to fill her.

His groans had her hands moving for her pussy, and orgasm ten hit her as she sucked the cum out of his cock.

When he finally pulled away, his cum was still dripping from her lips and falling onto her chest. He smirked, and rubbed it into her skin as he breathed hard above her.

Norya just looked up at him in a daze.

After a few minutes to catch his breath, Tristan forced her jaw into his hand, and turned her to look at the bed. "Look at the mess you made, Norya darling."

Continue the story in
With the Storms Catching Dusk...

DON'T FORGET TO REVIEW!

Thank you so much for finishing your read! Don't forget to leave a review or rating on all platforms as it helps me as an author more than you can ever imagine!

Amazon and Goodreads ratings help the most but feel free to talk about it everywhere else too—including social medias, blogs, Youtube reviews, and most importantly—word of mouth, and more.

FOLLOW NELLY'S SOCIAL MEDIA

Follow Nelly's social media to get the scoop as it's happening!

- tiktok.com/@authornalikyan
- instagram.com/authornellyalikyan
- youtube.com/NellyAlikyan
- amazon.com/author/nellyalikyan
- goodreads.com/nellyalikyan
- pinterest.com/insinpublishing
- facebook.com/authornellyalikyan

JOIN MY AUTHOR NEWSLETTER

Sign up for Nelly Alikyan's newsletter to be the first to know about new releases and cover reveals, receive exclusive content —like a special scene or two—and be up to date about any other exciting news, i.e. events, signed copies, etc.

www.nellyalikyan.com

ACKNOWLEDGMENTS

We've got another Catchers story down, and this one had barbarians. The bigger inspiration—which I truly hope came through—was our world's vikings as the Catchers Islanders. There's just something sexy about the barbarioness of it all.

There is continued thanks to everyone who was part of the process in finishing this book—cover designer, editor, betas, and me! The story wouldn't be possible without every part.

And another thank you to Maria V Snyder. This book is nothing like your books, but reading the Poison Study trilogy was what got me thinking about twins and different lands and an assassin falling in love with a magician. Your trilogy was what inspired novel one in this series and without novel one, there definitely wouldn't have been a novel two.

Always a thanks to my family who support my crazy dreams of being a big-time author. We all know it's going to happen!

And the biggest thanks to all of you, my readers. Without you, big-time author dreams are impossible. Without you, there aren't any Princesses meeting barbarians and falling in love. Without you, there aren't stories to get lost in. Without you, there is no world that, for at least a few hours, you wish to be a part of. No character that you wish was yours.

I'm in love with all of my men, but Sparrow especially has my heart. Which one has yours? I think Killian will be a really popular one!

Thank you to everyone for making this possible!

MEET THE AUTHOR

Nelly Alikyan is a girl from the Los Angeles Valley who's constantly on the move—from Boston to London to wherever she chooses next. She's the only reader in her family—not her only cause as the black sheep—and has dreamt of being a writer for as long as she can remember.

For more books and updates:
www.nellyalikyan.com